AYBIL

By

Kambon Obayani

ISBN: 978-0-9983940-1-5 Jasmaya Productions and Publications Tucson, Arizona, 85747

JASMAYA
Productions & Publications
The Eyes of Independent Publishing

Lovell Pendleton sat atop his burgundy Samsonite luggage. The San Antonio cicadas sang their nasal death hymn, and a humming bird twittered near his right ear. It was his special bird, Carrier, the bringer of worlds of words. Worlds of words and news. Sensual and tragic. He would miss Carrier. Miss the high-pitched bow of her wings, which greeted him each balmy Texas morning. It was not balmy this day. The heat rays yawned, its breath opening Lovell's sweat glands and a wet inhabitant visited his right temple, then jogged down his right cheek. He strode into his house backwards, watching the Samsonite, and extracted his last egg from the now empty refrigerator, then threw it into the street, amazed at the cackle and hiss, of the egg cooking. He would not miss the San Antonio humidity, nor the three shower daily weather, the cul-de-sac where his peach colored house sat, nor San Antonio College from which he had just resigned. Lovell closed the door to his home, still complete with wicker chairs, couches, paintings, appliances, and clothes, without looking back. It was the end to the Texas chapter of his life, and to seal it, he'd only taken three suitcases of books, which he returned to outside and sat upon, his silk shirt clinging for comfort, as he awaited their arrival. They were Kam Ha, the woman he'd been with for the past year, and Eduardo (Hibado) Longoria, his main man. Kam Ha's silver Mercedes turned the corner, stopped, lurched, stopped, lurched again, making a one two rhythm. Earth, Wind and Fire's "September" leapt from the car, and Lovell began to dance to his favorite song. Eduardo bounced from the driver's side, making duck movements; his arms open for an embrace. Lovell walked on his toes to every beat and threw punches, which didn't connect, at Eduardo's chest, in time with the music's horns. Spinning, he looked at Kam Ha snapping her fingers in the Benz. The music stopped and Lovell stepped back. Kam Ha had never allowed him to drive her car, and he didn't own one. Eduardo drove a BMW. Lovell watched Eduardo, watch him, watching Kam Ha. He pulled Lovell to him.

"She was crying and shaking so much that she couldn't drive. I like the feel of that huge Benz". Lovell returned the embrace.

"You've had the pleasure. I haven't."

Eduardo tapped Lovell's cheek.

"Don't be over sensitive."

Slapping Eduardo's hand away, Lovell thought to himself he wouldn't miss those words," Don't be over sensitive". They were Eduardo's favorite words to him. He shooed away those words with his hands and got his luggage. Returning to the car, he passed the passenger side and Kam Ha reached out to touch his face. He kissed her hand and continued to walk to the trunk where Eduardo stood. They put the luggage into the trunk, and as Lovell turned to Kam Ha, he reached out and wrapped her hair around his neck. His hand wound around the hair at her waist, he rolled it through his fingers, and up her back, until her head moved from his shoulder, then kissed those slivered lips, and tasted brandy. She only drank Pina Coladas. Leaning back, he looked into her face. The chiseled cheekbones, so high her eyes were like two knife slashes, pinched nose, and tan skin were still there. But her nose, which reddened when she wept, was still the same.

"We have to go Lovey. You have to be at the airport early."

Eduardo agreed, and Lovell, studying them, entered the car. Rolling down the window, he watched the streams of Kam

Ha's hair dance over the Mercedes headrest. Usually, when nervous or angry, she chewed the side of her lip. But today, she sat bobbing her head to Billy Joel, occasionally snapping her fingers. Once she and Eduardo had slapped fives. Lovell turned his head away from them and watched the one story mostly stucco homes of San Antonio pass. The Chicano homes lawns were always trimmed in squares and straight lines, and even in the poor neighborhoods, there was no garbage in the street. Everywhere he'd been in the river city he'd seen nothing but Chicanos, the occasional Puerto Rican, big steak fed Texas whites, and a spattering of blacks, who had all lived in integrated neighborhoods, and were very aware of their presence and position, in the city. He had never been to a black neighborhood in San Antonio. Had never been close to any. They had often referred to him as reckless. Some said wild; his hair loose ebony cotton balls, like Frederick Douglas, but without the part, moved with the wind, grew to his shoulders, and he often wore twisted braids, with beads to match the color of his clothes. Lovell, at times wore sandals with his suits, and at faculty and artistic functions, black people shied away from him, chuckling, giving him the once over, up and down, you must be crazy look. Lovell's black president, at St. Philip's College, had fired him, stating his appearance did not reflect the college's image. Lovell had looked down at himself closely in the president's office. He wore black Danish clogs, black and white pinstripe pants, a black butt length vest with Masai head shaped buttons and a white silk shirt. Looking up at the president observing him, Lovell Hitler saluted, and goose stepped from the president's office. Hibado stopped the car, then exited the Mercedes and smirked at Lovell. "This is the last Mexican meal you're going to get. Now stop dreaming and get out of the car."

[5]

Lovell smelled Kam Ha's Donna Karan perfume on
Eduardo as they passed. He thought they must have
embraced while he was dreaming.

They had come to Mama Cita's Inn on the river in San
Antonio. Lovell knew it was Eduardo's favorite restaurant
but he'd never been. Ahead of him, Eduardo and Kam Ha
were being led to their table, but as Lovell entered, the
maitre'd, smelling of Pierre Cardin, stepped in front of him.
"Do you have a reservation senor?"
Lovell stepped around him, walked to where Kam Ha and
Eduardo had sat down, and took a seat. The maître d had
followed him. "He's with us." Eduardo spoke looking at
the menu. The man turned and left. Lovell sucked his teeth.
Kam Ha cleared her throat. "They have wonderful fish
burritos here Lovey"
She rubbed her jade bracelet against his hand.
"Oh you've been here before. I thought this place had only
been open two weeks?"
Kam Ha wrinkled her nose and pointed to Eduardo. "He
brought me here last night just to look at the menu. He
wanted to see if you'd like it."
Lovell dropped his menu and turned to Eduardo. "Since
when did you need anyone to cosign what I like? You
know me well enough to know exactly what I like and
dislike."
Eduardo continued to look at his menu. He knew what they
knew about each other. Ten years of it. Ten years. First at
Oxford as young Rhodes Scholars, two working class
teenagers among England's finest, then as civil rights
workers. Lovell for SNCC sand Eduardo for Huelga,
boycotting grapes, Coors, Kroger's, fighting for the poor,
then as Ford Fellows at the Writers Workshop in Iowa,
where they'd met again and last, until this moment, as
Writers in Residence at San Antonio Texas.

"I did it more for her than for you. Now cool it and order those fish tacos. The tequila and beer should be here in a minute. I hear an edge in your voice. I know you didn't let that snotty waiter get to you."

Placing his menu on the table Lovell noticed the décor. Wooden tables with Orozco murals on the walls.

"Did he ask you two did you have a reservation?"

Kam Ha twisted the jade bracelet.

"It wasn't because you're black Lovey. That's his job."

Eduardo bobbed the menu up and down in agreement.

Lovell pushed his chair away from the table.

"How would either of you know. You're not black."

He rose from the table and walked to the toilet. He wouldn't miss these encounters in San Antonio restaurants where the Chicanos acted as if he had no right to eat there and Eduardo, and Kam Ha, always said it wasn't because he was black. He had realized early in his San Antonio experience that Chicanos were just as racist as whites. The only difference was whites, because of the laws, didn't show it. Chicanos, in San Antonio and being the majority, had no reason to hide their feelings. He liked it that way because there was no mistaking what they felt. What unnerved him was his best friend, a pure Texan, wouldn't admit it.   After three rounds of Tequila, chased by a glass of beer, and Eduardo and Kam Ha having half eaten their meal, with Lovell's still not having arrived, Eduardo called the waitress over and asked about Lovell's fish taco dinner, in Spanish.

" We'll bring it when it's ready."

She raised an eyebrow, stomped away, and returned with the fish taco dinner. No steam rose from the plate. Lovell pushed it away from him and putting a hundred dollar bill on top of the cold plate, sat it on the floor.

[7]

"I'll pay for my own so no one can say the reason it's coming late wasn't because I'm black."

Before Eduardo could respond, two guitarist and a percussionist with maracas, began to sing Juan Tala Mera and Eduardo's parents, Mrs. Longoria, tan from head to feet, and Mr. Longoria, or Sarge, gray Guayabera, shoes and slacks to match along with his cousin Nidia, and Ann, his girlfriend, arrived. He watched Eduardo's right eye twitch at his dad's head leaning to the right. It was a sign he'd been drinking. Nidia, clad in her white nun's smock and Ann, red waist length mane hanging over her left soldier, looking like orange sherbet, hugged Lovell as Eduardo's father pulled the next table over for them all to sit down. He snapped his fingers for a waiter, ordered a bottle of Tequila, and then raised his foot. The one hundred dollar bill and taco had stuck to his foot.

"This is some Negro shit. They must have not served you along with everyone else. That's the only way you'd do something like that."

Lovell raised his glass in affirmation. Mr. Longoria downed two shots of Tequila, then chased them with a glass of Beer and called the waitress over, raising his foot. "I seemed to have stepped in something. Could you assist me?"

The waitress turned, puffing out her cheeks like a snake ready to strike.

"Es el plato de este mayate cabron. El mesedo tee ayudere (That's the nigger bastard's plate. I'll get the bus boy to help you.)

Mr. Longoria took the 100 dollar bill, covered in guacamole, and stuck it in her apron pocket.

"He's a good tipper isn't he?"

[8]

She turned and walked to the kitchen. A bus boy, a man around thirty, returned and picking up the plate, held out his hand to Lovell, speaking in Spanish.

" Are you going to tip me too Mayate?"

Lovell dug in his nose, flicked a booger on the bus boy's shirt, and answered in Spanish.

"This is your tip mojado (wetback). It's what remains from the tip your momma gave me for fucking her last night."

The bus boy raised the plate; flame eyed, but froze, seeing Lovell's hand, knife tip between the thumb and first finger, ready to throw.

" You don't want to do that man. He won't miss."

Eduardo stood pointing at the bus boy, which, repeating nigger, nigger, nigger, in English, returned to the kitchen.

Mr. Longoria twirled an empty tequila shot glass.

"I hope they treat you well in Africa Lovell. I hope so because you've had a lot of shit dumped on you since you've been here. It's because you're black, you dress differently and you're proud. Whites and Mexican Americans can't imagine why a mayate', and you know that means nigger, could possibly be proud. As Mexican Americans we're taught to blend. Black people down here are taught the same thing. You don't give a damn and that makes people hate you for being an uppity nigger."

Mrs. Longoria sighed.

"You shouldn't speak for all of us Felix."

Mr. Longoria slapped the table.

"I'll say whatever I want because it's the truth and you know it. Why most of us can't stand the idea of a black man being with a Texana. Every time you see a black man with a white woman you stare and if you're with your friend, you nudge each other. Shit, when Ruth Ann, your best friend's daughter fell in love with him, you told her it wasn't right and she'd have a hard time in life if she

[9]

married him. You and I know we'd never had any blacks in our house until he came with Eduardo. We accepted him because he was our son's friend. Otherwise we would have thought he was a weird mayate' to be stayed away from. He's leaving now mi amour, we don't have to pretend anymore."

He raised his finger signaling the waitress to bring another round. Ice settled over the table. A dribble of water appeared, when four women, their light eyes beaming, approached the table. They all held books. A tall one with freckles and full lips, rocked on her heels.

"Aren't you Lovell Pendleton, the writer and composer?" Lovell faced them.

"Yes, I am."

"We loved your book and we saw your play when it first came out and the movie on T.V. last week. Reading your book and the play was like looking at our life. None of us thought the movie did the play or you any justice. We liked the music though. You're a genius. Would you sign our books?"

Lovell pulled out his pen.

"I'd be honored to ladies. And may I buy you ladies a drink?"

The women, throwing their heads back, gave high full-bellied laughter. She winked at Lovell.

"That's sweet of you, but no. We've drunk half of Texas. Anymore and I'd be flowing like the San Anton river and ready to pour some of it in your handsome mouth."

They slapped fives. Lovell pointed to the Tequila and beer on the table.

"And as you ladies can see. I like to drink." The spokeswoman flipped her hair, opened her purse and taking out a gold case, extracted a short gold pen, wrote something

and handed it to Lovell. "Well when you get thirsty again, give me a call. I've got lots of juice."
She touched Lovell's goatee. Kam Ha slapped her hand away.
"You can speak but don't touch Goldie Locks."
Lovell had finished signing the books. One woman touched Lovell's shoulder, another his hair, and the last his face, all with eyes hard on Kam Ha. Freckles white knuckled her book.
"Thank you Mr. Pendleton. You can reach all of us at that number. Let's go girls before we start the Vietnam war again. And this time we'll win."
Giggling, they strolled out the restaurant. Mr. Longoria cleared his throat.
"I want to drink a toast to you Lovell. You're the craziest man I've ever met. You have rich white women throwing themselves at you. You fight through all this caca for two years, become famous, and then when you make it, you leave. If I didn't want to insult you I'd call you stupid."
Mrs. Longoria lifted her beer.
"I'll drink to that. And Felix, if Texans are so prejudiced, what were those women doing over here, my love?"
"They want some of that big snake in his pants. His being famous makes it easier. They'd sleep with him but they wouldn't want to marry him."
Lovell leaned across the table and slapped fives with Mr. Longoria. They, Nidia and Ann were the only ones to laugh. Mrs. Longoria patted Kam Ha on the arm.
"Don't worry. Those were whores. No decent woman would do that. My husband's been drinking."
Mr. Longoria pointed his first finger.
"Watch your mouth woman. I've heard you and your slut best friend talking about how big he is. We've all got eyes."

[11]

Mrs. Longoria pushed her chair from the table and hand to mouth, shuffled from the restaurant. Kam Ha followed. Eduardo stood. Mr. Longoria poured the Tequila into the beer and stirred it with his finger.

"Don't look at me like that Hijo. You know I'm right. Plus, you don't want me to start on you. I know what you've been up to."

Eduardo, head to his chest, left the restaurant. Prickly needles flooded Lovell's chest. Touching his heart, he tried to grasp the feeling, but, along with the needles, it had vanished. He excused himself and entering the first bathroom, sat down in the first stall, after pulling down the toilet top. He allowed himself one tear. One tear of acknowledgement, confirmed by Mr. Longoria, for the past year. Yes, in the mind of all, he'd made it. Writer in Residence, novel published, play produced and made into a movie, writing his own score, now included in the national and international writer's reading circuit. He'd been offered a full position at San Antonio College. However, an anchor carved in sadness, lodged beneath his entrails, leaving him sometimes short of breath. A white dress entering the stall sliced his already halted breathing. Leaning back, Lovell gasped at the bald glistening pubic area in front of him, lowering onto his lap. Through the white linen dress he smelled lavender, and allowed his pants to be opened, and cringed with pain, as he was straddled, and sat upon. The movement was measured, but the cross licking his face was disturbing. A mahogany hand moved it and the elbow brushed Lovell's forehead. He finger tipped the moist spine beneath the white linen dress, and nibbled at the mangoes in front, held beneath it. A reservoir opened over his member as the two weeks of nights alone leaped from him. "I have given myself to god all these years and I have never been satisfied Lovell. Now, I have given myself to you

[12]

because I've loved you from the first moment I saw you. It is my time Negrito. In nine months, I will give you a son. I can't live a lie any longer."

Taking toilet paper, placing it between her legs, rising then cleaning his organ with her mouth, she shared his and her semen, and left Lovell leaning against the steel toilet handle, which gave no sweat. Lovell, reveling in the lavender's warmth, which covered his fingers, smelled his hands, and as he booted the door open, Ann stood outside. "Don't go out too soon. You smell like lavender. The old Sarge would kill you if he knew what just happened." Lovell glanced at the Sarge who sat alone fingering his cross.

"Maybe I should kill myself for making love to a nun in a bathroom."

Ann cuffed Lovell's cheek.

"Don't give me that Lovell. You know, I know, you're incapable of guilt." He smelled his hands. "I don't know what the fuck I feel right now."

"Feel loved, by Nidia, Lovell. The move she's making is going to cause hell. Especially from Mrs. bird faced Longoria. Do you know what that old bitch said to me? We've had whites in our family for a long time. As if I give a shit. These Chicanos are worse than crackers like my family have ever been. I wanted to tell her your son and I haven't had sex in two weeks, so I'm not the one she should be talking to."

Nidia, winking at Lovell, exited the women's bathroom, and took Ann's arm, who'd lit a cigarette, and blown the smoke on Lovell. They returned to the table as a throng of people, shaking percussion instruments entered the restaurant. "Lovely Lovell, Lovely Lovell, Lovely Lovell!" The group chanted and circled the table. It was the San Antonio Arts Commission, better known as the Gang of

[13]

Four, Armando Ruiz, Nancy Silberman, Dora Katacolis and
Nacho Sams. Armando, "El Topo", always in black with
Zorro hat, bloused sleeved shirt, silver buckled with
rhinestones down the side of stove piped pants and Tony
Lama boots, stepped forward, with a portable microphone.
Mr. Longoria cleared his throat.

"Lovell, isn't that the queer from that queer arts group
whose jaw you broke?"

El Topo gave Mr. Longoria the finger. Lovell could see his
mouth moving but couldn't hear a word. He thought about
the night they'd first met. He'd been invited to a party at
Nancy's house, being the new artist in town. He and
Eduardo had drunk a bottle of Tequila and smoked about
ten joints to celebrate their introduction into the art world.
El Topo had come upon Lovell, drunk and passed out in
Nancy's bedroom. Lovell had thought he was dreaming
about having sex and an orgasm, and had awakened, to find
Armando giving him head with Lovell coming in El Topo's
mouth. Lovell had kicked him off, semen still squirting,
and then proceeded to thrash him with left hooks, shouting.
"How dare you take advantage of someone defenseless you
pile of shit!"

Accenting each word with a blow, until Eduardo, with the
rest of the group, who had been standing guard and taking
turns watching, had come in and stopped Lovell from
killing him. El Topo, jaw hanging had screamed, spitting
blood,

" You should be honored I want to suck your black dick.
Your life in San Antonio in the arts is dead," as they carried
him away.

They had taken Armando to the hospital, his jaw broken,
but had been unable to press charges because they knew,
and knew Lovell and Eduardo knew, what had occurred.

[14]

Reality, with Ann and Nidia trying to hold Mr. Longoria, shook him.

"I'll kick your ass, you muthafukin' gota, maricon, fudge packin' ass fucker. You can't fuck with me the way you fucked with Lovell. He broke your jaw and still won. I'll kill you."

Eduardo pushed Mr. Longoria backwards into his chair and Mrs. Longoria sat on his lap, kissing him on both cheeks. El Topo handed the microphone and a plaque to Nacho Sams and left.

"And you, you white Mexican, you're no better. My son and Lovell saved your ass when those cholos were going to peel you like a banana, and how did you repay him? You never supported him, or voted for him to be an artist in residence here. You're all a bunch of goddamn hypocrites. If I were Lovell I'd shit on all of you. And you!"

He pointed at Eduardo.

"How could you allow these clasistas to be here when you know what they tried to do to your friend who'd die for you? I didn't raise you to be a back stabber and that's what you've become. A fuckin' Judas. I'm out of here before I puke."

Mrs. Longoria looked at her feet. Mr. Longoria walked over to Lovell and kissed him on the cheek. "Negro, I love you dearly and I'd be proud to have you as my son. I'll miss you and I wish you all the success in the world. You deserve it. You've never become bitter and you've made all of us eat your shit. I hope people outside the U.S. appreciate you the way we haven't. Nidia, you have every reason in the world to love him. Listen to your heart Mija. Eduardo, be a man!"

He, with Mrs. Longoria holding his arm, walked at the gang of three, who pressed against the restaurant wall. Nacho placed the plaque on the floor and lead the group

[15]

out. Nidia and Ann, looked at Eduardo, who stared into his cupped hands. Kam Ha leaned over and placed her arm around him. Lovell noticed they both wore sky blue clothes.

"I have to catch a plane."

Kam Ha reached for her purse, but Ann threw a stack of bills on the table as they all rose and left, with Nidia kicking the plaque. Lovell sprinted from the restaurant to Mr. Longoria. The gang of stood huddled, leaning against Nancy's white Mercedes sedan. Plaz Johnson, owner of a cable station, stood rocking in front of them. Lovell reached Mr. Longoria who turned around.

"Mr. Longoria, I didn't get a chance to thank you and tell you that I love you."

He and Mr. Longoria embraced. Mrs. Longoria stood to the side. Lovell began to shake. Mr. Longoria, the Sarge, increased his steel embrace. He whispered to Lovell.

"Don't let them see you cry. Cry on the plane, not in front of these assholes. Now calm yourself and turn around quickly. Plaz is drunk again and he's holding those pendejos with a knife."

He spun Lovell around and marched away. Mrs. Longoria trying to catch him. Lovell turned to see Plaz, moving his arm back and forward in front of the gang of four, who held hands.

"Put the knife away Plaz, there's no telling what might be in their blood."

Nidia spit. "Don't put it down Plaz. Stick them muthafuckas." Dora fell to her knees.

"Jesus, lord god have mercy. Please don't cut me. Nidia you're a nun. You should be asking him for mercy." Nidia spit again. This time at Dora.

"I walked away from the convent four hours ago, so I'm not a nun. And even if I were I wouldn't ask anyone to

[16]

spare you. You cunt loving snake." Eduardo stepped
forward. Nidia pushed him back.
"Haven't you done enough already, primo?"
Eduardo, with Kam Ha behind him, walked to her car and
got inside. Lovell stepped in front of Plaz. "Put the knife
away cracker and give me a shot from your flask."
Plaz blew snot from his right nostril onto Dora, wiped his
hand on her dress, and switching the knife to his other
hand, took a flask from his seersucker jacket pocket,
handed it to Lovell, then shoved Dora backwards with his
foot.
"I want each of you to hold out your arm so I can cut you. I
don't want anyone to ever say Plaz Johnson pulled a knife
and didn't use it."
The group, which now included Dora, held out their arms
to Plaz, who cut Nancy first. Nancy with the lopsided face,
Lovell called her. Polio had made the left side hang and it
gave her speech a swishing sound. Half Chicana, half
Jewish, she'd inherited dog food and animal feed factories,
and was married to Elmo Johnson, a master violinist who
played first chair with the San Antonio symphony
orchestra, but loved jazz. Nancy paid him a salary, to keep
him from going out at night, with women and as part of
their arrangement. She could have her women at the house,
and he could have his women, as long as they only did it in
the house. After Lovell had beat El Topo, he'd gotten a gig
at a club Plaz owned. El Topo's cousin Juanito was the
leader of the house band. The group, with Lovell fronting
had played well until Thursday night, which began the
weekend in San Antonio clubs. El Topo had gotten his
cousin another gig at a club, which started on Thursday,
which had left Lovell without a gig, and Plaz without a
band, for the weekend. Elmo had heard the gang of four
laughing about what had been done. He'd called Plaz, who

[17]

was his cousin, and had brought in a band. Nancy had been unable to say anything because he wasn't with women when he was playing. Plaz had never forgotten. He'd also not forgotten Dora, his first wife, and mother of his three daughters, who he had custody of and raised. That was the deal he'd made with Dora when he'd caught her in bed with Nacho. That's why he hated Nacho, who'd been his childhood friend. She received a yearly stipend until the girls were eighteen, an apartment building, stocks in the radio station and T.V. station, on the condition she'd never come near his girls, who thought another woman was their mother. He also hated homosexuals. It was rumored he'd been molested. The gang and Plaz were all from the same land owning, pioneer business class of San Antonio. Plaz was even more. He was a Johnson, from the Johnson's of Texas, as was Elmo, but from the black side. Plaz, sliced Dora last and kicked her in the ass as she walked past him.
"I regret the day I put my dick in you slut."
She was the first to run. The other's followed. He turned to Lovell, taking the flask.
"You should have done that a long time ago."
Lovell took a hit from the flask.
"For what? They didn't do anything to me that I didn't put myself in the position to let happen."
Plaz put the flask in his pocket.
"You would say some shit like that. It's the Christian in you."
He hugged Lovell with his six foot four blubbery body. His red beard with blonde streaks was wet with perspiration and tears.
"I won't be here whenever you return to the states. My alcoholic life has finally caught up with me. I'm putting a check in your pocket for the movie. I took some of it and invested it in my family's stock. It's diversified so you'll be

[18]

getting a lot of different checks. If you leave it alone, you'll never have to work again."

Releasing Lovell, Plaz two stepped towards his limousine, shouting over his shoulder.

"I still think you're the worst saxophonist I ever heard." Lovell shouted fuck you. That was their joke and how they'd met. Lovell, had been in San Antonio a week and sat in with Juanito's band, at Plaz's club and had been playing a set like the Art Ensemble of Chicago, abstract. Lovell had fallen right in and soloed. It was a Tuesday and not crowded. Plaz had reeled towards Lovell and told him he was the worst Sax player he'd ever heard and needed to play licks. Lovell had given Plaz his horn and told him to play a lick. Plaz couldn't.

"Since you're not a musician, and drunk at that, you can't tell me anything about music."

He'd then called *A Night In Tunisia*, and had soloed for fifteen traditional minutes. Plaz was asleep and snoring. Lovell had taken a match and put it in front of Plaz's mouth. He'd awakened swinging at the match.

"You must be fucking crazy and have a lot of balls to put that match in front of my face. Don't you realize I own this club?"

Lovell had stricken another match.

"Well, I thought since my playing hadn't lit you up, maybe this would."

" I heard every note you played. You listened to Jackie McClean and Wayne Shorter."

Lovell had stood in amazement.

"Yes I did." Plaz stood holding onto the table for support. "You better watch your step in San Antonio. People down here aren't used to a black man who doesn't fear them. But you're crazy like I am. We're going to be friends."

[19]

They'd met regularly, after that. Especially after the club incident. Plaz enjoyed sitting in the one room apartment with the flat board for a table held up by books, with round pieces of wood for chairs, also held up by books and laughing at the expensive stereo, records and tapes lining the walls. When the gang had blocked his getting a job at Trinity University, Plaz was able to get him a job, though part time, at San Antonio College. Unable to keep a steady band because the classical musicians were busy with the symphony, Plaz, who'd discovered Lovell had a Master's in psychology, by accident while looking for a piece of typing paper and had found the degree sitting on the table, had gotten him a job as a counselor, working with youth in the prison system. They'd edited an anthology together of Youth Prison Writings, which was in its second printing. The anthology's success had led to Lovell being nominated for the artist in residence. But when the gang had blocked it by voting 4 to 0 against him, the state board had given Lovell a state Artist in Residence, and he'd selected San Antonio. The state had recommended Lovell for a National Endowment of the Arts grant, which he won, and through Plaz he'd met his literary agent, had the novel published, won the Texas State Fiction prize, and though there'd been numerous offers which paid ten times the amount, had given his play to Plaz, for his small T.V. station, and had allowed Plaz to be one of the major producers of the film. That's when the gang had come around, inviting Lovell to parties and affairs. He would accept the invitations but never showed. Lovell watched Plaz's limousine pull away, with Plaz's middle finger held in the air. Ann and Nidia, each took an arm. Walking to the car, cement filled his shoes. Ahead of him sat the happy couple. Eduardo and Kam Ha, dressed alike, sitting in the front seat of her car, mouths turned down in disgust, waiting for him.

[20]

" They look good together don't they?"
Ann squeezed Lovell's bicep. Lovell patted her hand three times.
"Yes, they do. I'd never noticed it before. I guess that's where he's been for the last two weeks and why I've developed a good relationship with my vibrator. How long has it been since you've seen Kam Ha at night?"
" Two weeks. And Hibado and I have only hung out during the day."
Releasing the women's arms, Lovell walked to the driver's side of the car.
"I'm going to ride with Nidia and Ann."
Eduardo opened his mouth, but was silenced by Lovell's kiss on the lips. "Hush now, don't explain. You know the words to the song."
A feathered lightness filled Lovell's chest as the three of them skipped to Ann's Lincoln. Her family was nouveau riche', and had to buy their way into places others, unlike Plaz and the Gang of Four, were invited. That class smirked that even the cars, Cadillacs, Lincolns, 225s, showed their class. Ann, who wrote like Carson McCullough, and had also been at Iowa, where they'd all met, pretended not to care, but she did. It showed in the venomous way she spoke of them. If you didn't care, Plaz had told her once; you wouldn't spend so much time talking about them. Lovell had agreed that day, but couldn't today, with Ann's tears, which made rivulets through her make up. Nidia, sitting in the passenger's seat, patted Ann's shoulder, which hung like a dead carcass.
"All he had to do was tell me. Why couldn't he tell me Nidia? He's your cousin. Tell me. Why couldn't he at least tell me to my face, instead of me finding out like this? And how could he do this to his best friend? And with her! She's a shallow, materialistic, air head."

[21]

He wondered what he'd seen in her, Kam Ha, himself, then answered his own question. She'd been the only Asian at the party that first night. Later, before the jobs came through with Plaz. She'd seen him sitting at a table on the San Antonio River, nursing one pitcher of beer all night. It was his last fifteen dollars, after the bills were paid, and he was down to one bag of popcorn. She'd asked if she could sit down, then preceded to ask to him about the night with El Topo. When she took him home, he didn't invite her in. However, she'd come the next day, and he'd heard her open his empty refrigerator while he was in the toilet. Exiting, she was gone, but had returned in a few minutes with a bag of groceries. That's what had attracted him to her. She was there for him, and he appreciated it. There was never that spark though. Never that I look forward to having her come over to sit and talk, or just laugh, hang out, or make love. He had never wanted to spend a day in bed with her. Physically he knew what that was about; he was a butt man. Loved big asses. An ass and a personality that kept him on his toes and wouldn't take any shit from him. It was a lesson he'd learned about sex; it began in the mind. Kam Ha was supportive, elegant, always in silk, Parisian stylish, but not a reader, or a thinker, which bored him, even though she spoke French fluently. She looked as if she'd been carved from a piece of gold jade, looked good on his shoulder and pissed Asians and whites off when they were together in public. He'd always said to himself, "She was with me when I had nothing. Now that I'm getting something, I'd be wrong to dump her." Eduardo, Hibado, had repeated these words over and over. Kam Ha wasn't Lovell's type. Lovell wanted to say this to Ann and Nidia. He wanted to tell Ann. Eduardo had tried but couldn't bring himself to shatter her even more. He remembered the moment his brother, friend had revealed himself. Lovell

had not been given the Artist in Residence and Eduardo
had. They were sitting in Ann's study, which was the size
of Lovell's one room. Ann had cursed the committee. She
was also an Artist in Residence. Kam Ha was sitting next to
Eduardo.

"I'm glad I got it and I'm also sad for you bro. I think
you've brought it on yourself though. Look at you. Your
appearance makes a statement. The sixties are over but
you're still walking around not conforming. It doesn't work
anymore. You have to give. You didn't have to beat El
Topo. You did and now look what it's cost you. I don't
think it's worth it. I don't want to live your life. I don't
want to live in a one room like you. I deserve more."

"You don't have to Hibado, you're a Chicano."

"That's crap Lovell and you know it!" He'd slammed down
his glass.

"You're not getting shit because of your color. It's because
of what you've done and how you act. That color shit is all
in your head."

Lovell had stood over Eduardo.

"In my head huh. What about James Edwards, the painter?
He knocked Nacho out for touching his ass and they still
gave him a residency. Ann called Nancy a pussy-loving
bitch in front of the director of the National Endowment of
the Arts and they still gave her a residency. And how am I
supposed to act. Inferior? Gracious? I've worked as hard as
everyone else. Plus, to keep it real, I have more
publications and productions than any of you!"

He'd sat down stamping his foot. Ann, who'd been fixing
drinks, which were ready to be delivered, paused with a
tray of Manhattans.

"I agree with Lovell. The first thing they always say is he's
an uppity black bastard who doesn't know his place. His

color always comes first. And truthfully Eddy, he has done more than all of us combined."

She'd moved around with the drinks, which Kam Ha refused, moving closer to Eduardo.

"Well, I agree with Eduardo. They like him because he's suave. After all, he wears Yves St. Laurent and he's pleasant. I love you Lovell, but you're proud and you dress unconventionally. People notice you're black. Eduardo's like them."

She and Eduardo had slapped fives. Ann, her drink in midair snorted.

"You mean Eddy's like whites, don't you? Is that supposed to be something good? And in case you hadn't noticed Ms. Frenchy, he's obviously Chicano, not white and people notice it but it's not an issue to them. Being black is. I'm surprised at you Kam Ha. The man you've just said you love wears Pierre Cardin, and looks damn good, too."

Kam Ha and Eduardo had both sighed, exchanging a glance. Lovell had asked if Eduardo didn't think he, Lovell deserved more. Eduardo had said yes but he was never going to get it acting as if he owned the world. Kam Ha had agreed. Once again they'd slapped fives. Lovell and Eduardo had seen less of each other after that. Once, Lovell had gone to Eduardo's house and looked through the window and seen El Topo giving him head while Dora sat on his face, humping. He'd never mentioned it to his best friend.

"You don't know him very well do you Ann?"

Nidia leaned her back against the door facing Ann and glancing at Lovell.

"If you did, you wouldn't be surprised at him being with Kam Ha. Our family's not progressive. Very few middle class Mexican American families are. We're taught to get a good job, find a partner for life, buy a house, and seek

[24]

stability, like everyone else. Even more so because we live with the reality that this was all once Mexico, and feels ashamed we lost it. She'll only be able to keep him for so long. As soon as a middle class Chicana comes along, he'll follow her like a puppy running after a bone. Just look at my aunt and you can see what kind of woman he wants. You've had blinders on. Both of you, even though he was all-revolutionary he still wanted to be part of the middle class. We Chicanos always wanted to blend and be part of whites, not change anything. We're basically very conservative."

Lovell knew she was correct.

"Blacks too, Nidia. Middle class blacks are the same. Eduardo tried to tell us what he wanted. We listened but didn't hear. How long have you known?"

Nidia turned her back to Lovell and looked out the window, away from Ann. "Six months!" Six months! His life had climbed a lush hill full of tropical fruits and flowers. Kam Ha had been by his side, but his dreams had been of Nidia, sitting on lotus pads, in the lotus position, naked. She'd called him nightly and he'd even lay in bed with Kam Ha and had three-hour conversations with Nidia about everything imaginable. He'd never spoken with Kam Ha more than fifteen minutes at a time. She loved to sit as he worked and delighted in telling people she was present when the play and book were written. However, Lovell mused as they turned into the airport, he'd never read anything to her. He'd read everything to Nidia, over the phone from the convent and relied on her feedback. Stopping the car, Ann extended her hand to Lovell.

"I'm not strong enough to get out of the car black man. I just can't let them see me cry. Please write to me." Lovell kissed her hand.

[25]

"Great writing country Texas sister. You know I will and I love you dearly. Don't be too hard on Hibado. He tried to tell us but we weren't paying attention." Ann slapped the seat back.

"What's wrong with you? He's been stabbing you in the back for six months and you still defend him! I'm not like you. I fuckin' hate his cowardly ass!"

Lovell exited from the passenger's side, where Nidia sat. Closing the door, Nidia wrapped both arms around Lovell's waist and spoke into his chest. Lovell noticed streaks of gray in her scalp.

"I know that you will write to me. Think of me at night and we will be able to talk, like we used to when you were here."

She placed his hand on her stomach.

"Someone grows here for you Negrito. No matter what happens, stay alive so your new life will be able to appreciate you in the flesh. I will send you my address through dreams."

She opened the car door, still facing Lovell, placed her first two fingers to his lips, then got inside the car, as Ann pulled away. Neither looked back. Eduardo, or Hibado, as Lovell called him, and Kam Ha, waited, with Lovell's bags. Lovell approached them with open arms then embraced them. Kam Ha wet Lovell's shirt in front and Eduardo the side of his face.

"I knew you would understand Negro. I tried to tell you but I couldn't. I tried. They're right about me. I have been a coward. I'm sorry."

Lovell stepped away from them and picked up his suitcases.

"There's nothing to be sorry for. You two look good together. Thank you for all your help Kam Ha. I'll never forget it."

He walked into the airport, and like Nidia and Ann, did not turn around. Entering the first class section on the Air Italia flight, Lovell sat and got a final look at the San Antonio airport, and hummed. He'd taken his own money and upgraded the coach seat bought by Al Fateh University. "Friends no more." A whisky voice, full of gravel, called him away from San Antonio. It belonged to a shined copper chisel jawed man, with a mustache, goatee', bald head, up turned nose with elephant ears. The mustache hid a non-existent top lip.

"I had a girl, good little girl was she. I had a friend, best of friends were we. My friend took my girl away from me. And I know they're in love, But I was too blind to see. And we are, friends no more. Friends no more! I understand! I understand more than they think I do. I can plainly see that she's the girl for you."

Lovell stopped him with an open palm.

"You don't need to sing anymore. I didn't realize I was humming that song. It's the Intruders, Friends No More. The flip side of "Cowboys to Girls". I'm Lovell Pendleton."

The man slapped his leg

"I thought so. The great Lovell Pendleton, one of the writers in residence of Texas. I've seen your movie and heard you play. I'm Matt Johnson." Lovell stared at the ears.

"One of "the" Texas Johnsons?"

Matt flipped an ear.

"Yea buddy. Can't you tell old man Johnson marked us all? My cousin said you're a bad nigger. If your cousin's Elmo. He's the one who's bad! No, the word is great. He saved my ass, a couple of times." Matt raised a closed fist.

"Yea, I know. I was there and he told me. You don't know it but he was on the plane before us."

[27]

Lovell watched the stewardess on the screen, giving seat belt and life jacket instructions.

"Where are he and Nancy off to now?" Matt let loose a laugh which turned the few heads in first class.

"Nancy's not going anywhere. He took all his money and left that bitch. It was about time!"

Lovell gave a restrained chuckle.

"Yes, they were something."

Matt, his mouth now a thin line reached into his pocket then handed Lovell a stack of warm photographs. They were a series showing Lovell hugging Kam Ha and Eduardo, walking into the airport, then Kam Ha and Eduardo jumping in the air, in each other's arms, and kissing. He hummed again and stared down at a fading San Antonio. Matt placed a light finger on Lovell's knee.

"Wasn't he your boy?"

Lovell hummed louder.

"That's just like Mexican."

Lovell's inhale made Matt lean away.

"What's that supposed to mean Matt?"

Matt smirked licking his lips.

"I didn't mean to hurt you man. I mean, sometimes it's better we see the truth. It helps us to get closure. I grew up in San Antonio and my experiences with them have always been cutthroat. I can see from your face you don't agree. You'd probably say his being chicken shit had nothing to do with his being Mexican. "

The stewardess came to their seats. Matt ordered double vodka and a glass of Merlot. Lovell had stopped humming.

"You're right. I would say that; so let's leave it. Are you a photographer?"

Matt's finger moved like a windshield wiper.

"No, I'm a mechanical engineer and I've just resigned as county commissioner in San Antonio."

[28]

Lovell blew a low whistle.

"Damn. That was a good six-figure gig! Where you headed?"

The stewardess had returned with the drinks. Matt and Lovell touched glasses.

"To Aybil. Just like you."

CHAPTER TWO

Screaming awoke Lovell. The plane rocked and the fasten your seat belt sign blinked. The few passengers in first class all looked to the left where Lovell sat. Looking out his window, he saw black, thick smoke spewing from the wing. Matt sat upright, staring straight ahead, his eyes focused on the cockpit door. Lovell's left foot began a rat-a-tat-tat on the floor. Matt grabbed it.

"Don't worry man. This baby's not going down."

Lovell couldn't see the wing for the smoke.

"Passengers, this is the pilot. We're having a small problem and will be landing in Chicago immediately. Please remain calm. We have everything under control."

Matt gave Lovell a thumbs up. The plane slowly descended and stopped quickly. A rescue team began to spray the wing as the doors opened and everyone in first class was let out first and was hurried onto a waiting bus, which quickly pulled off, taking them to a hotel. They were told they'd be leaving in the morning and given a first class private room. Lovell and Matt got their rooms and met in the bar. They ordered wine and a double vodka. It was still daylight. Matt downed his double and ordered another. Lovell sipped his Merlot.

"You were as cool as ice up there. I was scared shitless. How'd you do it?"

Matt finger stirred the double, then stroked his goatee with the same hand.

"The smoke was coming from the bottom of the propeller. That meant it was in the fuel line and wasn't affecting the propeller directly. I was in Nam and saw planes hit worse than that and still make it."

Lovell watched a shroud cover Matt's eyes.

[30]

"Nam, huh."

Matt stirred his vodka again.

"I know I'm going to heaven cause I served my time in hell. I went to hell three times. Damn Negro, aren't you ever going to finish that wine?"

Lovell downed his wine and ordered another. Matt looked around the mirrored, gold carpeted bar and hotel. A white musician played Misty on a piano.

"I hate hotels and I hate Chicago even more. It's the most boring city in the world."

Lovell studied the hotel in the bar's mirror.

"The West side has some good blues."

Matt pushed his drink to the side.

"I can only take so much blues."

It was not the same for Lovell. His mother had played it constantly and had called B.B. King, Daddy B.B. He'd been raised hearing stories of B.B. King standing on a corner in Mississippi, in overalls, singing with his guitar and his foot on a crate. He'd learned to play bass and saxophone by listening to blues records and had first tried to imitate Bobby Blue Bland and Junior Parker, when singing the blues, and Eddy "Clean Head" Vinson, on the saxophone. He watched Matt nervous his mustache on the ends.

"I tell you what. My family's close to here. You want to take a ride Mr. Johnson?"

" I don't mind if I do Mr. Pendleton."

They walked to the car rental. While Lovell filled out the rental form, Matt went to the bathroom. The receptionist, auburn haired with an unabridged nose connected to both eyes, held his American express card then asked for his driver's license and another form of I.D. She took his card and I.D. and went into an office with a large window, closing the door. Matt returned and he and Lovell watched

[31]

her speak with another man who could have been her brother. They watched him make a phone call. Matt paced. Lovell drummed the counter. The man returned with the woman behind him.

"Mr. Pendleton we're sorry."

Lovell snatched his card and I.D. from him, banging his fist on the counter, leaning close enough to smell menthol Certs.

"Cracker box! You have O.J. Simpson running through airports for your damn commercials, and you act as if I stole the card or shouldn't have it! You've just lost a customer and if I wasn't leaving I'd slap a lawsuit on your ass faster than you'd be able to close your zipper."

The man stepped back, and inhaled, his face matching the company's uniform.

"I'm sorry you feel the delay is racially motivated Mr. Pendleton. I swear, I mean, I guarantee you it's not. Miss Ellis is new here. To be exact, this is her first day working the desk alone. She's never encountered an American Express card before and didn't know what to do. Our company has a nondiscriminatory policy."

Lovell cracked his knuckles.

"There was a woman before me who used an American express and she didn't ask her for any I.D. She didn't ask you for help with her?"

The man rubbed his palms together and then turned to the woman.

"Is that true Miss Ellis?"

The woman touched him on the arm.

"He requested our largest Mercedes. I thought, for security reasons, I should check. In the office you said I'd acted properly and now..."

"Mr. Pendleton, we're sorry for the delay and I assure you this wasn't racially motivated. You may have the Mercedes,

[32]

with the compliments of our company, for half the price. Miss Ellis, please give Mr. Pendleton the best prompt service."

He spun and trotted into his office, closing the blinds.

The woman, hands shaking and crimson faced, looked at the form, and wiped at her chin. Lovell smelled Alberto VO5 shampoo.

"It's something when you get caught and your men leave you hanging, isn't it."

She turned the form toward Lovell, motioned with her pen, where he was to sign, the counter now wash with her emotions, she handed Lovell the keys and pointing to the right, sniffled,

"The car lot is outside about twenty feet."

As Matt and Lovell turned towards the parking lot, the auburn hair came from behind the counter and purse in hand, body convulsing, walked in the opposite direction.

CHAPTER THREE

Lovell took I-95 and drove toward Harbor Bend, Michigan. Matt had been contemplating his beard since they had left the airport and was now rubbernecking. Neither had spoken for an hour and they had just turned into the city.

"Matt! What's up Mr. Johnson? "

Matt began to laugh until his amusement spilled over. He removed the joy pointed at Lovell.

"Every other building I've seen has either Pendleton, or P and something. You own this town don't you?"

Lovell's bowing head answered Matt.

"This is nothing compared to an uncle who's a president and owns half of Texas. There are only 6,000 people here." Matt sucked in his breath and raised an eyebrow. "I'd rather be a big fish in a little pond than a big fish any day. You have more control."

Lovell had heard this from his family many times. Big fish in a little pond. Control! Have everything within arm's reach and that way you can keep control. He only wanted to control himself and his life and had often told anyone who asked what he wanted most in life; I want some peace and the freedom to live my life as I please. Doing what I love most. Writing and music. He had tired of psychology. Tired of spoon feeding people's brains and replacing what had been sucked out by lifestyles and choices they'd made. He turned left, instead of right, which led to his parent's home. The homes faded and peach, cherry, plum, raspberry, strawberry and apple orchards, completing the Southwestern Michigan lavender canvas, extended from the sky. He passed the Baron cemetery and turned into a lane, with a sign saying "Peaceful Pendleton Pastures". Matt turned around, looked at the sign, and winked at

Lovell, who stopped the car and got out. He stood and watched a bull- necked six foot seven man, with cotton colored hair and mocha skin, in overalls, walking among the graves. It was Mr. Myas, his father's assistant at the mortuary and his most devoted deacon. He had always looked uncomfortable in his undertaker's three-piece suit. Wearing the blue overalls, a red and white-checkered shirt, with the red patches on the seat, Deacon Myas' face shined like sparklers in the night. His body moved with the rolling graves and as he whistled, three beagles ran towards him, sniffing the ground. Lovell noticed the shotgun angled across his back. The deacon let out a shout, "Thank you Jesus", his head straight towards the sky. The beagles yelped and leapt into the air. It was at that moment he realized why Mr. Myas had always looked uncomfortable in the suit. He belonged outside, in overalls and with his dogs. Deacon Myas, knew why Lovell had come, and moved his arms in a welcoming half circle, then pointed to two, fresh, four-foot pyramid shaped obsidian headstones. They were his parent's body's resting place.   He took one step towards the graves and pins began to stick his thighs. Two more and his calves turned to jelly. On his knees, Lovell crawled to the graves, and placing an arm around both headstones, face on the ground, his loss escaped in a scathing high pitched moan, watering the grass, which covered his face.   Prostrate, his reservoir of sadness emptied, and kissing both graves, he gathered grass from both, put it into his pocket, stood rubber legged, then with Matt and the deacon's arms under his, staggered to the car. He sat in the car, felt the deacon pat his shoulder, and before driving off, banged his head three times on the steering wheel.   Dusk, when night and day equally share the sky, yawned as he drove. Matt had turned and faced him, holding his handkerchief. Lovell ignored the offer,

[35]

and drove to Baird St., in Harbor Bend.   He accelerated,
seeing the moving vans, and men in blue work suits,
moving furniture from a mint green, three bedroom home,
with yellow, white and red rose bushes in the yard. He
exited the car, without turning off the ignition, fist balled
and swinging at the first man he encountered, who melted,
unconscious from the blow. A honey colored man, face
like the Native American on the nickel, with pointed cow
licks, wisps of hair on the top, thick on the sides, ran from
the house and bear hugged him.

"Don't do that boy, these men work for you. Can't you see
the Pendleton sign on their uniforms? You know what it
means. Now stop it before I have to beat the hell out of
you!"

Lovell placed his head on the man's shoulder. Sobs echoed
off the trucks and boxes in the yard. Matt and the workers
looked away.

"You've been out to that cemetery. They told you not to go
out there because they're not there. That's just where their
body rests. I thought you understood that!"

He massaged Lovell's scalp, rocked him, and then began to
shake him.

"I'm your uncle. Now listen to me. They're gone and you
have to accept it. We sold the house. That's why I'm
moving everything. You know I wouldn't let anybody take
his or her things. Pull yourself together."

He released Lovell, allowing him to cover his face and
handed him a handkerchief.

"And wipe that mamitappin' dirt off your face. I'm not
going to have you walking around before you leave this
country wearing some dirt death mask."

Lovell cleaned his face, blew his nose and pocketed the
handkerchief.

"Damn, where'd that come from?"

[36]

The older man faked a punch.

"I'll allow you to take my hanky. Don't say I never did nothing for you."

The work crew, Matt and Lovell laughed. He walked to Matt, open handed.

"Matthew Johnson, national middleweight golden gloves champion, nineteen sixty two to nineteen sixty-six. I'm Mack Pendleton, this crazy Negroes uncle. I was Michigan State commissioner on boxing when you were fighting. You could have been professional middleweight champion of the world."

Matt stirred the ground with his foot. "Thank you sir."

"Why'd you stop boxing, son."

Matt still stirred the ground. "Young, dumb and full of cum." Uncle Mack spit.

"Well, I guess we all been that at one time or another in our life."

Three workmen had walked from the house. Only one carried a box. Lovell sat next to the worker apologizing. Uncle Mack waited until he had finished, then told all the men he'd see them in Lansing. Matt and Lovell followed him inside. Lovell stopped and looked around the now empty house. Three picture size light colorations, where the photographs of he and his parents had hung, held him, until his uncle pulled him away. Walking from the living room to the kitchen, from hardwood to carpet, sent sizzling electric currents through his legs. He and his dad had laid it in the kitchen when his mother, losing the feelings in her hands, had begun to drop dishes, pots and pans. It was the first sign, something was wrong. Uncle Mack kept Lovell moving. Down the steps to the basement, which used to have a pool table, T.V., bar, living room set, complete with stereo, all in the front room, with the freezer, washing machine and dryer, cabinets for canning, fishing and

[37]

hunting gear, in the back. The bar, with all the liquor, remained. Lovell and Uncle Mack sat down. Matt moved behind the bar, and took out three glasses. [SEP] "Uncle Mack, what are you drinking? I know what Lovell wants."

" Bourbon. There's no ice for whatever you want."

Matt sang Thelonious Monk's "Straight No Chaser" and they all laughed. Lovell could see Matt studying the crosses and ankhs, which had been burnt into the walls. After the toast Matt opened his mouth, and then closed it. Lovell touched Uncle Mack in the ribs with his elbow.

"Matt's wondering how a preacher, with crosses and Egyptian symbols burnt into the walls, could have a full bar in his basement?"

Uncle Mack sipped his bourbon and rubbed the few strands of hair, atop his head.

"He was a man first and a preacher second that's how. And until you were born, when he was fifty-two, he was the biggest pussy eating cock hound this side of the Mississippi. And you can believe that. He was my baby brother and I loved him. But I'm a tell you. It took Gloria, your mother, threatening to take you away and him never seeing you again for him to stop. Shit, by that time, he'd probably tagged every woman in his church and all the churches around here. But the thought of losing her and his only son scared him. Most men are like that. It's not until we either lose that special lady, or are faced with the prospect of losing them, that we change. It's a dick thing and all the men in this family have big ones and they stay hungry all the time. I'm eighty-six years old and my dick still gets hard every day. I keep me a young girl near and when she comes over I wear her tight skinned ass out. Your daddy was the same. He stopped running around but he still had him a young thang he saw three times a week, just for

[38]

sex. When your mama got sick she told him to go out and get him some young pussy because she knew how he was."
Lovell slapped fives with uncle.
"She has to be young doesn't she?"
Uncle Mack held his bourbon up to the light. "Having an old woman is like two dead batteries. I rub her. She rubs me and the wheels turn slow. With them young thangs, as soon as she takes off her clothes, sparks start to fly."
They all did high fives. Matt stared at a far corner of the room. Following his eyes, Lovell and Uncle Mack saw a 36x14 color picture of Lovell's parents. Uncle Mack placed his hand atop Lovell's.
"I didn't want them to take that. I thought I'd put it in my car. That was in 1926, they'd just gotten married."
Lovell's father wore a black three-piece suit with a high collar white shirt and black tie with a pearl stickpin in it.
"I've never seen that picture before. My mom looked a little plump. She was always slim."
Uncle Mack motioned for Matt to pour him another. "She was pregnant."
He covered his mouth as his eyes turned to the glass.
"Pregnant! You mean I have another sibling?"
He walked over and picked up the picture, looking into his mother's face. Uncle Mack snapped his fingers.
"Put that picture back where it was, sit down and listen."
Lovell returned to his seat, carrying the picture, still looking at his mother. Uncle Mack took it from him, sitting it between his legs.
"Your maternal grandfather, old man Rodgers, was a lascivious old fart. He felt he had privileges other men of color didn't have cause he could pass. He could say the word nigger with such contempt, it would make your skin peel off. Carried a pistol and didn't mind shooting a man of color because he knew the police wouldn't do nothing

[39]

because he had them in his pocket. That's the way he got away with all the shit he did. Had the numbers wheel, owned all the cat houses, all the land where colored folks lived, the restaurants, pool hall and the three mortuaries. That mamatapa had it so the city wouldn't give nobody else a license. In return, he gave them a cut of everything and all the free black pussy they wanted." Matt whistled.

"Is that why everything is named Pendleton?"

Uncle Mack pulled a pouch from his jacket pocket and rolled a refer.

"No. It's named Pendleton because we bought it from him. That comes later. This is some family history even Lovell doesn't know."

Lovell watched Uncle Mack lick the perfect shaped joint, light it, inhale, and then pass the pouch to Lovell. It was his way. Family came first. However, even if you were family and couldn't roll your own joint, you couldn't smoke with him. He, and Lovell's father were like that. You had to be independent or they wouldn't be bothered with you. Family or no family. Lovell rolled his joint and passed the weed to Matt.

"Old man Rodgers felt it was his right to break in all his daughters. Yeah, you heard me. He took all his daughter's virginity. And there were eleven of them."

Lovell looked down at the picture.

"Mom had ten sisters? She told me she was an orphan."

Uncle Mack used his fingers to extinguish his joint. "In her mind she was. Every last one of her sisters killed themselves in one-way or another. They all lived outside of Harbor Bend in the township. The old man kept them away from Negroes. That way he could do what he wanted without anybody knowing about it. Your grandmother, old lady Esther, found out what the old man was doing because one of the girls told. You see he'd knocked your mama up."

Matt choked. Lovell murmured, "Oh my god."

"When your mama started showing. Old Lady Esther sent
her to Mississippi to stay with her aunt. That's when she
met your daddy, who had just finished mortician school.
Like your mama, he was the baby. There was Sally, your
daddy and me. Sally had rooming houses all over Chicago
for musicians and Pullman car porters. She provided a bed,
clean sheets one meal a day and a woman at night if they
wanted. The rule though was, none of the men could bring
another woman to her house. She even pulled house rights
on all the poker and crap games that went on in the house.
She made them Negroes check their guns and razors at the
door though. With the money Sally made, she sent me to
architecture school in Canada, sent your daddy to college at
Tugaloo in Mississippi, and bought momma a house.
Momma never worked a day in her life. Never scrubbed or
did nothing for no white folks. Colored neither. Your
momma's aunt lived close to the school and your daddy
would see her everyday on his way. He told me she made
fun of him because she said she could smell formaldehyde
on him. Anyway, she was obviously pregnant and she told
your daddy who the baby's daddy was. It didn't matter to
him because he loved her. He graduated just before she was
to give birth and being as crazy as he was, took her on a
honeymoon, down there. He couldn't get a car to take him
up in the mountains where the resort was so he took her
himself. Your daddy had some funny ways boy. He had this
albino mule. That mule was the meanest joker you'd ever
seen. Couldn't anybody get close to him except your father.
I mean he'd kick and bite anybody who got near him. But
he was like a baby with your dad. Your father gets a car
and attaches a carrier to the back, where he puts the mule.
He travels as far as he can, then puts your mother, her belly
as big as a pumpkin, on the mule and carries her up the

[41]

mountain to the resort. Your grandfather gets wind of it and sends two tar babies up to the resort, and they beats the baby out of your mother, and nearly kills your daddy. They were both in the hospital for a month. That picture was taken the day your father graduated which was the same day they got married."

He sipped at the last of his bourbon.

"To answer your question Matt, there was nothing my sister loved more than family. When she saw what the old man had done to her baby brother, she sat out to get him. She used the gangsters she knew in Chicago. White, Colored, Italian, Polish, and had them do everything to destroy what the old man had. They shot the police, robbed the games, killed all his numbers runners, poisoned his livestock, and planted dead dogs in the old man's freezers so people wouldn't eat in the restaurants. Every time that white nigger closed a business, she'd buy it, and put our name on it. She convinced Lovell's dad to take over the mortuaries and I took care of everything else. The price she paid though was she had to allow them gangsters to use Harbor Bend as a drop off point for whatever they wanted and she didn't get a cut. That's why this little sleepy town is so full of drugs now. They drop part of their shipment here going to Chicago one way and Detroit the other."

The empty bourbon and wine bottle sat on the counter, with the weedless pouch. Lovell lifted the picture and kissed his mother's face.

"So what happened to my grandfather and aunts?"

"As your grandfather began to lose everything, he also lost his protection from the police and authorities. He'd done so many darkies wrong they got back at him in the way they knew would hurt him the most; his girls. Jiggaboos would be waiting in the bushes outside his house or lying wait on the farm and they raped them every time they saw them.

[42]

The old man couldn't do anything about it because he couldn't catch them. One day a group of darkies confronted the old man directly and he chased them with a shotgun. That was just what they wanted him to do. Another group of darkies went into the house while that old bastard was thinking he was having a shootout with a bunch of niggers. The others were running trains on his wife and all his daughters. He came home feeling as if he'd done something and discovered he'd been hood winked. He went to bed that night and when he woke up in the morning, his wife, your grandmother, and all his daughters, your aunts, had drank poison and were dead. That old muthafucka came crying to your father to fix them up because the poison had disfigured all of them. Your father did a good job. Your mother, god rest her soul, insisted on sitting there and watching while he embalmed all of them. Then she dressed them and sat with them by herself for an entire night and not one iota of water dropped from her eyes. That white nigger, your grandfather came and picked up the bodies the next day. Your dad said your mother watched him from the mortuary's upstairs window. People said he buried them all out there on his land, which is now yours. I know you're going to ask me when he died. You were still in school. It was five years ago, 1974. He was ninety years old. God punished his ass. He spent forty- six years out there by himself. Now my mouth is dry and I'm tired of talking. You know the whole story now. Wrap it up in your pocket and take it with you, along with those stones you're walking on."

Lovell opened his mouth but was silenced by a voice and footsteps coming down the stairs. Matt snatched the pouch, placing it in his pocket. "Hello?"

A five foot four man with blond shoulder length hair, wearing a physician's jacket, and smelling of vodka, stepped into the basement.

"I'm Doctor Mark Winiford, and I've, I've, come to say I'm sorry. I know what's been going on at the hospital with Mrs. Pendleton's death certificate and I just can't live with myself and be part of all this. We made a very terrible mistake. She didn't have to die. We were looking for everything but the obvious. People haven't died from intestinal blockage since the thirties. I'm very sorry. They're holding the death certificate until the statute of limitations runs out. I've done enough already and refuse to be a part of it. If you decide to sue, I'll testify on your behalf, even though it will hurt my business and reputation."

Screaming, Lovell snatched the wine bottle and breaking it on the counter, was on the doctor. He pounded the doctor's head against the floor with his left hand while holding the fractured Merlot bottle with his right. Uncle Mack reached for Lovell who turned and swung at him. Uncle Mack and Matt took two steps back, and then froze.

The doctor shouted,

"Kill me! Kill me! I deserve to die."

Lovell held the bottle to his jugular vein. Uncle Mack took two steps forward.

"Lovell, put the bottle down son. I know how you want to kill him and so do I. But that's not going to get us anywhere. If you kill him you'll be facing murder and this is still the U.S. and he's still a white man. They'd like nothing better than to put another successful black man in jail. You know that. You have your whole life in front of you. Don't throw it away son. If you kill him they'll be four lives gone. Your parents, this shit head doctor and you. Let me get him and the whole hospital son. That's what your parents would want you to do. Think about them and how proud they were of you. They would be disappointed to know you threw away your future behind some ignorant crackers."

 Snot dripped from Lovell's nose. His breathing came in staccato spurts. Placing the half bottle next to the doctor's face, he got up, took the picture and embracing it, sat on the floor rocking. The doctor lay on the floor, both hands over his eyes. Matt rushed over and snatched him up. Uncle Mack spun him around and pushing him up the stairs, kicked him in the ass. "Get your monkey ass out of here before I change my mind and kill you myself. I'll have someone watching every move you make so you better not try and leave until I get a deposition from you." The doctor ran up the stairs and vanished. Matt sat on one of the bar stools sighing. "I wondered why you were leaving Lovell. Now I know. That little shit they tried to do to you in San Anton wasn't shit. This shit is real. If you stay here you'll end up killing a white man."

Uncle Mack, heaving, exhaled in agreement, and helping Lovell up, took the picture from him, and led the younger men upstairs and out the house, locking it behind him. Lovell, Matt and Uncle Mack, reclined on white brocade French provincial furniture, in the lounge of Uncle Mack's fifty-foot yacht, sipping champagne and Merlot. Lovell stared upward through the skylight watching the stars do somersaults. They were on their way to Chicago. Lovell had turned in the Mercedes at the Hertz rental office in St. Mary, the twin city to Harbor Bend. Matt had noticed the two and three story houses, numerous businesses, shopping Malls and whites in the streets. He had seen no whites in Harbor Bend and except for the row where Lovell's family owned businesses, there was only boarded up houses, and empty lots. Uncle Mack had told Matt that's why they

[45]

called the bridge between the two cities the longest bridge in the world. Harbor Bend had 85% unemployment, while St. Mary had 85% employed and 90% of those people were professionals. He had insisted they ride with him to Chicago and when Lovell had gone to the john had told Matt how water always calmed Lovell, who had been born on a rainy day and whose mother had taken Lovell into the bathroom whenever he wouldn't stop crying and turned on the water, which made the infant, then a little boy and ultimately a teenager, and man, stop. The family had a small fountain in Lovell's room and in the living room, which was never turned off, while he was at home. Matt had told Uncle Mack about the stories he'd heard of Lovell sitting for hours at the San Antonio River. Sometimes spontaneously playing his horn, to the delight of the shop owners on the river and subsequently, Lovell never paid for food or drinks anytime he was there. Lovell, eyes staring into his chest, had retreated to somewhere neither Uncle Mack, nor Matt could reach, embracing his parent's picture. It was only when the boat began its gliding journey, did he ask his uncle to tell him the truth about his parent's death. He had only been told his mother had died from malpractice and his father had had a heart attack shortly afterwards. Lovell had just returned from seeing his mother, and his skin had burned once he'd stepped out of the elevator, onto the floor where his mother's room was, because he'd heard her screaming from the pain. Entering the room, he'd counted eight machines connected to her, and his father collaring a nurse, who eyes were ablaze with fear, was promising to do more for his mom. Lovell had pulled his dad off the woman and together they'd walked to the nurses' station and raised so much hell, the same young doctor who'd come to the house had appeared and tripled the amount of morphine, his mother was receiving. He and

[46]

his dad had then sat, beside her bed holding hands, her face looking as if she had pancake make on and praying for God to take his mother home.

"Why didn't you tell me mommy was sick, dad?"

His father had leaned into the gray silk handkerchief, which matched his suit.

"I didn't know she was sick son. We were standing in the kitchen and she turned to say something to me and dropped to the floor."

Lovell's mom had opened her eyes at that point. "Boy what are you doing here? Don't you have a premiere to go to?"

He'd rubbed her hand.

"That's not important mommy, I…"

She'd sat up.

"What are you going to do, sit here and watch me die? That won't make it easier for me baby. It'll make it worse. What have I always told you? You throw that dream of yours out there and you go after it. That's what life's about. Now I want you to get up right now and go back to San Antonio. No telling what them nasty folks you've been fighting with might do if you're not there. Now go on before I have to get out of this bed and do some butt warming. You know I'll do it too."

Pushing the morphine button, she'd motioned for him to come closer and embraced him.

"Remember baby, all you have to do is close your eyes, think and I'll be there. This old body is tired and ready to rest. I'm proud of you baby. I want you to take care of your father. You know how weak he is. Now let me get one last look at you and you at me. And remember to wear a dark suit tonight it looks more professional. And put some grease on that wild hair."

She'd pulled his left ear, the way she did when he was a child and pushed him away from her. He'd left the room,

[47]

after kissing his father and without looking back. He had flown to San Antonio, holding his ear, and a lock of her hair she'd slipped into his pocket. Lovell was dreaming of his mom wearing an aqua summer dress with sunflowers splattered over it in the yard, barefoot, spraying her roses, in time for his movie premiere. When he'd returned home, alone, Kam Ha and Eduardo both having had something to do afterwards, his father had called and told him she'd gone home, as African Americans called it. He'd then gone to Eduardo's house, wanting a shoulder to hold his head, but his buddy had opened his door and before Lovell could tell him, had said he was fuckin' and to call him later. Kam Ha was also not home, so he had called Nidia, disguising his voice with a Mexican accent, claiming to be a relative with an emergency call and had released his sorrow into the phone, talking to her until the sun opened its eyes welcoming a new day. Later, he'd just gotten out of the shower when Eduardo had arrived, face flushed, and held Lovell, who dry eyed, had not returned the embrace, until Eduardo began to sing his mom's favorite blues song, ("You Use Ta Luv Me"), by B.B.King. It was then he'd clamped onto his friend and choked on the grief, which salted Eduardo's shoulder. He'd ridden with his Hibado, Eduardo, (country boy in Puerto Rican Spanish), to the airport, not remembered the flight, and had been met by Uncle Mack, in Chicago, who'd told him of his father's death. Lovell and Uncle Mack had had his parents cremated, per their instructions, the same day and had, also, per his father's instructions, played a video tape, of his father talking to his congregation, at the funeral service, about his passing and what he wanted done at and with his church. Watching the sky, splattered with stars, Lovell listened as his uncle explained how his mother had opened her eyes and told his father that her seven sisters were

[48]

around the bed, ready to take her, but couldn't because he was there. She had told him to go into the bathroom, but leave the door open so she could see him, and as he stood, she raised one hand, as if she were taking someone else's hand, had waved to him, and closed her eyes. Uncle Mack had watched this from the door of the room, and then had entered once his brother had lain next to his wife on the bed.

"Mackie, I can see my baby. She's wearing that pink dress I bought her with the red roses and she's telling me all I have to do is walk through this door to join her. I'm going Mackie. Look after my boy for me."

He had taken his brother's hand, and smiling, died. Lovell knew none of this. He had only been told his father had had a heart attack the same day his mother had died, and his uncle was suing the hospital. Downing his Merlot, Lovell gave Uncle Mack his parent's picture and taking off his shoes, curled into a fetal position, and slept until the boat docked, in Chicago. Uncle Mack pulling his ear, awakened Lovell. Standing, Uncle Mack guided him to the bathroom. "We're at the port. Now you have plenty of time so I want you to go in there, take a shower and wash that grief off you. I left a bad vine in there for you to wear."

Obeying, Lovell showered and emerged in the burgundy three-piece suit with a pink collarless shirt. His initials were embroidered on the breast pocket and the sleeves. Uncle Mack pointed to three pieces of new Samsonite luggage.

"I know you Negro. You left all your clothes and you only have books in your suitcases. Now look. I want you to leave the books at the front desk of the hotel and I'll send them to you. I've had some vines and leisure suits made for you. You gots to be clean when you hit Africa. You don't want them to think we don't rag here. Don't worry, they're all in your style."

[49]

Pulling Lovell to him, Uncle Mack patted him on the back three times.

"Don't try and change the rules baby. It's their land. Bend, but don't break. I'll see you when I see you." Kissing Lovell on both cheeks, he walked with Matt and Lovell to the dock, slapped hands with Matt, kissed Lovell again and pimped back to the boat.

"I know you Negroes won't forget how to walk while you're there will you? Oh yes, be careful, I've been told, them suckers are real funny about their women."

He saluted, boarded his yacht, and held his glass of bourbon in the air, saluting them, as he disappeared into the night. Lovell and Matt carrying the suitcases took a taxi to their hotel. Walking to their rooms, Matt stopped before going into his room.

"People in San Antonio don't have a clue where you come from. They think you're this artist, with a degree, who always has his ass on his shoulders. You have a right to be proud nigger. Just like me. The difference is I don't have the personality to scare people. You do. Especially white folks, and they'll always come after you because they can't stand to see a proud nigger who doesn't mind letting them know, he doesn't need them and he's superior. You got a hard row to hoe, nigger. But I got your back."

They slapped hands, and slept their last night, on U.S. soil.

CHAPTER FOUR

Sitting in the first class section of Alitalia, Lovell
watched the mint green clad workers load the plane. His
saxophones, alto and soprano under the seat, he chuckled at
Matt, who'd already gone to sleep. They'd walked out of
their rooms at the same time. Matt was accompanied by
one of the call girls listed on the special menu in the room's
special drawer. He'd been surprised she was Asian, having
never seen an Asian call girl before. Matt had seen his eyes
rise. "Black is alright, and brown is better. But me, I like's
em yellow." Those were the lines from a Blind Lemon
Jefferson song. High fiving, Lovell had pushed Matt.
"Damn bro' she fucked you to death".
Matt had made a rocking horse motion, then had
immediately fallen asleep in the airport van, and later,
stumbled through check in, slept before boarding the plane
in the airport lounge, and had knocked out as soon as
they'd sat down. Lovell could smell the Vodka coming
from Matt's pores. He took a blanket from under the seat
and placed it over Matt and watched while he rubbed his
head, beard, then snored with a hushed tone. Lovell smelled
a familiar fragrance. He looked up to see a guitar shaped
woman, in white high waist pants and Bolero jacket,
helping a stooped, ponytail silver mane man wearing a
cream silk suit and shoes, down the aisle and into his seat.
Lovell knew that walk. He had seen the pumpkin sitting on
her back before. Had smelled the Joy perfume, which she
patted in three spots on each cheek. His eyes had devoured
the red strawberry birthmark on the right cheek, shaped like
an open palm. His hands had run their fingertips over those
cheeks, had held them like a newborn infant and had
fingered tipped the 22-inch waist. They had circled the tan

[51]

back with black moles on the back of each shoulder, with a finger sized one in the center. His palms knew it bothered her when wearing a bra. That's why she didn't wear one. The coal black hair still hung to her shoulders. But he noticed a few strands of grey, just around the ears, and those golf ball sized twenty-four carat gold hoop earrings. He'd bought them with the money Sleepy the pimp had given him for telling him John L, another pimp, was waiting in the hallway of his apartment building, his pistol ready to fire. She turned around, the white V neck silk sweater welcoming two hands full of breasts, with the strands of hair between, after seating the man, who wheezed. The full moon liquid pools of eyes were the same. The pinched mouth and natural pyramid shaped eyebrows. Seeing Lovell, alabaster white teeth showed with the gold inside and the arms, before hard from the one hundred push ups she did daily, still firm, went to those hips. He understood those hips too. Understood them well enough to know how each muscle moved, and watched as they bent slightly to the right, along with that almost full face, cheeky he called it, as she blinked three times. That was their signal for I love you.

"Do you still love candy mon ami?"

Lovell blinked his eyes three times.

"Now, more than ever because I've learned how to appreciate it."

She ran her hands over the sides of that pumpkin. "We shall see, mon ami. The plane is about to take off. We shall talk as we're in the air. Yes? I must calm my husband."

Winking, she turned and sat down. He saw the rigid arm muscle place a blanket over the man's shoulder. Shuddered at the missing top half of the pinky, remembering the knife fight, which caused it to plop onto her hardwood floor. Smiled as she extracted an oxygen mask, placing it over her

[52]

husband's mouth. And held the throbbing beneath his
pants, for the forty seven year old woman, he knew as Miss
Marguerite. Nudging Matt, whose gurgled snoring had
begun to turn heads, Lovell waited for Miss Marguerite to
move the oxygen tank brought into the first class cabin,
into the row of seats, where her husband had reclined. Matt
gulped, wiping away slobber.
"Why'd you wake me?"
"Your snoring kept everyone awake."
Matt swiveled his head.
"Was I that loud?"
Lovell made a drum roll motion, as Miss Marguerite, stood
and blinking, walked toward the lavatory. Matt grabbed
Lovell's arm.
"It's amazing who you see in first class. Do you know who
that is?"
Lovell opened his mouth, and then shrugged his shoulders.
Matt lightly tapped him upside the head. "What world do
you live in? They've been writing about her for the past
year. She's Marguerite Jean Baptise, the wife of this old
Italian count who's supposed to be the only surviving
member of the Medici family and worth mega billions. He
met her at a hotel when she was a bartender about ten years
ago. He was this aging playboy and got drunk one night,
without his bodyguards and fell into the pool. She saved his
ass and refused the muthafucka's reward. This blew his
mind and he pursued her for two years until she finally
married him. Now the old geezer's about to die and she's
going to inherit all the family money because he has no
family."
Lovell looked back at Miss Marguerite who stood annoying
her hair ends, staring at him. Matt noticed and hit Lovell in
the arm.

[53]

"If I was you I'd go see what she wants. You never know what might happen. That old dude's going to die soon. He's so crazy and paranoid sometimes he won't even ride on his own jet. That's probably why she's here. Go on!"

The Count gagged and Miss Marguerite came running down the aisle, turned the Count over and wiped his mouth. She focused on Lovell by pulling at her ear.

"Mon ami, you were never one to make me wait. Come here. It has been years."

She spoke to Lovell in French. Matt's mouth left an open space.

"You know her man?"

Lovell stood and eased past Matt. Miss Marguerite cursed in French.

"I've known him almost all his life young man. In ways you can never imagine."

Matt slapped himself upside the head and called the stewardess for a drink. Lovell took Miss Marguerite's hands, knelt, and kissed them. Mascara railroad tracks appeared on her face.

"I am so proud of you mon ami. I have followed everything you've done. You'd be surprised to know I'm the silent contributor of your film. Giuseppe and I that is. He loves your work."

She smoothed the tears from his face.

"I'm sorry about your parents. Are you vacationing?"

She glanced around the hallway at the Count. Lovell noticed an age line on her neck.

"No ma'am. I'm going to teach in Aybil." Marguerite's face darkened and she slapped Lovell.

"Why, what the fuck are you going to teach there for? Don't you know he's a dictator and people disappear there all the time? I won't let you Lovey. I won't let you. I've just found you again and I don't want to lose you."

[54]

She held onto Lovell, her face in his shoulder, and shook. The other passengers turned and looked, while the stewardesses scurried about, their heads bobbing. Lovell swayed back and forth with Miss Marguerite.

"How could I go wrong, when I've learned all I know from you and my parents?"

Marguerite loosened her grip on Lovell.

"You're right. You have always been a man. Ever since I first saw you, you carried yourself like a little man. Now you've grown into a hunk of a man. How does it feel to be famous?"

Lovell ran his thumb across her chin.

"It is not I who is famous. It is you, Countess."

The Countess looked around, stepped close to Lovell and in one swift motion squeezed his penis and let go.

"I will tell you about what people perceiving as fame later. Guiseppi will be awakening soon."

Kissing him on both cheeks, she swayed to her seat, behind the Count, who sat up and removed the oxygen mask. The Countess Marguerite sat beside him and pushed the button for the stewardess, as Lovell, hand in pocket, stiff legged it to his seat, where two Merlots and Matt, awaited him.

"I know you don't want an ass whippin' do you?"

Lovell pretended to cover his head.

"No massa sir."

Matt raised his hand as if holding a whip. "Then tell me how you know that fine, foxy, classy woman."

Lovell mused his Merlot.

"I was ten when she moved across the street from us. She had no children, no husband, and as the moving truck unloaded her furniture, my mother commented she had expensive furniture and wealthy taste. I never saw her work during all the time I knew her, but she always had tons of

[55]

money. I know because I worked for her and saw where she put it. It was in the freezer, inside ice cream boxes."

Matt watched the Count and Countess kissing.

"You worked for her? What did you do?"

" I cleaned up her yard, cut the grass, shoveled her snow, and rode with her to the grocery store to carry her groceries."

Matt watched the Countess order a bottle of champagne.

"I saw her grab your dick. You must have been doing another kind of working too."

Lovell watched the Countess, whom he had known as Miss Marguerite, pour her husband a glass of champagne, clink glasses with her husband, down it, pour another, and then motion for Lovell to join them.

"She was my first and taught me how to be a considerate and good lover. I'll tell you more later."

Moving past Matt, he joined the Count and Countess. Lovell expected a shattered whisky bottle sound, full of halting breaths, but was surprised at the full baritone, emanating from his skeletal body. Like the Countess, he spoke to Lovell in French.

"Your work is the bowed strings of a hand carved cello, played in a garden of orchids and petunias. I salute you."

He raised the champagne glass and touched the champagne with his tongue.

"And now, my wife tells me, you are headed to Aybil. I hope you are ready to live under a boy ruler. Do you have a death wish?"

His pale green eyes, whitening around the edges, were hollow, with knuckle deep black hollows around them. The Countess wiped his dripping nose.

"I think not. I think it is the wanderings of a young man in pursuit of the unattainable peace. She is a filthy slut and we've all had her momentarily and she has left us all, with our dicks in our hands, and our hearts in her mouth. You will never have her my young friend. Never! Death knocks at my door and I still can't find the bitch!"

He laughed and choked. Miss Marguerite covered his face with the oxygen mask. He removed it and pointed a gnarled finger at Lovell.

"I know you from your work young man, and my wife's ravings about you. I shall watch over you in Aybil. After all, the boy ruler, at heart, is a peasant, who desires riches and power. He is easily swayed by trinkets, symbols, and anything, which moves in straight lines and squares. I know that type of man. They are afraid of what squirts from between their legs. I shall see you at my estate after we land. Go back to your seat."

Heat rose in Lovell's ears. Miss Marguerite touched him with her knee. He rose and backed to his chair, still watching the Count, who returned the look, then stumbled over Matt's legs, falling into his chair. Sitting up, he watched the Count recline with the oxygen mask. Miss Marguerite placed a finger to her lips. Lovell nodded and cursed. Matt patted his thigh.

"Old men, especially those who've grown up with everything at their disposal, have some shitty ways man. Don't take it personally."

Lovell watched the cotton fluffed clouds moving outside the airplane window. He was interrupted by the fasten your seat belt sign and the pilot announcing, they were approaching Rome, Italy. He drank the last of his wine and waited for the plane to land. Once the plane stopped, the door opened and three men, in high-buttoned grey suits, came aboard with a wheel chair. The Count spoke to them in Italian and as he was wheeled from the plane, the Countess following, one of the men told Lovell and Matt to follow them. They were met at the foot of the stairs by a limousine and driven from the airport, without going through customs, to a dock, where Lovell thought, an ocean liner awaited them; it was the Count's yacht. Once aboard, he and Matt were shown to two separate living room sized rooms, complete with shower, bar, bed, stereo system, movie screen and refrigerator. Stretching out on the bed, a syrup colored, red headed woman with midnight eyes, walked toward him, letting a black sheer robe fall to the floor with each step. Later, he awoke to the smell of Joy. "We're here mon ami." She glanced at his dick. "Giuseppe's an old man Lovell. Don't take anything he says seriously. Except for looking out for you. Be cool." She ran from his room. Exiting the room, Lovell picked up the robe, smelled it, then folding it neatly, placed it in his bag, and walked up the stairs to the top deck. Matt made an in and out motion with his arm. Lovell gave him a high five and they were led down the gangplank to a waiting limousine. The sign at the dock said Ischia Porte. The roads snaked upward and ended with a plateau which had a thirty-foot wrought iron fence covered with ivy. A four-foot gold "M" was on the gate, which opened allowing the caravan of limousines enter. They rode through two football sized courtyards with fountains, sunflowers and lilies. Lovell knew they were Miss Marguerite's favorites. Lovell and Matt sat in the back of one limousine and heard Miss Marguerite's voice come through the speakers. "Mon ami, I'll see you in the evening. We're having guests. I'll send a tailor over for you and your friend."

Matt gave Lovell the thumbs up sign. They were driven to a 6th century castle with angels fighting gargoyle statues in front. Water came from the gargoyle's mouth. The twenty-foot doors were opened and a dough bodied Italian woman, in her early thirties, in a white cotton uniform, with ringlet hair, greeted them with bubbling eyes. Walking in front of them, Matt pointed to her behind and made a round hand movement. Lovell had seen it too. The woman was around five foot four and had a bubble butt. The walls of the castle were adorned with Salvador Dali originals, and gothic scenes of angels, gliding through the skies. Long woven rugs covered marble floors, and lifelike knights in armor, stood beside each door. The woman stopped in front of a ten-foot wooden door, and turned the brass handle, opening it.

"This is your room Mr. Johnson."

Matt walked into the room. "And what is your name Sicilian?" The woman curtsied.

"My name is Juliana and I'm from Naples, not Sicily."

Matt looked at Lovell and said Hannibal before closing the door. She then led Lovell to a room farther down the hall, opened the door and entered before Lovell. His bags sat near a window, which opened onto one of the courtyards. A baby grand piano sat in the middle, with a sofa, rectangular coffee table, lounge chair, desk, eight foot entertainment unit, bed and pool table, all made of redwood, arranged in a circle. Juliana opened the entertainment unit and sat the remote on the table. "If you need, or want anything senori, push the red button on the remote. The blue button opens the bar, which also has refreshments. We are here to serve you senori." She turned to leave.

"Juliana?"

"Yes, senori?"

"I'm hungry. Do you have any fruit and calamari?"

"What kind of fruit senori?"

Lovell walked to the window and saw the limousines being driven across the courtyard. "Melons, like watermelon, grapes, pineapples. That kind of fruit." Juliana rubbed her hands together. "The Countess has fresh strawberries and cherries senori. She told us you'd like them. Shall I bring

[59]

them with the other fruit you requested?"

"Yes, and some fresh grapefruit juice."

"It shall be here immediately senori."

She left and Lovell's attention was drawn to the fifty-four inch television coming on. He watched as Miss Marguerite undressed, dropping each garment to the floor, then standing unclothed, she blinked her eyes three times, and climbed into a sunken bathtub, with mounds of bubbles. The four foot four tailor fitted Lovell in a three-piece royal blue suit. Emerging from his door, he saw Julianna, leaving Matt's room, pinning up her hair. He waited outside and Matt, dressed in dark purple, exited his room, smelling his fingers.

"Good lunch huh?"

Matt licked his fingers.

"I hope I don't go sleep during dinner. Man, I swear, being with you is something. This will all end once we get to Aybil, you know."

Lovell stopped Matt with his hand.

"What do you mean?"

" Negro, didn't you read the last page of the brochure? There's strict religious laws in Aybil. Unless we get lucky, this is the last pussy we're going to get. For a brilliant coon, you sure don't pay attention to details sometimes."

Lovell walked past Julianna, who smiled at Matt as they exited the castle and entered the limousine.   Six saxophones to the right, and six trumpets to the left, playing in parallel fifths, sounding like a gospel horn section, blasted Curtis Mayfield's " We Are Winners", as Lovell and Matt were escorted from the limousine to the main building of the Count's Estate. They entered an auditorium sized ballroom and, what Lovell thought to be a thousand people, began to cheer and chant his name. The Count, in a white tuxedo, maneuvered his electric wheelchair down a

[60]

red carpet, with Miss Marguerite, in abalone, the Countess by his side, met Lovell, bowed his head to Lovell, then allowed Miss Marguerite to turn him around and lead Lovell to a massive banquet table, where Lovell sat next to The Countess Marguerite, as the guest of honor. He could not count the courses, toasts, nor the roasts by people who had only heard stories of him, and was enthralled by the standing ovation he was given, after dinner, when the gala watched his movie.   Walking to a podium placed above everyone, his book in hand, to read from it for people whose second language was English, but had read the book in translation, by the Countess. Lovell saw his mom and dad, both with arms outstretched, beckoning him to come, their crystal eyes ablaze with pride. He reached the podium and had just said thank you in French, Spanish, Portuguese, the languages he knew, and Italian, which he didn't know, when the Count, oxygen fitter around his nose, slumped in his chair, blue faced. Miss Marguerite began to scream as doctors rushed to the Count's side and rushed him away. The guests stared at their drinks, then filed out of the ballroom, to their awaiting cars. Lovell read to Matt in the limousine, as they headed to their small castle. Alone, in his room, he stared at the television, until Miss Marguerite appeared, still dressed.

"Mon Ami, he's not dead, but he's close. I don't know if they can save him this time. I didn't want to come to you tonight, my dear. However, I have to be here. I give you all my love and kisses mon ami, and I will pray for your safety in that hellish country you've decided to go to. I'm still angry with you about that. But, then again it is you who must live your life, not I. Write to me love. My address is in the lining of the aqua suit I had placed in your suitcase. Those dreadful Muslims have their first Eed around

Thanksgiving. I shall expect to see you then. Yes, Mon ami."

Lovell blinked three times.

"Guiseppi does not say something and not follow through. Remember that. I shall see you soon. Your friend has a very healthy appetite. I would suggest you do the same." She blew a kiss and the screen went blank. He showered and naked, sat on the ledge before the window, in the dark, listening to the estate's fountains. His door opened, the light was turned on, and a woman stepped out of a knit black poncho, with quarter size holes. She said my name is Ethiopia. The name fit her appearance, and the television screen came alive.

CHAPTER FIVE

Lovell and Matt had boarded the Alitalia flight first. The other passengers, dressed in suits and dresses, had begun ordering drinks as soon as the plane was airborne. Lovell and Matt, exhausted, fell asleep watching Midnight Cowboy. The plane's dissension woke them. Lovell grabbed Matt.

"Matt, the plane's been high jacked!"

Matt pulled out his knife, Lovell his, and standing, back-to-back, they surveyed the plane. All the women were covered with white sheets, revealing only one eye, and the men wore Kufis. The flight airman, ran down the aisle and stopped in front of them.

"Please signoris, put your knives away. We have not been high jacked. This is the required dress for the women in Aybil. The country lives under Sharia, strict Muslim law. Please sit down and put your knives away. We are about to land."

The two men pocketed their knives and sat down. Matt stared at the sheeted women.

"Man, they didn't put this in the brochure. We've stepped into another century."

*****

Lovell sat on his luggage while Matt paced. His luggage hadn't been found. Lovell's had been opened and two of the vests to the suits his uncle had made for him were missing. They walked to an office marked luggage. Inside a middle linebacker sized man, unshaven, and wearing a wrinkled A-Italia uniform, dosed. They smelled Cutty Sark. Matt hit the table.

"Excuse me, I've been waiting out here for a half an hour and my luggage still hasn't arrived. I'd like some help."

[63]

The man opened his eyes, muttered "buckra", and closed them again. Matt hit the table with his fist. "What the fuck you mean buckra. It's hot. I'm funky and hungry. I went to shit and there wasn't any toilet paper so I had to cut my shirt, and you're going to tell me buckra, later. Bullshit!" The man jumped to his feet.

"You use that language again and I'll throw you out of here. This is a religious country. We're Muslims."
Matt walked over to the trash and opened a paper bag, pulling out the bottle of Cutty Sark.

"Well look, drunk ass Mr. Muslim. I need my--"
The man reached across the desk and grabbed Matt by the shirt. Matt uppercut the man's elbow, breaking his grasp, snatched him by the tie and lifted him into the air, bringing him down on Matt's knee, in the center of his back. Cutty Sark and mucus, shot into the air. He hiccupped, trying to grasp air. Matt raised a closed fist.

"Don't make me have to kick your Aybil ass muthafucka. He released the Alitalia worker who crawled on the floor coughing, then sat on his butt, cleaning his mouth with the heel of his hand.

"Go down the hall, they're probably inspecting it." Lovell put his suitcases on a trolley outside the office. He and Matt walked to an office with a closed door. Matt opened it to find four men, all in their early twenties, with one of his Playboy books in hand, jerking off. Lovell fell to his knees laughing. The young men put the Playboy over their penises.

"Please sirs. Don't tell on us. We were just, we were just…"
Matt walked over and closed his suitcases.

"You all were just beating your meat that's all. Keep the magazines. We just want to get to Jami- Al-Fateh."

[64]

The young man, still flushed, stared at the door. "Did the
Hajj down the hall come with you? I mean did he see us?"
Matt laughed until tears wet his beard.
"That muthafucka's too drunk to see anybody. He probably
went back to sleep."
They turned to each other, their mouths open.
"The Hajj, drunk?"
Matt motioned for them to follow. They tried the Hajj's
door but it was locked. Matt got to the floor and beckoned
to the young men to come down. Under the door, they
could see the Hajj asleep on the floor. The bottle of Cutty
Sark beside him. Matt stood.
"I'm Matt Johnson. This is Lovell Pendleton. We'll both be
teaching at the University."
The young men's faces brightened. A tall one, favoring
John Travolta, except with yellow skin, extended his hand.
"I'm Ramadan, he's Malik, this is Ali and that's Ali. We
were students at Jami-Al Fateh. Now we work here in what
Aybil calls customs. We'll get you a taxi. But first, Ali, go
get the vests."
Ali, reminded Lovell of a young Ricardo Montalban. He
returned with the vests and handed them to Lovell. "You
guys like the vests, keep them. Now you owe us."
Their brows pulled together.
 "What do we owe you sir?" Matt held out his hand. "A
favor when we need it. Now help us get a cab."
Ali, a David Ruffin clone, and Malik, Clark Kent like
twins, waited while Ramadan and Ali took Lovell and Matt
to get a taxi.   They talked to the taxi driver who drove
them, in the night, to Al-Fateh University. Stopping at the
University's gate, which had armed guards, Lovell and
Matt saw the two-story portrait of the Colonel, the
country's ruler, surrounded by colored lights. Even in the
dark, tall palm trees were visible. The taxi driver refused

[65]

the dollars they offered, pointed to a building and said
"professor", in English. They got their bags and standing
outside a red stucco building shouted,
"Does anyone speak English?"
A voice came from a second floor balcony.
"No, but I'm fluent in American."
Lovell and Matt bumped fists.

*****

Six-eight at a minimum, a hairless chalk colored Abe
Lincoln, with a patch over the left eye, stood wide legged
wearing black Viet Cong pajamas and shower shoes.
Smiling he walked toward Lovell and Matt, then stretched
his neck forward, looking at Lovell, moved his head back,
and fell to the ground crying.
"I knew you'd come back buddy. I knew it. I didn't know
what form you'd be in, but I knew I'd see you again."
He rocked back and forth on his knees, face prostrate to the
ground, then jumped up, and saluted.
"Sergeant Major Jim Ellingsworth reporting for duty sir."
Matt clicked to attention and saluted.
"Lieutenant Major Matt Johnson. At ease Sergeant Major."
Jim/Abe Lincoln spread his legs, placing both hands behind
his back.
"Stand down sergeant."
Jim reached for Matt's bags looking up at Lovell. "Hey,
buddy."
Lovell extended his hand.
"Hey Jim, I'm Lovell Pendleton."
Jim lifted Matt's suitcases, two in each hand.
"So, you've come back with the name Lovell Pendleton.
Before you were Michael Ellingsworth."
Lovell opened his mouth but Matt stepped between them.

[66]

"Soldier, we're tired, funky, and hungry. We need to get to our rooms and crash."

Jim made an about face and marched with the suitcases. Lovell made a crazy signal. However, Matt ignored him. They entered a lit, pale yellow long corridor, painted with pictures of the ruler on both sides, and newly waxed floors. Matt carried two of Lovell's suitcases and as they ascended the stairs, Jim, continued to turn and look at Lovell. Reaching the second floor, they walked past a room and the smell of stale acid urine, and rank feces, assaulted their noses. Jim didn't turn around.

"You know what that is."

"The latrine."

Matt barked. They continued past four rooms and turned into an open door. A red bulb lit a mosquito net hanging over two single beds pushed together, to the left. Matt surveyed the room and removed his shoes. Lovell copied Matt, who took his shoes and placed them beside the now closed door. Jim, barefoot, had put Matt's bags beneath a high rectangle table.   Lovell carried his suitcases over, putting them next to Matt's. Matt and Jim moved to the other side of the room, which was only slightly lit from the red bulb, and sat, cross-legged, on a sofa draped in a thick black and white tiger cloth. Jim reached over and passed a round bamboo basket to Matt, who took some bread, cheese and grapes, then handed it to Lovell. He took some apricots, two oranges, and a handful of kumquats and the remaining green grapes.

"This is all the rations I have. The cafeteria will be open in the morning. If you have to go to the head, turn to the left, that's the one I use. It's clean. The others are filthy. The Aybil soldiers are still here. They'll clean everything, but the toilets. Don't ask me why because I don't know.

[67]

They've let me use this one. Don't know why. Once they knew I was using it they never came back."

Matt got up and leaving the door open as he departed, turned to the left. Jim rubbed his hands together.

"Did it hurt buddy?"

Before Lovell could answer, Matt walked into the room.

"There's shit piled up in every stall, only one sit down toilet, and it doesn't have any toilet paper. I thought you said the john was clean?"

Jim nervously scratched his slick skull.

"I guess the water's gone off again and they used the toilets. There's only one sit down in each head. They all have boot prints on them because the Arabs won't sit on them."

Matt paced.

"How often does the water go off?"

"I've been here two weeks and it's been off more than it's on. That and the hot water. It only comes on once a day at different times."

Matt rubbed his palms together.

"Well, I guess it's back to basics. Is there a room where the main fuses and technical shit is?"

Jim stood and walked towards the door.

"I'll show you."

Lovell's eyes slowly adjusted to the room's darkness. Bamboo baskets hung from the ceiling on hooks. He touched the walls. They were cinder blocks. He moved past a round, knee high table, to closed shutter doors and opening them, took a deep breath, in awe of the North African moon, which, at only half, covered the entire bottom of the sky. Lovell held his hands, palms up, giving praise and thanks to forces greater than he.

******

[68]

Matt and Jim returned laughing and then settled in. Matt next to Lovell and Jim in a chair. Jim again, stretched his neck forward and back, looking at Lovell, marveling at the moon. Matt noticed it for the first time.

"Damn, look at the size of that moon."

Lovell held his hands up again. Jim cleared his throat.

"He used to do that?"

Matt patted Lovell's hand to pull him back to the room. "Your buddy?"

Jim covered his mouth. "Yea."

Lovell heard fragility, creep into Jim's voice.

"They put us together in boot camp because we had the same last name. He joked with me and said I was his cousin. I thought there must have been something to it because I rarely meet anyone with that last name. The strange thing was his grandparents were from Vermont and had moved to New York and I'm from Vermont. The same city, Burlington. That's more than a coincidence. He made me feel bad when he said his people were probably my slaves. Something like that's hard to admit especially for a white boy from Vermont."

Matt reached over and slapped fives with Jim. "We're all connected in more ways than we care to admit in America. That's the problem." Jim pulled a joint from the chair's cushion, lit it, passed it to Matt, then got an incense from one of the hanging baskets.

"That's something he said all the time. We're connected. I can't count the amount of times he saved my life in Nam. He and I even went to the same club, a little hole in the wall there. I can tell you were there Matt. So you know, all the clubs were segregated and anybody who crossed the color line in a bar, got their ass kicked."

Matt gave an Amen.

[69]

"He always told me to relax and stop being so fidgety. I couldn't sleep. Wouldn't take off my gun, even to get some pussy. He broke me of all that craziness just by taking deep breaths, in any kind of situation, chanting Sat Nam, even when we were under fire, and always stretching his head forward and looking into everybody he met. He said he could see the child in them and that's what he dealt with, because everything else was the shit the world had put on them. We were in the airport, getting ready to get on the plane to go home and he went to the toilet. It was rigged and killed him. The last words he said before he died was we're connected and you'll see me again, so pay attention. Lovell, you look just like him. You even move like him. I didn't mean to scare you, buddy."

Jim covered his face and wept like a child. Matt placed his arm around Jim.

"I lost a lot of buddies too. You still have night sweats?"

Jim walked to the balcony and blew his nose, letting the grief fly.

"Yea, less and less because I've been able to focus in on the dream that's causing them. I'm in that airport and digging through the rubble for my buddy. I can hear him moaning but I can't find him. When I do, and turn the body over, it's me."

Lovell had been holding the joint and listening. It had gone out.

"That means you wish it had been you who'd died."

Jim lit the joint for him.

"That's what I'm coming to terms with. I always thought he was a much better person than me and didn't deserve to die."

A knock on the door froze them. Jim took the joint, walked to the balcony, and using his fingers clipped off the flame,

[70]

letting it drop. He pocketed the roach. "Who is it?" They heard a woman's voice.

"I, uh, smelled the incense and thought maybe there were some English speaking people here. I just arrived and don't know where to go."

Jim opened the door.

"We don't speak English. We speak American."

*****

She could pass for Natalie Wood, except for the white scarf covering her head and the same color Abiyah, covering her body. Natalie Wood would never wear that. She looked down first, and then her eyes darted around the room. Inhaling, she kicked off her sandals, and peering down the hallway, in both directions, walked past Jim and sat in the chair he'd occupied. Blinking, she covered her face. "Now that my eyes have adjusted, I'm Doris Johnson."

Her voices twang made Matt sit up.

"And you're from Houston Texas, by way of Johnson City Texas."

Doris, who'd sat down, her feet not touching the floor, pulled up her legs and sat cross-legged in the chair, covering her feet and legs with the Abita.

"And you're also from Houston, but I hear something else."

Matt stood and shook her hand.

"San Anton's cousin. I'm Matt Johnson." Doris covered her mouth.

"Your mother's name was Edna. I heard about you and your brother."

Matt stopped before sitting.

"I don't have a brother. I'm an only child. I was raised with a cousin who's like my brother."

[71]

Doris fidgeted.

"His name's Elmo. He's not your cousin. He's your brother. Edna was his mother too. Your father's uncle Lyndon."

Matt rubbed his hands together and stared into his palms.

"I thought my father was his brother Sam."

"You thought like lit. Thought you farted but you shit. We'll talk about family later. Now, one of you pass me the joint. I've been under wraps for three years and feel like bustin' loose."

They all cracked up. Jim took a new joint from one of the hanging baskets and passed it to Doris.

"I'm Jim Ellingsworth and that's Lovell Pendleton."

Doris fired up the joint, hit it, but didn't pass it. "Well, well, well. I finally get to meet the man of the hour. I heard your name every day in England from Dr. Faturi at the recruiting office. You've given the Ministry of Education and the Department of Education at this university a newfound prestige. You must be the craziest muthafucka in the world." Matt stared at the joint Doris still hadn't passed. Jim's fists opened and closed.

"What's wrong with you woman. You've just met this man and you've insulted him already. Give someone else the weed. You can't handle it."

Doris gave Lovell the reefer.

"I meant no harm. According to Faturi, he's this famous writer. Therefore, he could probably teach anywhere in the world. Why come to a country with a dictator, renegade and murderer, who stringently enforces Sharia and where the both of you will be lucky to get some pussy? Here they're only going to use him as a symbol of some disgruntled black American, who came here seeking freedom from America, which doesn't exist here. The money's good here but that's about it."

[72]

Jim slapped his palms. His grinding teeth were audible.
"And why are you here?"
Doris reached for the joint.
"I married an Aybilian and he's been fucking me in the ass and beating my ass for three years. I finally ran away and I need some money to get started."
Jim snorted.
"That sounds stupid to me. You run away from your husband and go to England where you get a job and come back to the same country where your husband can still find you."
Doris took a long drag and coughed.
"He can find me but he won't do anything because I left my five children with him. Plus, I'm sucking Faturi and he has all my papers. I'll have to give up a year of head to get free. That's nothing. At least I won't be walking around with a sore ass, lumps on my head and locked in a house every day."
Matt, Lovell and Jim all cursed at the same time. Doris gave the weed to Jim.
"I'm tired and we all need to go to sleep. We have registration tomorrow. I saw all the soldiers gawking at me, so tell me where I can sleep. If I find another room alone, they'll try and rape me. I know none of you don't want any white pussy."
Jim moved one of the beds into a corner. Doris pulled the Abiyah over her head and used it as a cover. She wore blue jeans and a long sleeve white cotton blouse.
"Oh yes, my fellow American men. I saw some Eastern European women wandering around. You should go and find them before the soldier's do. The room next door's open and they can sleep there. Lock them in from the outside after you get a quick fuck."
She covered her face with the white garment.

Matt and Jim got up.

"We're going to find those women. Lovell, you coming?"
Lovell watched the half circle marble moon, which he thought had dropped.

"No, I'll pass. I'm tired."
Matt pointed to Doris, who twitched in her sleep. "Watch out for her. I don't have to tell you. If she goes to the bathroom, go with her. We don't know when we'll be back."

Jim angled his head at Doris and made a crazy signal with his hand.

"Take the other bed. I have a sleeping bag in the closet."
They left laughing. Lovell ran to the men's room, rushed his pee, and trotted back to the room, locking it from the inside. Doris was still asleep. He went to the balcony and on his knees, bowed to the moon again. Rising and turning out the red light, he removed his clothes and climbed into the single bed only getting a glimpse of the sky. Unaware of how long he'd lain watching it. The door opened and Jim entered, taking down one of the baskets.

"We found them and they have Polish and Russian Vodka. We'll be next door."

Lovell squinted in the darkness.

"I'm cool. Have fun."
The door closed and he could hear voices, and muffled music. Matt's baritone laughter eased through the walls. The door lock then clicked secure. He knew he and Doris had been locked in from the outside. Rising, he brushed his teeth using one of the bottles of water from Jim's shelf. Lovell closed his eyes. He awakened to a man singing" Ah- Ah- Ah-Allah Akbar," a grey hazed morning, and birds. Doris stood over him, naked, clutching her breasts.

"I'm cold and frightened Lovell. May I lie with you?"

[74]

Lovell pulled back his covers, turning on his stomach because he always slept naked, then sideways as Doris climbed in the bed. She spooned with him, her body jittering.

"He sodomized me every morning at the first call to prayer. It still spooks me."

Lovell whispered I'm sorry, and turned to embrace Doris. She eased under him, placing her left leg over his side, then urged his body up with her fingertips, and slid one leg under him. Guiding him inside, she whimpered.

"Please don't hurt me. I haven't had real sex in four years."

Lovell tried to move back, but Doris pulled him in, biting his shoulder.

*****

The banging at the door caused Lovell and Doris to sit up. She hurried from the bed, grabbed her Abiyah tossing it over her head and ran to the balcony pulling the shudder. Lovell picked up her clothes, placed them under the covers, and slipping on his pants, walked to the door. He could hear the sounds of boots marching down the hall and people banging on doors. Stepping on her shoes stopped him. He kicked them under the bed and was about to open the door, when he heard Matt's voice.

"Are you crazy, knocking on my door at six thirty in the morning. We're not in the damn army, you are." A voice said,

"Women, women."

"There aren't any goddamn women in here. And if there were, it wouldn't be any of your damn business. This is the professor's dorm and you're nothing but a damn private. Now get the fuck away from here. Or do you like looking at my dick."

The door slammed and boot sounds grew fainter down the hall. He watched the shutter door move, then Doris crawl into the room on her stomach. Lovell tossed Doris her clothes. She dressed still on the floor and then waited until Lovell closed the shutters.

"Welcome to the Jamahariya."

Matt and Jim opened the door.

"Doris, go next door quickly."

Doris ran. A door slammed. Matt paced.

"Cock blocking muthafuckas. They couldn't get no pussy and don't want us to have any. So that's the way it is here."

Someone tapped on the wall three times.

Jim pulled Lovell.

"Let's go."

Two sandy haired women, 5'10, and Doris, scurried into the bathroom. Lovell, Jim and Matt stood guard. The showers started and gasps echoed on the tiles. Jim doubled over, laughing.

"How do you like that cold water ladies. What a wake up!"

A squadron of ten green clad soldiers, with black berets, led by one wearing a red beret, with three gold stars, marched down the hall. Matt called over his shoulder.

"Jump to it ladies. We have company."

Lovell heard Doris shout,

"Cover your heads with your towels and look down when you pass them. Don't stop walking. They won't touch you."

The squadron stopped in front of the three men. The red hat stepped forward. They were all tanned to the point of looking crimson, with thick black eyebrows and small features.

"Show me your documents."

His accent was British. The three women exited from the bathroom, fully dressed, heads down and covered, walking

[76]

around the Americans and away from the Aybilians. Red hat followed them with his eyes.

"Are those your wives?"

Matt brushed past him and went into the room closing the door. Jim, arms folded, stared down at red hat.

"I thought you asked for our documents?"

"I asked you two questions."

Matt walked between the three-starred red hat and Jim put the passports against the soldier's chest. They fell to the floor. One of the other soldiers came, and picking them up handed them to his superior, whose eyes never left Jim.

"No, they're not our wives. Two are doctors at the university and the other is a professor. You'll see our documents are in order, captain. We're new professors here."

Three stars pushed the passports against Jim's chest. Jim didn't move.

"This is a religious country and fraternization between men and women, unless married, isn't allowed."

Jim snatched the passports.

"Define fraternizing?"

The leader turned away from them and marched. "You are the professor. You define it."

They watched the caterpillar of soldiers moving along.

Matt gave them the finger.

"I think we just made an enemy."

Jim still stayed where the soldiers had been.

"Yea, we did the worst thing you could do to a soldier; we addressed him at a lower rank and disrespected him in front of his men. He's not going to forget it."

Matt walked in a circle.

"We did one more thing and that was probably the worst.

They noticed Lovell's eyes pulled together in confusion.

[77]

"We didn't show any fear Lovell. They're accustomed to giving orders and controlling civilians with fear. Now that he sees we're not afraid, his only recourse, in his mind, is to kill us."

The three women came from their room with Doris leading, wagging her finger.

"And he will. That's Ibn Muktar Mustapha. He's in charge of the southern brigade, which lives in the desert and is always fighting the Berbers, who hate the Arabs. He's even had clashes with the Chadians who wiped out three-fourths of his platoon. Those you saw there are only the survivors."

Lovell watched Matt and Jim's jaws working and Doris, her foot tapping.

"What would a desert fighter be doing at a university?"

Doris closed the door.

"That's what worries me Lovell. That's what worries me."

Jim started doing jumping jacks.

"How do you know so much about him?"

Doris removed a scarf from her purse.

"He's my brother in law. He hung his wife because she refused to comply with Shari. She was an American from New York."

One of the eastern European women, who had stood chewing gum, smirking, paused mid bite.

"What did they do to him? After all she was an American."

Doris adjusted her scarf, making sure no hair showed.

"He lied and said she'd been killed in an accident in the desert and her body was burned. The embassy accepted it as such because they had no recourse."

The other woman moved toward Doris.

"Does he know you know this?"

Doris bobbed her head.

"Did he recognize you?"

Doris focused on Jim.

[78]

"A man like that doesn't forget anything or anyone. He'd never let you know it though. That's why he's so dangerous. People can't read him."
Jim and Matt went into the room and returned with towels and threw one to Lovell. "Hurry we have to go register." They entered the bathroom as Doris and the doctor's left.
*****

Lovell emerged from TM feeling airy. He dressed in a white leisure suit, with white sandals, a gold bracelet, earrings, chain, diamond ring with watch to match and carrying his valise, left the faculty dormitory. Matt and Jim had already left. Leaving the building, he was struck by the limestone colored buildings, which caused the sun to bare its teeth and flash a smile for the world. Lovell donned his Ray Ban glasses and opened the university map. Walking up the hill, the student and faculty cafeteria posed to the right. Across the street, pantheon shaped with marble columns and crimson figures dressed in knee length garments, bent, bearded hair to shoulders, all laboring with picks and forks, surrounded by orange trees, was the Department of Agriculture. It was the arena, molded on the coliseum, with ten foot glass windows and visible exercise equipment. Outside the arena were the basketball courts, which caused him to stop. He and whom he saw. Three seven footers, molded from caramel with afros and blowing whistles, training what some would mistake for tall South Americans, but they were Aybilians, in their national green uniforms with the black and red stripes across the chest and down the sides of the trunks. One of the Afros, checking them out blew a whistle and walked over to Lovell, ivory teeth a glow.

"A salaam alaikum my brother. I'm Madusun, from the Sudan, and the coach for the Aybilian National basketball team. Do you need some help?"

Lovell looked up into a George Foreman face.

"I'm going to the Department of Medicine. Am I headed in the right direction?"

The face continued to smile.

"Walking up this street is the long way. Cut through the orange grove to your right and pass the building on your left. You'll know it's the school of veterinary science because you can smell it. Continue on that path and you won't miss it. It's the largest building on campus. The Aybilians favor the medical students most because they think they're the brightest."

Lovell thanked him and turned to leave.

"What's your name Brother?"

"Lovell Pendleton"

"Do you play basketball Lovell?"

Lovell noticed Madusun kept glancing at his earrings.

"I used to."

"Did you bring a wife with you?"

" No"

"Then you play again, and a lot Lovell. We will be here at five o'clock if you want to play. I will get you some gear."

Lovell extended a hand, which was met by a grainy palm, which engulfed his.

"Thank you brother Madusun. I will see you at five."

He walked across the street and glancing back saw Madusun still watching him, until he reached the smell of animal dung contrasting the sweet acidic tang of orange trees, like brown open hands, with mint green shrouds, holding juicy bulbs, in an offering to God, he realized in this land, they called Allah. Walking, Lovell wanted to pray, to again prostrate himself in humility and

[80]

subservience, in awe of what something must unfathomably larger than he, had created. His head and arms arched upward as he repeated the few words aloud he knew in Arabic, Bis mahla, misha-allah, al-hum-do-allah, and began to sing Pharaoh Sanders and Leon Thomas' Um Allah- Ye-eh, Um Allah, Ye-eh, Um Allah, oh-oh-oh-um-Allah. Prince of Peace, won't you hear my plea. Ring your bell for me, let loving never cease."

He had stopped and closed his eyes, when clapping startled him. A class of male students stood at a window, their eyes aglow with wonder, watching him. Lovell hurried into the building and was met by Abubakar Faturi, in gray suit with a tie, the balding glass eyed director of English services, for the University of Al-Fateh, who kissed him on both cheeks and took his hand, guiding him to the first office for registration. Lovell sat down in a fluffy white cushioned chair with green pillows. Faturi pat him on the shoulder.

"I'll see you after the last office. Be sure and stop by to see me."

Lovell stood and shook Faturi's hand. A sweating sow faced man, in a white shirt and tie, came from a back room and paused, then put his hands to his ears. Lovell turned his head to see Faturi shrugging. Perspiration bubbling from each pore, a limp hand was extended. Lovell grasped it firmly and pig face smiled.

"I'm Fuad Abubakar, Director of Faculty Registration, please fill out these forms, and then go to the next office." He stood, leaned across the desk, glancing at the door, then sat, and taking a flask from one desk drawer, took a swig, then from another opened a bottle of Listerine, drank, gargled, spit into a waste basket, crossed his arms and fell asleep. Lovell took the papers, went to the next office, filled out more papers, was photographed and finger printed five times, until the last office, which produced the

[81]

I.D. card, covered in plastic. He noticed all the surnames were Abubakar. The last one, not much older than Lovell, and glassy eyed, put the I.D. card in his desk.

"That's enough for today."

Lovell had begun to wipe at the riblets which had already claimed his clothes. It was more than a hundred degrees and though the offices were vented, he felt no air conditioning.

"I don't quite understand. I was told without my I.D. from the university, I can't leave the campus."

He looked at the wet strands of hair clinging to the young man's sideburns. His hair was kinkier than Lovell's, though he had what people thought of as the Arab snout.

"This is true. However, we've done enough official work for today."

He closed the door and faced Lovell.

"Now everything is unofficial."

Hand in his pocket, Lovell opened his pocketknife. "What do you mean, unofficial?"

The young man had never introduced himself. The nametag, on the desk, said Salim Abubakar, in English, but had Arabic writing.

"Do you have American dollars?"

He rubbed his palms.

"I have a few."

"You'll need more than a few to get your I.D."

Lovell fingered his bankroll and pulled a hundred dollar bill from the inside.

"Will a hundred be enough?"

Salim jumped.

"A hundred!"

He sat down, his fingers twitching.

"Yes, that will suffice. This time."

Opening the desk he handed Lovell his identification.

[82]

"You do realize where you are don't you?"
Lovell nodded.
"And everything you do has to be approved by this office.
You also understand that don't you?"
Lovell stood, saluted, and goose-stepped from the office,
closing the door behind him. Dr. Faturi waited for him
outside his office. Lovell smelled Listerine as Faturi
studied Lovell's face, the one eye moving, the glass one
still, and taking his hand, showed him the air conditioned
classrooms and labs, in the school of medicine. The
students stood as they entered each class. That is except the
last class, which Lovell recognized as the group of
students, who'd applauded him. They sat, their arms folded,
waiting for Faturi to speak. Faturi introduced Lovell as
their professor. They still didn't move, until one, wearing a
blue kofi, and white cotton robe, called a JalAbiyah, stood.
"Professor Pendleton. Are you a Muslim?"
Faturi moved his feet and looked down. Lovell answered,
as he'd been taught by his father when anyone asked his
religion.
"I'm a believer."
The class erupted into applause and Faturi ushered Lovell
to his office, using the back of his hand as a handkerchief.
 "You are a very wise man Lovell."
He stopped in the hallway, placing both hands on Lovell's
arms.
"Why, Dr. Faturi?"
Dr. Faturi pointed at the class with his thumb, facing his
chest.
"Muslim, means believer."
"And why are those students different from the rest?"
Faturi leaned close to Lovell.

[83]

"Those are the sons of the highest ranking military in the country. Some of them don't have the grades to be in this college but are here because of their powerful fathers."
Lovell placed his forehead against Faturi's.
"Would one of those military officers be Ibn Muktar Mustapha?"
Faturi twitched.
"You don't even want to say his name aloud. And yes, one of those boys is his son. Even I don't know which one it is."
Butterflies fluttered in Lovell's stomach
"Let's go have a drink Dr. Faturi."
The doctor stepped back from Lovell and winked. "This is a Muslim country and I'm a good Muslim. We don't do that here."
He walked away from Lovell without looking back. Lovell walked from the building, his stomach doing somersaults. Passing the class, he focused his eyes on Matt and Jim, standing in front of the veterinary college. He noticed this time, the green clad armed soldier standing in front of the school. Matt held up a twenty-dollar bill, Jim a twenty and Lovell a hundred. Cursing and walking together Madusun waited for them at the street. Matt said, "Oh shit!"
Lovell didn't hesitate.
"He's cool. He's a Sudanese."
Lovell introduced Madusun to Matt and Jim. He fingered a pencil mustache.
"The first day is a real introduction to Aybilian ways. They're bloodsuckers. Don't worry brothers we're all here to get their money and leave. Whatever you had to pay today, you'll get back a hundred times. Did they tell you about the final registration downtown?"
Lovell, Matt and Jim stopped.

[84]

"Come, I'll take you downtown. Look for the name Faturi in each office. They're the cheapest and all from the same family."

Jim began to trot towards the faculty dorms, shouting over his shoulder,

" I'll be right back, wait for me."

Lovell saw Jim's left leg didn't fully extend, giving him a galloping motion. He wondered how anyone could run in this 100-degree weather especially wearing a shirt and tie. Matt, Madusun and Jim, all wore short sleeves and ties. He remembered Matt, besides his watch, had a silver chain bracelet, to match the silver obsidian ring he wore. The ring and chain were missing. The sun ricocheted off his twenty-four carat gold earrings and he thought of Madusun's eyes, Fuad Abubakar's motions to Faturi, his limp handshake, and Faturi's shrug. Realization bucked his knees. He grabbed a hold to Matt for support.

"They think I'm gay because I wear jewelry. Madusun you were watching me to see if I switched because I wear jewelry."

Madusun and Matt exchanged a knowing look.

"I wanted to tell you that Lovell but I forgot. The Arabs think men who wear jewelry are funny. Jewelry is for women and given to them when they married. It's a sign of prestige. You should have read the brochure."

"I am not Arab brother Lovell. We are tall, we are black, and we are African. My religion is Islam. We also think that. You're right, that is why I watched you walk. I wanted to see if you were a he/she. The Aybilians are worse because they're one step away from the Stone Age. If it weren't for the oil, they'd still be sleeping in tents with their sheep."

Lovell spit.

[85]

"Will they treat me differently because I don't dress like you two?"

Madusun placed a hand on Lovell's shoulder.

"They will not respect you."

Lovell thought of the class not standing.

"I thought this was an Arab Socialist Republic."

"Those are only words my brother. Only words."

They heard a whistle and saw Jim plodding with a brown bag. Their attention was cut by a voice screaming in Arabic. Madusun ran toward the Veterinary School.

" Someone's shouting for help."

They followed Madusun who turned into the one story building, continued through the hallway with classes on both sides, through a back door, out into a pasture, then veered right following the shouting and soldiers gathered in front of a barn. Lovell, Matt and Jim, moved around the crowd and eased to the side of the barn, near the entrance. Some soldiers laughed and moved away, carrying their rifles. The three Americans maneuvered to the open door to see a mule, foaming at the mouth, teeth gnashing, moving its head from side to side, with all its muscles taut. It lurched at anyone who approached. Behind the mule, purple faced, a soldier writhed. Madusun pointed downward and they looked. The soldier's pants were around his ankles. The mule had backed the soldier against the wall.

"Do you see what I told you about the Aybilians? They're from another century. He was humping that mule and got trapped against the wall because the mule didn't like it."

Jim walked around Madusun.

"That's a horrible way to die. I'll distract him to the left. Matt, you run around and stick your knife as deep as you can in that mule's ass. He'll move then."

[86]

He grabbed a handful of dirt, threw it in the mule's face, and then ran to the left. The mule snorted and eyes aflame with rage, turned its massive head towards Jim, chomping. Matt darted past the animal, and slammed his knife in its ass. Blood squirted in the air as Matt extracted the knife and the mule's eyes widened, head shook tossing slobber over the closest people, as it lurched forward. The soldier crumpled to the barn floor and Matt reached for his feet but jumped back when the mule kicked both back legs, its hoofs landing in the man's face. A crunching sound made Lovell turn away. He looked back to see Matt pulling the soldier across the straw covered floor, blood trickling from his ear, nose, and spurting with each gurgled breath from his mouth. Four streams of blood arched into the air, and he breathed no more. Matt glared at the mule, still focused on Jim, Standing against a far wall, a man wearing a white lab jacket rushed into the barn, running his hand along the mule's left side. He stopped and examined the open wound which still bled.

"Why did you do this to my mule? You no good fuckin' American."

Matt stood, wiped the blood from his hands on the man's jacket and took a step but the Aybilian grabbed his arm. Matt, hand closed, half circled his arm, breaking the grip. The white-jacketed man screamed in pain, holding his arm. Madusun moved in front of the man, as Matt left the barn and pointed down at the dead soldier, began to speak in Arabic. The mule breathed easier as the Aybilian flexed his right arm and stroked it with his left. The other soldiers carried their dead comrade out of the barn, leaving a trail of blood. The animal allowed Jim to pass. He, Madusun and Lovell joined Matt who kept his back to everyone. Jim hugged Matt.

[87]

"We've been through a damn war and it's still hard to watch a young boy die."

Matt wiped his eyes and he and Jim, arms circled each other's shoulder. The bag had dropped. Lovell looked inside. It was full of dollars. Madusun exhaled.

"Do you see what I mean about the Aybilians? They have to buy a wife and the price is very high. That's why they sleep with animals. That guard isn't for the school. It's to keep the Albanians from getting the sheep at night. Imagine how they'll be about their wife once they save enough money to buy one and they start having regular sex? I have been here for two years brother Lovell and I have seen many things happen to men who've tasted the Aybilian women. It was their last taste."

Matt and Jim rejoined Lovell and Madusun. A taxi, which had just dropped off a group of white men, stopped at Madusun's raised hand. Entering, Madusun gave directions in Arabic. The taxi took a right turn. Madusun shouted "Lah", which meant no. They had turned into an open flat area and a stirring crept into Lovell's arms. The flat land was a mass of brown clay with red streaks in it. He remembered his mother talking about the land in Mississippi so full of bauxite; people would eat the clay, when wet. He had never been to Mississippi. Never to his mom's roots, but something familiar about this patch of earth made his blood hum, sending tingles to both feet. He wanted to ask the taxi driver to stop, but Madusun and the driver were arguing. Then the taxi stopped and its driver said "gary-gary".

Madusun took hold of his head and banged it four times against the steering wheel. The driver raised his hands, a baseball sized purple knot above the right eye. Madusun pointed towards the road and the driver, one hand rubbing his head, drove them back to where they'd begun and screeched away as they exited. Madusun walked in circles, his eyes squinted.

"If you hear anyone say gary-gary, you and Matt must fight. It means nigger."

Jim swung at an imaginary foe.

"Here fuckin' too huh."

Madusun took Lovell and Matt's hands.

"We are tall, we are black, and we are African. The Aybilians are Arabs. Do not be fooled."

A Mercedes stopped. Madusun looked into it and laughed, speaking in Arabic.

"Come, he is Sudanese."

His mother would call the driver's head buckwheat because he had tiny chukka bugs. Others, in the black community would be less gentle and say he had nappy hair. Nappy hair and blue black. Matt whispered to Lovell the driver looked like Stephen Fetchet. Lovell agreed. They could be twins. Sleepy eyes and all. Madusun introduced him as Dr. Ahmed Hamsa. He shook hands and drove.

"Except for you, Madusun and Mr. Pendleton, everyone in this car is a doctor. Mr. Pendleton's close because he has a terminal degree and publications, it's comparable to a Ph. D. You're the low man in the group."

Madusun slapped the dashboard laughing.

"And you are my cousin good doctor and if you say another word I shall thrash you as I did when we were children."

He faked a blow and Ahmed covered. Lovell was enthused by the humongous palm trees lining the road and the students, men and women, dressed in blue trousers, dresses, white shirts and blouses, all long sleeve. The women wore scarves, covering their heads. Leaving the campus, traveling on a paved highway, orange, kumquat and lemon trees dotted the landscape. Cotton white apartment buildings, like ghetto projects, were at first sparse, then appeared in succession, as they neared the city, Ripoli. Unfinished buildings, like half-dressed skeletons, stood boldly in every block. The ruler's two-story portrait loomed in the distance and before they reached it, the musk of ripened fruit, made Lovell's tongue itch. Ahmed pointed to the fruit trees.

"Oil makes people wasteful. Look at all this fruit. It's long been ready to pick but the Aybilians just let it sit. They could sell it at the market or use it for export."
Madusun sniffed.

"They couldn't export it because nobody wants to trade with the boy ruler. He's made himself the world's worst enemy."

Driving through the heart of Ripoli, the traffic crawled. Drivers shouted from windows and people, mostly men, dressed in western clothes and moved, shoulder-to-shoulder. Open cafes abounded, and men sat outside, drinking tea. Towering above all the structures was the IBM building. The Americans turned their heads to see white men, in their white IBM jackets, leaving and entering. Matt spoke for them.

"I thought all western businesses had been thrown out of this country."

Ahmed threw a cigarette out the window.

"All except them, they're too valuable."

Turning to the left, they approached the souk. Multi-hued dresses and material swayed from small stalls. Chickens, hung upside down, or in rows circling in roasters, and cow heads, swarming with flies, were posted outside shops.

"You can find anything and everything inside there."

Ahmed lit another cigarette. Madusun fanned the smoke.

"Everything except a woman."

Ahmed let loose a loud guffaw.

[90]

"I've been everywhere in the world and this is the only place I know which doesn't have a whore house. Poor Aybilians, they must have calluses on their hands as thick as concrete and their sheep must stay sore."

The men laughed until Matt stopped them.

"Look what's next to us."

A small van with an Aybilian driver and full of Asian women, kept pace with them. Matt waved and one of the women returned the greeting. "Ahmed, please man, follow them."

Ahmed allowed the van to pull in front of them. Madusun read the writing on the van's door. "They're from the city hospital and are probably North Koreans."

The van stopped at a five-story apartment building. Ahmed parked the car down the street and watched in the mirror, waiting until the driver had let the women exit. He walked them to an iron gate, making sure it was closed and then pulled off. "Everybody down."

Ahmed's cigarette smoke was the only visible sign someone was in the car. Matt started to rise.

"Don't get up. He'll come back around. I'm sure he saw my cigarette."

Lovell heard the cigarette being smashed out. No smoke showed. The purr of a Volkswagen engine creeped past the Mercedes. No one moved. They waited a few minutes, then sat up. Ahmed opened his door and stepped out.

"He won't come back. There's too many Mercedes in this area. Guys, you're in luck. Look!"

Matt and Jim followed Ahmed's eyes. The gate was open and two nurses beckoned them to come. They took off running. Lovell pulled back the back seat Madusun held for him.

"Aren't you going brother Lovell?"

[91]

" No, I want to get all my papers straight. They'll be here just like we'll be here. What about you two?"

Madusun and Ahmed, sitting down, closed the doors.

"We're married. My wife's in the faculty hostel and Ahmed's will be here tomorrow. Otherwise, we'd be running too. You don't miss an opportunity to have a woman in the Jamahariya brother Lovell. The opportunities are rare."

Lovell looked at his faculty identification.

"I'll take my chances."

The Sudanese cousins faced each other. Jim interrupted their unspoken understanding by knocking on the window.

"Lovell aren't you coming in, there's a lot of hungry, horny Korean nurses in there. Come on."

" I'll pass man."

Jim rubbed his chin, nodding.

"You're so familiar it's crazy. You want an Arab woman, don't you?"

Lovell picked up the bag.

"You forgot this."

Jim waved him off.

"That's what I came to tell you about. That's counterfeit money. I've been using it all over the world. Give it to those ass holes in the registration office and hold the rest for me. I'll get it later."

He tapped the window and trotted down the street. Ahmed pulled away and they drove in silence. Turning into a street Lovell thought he could have been downtown in any city. The edifices were spaced, unlike downtown Ripoli where one touched the other. No paper littered the street. They were new, clean, and even the leader's portrait seemed newly painted. Flags from various countries billowed. Mercedes vans, with drivers waiting outside smoking, were parked like soldiers at attention. Lovell tucked the bag under his arm. Ahmed approached him.

"Give me a fifty dollar bill, your I.D. and let me do all the talking."

They entered a circular building with an enlarged photograph of the leader/colonel, in front. The floors glimmered and air conditioning cooled the halls, all lined with the colonel in western clothes, fatigues, robes, holding children and speaking. Madusun whispered for Lovell to sit while he walked along the left, looking into offices and Ahmed to the right. Ahmed entered an office, stayed for a few minutes and then poked out his head, calling Lovell. He opened and closed his hand five times. Lovell reached into the bag, felt two small cards, and pulling them out, realized they were Matt and Jim's I.D. cards. He removed five fifty-dollar bills, and pretending to shake Ahmed's hand, handed him the cards and money. The office, large dining room sized, had gold leaf legged embroidered furniture, with cedar desks and tables. A graying, completely bald version of Dr. Faturi, except both eyes moved, and bearded, sat behind a desk, in a cream three-piece suit. Pierre Cardin cologne hung in the air and Mozart's Eb concerto for a string quartet, played on a small recorder.

"I am Dr. Abdul Faturi. I've heard my son mention you. Welcome to Aybil. Here are you and your college's documents. Always come to my office for whatever you need. That includes an exit visa, travel documents, military taxes, etc. I am the director of all these departments. Believe me, your contributions will be more appreciated here than elsewhere. I will see my son tonight and I'll tell him you are more than what he thought you would be. I studied in the states as a young man and my son was born there. Unfortunately, his mother, who was also an

[93]

American, lost her life in a car accident once we returned here. That was before this man seized power from the Italians. I know you know, my son and his wife were educated in the states. That is why these boys who only care about people walking in a straight line can never deny him. Soon, he will be president of the entire university. Mark my words. Have some tea."

Lovell, Madusun and Ahmed sat at the round cedar table. The senior Dr. Faturi pushed a button. A diminutive smooth faced slight boy in the traditional Aybilian green sashayed into the room. "Pour our guests some of our special tea."

He twitted out and returned in an instant with four small gold trimmed teacups and saucers, with a little steam rising. Dr. Faturi raised his cup, saucer in lap.

"The true appreciation of this tea resides in it being drank in one swallow. Your insides will be delighted."

They drank together. Lovell's insides quivered. It was brandy and he had not eaten anything today. Dr. Faturi rose and brushed past the boy who bent over to retrieve the teacups.

"Thank you gentlemen. I am always at your service."

Madison and Ahmed waited until they were outside to double over laughing. Tears danced from Ahmed's eyes. He mimicked the older Dr. Faturi. "Your contributions will be more appreciated here. Did you hear that? And then rubbing the ass of that sweet Pakistani boy. My god, these Aybilians. This man is a doctor, still takes bribes, he obviously has a wife, and likes going up some boy's ass. I tell you Lovell, we are not like these people. We only share the same religion that's all."

They snickered all the way to the car. Lovell sat in the back seat, feeling woozy. "Thank you brothers for your

[94]

help. I'm sorry but I'm starved and that brandy has my head spinning. I haven't eaten all day."

Ahmed, still wiping his eyes, cleared his throat.

"I wouldn't eat at any of those cafes downtown if I were you. The Hilton's hidden inside that building at the end of this lane. The Aybilians can't go in there because it serves alcohol. We can eat there and get some more refreshments."

Madusun blew his nose out the window.

"This is where you should always come Lovell. No Aybilians!"

They stopped in front of a pyramid shaped glass building, without flags or the colonel's face. A teenage Sudanese boy took the keys and drove the car away. They strolled into the lobby of luxury. Lovell paused hearing a pianist playing "Misty." He followed the sound into a brightly lit lounge with tables seating six, cushioned, with booths. A baby grand piano sat in front of a mirror and a five foot hazel eyed tan skinned man with wavy sand colored hair, sat on phone books, with a pillow on top, playing Lovell's favorite song. He played arpeggios with both hands and ended the song. Lovell asked the waiter, Madusun identified as an Egyptian, if the pianist could play "*Willow Weep For Me.*" The waiter left the menu, spoke to the musician, who launched into the tune. Ahmed and Madusun fidgeted. Lovell noticed their discomfort.

"What's wrong?"

They stood.

"It's time for us to pray."

" But aren't you hungry?"

"We'll eat after we pray Lovell."

Lovell stood. Madusun held his shoulders.

"You don't have to leave. We'll come back after prayer. We'll probably see Matt and Jim downtown. That's where the nearest mosque is."

"What can I do for you brothers besides buy you dinner and get you drunk?"

Lovell had never seen two men smile wider. He counted all their teeth. Madusun nicked Lovell on the chin.

"My wife's birthday is tomorrow and I want to have a nice gift for her."

"And my wife, her sister is coming tomorrow and her birthday is also tomorrow. You see we married twins."

They slapped fives. Lovell reached in his pocket, pulling out his bankroll. Madusun stopped him.

"No brother. We will buy gifts with the other."

Lovell counted a thousand dollars and handed it to Madusun. The three embraced and the two cousins left. Lovell ordered two orders of escargot, sea bass, salad, a bottle of the most expensive Merlot, steamed carrots with string beans and sat back to enjoy this fine musician who played like Art Tatum. He'd finished the escargot, as the song ended, and called the musician over. The pianist, taking out his handkerchief, wiped down the keys, and placing the handkerchief his pocket, swayed over to Lovell. Sitting at the table, crossing his legs and extending a tiny hand, a high-pitched voice and liquid marble eyes, held Lovell.

" Hello, I'm Penny Marshall, from Trenton New Jersey, by way of Baton Rouge, Louisiana and you're Lovell Pendleton, from San Antonio, Texas."

Lovell held his fork. Penny called the waiter over. "I eat the same food as you and don't get paranoid, I asked Dr. Faturi if he'd hired anymore Afro-Americans and he mentioned you and Matthew Johnson.

He wasn't sure about anyone else."

[96]

Lovell's shoulders dropped.

"How long have you been here, Penny?"

" I got here yesterday and slept here last night. I couldn't get my I. D. card from Faturi's nephew, so I came back down here."

"What did you offer him?"

Penny's mouth pinched.

"I didn't offer him anything."

" That's why you didn't get your I. D. They want U.S. dollars."

Penny took out his wallet and opened it.

"How much?"

Lovell smirked.

"I gave him a hundred. I think you can get by with fifty. He's the first bribe. Then there's Dr. Faturi's dad. He won't accept less than fifty."

Penny said damn and looked at his watch.

"How long have you played here?"

Penny leaned back in his chair.

"I started last night. They hired me on the spot."

Lovell acted as if he were playing a run.

"I can see why. Art Tatum, Oscar Peterson, McCoy Tyner, Fats Waller and you."

Penny winked and returned to the piano.

 "You forgot about Scott Joplin and Mozart."

Rubbing his hands, he played "*The Tremonisha Suite*", fused with choruses from Don Giovanni. Lovell and Penny had finished four bottles of Merlot when his four friends entered. Lovell looked at his watch. It was seven o'clock. They sat down and Matt pointed at Penny.

"How in the hell did they get someone that good here?"

Lovell waited until Penny had finished his tune, wiped off the piano and approached the table. The waiter stopped

[97]

him. He told Lovell he'd be right back and left the lounge
with the waiter. The four men leaned toward Lovell.
"He's a he/she. Little dude's a faggot."
Lovell's jaw flexed.
"I don't care what he is. He's fantastic pianist and a black
man just like us, in Aybil. I don't want to sleep with him
and neither do all of you. So why let his sexuality bother
you? You don't even know what kind of person he is."
They all sat back, studying Lovell. Penny returned and
pulling his chair away, sat at the table.
 "My names Penny Marshall, how are all of you?"
The four men nodded. Penny sighed.
 "I guess you he men are afraid of a faggot. Tell me. What
makes you think I want you?"
A red flame crept across those green eyes. He pushed his
chair farther back.
"Lovell I'll see you at the university. Fuck all of you."
Matt stood, his hand out.
"You're right man. I know I'm trippin'. I'm Matt Johnson."
He and Penny shook hands. The rest introduced themselves
and also clasped Penny's tiny fingers. Penny sat down and
ordered a round.
"You all won't believe what's going on upstairs. There's a
crew of stewardesses having a party and they want me to
entertain them. They're single and very alone. Anybody
want to come?"
Matt and Jim jumped to their feet, volunteering. Lovell
continued to nurse his Merlot. He rose to hug Penny, but
fell backwards into his chair. They all looked at him.
"How much has he had to drink?"
Penny patted his cheek.
"He knocked off most of four bottles of Merlot."
Lovell's head felt clear, but he couldn't stand. "We'll take
care of him."

The Sudanese sipped from their Vodka. They drank it straight. Penny waved at Lovell.

"Get some sleep. I'll see you at the faculty meeting tomorrow. It's mandatory."

He took Matt and John's arms.

"Come darlings. Don't you know a faggot's a woman's best friend? Stick with me and you won't wear your hands out in the Jamahariya."

Matt and Jim walked like two schoolboys being led by a teacher. The Sudanese sucked their teeth.

"He's old enough to stop that. We wouldn't allow that in our country."

Lovell heard himself slur. "What would you do to him?"

They spoke in unison.

"His family would banish him and he wouldn't be able to return to his village until he had a wife and stopped that."

An anchor dropped in Lovell's forehead, his chest and his chin's resting place.

*****

He awoke, lying face forward, covered by a blanket, the bag of counterfeit bills on his chest. Cotton mouthed, he rinsed it with Jim's bottled water. Staring around the red lit room, he realized Matt and Jim hadn't returned. Trains running through his head and slipping on his shower slippers, Lovell walked to the bathroom and bumped into Doris, wearing a long black housecoat buttoned to the top.

" Smells like someone's been having a good time. Did you bring any for me?"

Each word rim shotted behind his eyes.

"No, and I'm never going to drink that much again."

She took his arm.

"Sure you aren't. Come and let me fix you some tea."

[99]

Lovell rubbed Doris' hand and tried to move past her. "I have to go to the head first."

Doris turned him around. "You can't go in there!" It's been made into a women's bathroom. The men's is down the hall and around the corner."

He turned back around and stepped toward the bathroom. Women's voices came from inside and he smelled perfume. He faced Doris.

"Whose decision was that?"

Doris placed a small arm around his waist.

"The women's. That's the idea of the Socialist Republic. All individuals are supposed to be responsible and organized collectives. Men and women have to develop clean up duties too. Theoretically it's supposed to be a classless society."

She led Lovell into her room. Pink sheer material loped from the ceiling and hung like a canopy over the two single beds pushed together to make a double bed. It covered the walls and was used as a bedspread. Pink throw rugs with brown-striped tigers concealed the floor. The far left corner held a waist high refrigerator, and next to it, silk pink and brown polka dot fabric concealed a same height table where two double burner hot plates sat. Against the far right wall, the polka dot cloth rested on a sofa and in front of it a rectangle glass coffee table with cocoa brown legs reflected the dots on another table where a portable record player and big Sony shortwave radio, its long antennae pointing toward the open balcony doors, resided. Two mocha brown chairs were placed in front of the coffee table. Doris ushered Lovell to the couch and turning on the burner, began to stir something in a small pot. Lovell smelled ginger and burnt eggs. Doris brought Lovell a small cup and saucer.

"Drink it straight, it'll get rid of your hangover."

[100]

Lovell drank. His throat caught fire, eyes began to water and his nose ran. Doris handed him a Kleenex and after he'd blown his nose, his head had cleared. "What was that?"

"Ginger tea and desert herbs. It always does the trick."

"You surely didn't learn that in Texas, home girl." Doris clapped her hands. "Certainly not. That's one of the many wonderful remedies I learned in the south of Aybil, where you'd probably be surprised to know, most of the people are black."

Lovell snapped his fingers.

"It's close to Chad and Niger."

Doris sat in one of the chairs, her feet barely touching the floor and unbuttoned the top buttons of her robe. Lovell could see the inner shape of one breast.

"Has anyone ever told you how much you look like Natalie Wood?"

Doris lifted her little feet onto the chair. Her milky thighs showed.

"I've heard that all my life."

" How'd you get settled in so quick? It looks like you went shopping already."

Doris moved over to the couch but positioned herself at the far end.

"Most of this stuff was already in the room. I went to the souk and bought the material. Do you like it?"

"It's like the chamber of a queen."

Doris moved closer.

"Does your head feel better?"

Lovell could smell Doris' perfume. It tingled the roof of his mouth.

"Like brand new."

Next to him, he smelled ginger.

"Do you want to feel better Lovely Lovell?"

[101]

He breathed deeply as her lips warmed his cheek. "Of course I do Doris. But, you know, I'm not serious lady. I mean, I'm not interested in any relationship and I don't want to ruin a friendship."

Doris touched him between the legs.

"What was last night, a sympathy fuck?"

Lovell leaned his head back against the material on the wall. It smelled of Patchouli.

"No, it wasn't a sympathy fuck. It was real and I was moved. There's someone else in my life, Doris."

She massaged his scalp.

"She's not here is she?"

" No"

"Then what's the problem?"

"What will you do if you see me with someone else?"

Doris snorted a laugh, covering her mouth.

"What will you do if you see me with someone else?"

Lovell tickled her ear.

"Nothing"

"Then you have your answer Lovell. I told you I've been a prisoner for years. I need a close relationship like I need a hole in my head. I grew up in the sixties more than you. Having you ever heard of FTF?"

He leaned away from her.

"What's that?"

"Friends that fuck. That's all I want Lovell. A friend I can fuck sometimes. Can you handle that?" Raising her head, he ran his tongue over the slim lips.

"Of course I can!"

Doris stood unbuttoning the robe.

"Let me make sure the doors locked."

Lovell walked to the bed, behind her.

Later, her munchkin finger circling his nipple, Doris smelled his chest.

[102]

"Tell me about her".

Lovell blew into her hair.

 "About who?"

"About the lucky woman who has your heart."

"Nidia. She's like a ray of sun in my life."

Doris tickled Lovell's stomach. He wasn't ticklish.

"Professionally she's a pharmacist, but she's been a nun ever since she finished pharmaceutical school."

Doris raised herself.

"You're in love with a damn nun! Are you crazy?"

Lovell patted the bed and shushed her with a finger across both lips.

"She left the convent the day I flew from San Antonio. Before that we talked on the phone every day and I saw her at holidays. That's how we met."

"How do you meet at a holiday? Don't tell me she's a relative."

It was Lovell's turn to tickle. Doris squirmed.

"She was who I thought was my best friend's cousin. I'd see her at his parent's house. From the first moment we met, there was this chemistry. It was like a canal opened inside me and flowers flooded my heart. We could never be alone though. Her family sensed something so they kept us apart. The only time I got to touch her was when I went to a movie with them and in the dark, she took my hand and placed it on her heart."

Doris placed her hand on Lovell's heart.

"It's beating faster, Lovell."

His hand covered hers.

"Just thinking about her brings those flowers back."

Doris crossed her legs and rocked.

 "Lovell, you're in love with a woman you barely touched".

 "That's how I know it's real, Doris. I'd be erect every time we spoke on the phone and afterwards I'd have these erotic

[103]

dreams of making love to her. We'd speak the next day and she'd had the same dreams. It finally happened for real in the bathroom of the restaurant where I had my last meal in San Antonio."

Doris slapped her cheek.

"In the bathroom! Well that's romantic! Couldn't you find somewhere else?"

Lovell fingered the silk laden wall.

"It just happened and that was the only place. What can I say?'

Doris too, played with the wall.

"You don't have to say anything. I know how shit can happen. My husband and I were standing up, in a closet, at a party full of people when we first did it. Of course, we were very young, and he was much different then."

Her head dropped. Lovell stroked her cheek. "Different how?"

"He was alive, free, and vigorous. It wasn't until we came here he turned Muslim. No, that's not right. He was always Muslim. It wasn't the center of everything and it didn't control him. Now that I think about it, it was being here, in the midst of all these cages that turned him into the animal he became and is now."

Lovell watched Doris' body fill and empty with each inhale, and exhale. He reached for her miniscule hand and kissed it.

"Love, she's a bugger, isn't she?"

They smacked high fives. Doris went to a cabinet drawer and threw Lovell a key.

"Here's a key to your room. It's two doors down. I left a sheet and some blankets for you. It gets cold in the desert at night."

She stood naked in front of her door. Lovell gathered his clothes and dressed.

[104]

"I know when I'm not wanted and I've worn out my welcome."

Doris stepped in front of him and placed her arms around his waist.

"It's not that I don't want you. You should be able to feel that. I'm supposed to be Miss Independent. I've just made love with you and then listened to you talk about the woman you truly love. My head tells me it's okay but my heart wants you and I feel like crying. I don't know if it's for myself, from thinking about my husband, or for you, who I know I can't have and am not ready for. Therefore, when in doubt and confused, as the song says, take a trip through your mind and see what you may find."

She cracked the door, peeked out and then opened it wide enough for Lovell to pass. She planted a kiss on his arm as he left and closed the door. Leaning against the wall, he heard Doris sobbing. Walking down the hall, the smell of curry wafting from some new arrivals room, Lovell thought of Nidia and what she'd told him once about Ann, who'd always considered herself a modern woman in accepting Eduardo's philandering with the attitude, I don't care what he does as long as he comes to me when I want him. Nidia had said women only give lip service to those kinds of ideas. However, inside, they always hoped the man would change and were secretly waiting for him to do so.

Rounding the hallway corner, rancid stench dissipated all thoughts of women. He walked into the toilet and noticed first, the hordes of swarming flies, someone had taped plastic over the urinals. Opening each stall, piles of feces, and flies greeted him. He backed out of the funk, trotted to Jim's room and carried a long coiled water hose, bleach, a bucket with cleaning supplies, and walked back to the bathroom. Splashing bleach and powdered soap on the floors, cleanser in the sinks and on the floors, he connected

[105]

the water hose to the largest sink, he assumed was for clothes, and turned on the water. Opening each stall he washed the feces away and tried to drown every fly. Soon the smell of bleach and soap filled the air. Doors began to open and three men, two blonds and another dark haired, walked into the bathroom, carrying push brooms. They rolled up their pants legs and scrubbed the floors. They had that long angular face Lovell associated with Eastern Europeans. Another, fat European man with marble blue eyes and a mustache, came into the bathroom carry a tool case. He said something to the other men and departed. Lovell heard him going down the steps. Lovell opened the shower doors and splashing bleach and soap powder, sprayed the walls and floor. Within minutes the showers began to run. They worked together in silence until the walls, floors, toilet stalls and showers were clean. One of the blonds flushed the toilet. They all shook hands as the fat one returned sweating.

"I'm Rhinehart, this is Claus, and Jerzy."

Lovell noticed Rhinehart's oily hands.

"How'd you get the water running?"

"I found the line coming to our bathroom and rigged it. It was easy. Looks like someone already did it for the women's bathroom."

"That was Jim. That bathroom wasn't always for women. He cleaned it by himself and turned on the water."

They didn't blink.

"We thought it was better to give the women the clean one."

"Well, he'll say you should have asked him first. It's right outside his room and he did the work."

They nudged each other.

"He must be an American."

"Why do you say that?"

[106]

Rhinehart began to wash his hands and speak over his shoulder.

"Because Americans feel anything they do, they have a right to."

Lovell looked around the now clean bathroom. "And how do Europeans feel. No, don't answer. Tell me this. Now that we've cleaned this bathroom. Anyone can come in here, dirty it up, and you'll be okay with that."

Rhinehart spoke and the others mumbled for them. "No, we won't be ok with that."

"Then you're the same as Americans."

All four men shook hands. Klaus spoke English with a very thick German accent.

"And we have to guard our bathroom. These two wings are all professors and mostly couples. I haven't seen anyone but Europeans and Americans. We can keep our toilets clean as long as we keep them out. "

Lovell watched their faces but detected nothing. It was something they understood but he didn't.

"You mean the Aybilians?"

Rhinehart wagged a finger.

"Them and all the other Arabs. If they're near our women, it's okay. If we're near theirs it's a problem. I know because some of our people just finished a contract here and they warned us."

Lovell remembered Ahmed's words.

"It's always a question of women, isn't it?'

Rhinehart took the cleanser, sprinkled it into the sink and began cleaning away the oil.

"That and other things. You'll see. The first thing we have to do it remove all the containers. That will keep them away because we won't have any toilet paper in here any canisters. They won't use a toilet without a canister or toilet paper."

Lovell began to gather the cleaning supplies.

"Is there a way we can lock the door and give only the people on this floor a key?"

Rhinehart opened his toolbox.

"I'll have it done tomorrow."

They all returned to their rooms. Lovell slipped into his robe and returned to the bathroom. The sound of someone grunting stopped him because it came from the shower, but the water wasn't running. Turning to the right, he pretended to drop his towel and looked under the bottom of the first one. An Indian man squatted and defecated. Lovell gagged. The man continued, until he'd finished, then turning on the shower, let the turds wash down, then blew his nose in the shower, regurgitated and took a shower. Lovell waited until he'd finished.

"My name is Lovell Pendleton. Four other guys and myself just took an hour to clean this bathroom and you shit in the shower. Don't you realize other people have to use it?"

The Indian, graying chest and full hair, tried to move past him. Lovell refused to move. Rhinehart came out of his room, wrapped in a towel.

"What's wrong?"

"This gentleman just shit in the first shower."

Rhinehart stepped within smelling distance.

"I'm Dr. Rhinehart Schultz. This is Professor Lovell Pendleton. If you want to use this bathroom, you'll have to help keep it clean and not shit in the shower."

The Indian man walked over and blew his nose into the sink.

"Who are you to tell me what to do? This toilet belongs to the university."

Rhinehart backed him against the sink.

"We all have to live on this floor and we're supposed to clean the bathrooms ourselves. Now are you going to help

[108]

clean it or not? If you don't want to help then you can't use it."

The Indian tried to pass again. Rhinehart refused to move. "I'm Dr. Fakur Ali and I'm not some janitor. There's your answer, now let me pass."

Rhinehart dropped the towel from his shoulder. "Clean up that snot from the sink."

The Indian stepped back and squared his shoulders. "No!"

"Clean it."

"No!"

Rhinehart grabbed him around the neck, twisted his arm and forced his face into the snot in the sink. He rubbed the Indians face in it, and then turned on the water until the Indian began to gag. Rhinehart then pushed him backwards and snatched the Indian's towel from his waist. He covered his private parts. The snot dripping from his face.

"Now get out."

The Indian bent over, trying to conceal himself. "There are women out there and my children are in my room."

"I care as much about them as you care about this toilet, now get out. And every time you use this bathroom, and we catch you. You're going to eat shit."

The Indian backed out; covering himself ran down the hall and knocked on the door. The door opened and he closed it to a crack, speaking through the small space. It opened again and a pair of pants was handed out. He slipped into them and went inside. Rhinehart wrung his hands.

"I didn't tell you about them. Do you still have that bleach?"

Lovell ran to his room and returned with it. They bleached the shower floor, bathed and returned to their room. He slept in his own room, alone for the first time in Aybil.

*****

[109]

Screaming and shouting awoke him the next morning. His heart did somersaults as he tried to remember where he was. Jumping out of bed, he opened the door to see one of the Polish doctors dragging an Indian woman by the hair, down the hall and Doris kneeing another one, in the stomach, who had her by the hair. The Indian woman finally let go, and doubled over succumbed to left and right uppercuts, which sent her sprawling onto her back, exposing a black silky haired vagina. Lovell got a good look because Doris kicked her in the mouth, knocking the Indian woman cold, her legs spread. Doris threw a towel over the woman's body as two little copper skinned Indian girls cried over their mother. Slipping on his pajama bottoms, Lovell watched the Polish doctor kicking another Indian woman, crawling on her hands and knees, down the hall. Doris pulled a few loose strands of hair, from her head.

"Boy that felt good. I haven't kicked any ass in a while." The unconscious woman stirred, sat up wobbly and realized she was bare breasted, covered herself and with the children's assistance, rose and staggered down the hall, wearing her sari.

"Isn't it a little early to be fista cuffing, Doris?"

Doris, breathing heavily, flexed her hand.

"Those bitches said they have servants to clean up after them and refused to clean up after their kids messed up the bathrooms. They left us no choice. I bet they won't be back."

The doctor returned limping. She'd hurt her foot. "My husband told me he had to beat one last night. Damn Paki's."

[110]

Something about the word, and the tone made Lovell's
back stiffen. He had no ideas they were Pakistani's. Doris
had turned red.

"They're just classist assholes. It's their society."
The Pole stormed off and returned to her room, to gather
her toiletries. As Lovell rounded the corner to the toilet, he
saw two Pakistani families, carrying suitcases and clothes,
moving to another floor.

*****

Lovell had showered and dressed in a tan short-sleeved
leisure suit with brown tie and shoes, when Doris' voice
called to him.

"Come on, we're going to be late. This is the most
important day of the year. You have to give a speech."
He emerged from his room to a whistle.

"Um, don't you look good enough to eat?"
Lovell took Doris' hand.

"Give me a bite of you. I'm hungry."
Doris pulled away.

"Don't do that."
Her face had changed color.

"Do what?"

"I know you're joking, but unless we're behind closed
doors, never touch me in public. You never know who's
watching."
Lovell looked around and saw no one. However, Doris'
tight lip communicated more than her words. She covered
her head with a scarf and took two steps.

"I didn't mean to snap at you, but you have to learn. It
could mean a flogging for you and me. You also have to
learn to take off those earrings. Do it now."

[111]

He removed both earrings and placed them in his pocket. They walked at a distance and exited the building. Lovell covered his eyes because the sun's glare temporarily blinded him. He ran back to his room and got his sunglasses. Doris waited for him at the street.

"There's something you must remember. Say A salaam alaikum, and all praise to Allah, when they ask you to speak. Wherever the female student's sit, don't look that way and thank the leader of the country, Dr. Faturi, the president, Saleh Humseen. Remember that order. First the leader, then the president and finally, Faturi. I'll leave everything else to you."

Walking he could see Eastern Europeans, Indians, Pakistanis, the Sudanese in their white robes, turbans, and the Egyptians, in their tailored leisure suits with ties, all going to various schools. Most of the faculty was men. The other women faculty hadn't wrapped their heads. Doris said they'd regret it. Lovell and Doris walking a step apart entered an arm shaped building for the meeting of English professors. Dr. Faturi and the President, Saleh Humseen, sat on the stage. Doris sat next to Lovell on the left hand side of the auditorium. She insisted they sit there because, she said, all the speeches began on the right and worked to the left. Once the first speaker stood and introduced himself, Doris whispered,

"Get ready for the ride; it'll be a long one."

Every professor was required to stand and give a brief welcome. After the first three men had spoken, the back door opened and Penny, Matt and Jim, arms linked, walking at an angle, came into the room. They spotted Lovell and Doris, who'd sat in the back, and sat beside them. Alcohol, poured from their pores and all had dark half-moons, under each eye. Doris nudged Lovell.

[112]

"Get them outside quick. Take them to the bathroom and spray them with cologne. Then do whatever you can to get them straight. The Aybilians won't forget it if they smell the alcohol, or, if they go to sleep". Lovell stood and grabbing each by the back of their collar, pulled them outside. Penny staggered, Matt perspired and Jim held his head. "Quick you fools into the bathroom!"

They followed Lovell into the nearest bathroom. He turned on the water.

"Okay drunk ass troopers, heads under the cold water, and fingers down the throat."

They complied and almost in unison started to heave into the sinks. Matt was the first to stand. "Damn that felt good".

Penny was still heaving. Jim kept flushing his nose. "Doris said we all have to give a brief speech and this is important. You brothers have to get it together."

Penny stood wobbly.

"I can't give a speech. I'm too sick."

Lovell reached into his pocket.

"I brought my cologne. I'll spray you guys so you won't smell like alcohol. Doris has some mints. If you can't do this they'll send you home."

Jim reached into his pocket and brought out a small jar.

"Well fellows. We need a bit of the hair of the dog."

Matt held up his hand.

"Man, I can't my nose hurts." Penny gave Jim the back of his hand.

"Hit me. I'm not ready to go back to the fucking states."

Jim poured white powder on the back of Penny's hand.

Matt held out his and they all began to snort. Jim held the bottle out to Lovell.

"Want some nose candy. The Danish stewardesses didn't want to take this coke back on the plane with them. They gave it all to us."

Lovell declined and in a very few minutes, the three men were wide-eyed and jabbering. Lovell sprayed them with his Pierre Cardin and they reentered the meeting. Sitting down, Doris gave them all the finger and passed out candy. Three hours later, the speeches still hadn't finished. Lovell began to count the nodding heads. He thought the Aybilians must have sensed the drudgery because they had students, dressed in the Aybilian green, passing out green tea. Lovell took one drink and gagged. It was three-fourths sugar. The tea made Matt, Penny and Jim, more active. They began to play tic tac toe, by passing the paper down the aisle, until an hour later, it was their turn to speak. They all began their speeches the same way, following Doris' instruction. When they'd finished, Doris stood. She addressed the meeting in Arabic and spoke for five minutes, all in Arabic. When she'd finished, all those who understood, stood and applauded. The meeting ended and the professors began to leave. Doris told Lovell to take his three friends outside and wait for her. They stood outside and watched as the professors left. Then the door closed. Matt marched up and down. Jim did exercises. Penny played an imaginary piano and tap-danced. They all stopped when Faturi and the president emerged smiling. Faturi nodded to Matt, Penny and Jim, then beckoned Lovell over to them.

"Dr. Humseen, this is Professor Lovell Pendleton". The Doctor, wearing sunglasses with finger thick graying eyebrows, a full mouth, and white mustache, extended his hand to Lovell, the way he'd seen the pope do to people. He saw Doris in back of them, motioning to him to kiss it. He pecked the doctor's sweaty hand.

"We are very honored to have you with us Professor Pendleton. Our national television will interview you in an hour. Please be at Dr. Faturi's office and be prepared, this is very important."

He and Faturi turned and walked away. Faturi looked back and winked at Lovell. Matt and Lovell, once the two Aybilians were at a distance, spit on the ground. Penny, seeing Lovell frozen, staring at the men's backs, walked over and took his hand. "It's nothing Lovell. Don't take it seriously. It's probably one of their customs. Don't let it get to you."

Lovell felt his body jerking and his neck hot. Doris glanced around and rushed over to Lovell.

"Snap the fuck out of it. It's a sign of respect and to put you in your place."

Lovell's face twitched.

"A sign of respect, or another form of ass kissing."

Doris slapped him.

"It's not ass kissing. Men do that to those in higher positions and people they admire. He's got a fucking ego Lovell and you'll probably never see him again after today. You're going to see him in another hour and you don't want him to sense your anger. He's a political appointee and you don't want to cross him, so cool it."

She whirled around at Matt, and Jim.

"And you two, especially you cuz. You know better. We've just met and I don't want to lose you. You can do whatever you want as long as you're cool. But you guys, they could have arrested you on the spot for being drunk and none of your family would ever see you again. Get it to fucking gether."

Doris spun on her heels and faced Penny, placing her hands on her hips and moving her neck.

[115]

"Look Miss Thing. I know you don't want to have your ass barbecued and a train run on you with no grease do you?" Penny copped the same pose.

"The only people who get in here are those I want."

Matt choked on his laughter.

"And one of who he wants was in there last night and going to town."

Penny walked towards Matt, licking out his tongue. "Well, you must have enjoyed it or else you wouldn't have been watching. And, if I remember correctly, you were deep in that woman's ass and loving every minute of it."

Matt bowed to Penny and the four of them began to walk. Lovell noticed Doris' walk.

"What's wrong with you? You're walking like your underwear are up in there."

The four men laughed. Doris continued to walk, her face flooding with tears.

"Not my underwear! The president was in there as I was giving Faturi some head."

She sunk to the ground, covering her face. Matt slammed his fist into his palm. Jim did a front kick. Penny stood next to Doris and glancing around, patted her shoulder. Lovell, biting his lips, let the floodgates of tears be free. Soon, all four Americans, in the Aybilian heat, were weeping, the men in a circle, protecting Doris on her knees.

*****

The Television lights caused Lovell to tug at his collar and dab his forehead. There was no makeup artist, no director, only a thirty something cameraman, who pointed to a chair, where Lovell sat waiting for someone to come. He had grabbed Dr. Humseen's hand with a vice grip and ignored Faturi's pleading eyes when arriving in the makeshift studio, once Faturi's office. Dr. Humseen had

[116]

coughed, given Faturi a brow pulled together glare and exited the office with the English director scuttling behind him. Now he waited, thinking of the brown spot, which had appeared on the back of Doris' dress after she'd been raised from the ground by Matt and Jim. They'd all walked to the faculty building with her, Penny entering her room, leaving Matt, Jim and Lovell damning the Aybilians. Alone, in his room, Doris had knocked on his door, and peeking her head in, reminded him of what he had to do. Jim and Matt had passed by shortly afterwards, carrying Matt's bags, and had said they'd given Penny the money to bribe the Faturis. Lovell, unwilling to talk, had given his friends a thumbs up sign, but kept his face in a wet pillow. Footsteps and the camera's white light, bleached away the dried blood. It was Dr. Humseen followed by Faturi, whose fingers nervously played with his tie. Humseen sat across from Lovell, cleared his throat and began to speak in Arabic. He then turned to Lovell.

"Aybil has a policy which welcomes those who America has not appreciated. Do you think our policy will attract more Afro-Americans who are the particular victims of America's practices?"

Lovell inhaled.

"I think most Afro-Americans, who have degrees like I do, will probably never go to any country because they've succeeded despite America's practices."

Humseen adjusted his dark glasses.

"But due to the racism in America, those Afro-Americans are not appreciated? Isn't that correct?"

" They're not appreciated by the government but they are idolized by their people."

" Idolized? By what people?"

" By other Afro-Americans! That's why they may or may not go to another country. They love their people and feel

[117]

loyal to them. Another country would have to offer them a lot for them to come."

A smile appeared and the doctor leaned forward. "And Aybil has obviously offered you something which has made you decide to come and work here. Could you tell the Aybilian people what that is?"

Lovell could see Faturi hands stop moving.

"I have only been here a short time and therefore I haven't personally had a lot of experiences with Aybilians. However, what attracted me here is what attracts most people to any country outside their own, respect and decent treatment. That is, respect as a human being without people using their power or position over them."

The president's back stiffened and he crossed both arms across his chest, before speaking in Arabic, and the camera light being turned off. The other white lights in the studio blinked off, one at a time. Black spots appeared before his eyes, he blinked, and realized the chair next to him was empty and the camera man's assistants were breaking down the lights. He walked outside to his four friends. The sunlight reflected off Doris' smile.

"You can dress them up but you can't take them out."

The three men's heads moved like toy dogs in the back of a car.

"What's that supposed to mean?"

She stared at the ground.

"Humseen came out with an attitude and his lapdog Faturi was trying to put a good spin on whatever you said. What took so long?"

Lovell raised his sunglasses.

"How long was I in there?"

"Ninety minutes. We were starting to worry."

He walked in front of them.

[118]

"I told him what we wanted, that everyone wanted to be treated with respect like a human being."

Doris bent over giggling.

"You sure know what to say don't you."

Lovell continued to walk. Matt coughed.

"Don't get an attitude with us Negro. We've come to take you to get some money."

Lovell turned on his heel and followed Doris. She was leading the way, across the street, between the sports pavilion and the basketball courts, which led to a small round red clay structure. Entering Doris made a sucking sound, stopped, crossed her legs, still standing and began to curl the few ends of hair showing.

"Hi, uh we're here to pick up our housing allowance."

Her voice was girlish and she swung her body. Penny, one hand to hip, covered his mouth. Matt and Jim sat down smirking. Though the office, equipped with calculators, adding machines and file cabinets was cool and air-conditioned, the man behind the desk, Omar Shariff's twin, began to perspire, his eyes fastened on Doris. " I, uh, I, uh, I, uh need your faculty I.D. card number and your name. Could you give me your card please?"

Doris handed him the card. He opened a drawer, took out a stack of checks, and dropped them on the floor. Doris bent down to help pick up the checks; they bumped heads, began to laugh, and then smiled into each other's eyes. Penny cleared his throat. "We'd also like our checks."

Doris and Omar stood, facing each other. He handed Penny the stack of checks. Penny took his check, then handed Matt, Jim and Lovell theirs. The accountant sat down and pulled up a chair for Doris. "I'm in building four. I mean my name is Yusef. Yusef Bahar. I'm the chief accountant."

[119]

He held out a trembling hand. Doris took his hand and held it.

"I'm Doris Johnson and I'm in building three."

Yusef leaned back.

"Building three is for married faculty."

Doris still held his hand.

"Those were the first rooms we found."

He let go of her hand and opened a large book. "There are some single rooms on the second floor. Are you in one of those?"

Doris put both hands in her lap. Her breathing was slow and measured.

"Probably."

He looked at his watch.

"You better hurry to the bank. The Aybilians always leave a half hour early, pretending they're going to pray."

Matt, Jim and Lovell walked out front and doubled over laughing. Lovell heard Doris ask where Yusef was from. He said Egypt. Penny and Doris walked from the office together. Once outside Doris' knees buckled. Penny pulled out his handkerchief.

"Do you want to put this between your legs to soak up all that juice?"

Doris took the handkerchief and wrapped it around her head.

"Oh my god. Did I make a fool of myself? Or did I make a fool of myself?"

Penny danced around her.

"You both made fools of yourselves. Tis love my dear. Tis love."

Doris took Penny's arm then stopped and let go.

"I must be crazy holding your arm. Let's go cash these checks and have some fun. They're the equivalent of $4,000.00."

[120]

Lovell awoke the next morning with trains running through his head, not remembering what had happened the night before. Leaving his room and shading both eyes from the sunlight, he met Penny, wearing sunglasses and a lime green robe, leaving the bathroom.

"Looking at you, lime sherbet ice cream, makes my head feel even worse."

Penny aimed a soft blow at Lovell's chin.

"Thank goodness we don't have any classes today. I couldn't take standing in front of a class. That's it for me and that snow. I can't swallow. How's your jaw."

He moved his jaw.

"It's sore. Why do you ask me about it?"

Penny removed his sunglasses. Bloodshot eyes with black craters winked a hello.

"You don't remember what you did?"

Lovell didn't have to answer. Penny started to laugh, then gagged and ran back into the bathroom, closing a stall and heaving. Lovell brushed his teeth and waited for Penny who reeled out and cleaned his mouth.

"Did you look at who was next to you, this morning?"

Lovell hadn't noticed.

"When you go back to her bed, she should be there. Her name's Danita Shumska and she's the new head doctor at the clinic. You went down on her in front of everyone and put on quite a show. You turned the evening into a real orgy. Even I had a sweet Polish nurse who's still sleeping. I'm going to go and get some of the hair of the dog. Meet me downstairs in two hours. I need you to take me downtown to get my registration card." Penny planted a kiss on Lovell's cheek and switched down the hall to the

[121]

right of the men's room. Lovell took a quick shower and returned to his room, to find a forty something blonde, with hazel eyes and a pointy nose, smiling at him. She pulled back the covers, displaying a full tanned body and beckoned him with her finger. He climbed in and had a hearty breakfast. Lying on his back, her face on his chest, she ran her nails across his stomach.

"I have never done this before."

Lovell couldn't look at her.

"What did you do?"

"I ingested cocaine and had sex with a man I'd just met, in front of my colleagues. I am a mother and a respectable doctor. I don't know how I'm going to face them."

She turned her body away from him, covering her head with a pillow. Lovell touched her back.

"From what I'm told, they joined in with people."

She still refused to look at him.

"But I'm their superior."

She turned and faced him, her right eyebrow raised. "What do you mean from what you're told? Don't you remember?"

He covered his mouth.

"I remember this morning, but not last night."

Pulling the sheet around her, Danuta dressed, and left the room without speaking. Lovell showered again and met Penny outside. The sun sent hammers pounding in his temples. He saw Danuta ahead almost running towards the cafeteria and could see Penny, from the corner of his eye watching his jaws running in place. Unable to answer, he held his stomach trying to squash the bile, beginning to gurgle. Unable to hold it, a green stream squirted from him. Penny backed away, hand to nose.

"Is it guilt or nausea Lovell?"

[122]

He let loose another gulf and thought of what his mother had told him. Guilt was about something you could do nothing about.

"I'm incapable of guilt."

Penny angled his body in Danuta's direction.

"She's not a freak, she nor Doris. She walked after a few lines. I don't know about you. Now come on! We both need to eat. Let's go to the cafeteria." Lovell gagged several times before they reached the cafeteria steps. He stopped, seeing the red berated major, leaving what he thought must be the kitchen area.

"I don't want to eat there Penny."

"But you're sick Lovell."

A passing car, painted with the Aybilian green, stopped. The driver, a teenager, hoisted a white taxi emblem, on top of his car. He leaned inside and secured it.

"Professor Pendleton, come ride with me. I'm one of the new student taxis."

They entered the taxi. The driver watched them in the mirror.

"I saw you on television. We're not like the Americans. We'll treat you with respect and dignity here. This is a fair Muslim country, unlike America. We don't have racism here. We have a saying in Arabic. Unta iquo. We're the same."

Penny gave Lovell a wide eyed, what the hell is he talking about look. Lovell, pretending to touch his moustache, shushed him with a silencing finger across the lips.

"Thank you. I'm glad to be in Aybil."

The young man put in a cassette. James Brown's "Payback" began to play and smiling, his head bobbed.

"Where are you going Professor?"

"Just take us downtown. We're going to walk." Leaning against the back seat he closed his eyes, trying to halt the

[123]

merry go round, playing in his head. He could feel Penny patting his feet to James Brown.

"Are you alive over there? "

Lovell gave an affirmative nod.

"How ironic it is to be riding in a taxi, in Aybil, listening to James Brown. I've never had this experience in the states. If Afro-Americans only knew how far our culture reaches."

Lovell patted Penny on the leg three times, signaling he understood.

"I'm going to write to my mom and tell her about this. Even though she thinks James Brown's music is the devil's music, she'll appreciate this."

Frog sounding words escaped from Lovell's throat. "She must be a southern Baptist."

Penny slapped Lovell's thigh. The light blow bounced from his forehead to the back of his skull. "She's not only a Southern Baptist, she's the minister of her own church."

Like a true southern Baptist Lovell raised his first finger. "I'm a PK too."

Penny fived Lovell's knee. "Then you know what I know. There's a big difference between the people, the preacher, and how people expect you to be. That's why most of us are bad. What they want you to be is something our preacher parents aren't. You get tired of that shit."

Lovell knew well what Penny had to say. People wanted preacher's kids to be pious and extra good, thinking they were a reflection of their mom, or dad. The person in the house was the same, but different from the person in the pulpit on Sundays, or the one who conducted prayer meetings and visited the sick. The man, or woman, they knew, was human. They drank, sometimes smoked, got angry, lusted, could be selfish, jealous, and wasn't always full of the Holy Spirit. What others saw was the servant of god, and they thought their children were an extension of that servant. Penny touched Lovell again with a finger.

"Was your choir director gay?"

Lovell confirmed.

"He was my cousin and he killed himself."

His stomach exploded again out the window, splattering the side of the taxi and the street.

"That's why you're so comfortable with gays. He must have been close to you?"

A trembling bottom lip told Penny more than his friend's words.

"He lived with us because his father, my uncle Mack, rejected him. I found him hanging from the tree in our back yard. He'd already written three symphonies. All he wanted as to be treated like a person; not like a faggot."

He heard Penny sniffle. The music had changed to Teddy Pendergrass' "Close the Door."

"My choir director was my first. I seduced him in back of the organ, on the side of the pulpit. I was supposed to be getting a music lesson. He taught me and I taught him a new tune that night. I'd been lusting after him since I was ten. It took me two years to make my move. I've never turned back."

The taxi stopped and opening the door, the smells of barbecued meat made Lovell lurch. He reached into his pocket.

"You don't have to pay me sir. I want you to tell the Americans who've mistreated you how Aybilians are. I'll see you around the university. My name's Basir. I'm in the physics department."

He pulled off waving out the window. Penny took Lovell's arm.

"Before I ask you what the hell you said. Which way are we going?"

[125]

Lovell pointed to the left and walking away from Ripoli's center, they headed for the Hilton. Each person they passed, nodded to Lovell. Some stopped and shook his hand, speaking in Arabic. A couple of men kissed him on both cheeks. Penny remained silent until they'd sat down in the hotel dining room and he'd winked at the waiter.

"You've been here less than a week and you're famous already. What did you say and why didn't you want to eat in the cafeteria."

Before he could answer, the waiter turned on the television and there sat Lovell with Dr. Humseen. Everyone in the hotel dining room stopped eating and looked at Lovell, who guzzled two bottles of Perrier and devoured the bread on the table. He watched his mouth move, but the voice was not his. The subtitles were in Arabic. Lovell occasionally refused to look at himself, fearing he'd vomit. Once it had ended, Penny gave Lovell his handkerchief, because Lovell's was soaked. Rage had lodged in his throat, causing it to contract. He gulped for air, the food in his stomach turned to acid, burned, making him double over, pass gas, then finding no real release, bubbled from his eyes and forehead. Blood oozed over his hand. He'd bent the fork he held, in half.

"That wasn't your voice. They overdubbed it with someone else's and made you sound like you were so grateful the Aybilians had hired you because the U.S. had treated you terribly. Don't worry about it. Anyone who speaks English can tell it was overdubbed because sometimes the voice and mouth weren't in sink. Calm yourself and stop grinding your teeth. You'll make yourself sick."

Lovell, shielded his eyes with dark glasses and went to the bathroom, to blow his nose and wash the two soiled handkerchiefs. He exited the lavatory seeing Penny

[126]

standing and speaking with two Anglo women, who
nodded and walked away as he approached.

"I guess I scared them away, huh Penny?"

His friend pushed him.

"They're from the American Embassy. They're having a
party Friday, which is the holy day here and wanted some
entertainment. I accepted and volunteered your horn.
You're okay with that aren't you?"

Lovell checked the people in the hotel, checking him,
checking them out, as he and Penny left, walking towards
downtown. As before the men nodded to Lovell.
Occasionally a sheeted woman with one eye showing,
walking with her head down, glanced at him. They'd
walked about four blocks, arm in arm, when Penny
squeezed Lovell's forceps. "Have you noticed people
acknowledge us, but they're not staring at us like there's
something's wrong. I'm holding your arm and it's okay.
There are men and walking holding hands and no one's
even looking. And look at all their colors, it's like being in
New Orleans, but there's no hostility from those who are
white. You know, I realize there's been a knot at the top of
my neck, next to my back from being self-conscious and
hunching up my shoulders and I've been walking like that
for years. I feel it starting to relax. I like it."

Lovell knew that feeling. He knew what it meant to live in
a country where your color was not just a color, it was an
issue. People treated it as if it were something bad or
wrong, and represented wretchedness. They recoiled in
abhorrence and fear. Here, it seemed, from walking down
the street, it was noticed, but was not significant. He paused
to tell Penny about gary-gary, then changed his mind,
watching his sweet friend's green eyes turn sky blue, with
glee. They turned into the building where the senior Faturi
worked. He was not in the office but the Pakistani young

[127]

man, his eyes aflame and smiling, filled out the papers and instead of accepting the bribe, gave Penny some Aybilian dinars, the local currency. Lovell waited outside the office for Penny, who emerged giggling.

"I think I've come to the right country. I'm in the Garden of Eden."

"Don't get bitten by the forbidden fruit Penny."

Penny patted his butt.

"They'll never be able to eat all this, it's too sweet."

They hailed a taxi saying Jami Al Fateh, and returned to the university gate, where the taxi was not allowed to enter and walking to the faculty building, saluted the ruler's picture. Some passing students clapped. Inside, they knocked on Doris' door, and heard sounds, but no one answered. Neither Matt, nor Jim were in their rooms, so they parted. Lovell sat on his balcony, watching the light u shaped building, now full of professors. Curry, chutney, ground black pepper, and boiled rice scents, mingled in the open courtyard. Pulling his balcony doors outward, so as not to be seen by the adjoining balconies, he removed his clothes and sat naked, watching clusters of stars, acting as acrobats above a close net. Taking out his soprano saxophone, he played within harmonic minor scales, which sounded Arabic and North African, singing a melody, through his horn, saying how easy it would be to swing on one of the cascading lights somersaulting through the reachable sky. He had never felt so close to it before. Never believed he was within arm's reach of the mysteries hanging above him. Closing his eyes and in his mind's eye, he extended his right hand, feeling for one of the sparkling embers. However, a knock on his door, left his hand empty, and he placed his soprano, on the chair, wanting it to bask in the night's presentation. Wrapping a sheet around his bottom, he opened the door. Danuta stood, still in her white doctor's

[128]

knee length coat, perspiring, with a pushcart full with two large packages.

"I'm, I'm sorry. I, I, saw your name on these packages and some letters for you, so wanted to bring them to you."

He helped her pull in the cart and turned on the lights. She stepped away from the balcony where she could be seen.

"Please, if you're going to have the lights on, close your balcony door. I don't want Aybilian eyes to see me here."

Lovell turned off the light and lit candles. Danuta sat on the edge of his bed and handed him the letters. He removed the big heavy packages from the cart. Opening one, there was a portable stereo, combination record player, cassette recorder and small television. There were also boxes of batteries and ac adaptors for the Aybilian current. The next package contained boxes of cassettes. Miles Davis, Coltrane, Thelonious Monk, Jackie McClean, Horace Silver, McCoy Tyner, Billie Holiday, Sarah Vaughn, all his jazz favorites and R&B fake books, which are hand copied songs, plus boxes of soul, pop, funk, R&B, and classical music. The letters were from Eduardo and Nidia. Inside both packages were letters from Miss Marguerite.

"Someone loves you very much to send you all this. Is it your wife?"

He sat the portable stereo system on the table, plugged in the adaptor, extended the antennae and flipped the switch. The BBC shook the room and he heard a balcony door close to the right.

"I'm not marriageable Danuta. Look!"

She stood and paced.

"I came to say I'm sorry for leaving the way I did. That was not polite. I want you to know, I'm not a whore."

Lovell walked to the balcony, rubbing his hand, and kissing his horn, placed it back in its case.

[129]

"No thought like that ever entered my mind. We just got caught up in a moment. That's all. Guilt is about something you can do nothing about Danuta."

She paused and approached him.

"You play very beautifully. I'd like to invite you to have some Polish liqueur, if you have the time?"

Lovell moved to a darkened corner, his clothes in hand.

"I'd love to. I need to dress first."

Danuta turned around and faced the balcony. Dressed, he blew out the candles, and seeing no one was in the hall, beckoned to Danuta who walked in front of Lovell, who pulled the cart. His steps were light and fast. She rounded the corner, almost sprinted past the men's bathroom, to the last room and opened the door. Gasping, he entered a wall to wall swarm of purple velvet and satin couches and cushions. He was in plush European living room with purple shaded lamps and even a coffee table with a purple velvet cloth cover. Removing his shoes, he followed her arm directing him to a color coordinated armchair, with gold tacks around the bottom and on the arms. Grieg played on a small cassette. Sitting, he waited while Danuta went behind a partition and emerged in a royal purple evening gown. Lovell swooned, stood and bowed. "I'm honored by your invitation, your highness."

Danuta curtsied, and then offered him two brown liqueurs on a tray.

"Sweet is on the left and a dry is on the right."

Lovell took the dry. She sat the tray on the table and offered him some dark cookies, then sat on her couch, lifting her legs onto it, only revealing her pink toenail painted feet. She took care of her feet. He recalled the smooth heels wrapped around his ankles in the morning, and crossed his legs, his groin rising, again hearing her coos and fingers throbbing in his scalp.

[130]

"Your quarters are lovely. Did you bring this lovely furniture from Poland?"

She raised her glass.

"Gindobre, no! I bought this at a special sale from the Polish embassy. They were remodeling their quarters."

The liquor was smooth, and made his mouth pucker a bit.

"Put a piece of the wafer in your mouth, it takes away the dryness."

Lovell obeyed, as Danuta changed the music. Her leaning over displayed a pumpkin butt. She noticed Lovell looking and batted her eyes. The music was Miles Davis, "Blue and Green", from the "Kind of Blue" album.

"You've gone from Grieg to Miles Davis. I like your taste in music, Danuta."

Her eyes softened and smiled.

"This was my favorite music when I was a student at the university."

He swayed to the music.

"Mine too. We have something in common. Would you like to dance?"

Her brow wrinkled.

"You can dance to this music?"

Lovell stood and embracing an invisible partner, moved around the room and sat down. Danuta, actually smiling for the first time, poured him another drink.

"I saw you on television. It must have angered you."

" It did. They-"

"They made you seem like a sniveling American. It was stupid though. Anyone could tell it wasn't you speaking. Anyone except an Aybilian."

"They're the ones it matters to most. Don't you think?"

She closed her eyes contemplating.

[131]

"To the government and the school yes, but not to anyone else. I wouldn't give it a second thought if I were you. I guess you've had your first lesson in Arab ways."

Lovell noticed her mouth curled.

"Arab, or Aybilian?"

"I understand that question Lovell. I've been here for two years and I've traveled most of the Arabic countries. The people aren't very different in the other counties, when it comes to foreigners especially Americans."

She raised an eyebrow.

"Why Americans?"

" They hate you but love what you have. I think with you it was something different though."

"You mean because I'm black."

Her head and eyes lowered, answering his question.

Someone knocking at the door made her head jerk upward and her eyes darted around the room. Grabbing the liquor glasses, she placed them under the couch and pointed to the back of the door. He did not move. Her eyes pleaded with him so he stood behind the door, his glass hid. She cracked the door, peeked out, sighed, and began to speak in Polish. He sat on her bed and she jumped when his foot touched her thick calf. She closed the door and sighed. Lovell stretched out on her bed then got up, seeing Danuta waiting for him on the couch. He sat in the chair.

"Why are you so afraid? This is the faculty dorms."

She snorted and mucus escaped from her nose. She covered it with her hand and grabbed a tissue. "Why? Don't be silly. I've been here two years and I've seen people sent home for being together. You never know when they'll come knocking at your door. Why last year a Polish man was flogged in public because he embraced a female student whose father had just died. That's why. You'll learn."

[132]

She stood over him, moving her finger.   Lovell refused to look up at her. Instead, he focused his attention on the paintings of snowy hills, with yellow flowers protruding and tan canvases, with ripples of colors streaming down. Danuta followed his gaze.

"That is the work of Jerzy Feiner. It was he and his wife who were at the door. They live in the next room. You should meet him. You are both artists."

Lovell glanced at the paintings behind him. One was a portrait of Danuta.

"How do you know I'm an artist? I haven't told you anything about me."

She stared into her palm.

"You played your horn last night and read from your work. You really don't remember anything, do you?"

"I'm sorry, I don't"

Pain trembled through both lips and eight fingers. He moved to the couch and placed his hand atop hers.

"Tell me about being a doctor in Aybil for two years." Danuta told him about the contracts between the Polish government and Aybil. The government took part of their salary and gave them the rest. She had a son and daughter whom she had raised by herself. Her husband, also a physician, had escaped from Poland, and gone to France with a French woman. Her door opened suddenly and a ten year old blond haired girl with glasses burst in and froze. Danuta grabbed her heart. Lovell felt his pants because a squirt had escaped. "Katia!" Danuta screamed at the little girl. Grabbed her by both pigtails and dragged her from the room. He could hear the little girl explaining in what he assumed to be Polish. Sitting in the room alone, he felt under the couch for the glasses and drank both the sweet and dry liquor. Danuta returned with the little girl, a balding, mustached, pointed nosed man wearing a painter's

[133]

smock and a wide faced waist length brown haired woman, in an evening gown, smoking a French cigarette, and a brandy snifter. They looked at him with amazed eyes. Danuta introduced them as Anna, Jerzy, and Kasha Feiner. Jerzy kissed Lovell on both cheeks and sat down.

"I heard you playing last night. It inspired me so much, I have painted all day."

Anna cleared her throat.

"Jerzy, we are interrupting Danuta and Lovell's evening. You will come and visit with us, will you not, Lovell?"

Standing, as he had done since they entered, he pointed at the painting with the tan top and the earth toned hues, like driblets, moving down the canvas.

"I'd be happy to visit with you especially with anyone who can paint like that."

Jerzy took the sifter from Ana and passed it to Lovell.

"That is the desert, it's not finished because I haven't grasped it yet. Danuta insisted I give it to her. I often take it back and add more, as I understand more about what's all around me. Here have some Polish brandy."

Lovell took the glass and drank. It was light, syrupy but poignant. Danuta scowled.

"You should not be drinking so openly. You know where we are."

Ana reached for the brandy.

"Unlike you, Danuta, I am not afraid of them. What can they do to me, send me home? I refuse to live in fear, like everyone else here. You forget we are still under the Soviet Union. This is nothing compared to that."

She led her family out of the room. Kasha let go of her hand, kissed Lovell, then wiped her lips, seeing if any color was on them. Her parents, their mouths agape, stood immobilized, their shoulders pulled together. When Lovell laughed, the three Poles laughed and relaxed.

[134]

"It doesn't rub off Kasha. I'm always black."

"But you look very light brown to me uncle, like tea with a lot of milk in it."

Danuta stamped her feet and rattled something in Polish. Lovell sat down while a brief conversation, somewhat heated he thought, ensued. The Feiners bowed, and left.

"That child must learn to stay in a child's place. She must not speak so freely, and her behavior, I'm sorry Lovell, it was very inappropriate."

Her pursed lips showed annoyance.

"She scared me when she came in the door. Other than that, I don't think she did anything wrong Danuta. She's only a child and children are often curious. I think this is the first time she's ever seen a black man."

Danuta gave him a wide eyed frozen stare.

"There are Africans in Poland, as international students."

"But this child obviously hasn't seen them. She meant no harm and I took no offense."

"I am glad you didn't. Still, she should not speak so."

"Children are children, you have to let them be."

Danuta lifted her head, her nose in the air. To Lovell she looked like a prissy school marm.

"Are you a parent? If you were, you wouldn't think that way."

"Her parents obviously don't think the way you do Danuta, and they're parents."

She chuckled, and turned away from him.

"Thank you for your visit. I have enjoyed your company. I hope you will come again. I go to bed at ten o'clock every night. My work day is very long. Oh, I forgot. You have another package. Will you be able to carry it?"

There was another large box. He hoisted it on his shoulder and walked to the door. She ran her thumbs across his knuckles.

[135]

"It is better for you to come here because I'm in the corner and it is not easy for people to see us. Believe me, we cannot be too careful Lovell. Anytime you wish to visit me, you may."

Lovell kissed her on the cheek and left. Carrying the box and approaching his room, he saw Matt and Jim standing in the hall, whispering. They stopped when he was within hearing distance.

"Go inside and check your room."

Lovell went into his room. Turning on the light, he surveyed everything. It was as he left it. He enjoyed the two men.

"It's just as I left it. What's wrong?"

Jim flexed his arms. The muscles rippled. "Someone's been in our rooms."

Lovell's stomach turned over.

"Are you sure?"

Their eyes, hard steel and alert, gave the answer. "We're splitting up. That way it will be harder for them to search our rooms. It's time to lay some boobie traps. He doesn't know who he's fucking with."

A stark eerie cloud covered and the butterflies in Lovell's stomach dive bombed.

"Who's he?"

They looked at him with squinted eyes and spoke together. "Don't be naïve. The major!"

They marched to Jim's room and closed the door, leaving Lovell alone. He sat in his room, observing the letters Danuta had handed him. Then his door opened and the two soldier doctor's walked in, in single file.

"Television star you need to keep your door locked at all times. Haven't you learned anything yet?"

He gave them the finger. Matt glanced at the box's labels. "The baroness from Italy, huh? You're one lucky guy."

[136]

Matt turned on the stereo, the BBC, belched from it. "He's not that lucky. What happened on the T.V.? It has everyone talking."

Lovell pushed one of the boxes with his foot.

"They interviewed me, then overdubbed my voice and turned around everything I said. I could tear somebody's fucking head off."

Jim stretched his arms.

"Who did it?"

"His highness fucking Humseen."

Jim gave Lovell a bear hug.

"Don't worry about it. Most of the faculty is laughing because they could tell it was a fake. I guess being a celebrity has its downside. Huh?"

"Kiss my ass Jim and both you fools get out of my room. I have an eight o'clock class tomorrow." They dragged their feet and stepped out the room but Jim stopped at the door. "Did he really make you look so bad you'd like to take his head off?"

Lovell acted as if he were wrenching away a top. Jim wrenched back and closed the door. Opening the first letter from Nidia. He reclined on the couch. *Dear Lovell, My heart is so full thinking of you. I find it ironic, I've left the convent and I'm out here in the world and you're not here to share this newness with me. Sometimes I can feel your presence. It's as if you were lying next to me in the bed and I can smell your honeyed scent. Sleeping where you slept. Sitting where you sat, inhaling the freshness of the clothes you left, brings you ever close to me. I feel a stirring inside me I've never felt before. It begins between my legs and crawls up to my breast, making my nipples stand. Sometimes I'm embarrassed walking because they're poised and throb all the time. Their throbbing is only for*

*you my love. I'm waiting and saving it all for you. I long to
be with you talking and sharing for hours and hours, like
before, but this time in person. I'm patient though and
know it won't be long. Believe it or not, one of the sisters
assisted me in getting a job at the hospital. I stepped into
the position as assistant Director of Pharmacological
studies at St. Mary's hospital. How strange it is to work,
this time for pay, with the same people as before, without
being a nun. The women still find it hard to speak openly
and do men talk around me. I let loose on them though
and they're often taken aback at how gritty I can be. Little
do they know, nuns have these conversations in private
and are ten times as nasty because of the restraints. Lovell,
I'm so glad I have none now. Then again, I do. I'm
restraining my passion because the man I love isn't here.
You told me you have a holiday for a week in October.
Where will you go? Will it be possible for us to meet
somewhere? I hope so. Send me a phone number so I can
call you. Yours always, Nidia P.S. Ann and I have gotten
really close. I see her every day and we spend lots of time
together. She sends her regards.*

He bent over rocking, clutching and unclutching his fists.
Her lavender smell filled the room and holding the letter to
his heart, he called out her name, visualizing, those
spooned out obsidian eyes, with the brown flecks around
the iris, and her onion butt which he'd only touched once.
She had once pretended to be taking a nap, at Eduardo's
parents' house. And as he was leaving the bathroom, in
front of the guest bedroom, she'd opened the door and
stood naked in front of him. The view was brief, but
enough to make his body rise and he'd had to pull out his
shirt to cover himself before he could join the party outside,

[138]

where the Mr. Longoria loved to barbecue. She'd emerged a few minutes later, first finger in her mouth, her hand showing, and Mrs. Longoria had scolded her and tried to force her to cover her head. She had refused and it was the first time he'd seen her drink. She'd insisted on dancing the cumbia with him. And though he'd kept a very visible space between, she'd managed to squeeze his penis once and had pinched his bottom all the time they'd danced. The Longoria's had eyed them close and before the dance ended Eduardo had broken in and danced with his cousin, spinning her and lifting her off the ground, much to her delight and the humor of his family, who roared with laughter until their sides hurt. Eduardo had patted him on the back after the dance, but had never mentioned what Lovell thought he might have seen. Kissing her letter and placing it in his underwear, he opened Eduardo's letter. *My brother, I know you were surprised to see a letter from me. I am surprised to be writing this letter to you. However, as we both know, life is and always has been full of surprises for both of us. Everyone here has been surprised by Nidia's actions. I shouldn't say everyone. The Sarge hasn't acted surprised at all. I wonder if he's known something all of us hasn't. I must say I was and wasn't surprised. I've always known she loved you. I knew you loved her and saw what she did to you last thanksgiving. What has surprised me is the ease which she has shown in adjusting to not living in the convent. She's working, has moved into your old apartment, with furniture and all, and has developed quite a friendship with Ann. I'm surprised at that. I never even knew they were that close. My life has been full of surprises. Kam Ha surprised me by turning into a total Vietnamese bitch. She took me to Houston for a weekend, put me in a hotel and stayed with her Vietnamese family*

[139]

and friends. Then she asked me to change my clothes when we were going to a party with them because I had on my new Toni Lama's, with a western suit. She wanted me to dress what she considered more formal. I changed, except for my Lama's, and then when we got there, she acted like I was just a friend and left me alone most of the time. It didn't take me long to figure out she was ashamed of me and had used me to get back at you for not treating her like the rich princess she was in Viet Nam. I was the only Chicano there. All the other Vietnamese women were flaunting their white boys. I guess I'm not as rich as she thought and I'm too ethnic for her. Her entire world was rich Vietnamese in Houston and the conversations went back and forth from French to Vietnamese. What struck me as odd was none of the white boys could speak French, I could, but they still drooled over them. I showed the bitch though. A fine Chicana swept me off my feet and I invited Kam Ha to a gathering, invited my home girl and Tex Mexed with her all night leaving Kam Ha sitting in a chair. I spoke Spanish all night and then made her take a taxi home (I made sure I gave her the money in front of everyone). I haven't heard from the bitch since. The Gang of Four surprised me by transferring my residency to Corpus Christi. They don't realize they did me a favor because I can go fishing more. Man, it's humid and boring here. However, I'm now an announcer on T.V. I handle the arts calendar and do features. Isn't life funny bro? You always said that. Man, I know I've been a pendejo. I guess I got confused and couldn't see I was being used. I love you and I'm sorry. We've been together too long to lose what we have over a woman. You, not being an ass hole, will surely do right by Nidia. She didn't make her move because of you but her love for you was the catalyst. Ann said she knows she's pregnant and wears your underwear every day. Remember the song; "If you want a do right woman, you got to be a do right man." You're both do rights. Your Hibado, Eduardo

He placed the letter on the table, went to the window and played My Funny Valentine to the moon, Nidia's most requested song, then opened, Miss Marguerite's letter. It was one line after the greeting.

Giuseppe died, I'm relieved, not sad, and I'll be here whenever you come through. I'll be watching out for you, Love Marguerite

Something fragile in his knees tore, and he stumbled, knocking over a box of cassettes. The cover broke and flattened against the back of the cassette jacket, Lovell saw a one hundred dollar bill. He opened all the other fifty cassettes and found the same bill in each one. His knees still weak, and cradling his horn, he climbed into bed, hearing Sarah Vaughan sing "My Funny Valentine." He awoke hours later, still embracing his horn. The faculty dorms were silent. Walking to his balcony, he thought he saw two figures running across the courtyard. Ducking he looked again, but didn't see any movement. Lighting candles, he stacked all the cassettes and moved the boxes. Though cardboard, they still had weight. Using his pocket knife, he split the sides of the boxes, and discovered, wrapped in protective material, albums. Music albums, jazz, classical, R&B, plus silk shirts and ties. Inside three of the albums were cards with names and addresses of the Italian ambassador to Aybil, the Swiss ambassador, and the

[141]

president of IBM, who, surprising to Lovell, had an Italian name. He placed the cards inside his passport, which he'd hidden under a loose board at the bottom on his cabinet and slid the cardboard under his bed. Arranging the albums in flat piles, he turned on the cassette recorder, and listened, this time in reality, to Sarah Vaughan singing "My Funny Valentine." His windows shaking from the sound of music, forced Lovell to sit straight up in the bed. It was still dark. He walked to the window and could see the other faculty members coming from their rooms, hearing the refrain. Allah Akbar, Allah Akbar, Allah Akbar. It ended abruptly and a voice clearing its throat began the call to prayer. Lovell looked at his watch, it was five o'clock in the morning. He dressed in his sweats and went out to run. Leaving the building and running past the cafeteria, he again saw the major, leaving the kitchen area. He stopped upon seeing Lovell and then hurried to his private car with the red flags on the front. Lovell turned into a dirt road and began to run across a sandy field, then through the dense orange groves, staying clear of branches; he slowed, thinking he heard panting. Stopping and squatting, he saw couples humping, leaning against orange trees. The girls were bent over and the boys had entered them from the back. Coughing loudly, murmurs, fearful exclamations and people running could be heard. He waited until the movement stopped and continued his jog, until he came to a clearing, and saw a village, which had been shielded by the orange groves. Men, in white and blue cotton Jalabias, with pants, carrying prayer rugs, walked to a small Mosque, in the distance. He zigzagged through the grove, increasing his speed, circled it ten times, then sprinted across the open field to his room, letting his clothes drop, walked to the shower where he met Jim, carrying a soiled towel, coming from the shower. He slapped fives with Lovell and

[142]

continued to his room. Lovell smelled oil in the bathroom and thought Jim had probably been working on the pipes again, because the hot water was on in every shower.
Back in his room, after meditating, he walked toward the cafeteria, responding to his stomach's calling. He strolled on his tip toes, back to the kitchen to watch the food being prepared. A young man with red hair, with what he now thought of as Arab yellow skin, stood smoking hashish in a small pipe and watched while another young man poured a green liquid into all the pots of rice and sausages, stir it, then blow his nose into each pot. Lovell recoiled, almost heaving. The red headed Arab turned around, placing the pipe behind his back.
"What may I do for you, sir?"
Lovell pointed to the green liquid in a clear container. The young man spoke in French.
"The green liquid is to numb everyone's sex drive"
"And why do you blow your nose in the food?"
Taking Lovell's hand, he walked to a wooden fence. Behind it sat a round small room. To the left of the room, clothes hung on a wired clothesline. Lovell could see, inside the room, ten single beds, lined and touching, with five young men asleep. A single light bulb hung from a chain and three other metal lamps sat in corners. Suitcases sat flat and clothes were folded in corners. It smelled of wet damp cloth and some of the sleeping men coughed. "We treat the Aybilians the way they treat us. We all have to live in this cave, without heat, with one toilet and shower, for all ten of us. Some of us are starting to get sick. They do this because we're Tunisians and we've come here to work."
" But not only Aybilians eat in the cafeteria."
"I don't care. They all treat us like shit. So we make them eat our shit."

[143]

Lovell's stomach growled.

"I'm Shariff. Your stomach says, Professor Lovell Pendleton the Afro-American writer professor who has come to Aybil seeking treatment as a human being, different from how they treated him in America is hungry." Lovell cracked his annoyed knuckles.

"Even if I were starving I wouldn't eat anything from here."

Turning on his heels, he began to walk. A firm hand on his arm stopped him.

"Come with me professor. We too have been used by the Aybilians. I know that was not your voice." He led Lovell behind the room. A red brick, six-foot structure, with a wooden door, stood next to three burners connected to a generator. Sharif removed the door. Food, fresh and canned, was stacked neatly. Lovell remembered his mother telling him about people who kept their milk and cheese fresh in something called a Shilo. Here it was. Next to the Shilo, were fifteen coolers. Shariff waved his hand.

"Breakfast patties, eggs, hash browns, what will it be for breakfast, professor."

Lovell looked at the last cooler and walked toward it because he detected a whiff of fish.

"I'd like some fish and eggs."

Shariff opened a cooler with fresh fish packed inside and another with eggs. He prepared Lovell a small plate and smoked while he ate. Lovell finished washed his hands with water from a container of clean water. Shariff cleaned out his pipe and smiled at Lovell looking at all the ice chests. "You can't get fish in the city because they give it all to the soldiers, but we have it because we're in touch with the Chadians. They have access to everything. Whatever you want, you can come to me, only you though."

[144]

They shook hands. Lovell waited while Shariff loaded his pipe again.

"And what can I do for you? You've been very kind to me."

Shariff lowered his pipe, smoke spraying from both nostrils.

"This is how we make our extra money to send home. We know you westerners like this. I won't ask you if you do. Send me customers, through you."

Lovell raised both eyebrows. Shariff choked, laughing.

"I am not the Aybilian secret police. How could I be living like this?"

Lovell looked worried and stroked his hair.

"Shariff, why does the major come here so often?"

Shariff, his eyes glazed, gave a full smile.

"He makes sure we're putting the dick killer in the food and he loves camel meat. Little does he know it's cooked in piss. He is very dangerous and hates Americans."

Lovell thanked him and walked to class.   He sat on the knee high wall outside the department of medicine, watching the students filing in. From his seat, at the far end of the wall, concealed by trees, he again saw the major's car stop behind the main building and squinted trying to see the face of a young man emerging from the car, hidden by the soldiers opening the car door. The classroom was a large auditorium with ankle deep water on the floor. Cushions had been arranged so he could jump on each one to reach the podium. The students stood as he entered. After introducing himself and having each student introduce themselves, he began to pass out the syllabus when the door opened and a student entered smoking a cigarette. The other students stared at Lovell, who continued ignoring the student. Passing out the last syllabi, he asked the student to step outside and smelled vodka on the round faced man, around twenty-three, with cross eyes and slits for lips, and a boxer's flattened nose.

"I know today is the first day, but I hope you won't be late again."

The student, took out a cigarette from a flat gold case with the Major's insignia on it. He lit the cigarette and blew the smoke away from Lovell. "Sure."

He ended his classes and was walking back to the dorm when the Major's car passed and someone flicked a cigarette out the window, hitting him upside the head. As he flicked off the cigarette, turning to look at the car, he heard Doris calling his name. She caught him and touched his right thigh wear no one could see.

"Lovell, I'm in love."

Her pale face glimmered in the sunlight. "We've been in each other's company ever since we met and we have so much in common. He loves country, and classical and Bonnie Rait, and boy can he eat some pussy."

Lovell snapped his fingers.

"I know that's a prerequisite. I wonder how you'll feel in two months once the newness wears off."

She stopped and looked up at him.

"Don't give me that socio-psychological crap Mr. Pendleton. I know the difference between what's real and what's not real."

She stamped away from him. Lovell strided, catching up with her.

"Hold on home girl. I just don't want you to get hurt. If I remember correctly, it was only a little while ago you were talking about not getting involved. Now you're in love."

Doris sighed and stroked her purse strap.

"I know Lovell. That was different because you'd just had me and were talking about someone else. I felt a little weird. Meeting him was like the first time I was with my

[146]

husband, before he became my husband. It's like what Stevie Wonder said. If it's magic, then you know it has to happen. It has. Oh god, here comes my drunk ass cousin and his partner in crime. I swear, those two are going to end up in the gallows."

Matt and Jim, in basketball shorts and shirts threw Lovell a gym bag. Matt high fived with Doris. "Boy, cuz, you're glowing what have you been doing?" Doris gave him her biggest cheesiest smile and curtsied.

"I've been being a nice girl, unlike you two. I've seen you two leaving campus every night. Found something huh?"

Matt did a Cleavon Little bow legged "Blazing Saddles" walk and the four laughed. The three men left Doris, walking to the dorms. They were crossing the street when an alarm sounded. Soldiers emerged from places Lovell hadn't noticed, running towards, the open fields behind the university. Matt said they were on maneuvers and kept walking. Inside the basketball gym, the Sudanese huddled together and the Aybilians sat in a corner, in a circle. The three Americans sat with Madusun, Ahmed and two others. Madusun whirled his finger. "They found Humseen about an hour ago in one of the oil wells. He'd been strangled and his neck broken."

All the men looked at Lovell. He lifted the basketball shirt, covering his face. Madusun pulled it down.

"He had a lot of enemies. Especially those wanting to be head of the university. It's a political post you know. They're replaying that interview you had with him Lovell. It was the last time he was seen on television. Be careful."

Lovell dropped the shirt. "Why do I have to be careful?" Madusun stood and bounced a basketball sitting on the floor.

[147]

"The Aybilians know what he did to you. They're vengeful and think everyone else is the same. They might think you tried to get back at him. That's why."

He dribbled across the court and with no effort, dunked the ball backwards. Seeing no dressing room. Lovell stripped and changed into his gym clothes and saw Matt talking to Ali, the David Ruffin look alike, from the airport. He played with the Aybilians, had moves like George Gervin, but jumped like Dr. J. He was the best player, dunking the ball over the seven footers, making jump shots from all corners, pulling up from inside and outside, taking guards off the dribble and making no look passes. Everyone, after a while, stood, open mouthed, whenever he had the ball, which was not often, because the other Aybilians, wouldn't pass him the ball. He was almost ready for the pros. The American Sudanese team, with Madusun at center, Jim, who couldn't jump high but could box out and therefore get rebounds and Ahmed at forward, Lovell and Matt at guard, one by two points to a younger Aybilian team. Ali had scored twenty-five. The game had just ended and everyone was shaking hands, when the major and ten armed guards burst into the gym. They came directly to Lovell. Jim stepped in front of him. One of the Colonel's men pointed the machine gun in Jim's face. He refused to budge and didn't blink. The rest of the group made a semi-circle, then placed a seat in front for the Colonel to sit down. He sat, crossing his legs. The Sudanese and everyone except Matt pressed against the walls. Matt stepped up next to Jim.

"What can we do for you, sir?"

The major had glued his eyes to Lovell.

"You can do nothing. I am here to speak to Professor Pendleton."

"We'll talk."

[148]

The Colonel placed a right hand on his gun. Lovell pushed past Matt and Jim.

"What is it major?"

The Major motioned for a chair to be pulled up and pointed to it. Lovell straightened his back.

"I prefer to stand, sir."

The Major refused to look up. Instead, he addressed his questions to a new man, whom Lovell had not seen before. He wore a ponytail and to Lovell, had a bird face. The man translated.

"Where were you last night between 7 p.m. and 9:30 p.m.?"

"I was having tea with Dr. Sumska."

The Colonel crossed his legs.

"Alone?"

"No, it was the Feiner's, Dr. Sumska and myself."

"How long were you there?"

Lovell sighed loudly.

"I just told you, from 7 p.m. to 9:30 p.m., I was there. I guess around two hours."

The Major stood and facing Lovell, spoke in English.

"When is the last time you saw Dr. Humseen?"

Lovell turned to the translator.

"Tell him the last time I saw him was in Dr. Faturi's office."

The Colonel turned his back to Lovell.

"Ask the American, was Dr. Faturi there?"

Lovell answered yes and the Major led his entourage from the gymnasium, after knocking over the chair. Madusun rushed to Jim and Matt.

"Are you two crazy? Do you know who that is? He can have you out of here tomorrow. And you Lovell, acting arrogant? He could have had you arrested and you would have disappeared. You Americans are too brave for your own good."

[149]

The other Sudanese, and the Aybilians, except Ali, who'd walked over to stand with the Americans, murmured their agreement. Lovell said what he knew Matt and Jim were thinking. If they let him intimidate them now, he'd do it forever. It was like standing up to a bully. The difference though, in this instance, was the bully had an army and a country behind him. Taking a step, his knee locked and he sat on the floor massaging it until he was finally able to move. It was an old ligament problem from high school, which sometimes occurred when he ran a lot. His knee often ached, and sometimes sent electric jolts up and down his left side, causing him to jump with pain. Limping, he, the Sudanese, and Ali, walked towards the faculty dorms. Matt, slapped Ali on the butt.

"What the hell are you doing in this country? You should be in Europe or the states playing professional ball."

Ali, seeing Lovell limping, had placed Lovell's hand on his shoulder for support. Lovell had kissed him on the cheek.

"That's my dream, sir. I think about it every day. Playing with the Aybilian team is okay because it's my country. But I'm much better than them and they know it."

"Is that why you have to demand the ball when you're open?"

Jim rubbed the straight line of knotted scars, stretching from mid-thigh to below the knee as he asked the question and limped more than usual. Lovell had learned they were from shrapnel and bullets; souvenirs, from Vietnam. Madusun, didn't allow Ali to answer.

"Yes, they're jealous of him and all want to be a star. That's what happens when you try and put everyone on equal footing. People strive to shine more and envy the one with talent. This socialism nonsense even affects sports. All that's going to change now that I'm the coach. I'm going to build the team around Ali."

[150]

Matt slapped Madusun on the butt and they all high fived. Someone clearing their throat made them all turn around. It was Doris and Danuta walking together.

"I see we have a little male bonding and posterior fondling. Are there some new relationships developing here?" She winked at Matt. "Cousin, with the way you're switching you're the only one who has anything new happening. Now get on before I smack you on your butt and get us arrested."

Doris smacked her butt as the men moved aside to let she and Danuta pass. Danuta turned focusing her eyes on Lovell's limp. Jim looked at Danuta from the back, and waited until they were far away. "Damn, she's got a big ass. I've never seen a white woman with an ass like that. I need to go to Poland."

Matt pushed him.

"You know you can't handle no big ass white boy. That's why you like them Asian girls. They small just like that acorn between your legs."

Jim faked as if to grab Matt's penis.

"Well, your pencil must not be much bigger because you prefer them too."

Laughing, he and Matt headed towards the cafeteria. Lovell halted them.

"Don't eat in there. I spoke to one of the cooks. He told me, your Major friend has them put something in the food to numb the sex drive. The Tunisian cooks also pee and blow their noses in the food."

Ahmed stamped the ground.

"I thought something was wrong. I ate there and when I got home, my dick was like a wet noodle. My wife accused me of doing something."

They all wondered aloud what they'd do about food. Lovell suggested they go directly to the cooks, especially Shariff

[151]

and have them cook for them for a small fee. Madusun and Ahmed said they'd go to the Sudanese market, which was illegal and hidden, but still functioned every day. Ali, listening to them had another suggestion. They could all go the Haba Shangira, the small village behind the university, where he was from and where his family still lived, and buy their food. They had reached the faculty housing unit. Madusun and Ahmed decided to go to the Sudanese market to see what they could find. Jim and Matt would go with them. Lovell, with Ali's support, limped to Haba Shangira. They walked towards the orange groves but Ali veered away from them.

" Night is coming professor. We don't want to disturb those who are having fun."

Lovell couldn't see anyone in the dusk.

"So that's where everyone has fun."

Ali took Lovell's hand.

"It's not anyone professor. They're all couples who've made promises to each other and the man doesn't have enough money to get married. It's also not just for fun. There are places to go for that."

His voice was like steel and seasoned with pepper. Lovell could see Ali's head, back and shoulders pulled back.

"I'm sorry Ali. I didn't mean to offend you by suggesting something about your people."

"You didn't offend me sir. I only wanted to make it clear. We do have sex for fun, but not out there. We go to the whorehouse."

Lovell stopped walking.

"I was told there aren't any whore houses in Aybil."

Night had eased its arm over the sky. He couldn't see Ali's face, but heard his laughter. "Whoever said that doesn't know this country. There are about ten in downtown Ripoli. The women are all Egyptian. Actually, they're Nubians."

[152]

"You mean they're black and Aybilian men like to have fun and get pleasure from black women."

Ali tugged at Lovell's hand and they walked again. "Yes sir, my father told me men all over the world prefer black women for fun."

My mother is Nubian."

He quickened his pace. Dogs began to bark. Ali picked up rocks and began to throw them in the direction of the barking.

"Never come out here alone at night sir. There are wild dogs out here and they will attack you. I lost my little sister to them."

They walked across the remainder of the field and rounded a bend. After about twenty steps, Lovell heard hammering and machines going. Then he saw three lit buildings in a semi-circle. Ali led Lovell to the farthest building on the right, which housed the sounds. They entered a closed door, Lovell heard Horace Silver's "Senor Blues" coming from unseen speakers, stepped down into a modern garage, with a raised hood Mercedes and the smell of French cigarettes coming from the engine. Two feet, in steel toed work boots, protruded from under it. Ali did not move. The feet disappeared and cigarette in mouth, what Lovell thought was an eight foot blue black man with sleepy eyes, a shiny bald head, tiny ears and a fog horn nose, in a navy blue mechanic's jumpsuit, stood above him, his arms open for an embrace. Ali walked, and embraced him.

"Baba, this is-"

A high pitched Smokey Robinson voice completed the sentence.

"Professor Lovell Pendleton"

The giant walked to Lovell, taking off surgeon's gloves, gave him the power shake with the right hand, which

[153]

covered Lovell's, and engulfed him with a left armed embrace.

"Welcome Professor. My son told me you'd met."

The accent was English. He stepped back and crushed out the cigarette in an ashtray, then emptied it in a trash can. Ali picked up the trash can and leaving Lovell standing, walked outside with it. The giant excused himself and turning, zipped down the coveralls and stepping out of them, revealing white boxers and a basketball shirt. He hung the suit on a wall rack, and still not facing Lovell, closed the door to a bathroom. Lovell heard a shower running. Lovell gasped at his massiveness. He'd never seen a man that huge. Ali returned carrying the trashcan and a plastic liner, placing it inside the can and putting the can in the exact place as before. Donning white surgeon's gloves, he cleaned each tool, placed in either a tool box, or hung them on a rack, then swept the garage clean. As the bathroom door opened, Lovell was being led to the center house, where, after removing his shoes, he was introduced to a small living room, with lounge chair, tables, loveseat, coffee tables, and sofa. The only difference, from any he'd seen in the United States, was the pictures of Nubian kings and warriors on camels and men and women working, hauling water, from the Nile. Ali returned with towels and a Jalabia. He threw them to Lovell, told him the shower was behind, and left with his own set of toiletries. The bathroom was black marble, from ceiling to floor, with black towels, scented soap, and large palms. A minimum of twenty bottles of cologne sat on a shelf. He washed, rolled his gym clothes into a ball and exited wearing a white Jalabiya. Ali called him and Lovell walked into an open archway and stepped down into a palm lined room with arm cushions and flat mats. A knee-high gold leaf round table sat in the middle, surrounded by larger floor cushions

[154]

and arm rests. Ali and his father, sat on cushions. Ali's dad smoked a long stemmed pipe. Lovell swore it was hashish. He sat down on a flat cushion and straightened out his aching knee, being sure to pull down his Jalabiya, so his underwear wouldn't show. Lovell smelled perfume but didn't turn around. He saw a figure in black out the corner of his eye and dropped his head as directed by Doris who'd given him specific instructions to lower his head if ever in the room with an Aybilian wife and to never give a compliment. He smelled chicken, rice, boiled greens, tomatoes and fried bread. The last dish was fish. His stomach spoke in expectation and he heard the father laugh. The figure, a woman left, and Lovell looked up to see father and son smiling. The father motioned to the food. Holding his left hand behind him, Lovell spooned out the food, using his cupped hand. Though he was the only one to eat the fish, he made sure some was left for someone else. After they'd finished, and the giant had burped aloud, like Lovell's father did after every meal, much to the consternation of his mother, the woman entered again and cleared the table, leaving finger bowls for them to wash their hands, a bottle shaped like a genie's lamp, and poured three small glasses.

"My son tells me you hurt your leg. I have something for it. Show me where it hurts."

A velvet voice spoke to him. Lovell, head to chest, pointed to his knee. The three family members choked on their laughter as the giant spoke.

"You can look up professor. My wife doesn't cover her face and you will not offend me."

 Lovell looked in the direction of the feminine voice and covered his mouth. She was black as tar with cheekbones so high, only a knife slice of eyes shown. And those lips, huge, red painted liver lips and skin like obsidian jade. Her

[155]

hair fell in long waves, from underneath a black silk scarf, and touched her waist. Hairless arms, hennaed hands, and a sheer top with a black under bra clung to the ebony skin. Weathered hands lifted his leg, bent it, and when he winced, carried a smoking urn, scooped out a handful of olive smelling avocado green cream, spread it over his knee. She wrapped it with a bandage and told him not to walk on it tonight. Lovell studied the narrow, long piano fingers and still wouldn't look at her face. "Welcome to Aybil Professor Pendleton. I hope you will visit us again." Lovell thanked her hands, and laughing she left. The giant pushed his glass over.

"You are very mannerable professor. This is not a typical Aybilian home. If it were, the wife wouldn't even come out. If she did she'd be covered. Relax."

Lovell bottomed up his glass and struggled for air as an explosion erupted in his stomach.

"What is that?"

Tears dribbled from Ali's eyes.

"That's homemade Nubian wine, made from rice. You drink another one and you won't be able to get up. We appreciate your consideration professor, but as my father said, you can relax."

Lovell exhaled.

"I'm sorry, I just don't want to do anything wrong."

The giant slapped him on the back.

"Don't worry about that my man. You're at home. I learned to speak and write English from black soldiers during world war two. They practically raised me."

Lovell's drawn eyebrows spoke for him. The giant continued.

"Haven't you heard the song, from the halls of Montezuma to the shores of" He didn't need to finish the song.

"I was a small kid. The American soldiers were here for a long time. They only left in 1967 when the group of seven pulled a coup d'état. They taught me how to be a mechanic and everything. The last one died two years ago. You could actually say, they were the only family I knew. My family was killed during the war."

Lovell sat up.

"I don't quite understand when you say they were your only family."

He poured Lovell another drink.

"I lived with them on the American base and went to DOD school. That's the Department of Defense."

Lovell could only shake his head in wonder.

"But you're still a Muslim, aren't you?"

The giant's smile vanished and he looked around. Ali also looked toward the door. They rose.

"Come walk with us."

They went outside and walked away from the house. It was so dark he could barely see his hands. He followed the white Jalabias. Lovell smelled sheep and cows. Stopping at a high wooden fence, and what he thought were three Great Danes ran to the fence. They didn't bark. Ali and his father patted their heads. Lovell stepped away from the fence.

"Let them smell you professor. You never know, there might come a time when you have to go outside. This leads to the desert. If they don't know you, they'll rip you to pieces. These are pure Nubian watchdogs. They can also herd sheep."

Lovell leaned against the posts and let the dogs, who stood at his waist, sniff him.

"Let me answer your question. I was born a Muslim, that's all. I was raised as a Christian and what people call a pagan, on the base. My closest friend was from the Carolina Sea Islands and he believed in African gods. Here

[157]

though, no one knows this. They see me as Muslim like them. It means nothing."

Lovell noticed Ali watching the house.

"Why are we talking out here?"

The father lit his pipe.

"I have to be careful of my younger children. Not both. It is only my daughter. My youngest son is more influenced by his brother and I. What she learns in school has become stronger than anything we can teach her. We have to be careful. This is how this man controls us all. He brainwashes the children, and they will report you to the community leader."

He touched his son's shoulder.

"My boy's quite a player isn't he?"

" He should be in Europe or the U.S. playing pro."

The father blew smoke through his nose.

"I know, that is why we must get him out of here. I made a mistake in letting him come back here. He went to private school in Italy and graduated from Pratt with a degree in aeronautical engineering. He's actually a pilot, but they won't let him fly because we don't have the family connections."

Lovell remembered his payments to Faturi.

"Can't you pay someone off?"

He saw the father's eyes from the match. They had reddened.

"I have my shop here and I work for the Italian embassy. I could pay, but it would bring more suspicion because they'd want to know how a mechanic and what they think is a driver, got so much money. It would cause me more trouble. He has only one choice to get out of the country and that could be very dangerous. We have to do it though because being here is a waste of his time. Now let us go back inside. My wife will not like it that you are standing

[158]

on that bad leg. Oh yes, my name is Ramadan. Call me R. S."

Lovell struggled to see.

"I'll call you Mr. R.S. What does R.S. stand for?"

He heard Ali snicker.

"My name is Ramadan Suleiman, or as you would say it in the states, Solomon. The G.I.'s call me R.S. for running smooth. I was quite an athlete. I can still take my boy off the dribble and dunk on him with my left hand."

Ali pushed his father and they tussled.

"You try and dunk on me old man and I'll break your arm."

They walked to the house and Lovell picked up his clothes. The father looked to the son.

"Where does he think he's going?"

Ali shrugged. "Professor?"

"Call me Lovell, Mr. R.S."

"Lovell there are patrols everywhere! You might as well be asking to go to jail being out this late at night."

Lovell looked at his watch. It was barely ten o'clock but he didn't argue. Ali sat in the chair and turned on the music. It was the Isley Brother "*For the Love of You.*"

"You can sleep in one of my bedrooms. This is my house and the other is for my parents. My little brother lives in both houses, my little sister, only with my parents".

Mr. R.S. left the two younger men sitting in the living room. That night, Lovell learned R.S. had gone to the Sudan on vacation and had hurt himself playing basketball for the Aybilian team and had been taken to the hospital. There he'd met the only Nubian nurse at the hospital. He pretended to be worse off and stayed extra days talking to her. Every chance he'd got, he'd returned to Khartoum and had gone to the hospital. His mother had been raised in a home run by missionaries and he knew her language because of the missionaries, who were American had

[159]

allowed the Nubian girls to speak it, as long as they learned to read, write and speak English, along with Arabic. It took his father three years to win her heart because the missionaries didn't like R.S. He wasn't a Christian. In fact, he was a Muslim and had to convert to win their approval. Ali told him his father had said he didn't care because he had no belief at all in any religion and would do anything to get his mother. Mrs. Sulieman was unhappy in Aybil. She was not allowed to work and hated not being able to go out at night or by herself. She had become even unhappy since his little sister had run after a ball and had been mauled by the wild dogs. They all wanted to leave, but hadn't been able to find away. Lovell listened until his eyes drooped. The call to prayer and a rooster crowing signaled an end to his meditation the next morning. He had practiced what his mother had taught him from a childhood; set your body clock with your mind and you'll awaken at the time you want, every day. His pattern had been developing; to bed by one, up for meditation by 4:45 and out and running before 5:30. After his toilet, he slipped on his gym clothes and eased out the back door. Standing and looking at the pastures, in the yawning dawn, and watching the desert, a flattened pale blanket before him, he heard someone talking and turned to see Mr. R.S. and Ali, prayer rugs in hand, going to the mosque. They waved at him and continued to walk. He trotted to them. "You two are off to the mosque." Mr. R.S. spat.

"It's the only way to keep peace with our neighbors and my little girl. They have her report if we don't go. I'd rather be in bed going for my morning ride with my wife. I'm sorry for you two, you've never had the pleasure. Your wrists must be very strong or you'll be broke all the time. "

He tapped Lovell, who'd stopped, with his rug. They were near the mosque and he'd noticed more than half of the men, had one pupil less eye.

"Many of the men here put sugar over one eye and let the flies feast on it, to keep from being conscripted into the Italian army. They can still see out of the eye."

Lovell's foot dusted the ground.

"And how did you escape the service Mr. R.S.?"

He patted Lovell again with the rug.

"I have to do my social duty now. Wait for us here, I'll tell you."

Lovell sat outside the round mosque and watched as the day opened its palms to the world. Haba Shangira was a one block village with close to thirty stores on each side of the half paved, half dirt street. Bulldozers and road paving machines sat at the head of it and the smell of garbage singed the air. Outside the village, before the orange groves, were stretches of shrubbery and open land. All the houses, half-moons and squares, were to the left of the street, like scattered pieces on a monopoly board, with smoke sifting upward from chimneys. The smell of fresh bread eased itself into the air from behind the mosque. He swiveled his head following the smell and saw a pastoral scene straight from one of the pictures he'd scene in Bible School, with the sheep in the pasture, lambs shadowing the mother sheep, dry arid land, a sheep dog squatting, tall bushes and a small boy carrying a wooden bucket of sloshing milk across open land towards a small white house. Once again, serenity visited him. The warm sensation of fresh cocoa pouring through his chest and stomach, sending peaceful currents through every limb, he fell to his knees, head prostrate to the ground, to thank forces beyond himself, for its majesty.

[161]

Someone clearing their throat brought him to his feet. It was Mr. R.S. and Ali, over him. Other men stood at a distance, pointing at him, smiling. He brushed the dirt from his forehead, arms, knees, and looked back at the pasture, mist forming at the corner of each eye. Mr. R.S. followed his eyes. "Beautiful isn't it. That is why I will miss this land so much when I have to leave. It is still untouched. But as you see, the world encroaches on it everyday. Soon, all this open land will be buildings and asphalt because our people have nothing to do and so they stay in bed a lot. And, when men and women are in bed, babies come, families grow, and they need more space. You know Lovell, the more children you have here, the more money the government gives you. What an incentive to do what we all like to do, heh?"

He winked at Lovell, placing an arm around his shoulder, beginning their walk.

"The next time you need to pray. And you pray in that position, come inside the mosque. I will show you what to do and teach you prayers. I do not believe in religion, but I do honor and respect something stronger than me. It is everywhere. I know how you feel."

Lovell allowed his joy to run freely from each eye. They walked toward the village as shops began to open. The head of a cow, blood still dripping, was placed on a hook, outside a glass window, where a cleaver separated its other parts. Men hung pails, baskets, turned on radios and displayed materials. Tables were placed outside an open café where team was being poured by a small boy, like the one who had carried the pail. They sat at a table near the dirt street, waiting for tea. The little boy, no more than seven, ran from the back of the shop carrying a tea kettle jumping from the raised platform where the shop sat. From around the corner, screeched a jeep full of soldiers

[162]

laughing. They did not see the boy who turned and headed to the sound, and mid stride, froze. Lovell jumped from the table in time to grab the boy and rolled away from the jeep which still sped past without stopping. He lay on his back, holding the child and looking at the smashed kettle. He heard footsteps behind him and someone took the boy from his arms. Looking up, he saw a pale man with deep green eyes and sandy curly hair, favoring Penny, hug the boy, then turn him over and give him ten hard whacks across the bottom, then shake him screaming something in Arabic. The child cried and the man kissed him, holding him to his breast, and rocking. He whispered something in the boy's ear, and put him down. The boy walked to Lovell, took his hand, kissed it, placed it to his forehead, bowed and picking up the kettle, without looking, ran back across the street and into the restaurant. The father sighed, shook his head, and extended his hand to Lovell, pulling him to his feet. "I am Basam Muhammed. Thank you for saving my son. I would like to buy you some tea. Come!"

Holding Lovell's hand they strode to the teashop. Mr. R.S. and Ali had pulled up a chair. The table was full with steaming glasses of tea. As Lovell sat down, the men all slapped the table. Basam ordered another glass of tea.

"I have something stronger to put in it at home."

Mr. R.S. looked at the other men in the café.

"So, do they. They're drinking so much tea to try and clear their heads. Good Muslims all of them." Basam slapped the table.

"You and my father used to say that all the time. Look at Bashir. I was coming from the studio last night and stopped by the hump house. He had one on each knee and a bottle between each of their legs. And here he was leading the prayer this morning. And Saleh, the Imam, has a special room in that new one behind the old souk. He pays her so she won't sleep with anyone else. I know because she was laughing and told me as I was riding her and devouring one of her humps. She told me his tail is so old and withered, most of the time it doesn't even work, so he licks and drinks her well water. I'm going to use this in my skit tonight."

Mr. R.S. reached over and bumped Basam's hand with a fist.

"Don't get carried away son, you know what they can do." Basam reddened and leaning close, knocked on the table three times.

"What more can they do to me?"

Mr. R. S. was about to speak when the boy, a new kettle in hand, came dashing through again. His father grabbed him. Some tea splashed on the floor, smoke rose. Basam spoke in Italian.

"He's been like this ever since, you know Ramadan. He won't complete any of his work in school and he's always in a hurry. Lovell chimed in, speaking a broken Italian, French Spanish.

"He must have had a devastating recent loss. He's afraid if he doesn't do everything fast, he won't have a chance because maybe he'll die too. It's insecurity and being a child, he doesn't know how to express it. You need to get him some help."

Basam's eyes turned glassy.

"There is no help here. Anyone with that kind of profession has either been killed or has escaped."

Ali leaned close to Basam.

"Hold your voice down."

Basam picked up his son, and kissing Lovell again, left the teahouse. Mr. R.S. spoke to Lovell in French. "His father and the boy's mother disappeared three months ago after doing a skit about the disappearance of the group of seven who pulled the coup d'etat. Only one remains, and that is our leader. The irony is he came on the T.V. and grieved in public. Then he gave Basam his father's show. Like father, like son. I guess that's why they say the tragedy of youth is that it's wasted on the young."

Lovell noticed the men at the two closest tables listening. They asked what language he was speaking in Italian. Mr. R.S. said gary-gary. The men laughed and resumed their conversation. Mr. R.S. signaled it was time for them to leave by rising. The men said gary-gary as they left and the café exploded in laughter. Mr. R.S. acted as if he'd stumbled and knocked all the glasses of tea to the floor, breaking them with tea and sugar spilling over the floor and on the men. Ali grabbed his arm and they moved from the shop.

"You know what gary-gary means don't you?"

Lovell grunted.

"I got careless there. Some of these men work for foreign companies, they could speak any number of languages.'"

Lovell blew in exasperation.

"I didn't know it was this bad."

Ali threw an arm around Lovell's shoulder.

"It's that bad and that good. My father told me many of these men killed their wives because the Italians would come and make them hold their hats while they made love to their wives. Only certain Aybilians were allowed in the city at night. They didn't care about my dad because they couldn't see him."

The three men laughed and smacked each other on the back.

"Damn, being a black man is no joke, is it?"

"They either hate you or they love you. The reality though son, is they all want you and envy your power."

[165]

Doing a three-man hug, they separated at the end of the village; Ali went to the airport, Mr. R.S. to his shop, and Lovell to the university. He realized he'd found a new family. Arriving back at the dorm, out of breath from jogging, from the village, he realized his leg didn't hurt. He walked up the stairs and turned to the right, instead of left to his room, and noticed a brown bloodstain on the floor outside the bathroom, which was closed and locked. He knocked on the door and Rhinehart's door opened. He walked out with a set of keys, handed Lovell two keys and turned to go back into his room. Lovell patted him on the back, pointing to the dried blood spot. Rhinehart showed him a swollen left hand.

"We went to war last night about the bathroom. They lost."
"Who are they?"
"Who else, the friggin' Packi's and the Indians. They wanted to try and use our toilet because theirs has gotten so filthy. They won't try that again. We gave them quite a lickin'. I changed the locks. You can't get in unless you have a key. This one and the one for the women. One of the greasy bastards actually bit me. He won't be biting anyone again because he doesn't have any teeth. I gotta go. It's time to oil me hot dog."

He closed the door to his room. Lovell heard a Bessie Smith "Lover Cat Blues" song and begin to play.

Finishing in the spotless toilet he rounded the hall and saw Penny pacing up and down, Doris looking out the dorm window and Matt leaning against the wall drinking something clear from a soda bottle. He had advanced half way when Penny saw him and fell against his chest crying. Doris trotted down the hall and slapped him upside the head.

"Where in the fuck have you been? We've been worried to death about you?"

[166]

She pulled Penny away letting him know that it was okay he's here now. Matt walked to him in even strides and once within arm's reach left hooked Lovell knocking him down. "Nigger if you pull that shit again, I swear to God I'll kill you."

Jim pulled him up, collaring him.

"Buddy, don't do that. If you're staying out all night you got to let us know".

Lovell pushed Jim away rubbing his jaw.

"What the hell is the matter with all of you? I'm a grown man. I'll stay out if I want. I don't have to answer to any of you. Are you crazy?"

Penny wiping his face was hiccupping.

"Lovell, there was a sweep last night. Jim and Matt had to jump out of the Polish doctor's windows because the Major's men raided their room. The Indians told them we had drugs and alcohol after the fight. They caught the doctors and deported them immediately. They made everyone on this floor stand at one end and went through every room. We saw them take someone covered in a blanket from the other end and when we came back your door was open and things were scattered inside. We thought it was you."

He held Lovell and shook.

"We're so glad you're alright."

Lovell rubbed Penny's curls and kissed him on top of his head.

"Thank's for caring guys. I spent the night in Haba Shangira with Ali's family."

Doris hugged him.

"We have to look out for each other Lovell. It's already starting to get crazy and all about a stupid bathroom. The Indians are sick. Have you seen their toilet? It's filthy.

[167]

They think they're too good to clean it and now want to come up here. I enjoyed kicking some ass."

Penny rubbed his hand.

"Me too. I hope I can play tonight. My left pinkie is swollen."

Lovell looked around at his friends.

"You Americans are crazy. Is the war over or has the battle just begun?"

Jim hammered his palm.

"That wars over. Who knows what's going to happen next."

Lovell walked into his room. The beds and couch had been turned over but they hadn't touched the stereo, records or tapes. He looked down to his hiding place. It was still untouched. His friends helped him make up the beds. Later, they had a meeting of everyone in the hall. The Poles and East Germans had the right wing and the Americans lived in the center. The left wing was left open. Keys were given to the women, to the women's bathroom, and the men's keys to the men's room. Work duties were organized with each group having certain days to clean. They pooled their money to buy supplies. The five Americans worked out a plan to keep each other abreast of where each would be especially if they'd be out all night. They made Penny promise not to have any Aybilian men in his room. Penny and Lovell discussed the evenings program. The first set would be the Mozart's "*Concerto for Bb Clarinet*," the second set a medley of Gershwin tunes, and the third set Miles Davis, Coltrane, Horace Silver, Hank Mobley and Duke Pearsom compositions. What Penny didn't know, he could read. The Fabulous Five, as they called themselves, formally dressed in black, took a Sudanese taxi from the front of the university to embassy row. Arriving early, they were searched at the door by a marine, then escorted to the

[168]

plush Ambassador's residence. Doris murmured "House and Gardens" as they entered. The ambassador's wife, a tall Texan with platinum blond hair, recognized Doris saying she was a friend of her family. Her smile dropped, and then rose again, when Doris introduced Matt as her cousin and uncle Lynndon's son. Jim turned his back, and then swung around, his patch lifted, showing an eye, minus a pupil, and the woman swooned the color draining from her face. Doris kicked Jim and helped her to a chair, getting a straight brandy for revival. She left the room holding her head. Matt and Jim headed to the liquor and downed three straight shots to get started. Penny and Lovell tested the piano, playing a Tiger rag duo, to the delight of the ambassador, a balding midnight faced Afro-American, who strolled in, with a bow tie, but jacketless, and began to tap dance and cut a rug. Jim and Matt set their drinks down, corrected their postures and approached the ambassador, who turned on Jim. "Let me tell you something muthafucka. Just because I'm in this position, don't think I won't take off this tie and kick off in your ass. Now you pull some shit like that again on my wife and I'll give you a sho nuff Afro-American ass whippin'. You dig where I'm coming from?"

Jim said yes sir, apologized and stood with his hands behind his back like a deacon at church. The ambassador turned to Lovell.

"And you, Negro. Brilliant ass coon, I know your momma didn't raise no fools. Don't let these mamatapas fool you and don't let your mouth write a ticket your ass can't cash. We all know how the States are with our people. But it's much better than what it was. They've shown you their ass already. So don't be silly. Now, I want you two extraordinaire musicians to represent us and show them how we party. And one more thing, the next time you party in the hotel, Mr. Benjamin Marshall, son of the president of Mt. St. Mary's College in Baton Rouge, Louisiana, find someone other than the local staff. These Aybilians don't like anyone sleeping with their people. Man or woman. The Faculty of Education at the university has an abundance of men with your persuasion. I say this because if you get in trouble for that, I can't help you. By the way, my name is Edward Daphne.

His wife freshly powdered, creeped into the room, looking at Jim. The ambassador gave them all an up and down glance.

"Hello darling, feeling better? I was just discussing this evening's program with Mr. Marshall and Mr. Pendleton, telling them how precarious it is for Americans in Aybil." She ran her tongue across her lips, walked over to the chair where she'd sat her drink on an end table, popped a pill and downed the half glass of bourbon.

"Shove it Eddie. I heard what you said to them. You scared the shit out of me you Cyclops dirt bag. You pull that shit again and I'll go real East Texas on you. You hear me you poor white trash shit kicker."

Jim smacked his lips.

"Yes ma'am, I'm very sorry. I'm not white trash."

She looked him up and down.

"I've heard of the Ellingworths of Connecticut, light Blue Bloods. Okay you're not white trash. But what you did is like a PWT. You got me a good one. Now let's all have a real drink before we have to start acting. Miss Johnson, pour us all a drink and help me prepare for these tight asses."

Doris obeyed and they all downed snifters of brandy. The ambassador and his wife disappeared. The friends looked at each other and howled.   The first guests to arrive were the diplomats from various countries. Jim took on the duty of passing out drinks and acting as a bartender. Men in suits watched them. Penny whispered to Lovell they were probably CIA agents. The ambassador from Italy raised his glass to Lovell. After the first set he introduced himself, mentioned the Countess and told him she'd be expecting a visit. He also asked Lovell to play for his next occasion, in two weeks.   Lovell and Penny were in the middle of their second set when a black couple entered, dressed in black. He was short and full, she was tall and thin. Lovell thought of Matt and Jeff. They moved through the party, nodding and speaking, and being very civil. Penny raised his eyebrows and lifted his head to signify snooty. They finished the set and walked to the ambassador's patio. Tall palm trees were placed around the perimeter of the open area. The short black man approached them.

"What's up black men?" He gave the shake.

"I'm Abdul Bibbs, from Philly. I'm the head accountant at Al Almajuwabi, the Aybil Oil Company. That's my wife Aisha."

Penny dropped his head and snickered.

"I thought you were stuff shirts and wouldn't speak to us."

Aisha reached them and embraced Penny.

"Hey sweetie. I knew you were full of sugar from the first time I saw you moving your shoulders like a miss thing. And you, you're playing the hell out of that horn."

Penny put his hands on both hips.

"I'm the original Miss Thang, not Miss Thing."

Aisha slapped him on the butt. "Well excuse the hell out of me."

The ambassador approached, brandy glass in hand. "I think it is quite inappropriate for all the black Americans to be congregating on the patio and not circulating. Look at the statement it makes. We've come too far to be thought of as segregating ourselves."

[171]

He looked at them with his nose flaring. Abdul clinked the ambassador's glass with his own.

"We were just getting acquainted."

The ambassador's foot showed annoyance with a slow patting.

"Then do it properly and not on a patio in the middle of my party, Negroes!"

He turned and puffed away. Aisha stuck her tongue out at him.

"We'd better go before he has a damn heart attack. We'll go first, you two follow. We'll hang out after this part is over."

They returned to the occasion in twos.   Lovell and Penny played the next set and sat at the piano, playing an Ellington duo medley, then finished the third set. They watched as Matt, Aisha and Abdul never spoke directly to each other, until all the guests, except the Americans, had left. Then the ambassador, his eyes apple red, who stood by the door, shaking hands with everyone, pimp-stepped into the next room, and returned doing a duck walk to Shorty Long's "Function at the Junction". Mrs. Daphne kicked off her shoes and joined him in the middle of the floor. That began the party and everyone danced until late to 60's Motown, Watts Stax and 70's Philadelphia sound music. Mrs. Daphne was holding court with the women, when the ambassador tilted his head, motioning for Penny and Lovell to join him on the patio. He handed them an envelope.

"Here's a small gift of appreciation. Go get Bibbs and Johnson!"

Penny went to get the two.

"Pendleton. I'm surprised, but not surprised, you're here. You represent, all of you represent, and the finest of what we have to offer. I was disappointed with seeing you on television, but that's how we learn. I know you won't put yourself in that position again. Believe me, other opportunities will present themselves. Vigilance is very much in order here."

Lovell was about to answer when Abdul and Matt, with Penny in tow, arrived. The ambassador raised his glass. "Black men, we represented this evening. I was pleased with your performance. I know that, on all future occasions, you will hold our banner high, and do your duty. I thank you. Now it's time for all of you to get the hell out of my house. My wife and I have a dance to do and we don't have to worry what we're wearing. But before you do Bibbs, show these black men the ropes. I want nothing to happen to any of them on my watch. Do I make myself clear?"

Abdul said yes sir.

"And how's that daughter of yours?"

" She's fine sir. The German specialist sees her weekly."

The ambassador unbuttoned the top button of his pants and belched.

"Good bye fellows. I'll be seeing all of you. Stay out of trouble and remember this. Don't steal from the Aybilans and don't mess with their women. Follow those two rules and you'll be fine. Now get out."

The four turned and walked to the living room, Aisha and Doris stood by the door, their arms folded.

"What speech did he give this time?"

Abdul took her by the arm.

"They represent the one race."

She patted her husband's arm, removed it, and took Doris' arm.

"Let's go all of you. It's late and the patrols will be out. We live a few blocks from here. You can go home in the morning, after I fix you all some grits and eggs."

Matt smacked his lips, and they walked to The Bibbs' huge Mercedes Benz. He awoke to the scent of scrambled eggs,

[173]

sausage and grits. Unfamiliar with the room, he tried to remember which relative liked Romare Beardon and played Donny Hathaway's "*Pieces of A Man*" suite in the mornings. The feel of cold marble on his feet brought reality to both knees, which acknowledged the cold with sharp electric jolts through his thighs. I'm in Aybil and this is Abdul and Aisha Gibb's home. Slipping on his trousers, and shirtless, he peeked his head out of the cracked door, glanced both ways, then retreated to grab his shirt and saw the bathroom, in black marble, to the left. He showered, finding the towel set, which had been left for him, and went downstairs, following the familiar smells. Rounding the curved marble stairway, also black, he walked across a marbled floor, through a flowered living room with low built couches and portraits of desert scenes and Tuaregs. He then turned left into a kitchen where a woman, asphalt colored waist length hair wearing sheer gloss legged pants with thigh length tights under them and a full arm length see through top to match, had her back to the door helped Aisha, dressed the same, but in white cook. He cleared his throat and the women turned around. His knees quivered and he wanted to grab his penis, which throbbed in seeing the moon eyes, grapefruit forehead, high cheekbones on an oval face and unblemished caramel skin with an owl nose and mole on the left lower cheek greet him. The woman turned crimson, dropped her eyes and lifted her hair, covering her face. Aisha looked from the woman to Lovell and chuckled.

"A- Salaam-A-lai-kum my brother, I thought home cooking would wake you up, the others are outside. Penny just came down too. I knew you two would be here last. That was a hell of a concert you played last night. Here's some fresh grapefruit juice."

[174]

She handed him the glass, which he took with trembling hands, his voice having gone between his legs. The woman had turned her back to him. He paused then glided towards Hathaway's voice, hearing the woman ask in an ashy voice who he was and Aisha say his name and ask,

"Homegirl what's wrong with you?" then laugh. He reached the veranda and Hathaway eased into the first words "hang on to the world as it spins around", of the song Someday We'll All Be Free, and saw Matt, Jim and Abdul, each with a hashish pipe, sitting at a long rectangle table, Penny placed dishes on while dancing. Jim offered him a pipe, which he refused.

"Abdul, who's the woman in your kitchen?"

Abdul gave a glazed eyed smile.

"That's Khadijah, Aisha's home girl."

"Homegirl? You mean as in the states?"

Abdul waved his hand clearing the smoke.

"No, as in best friend, she's Palestinian/ Aybilian. Beautiful, isn't she."

Lovell looked back at the kitchen.

"Disturbingly so."

Abdul put down his pipe, giving Lovell a closed mouth glare.

"She's not the kind of woman you have an affair with."

Jim placed his pipe in an ashtray.

"He didn't say anything about having an affair with her. He just asked who she was."

Matt had also stopped smoking.

"Excuse me brother Bibbs, you sound defensive. I was going to ask the same question. I thought Aisha was your wife?"

Bibbs played an arpeggio on the table. Penny stopped to listen.

[175]

"I, I didn't mean to sound defensive. I know how it is to be in Aybil alone. I guess I was just saying she isn't one of those women you screw around with. She's heart attack serious."

Jim and Matt reloaded their pipes.

"Well I guess that excludes us."

Penny paused with a dish in his hand, then sitting it down, walked to the kitchen. He and Doris returned whispering and carrying platters of sausage, grits and scrambled eggs. Aisha followed with biscuits. The woman emerged, her head down, carrying a pitcher of lemonade, the peel floating inside. Abdul walked to the head of the table and bowed his head. "In the name of Allah, all praises be, Buddha, Jesus the Jew, Krishna, the black Indian, and everyone else sacred who has walked this earth, bless this food and please bless the bottle washer because he has a job to do. And as my father would say, good food, good god, good meat, let's eat."

Everyone sat down. Aisha to the left of Abdul, Khadijah to his right, Doris next to her, Penny next to Aisha, Jim next to Doris, Matt next to Penny and Lovell next to Matt. Khadijah spoke with her head up but refused to look at Lovell who ate in silence, not remembering the conversation and refusing to look anywhere but his plate. He could feel Aisha's dark oval eyes peering into him, seeing his heart quivering, flopping back and forth, unable to find a comfortable reclining position. For a few minutes, he watched Khadijah's elf sized hands, and remembered he'd looked down at her. She must have been four ten or eleven. Her voice was high, light and bubbly, and she threw her head back when laughing, showing every tooth. He was the first to finish eating and looked at his own hands, which were small for a man. He'd heard jokes all his life about his small hands and feet, and enjoyed seeing the

[176]

surprise on women's faces when he undressed, because they'd already made assumptions about him. He looked up to see Abdul rise, and stood lifting his plate and reached for a now empty platter, Khadijah rushed around stepping in front of him, her body edging past him and a hand ever so lightly brushed the back of his; she took his plate and the platter from him.

"Don't do that. I'll do it for you. You sit down. Feesha? Would you like some tea?"

She spoke to him looking at the plates. His body rose, and he pulled out the bottom of his shirt to conceal the obvious, feeling her bubble butt, and the whiff of an unfamiliar fragrance, which made him blink, his head swirling. She twittered away, her hips undulating. He followed her movement, then looked back at everyone else, feeling all eyes on him. Lovell dropped his head, self-conscious. The others cleaned the table as he stood, alone, awaiting his tea, which arrived from Khadijah, who bowed as she handed him the cup and saucer.

"You must sit down and drink your tea. It's not good for you to drink standing up."

Group laughter made them both turn around, seeing six faces leering at them. Khadijah, hands over her face, ran into the house. Lovell studied his black tea with red berries floating inside.

"What you want isn't in there. It's inside her."

He hadn't heard Aisha's approach. She stood over him, her copper skin shadowed. The unhallowing of her white outfit and that bushy hair, similar to Lovell's cut in a shag. He couldn't see her eyes, but the voice caressed his racing heart.

"She's not-"

"I know Aisha, she's not the kind of woman you have an affair with. She's serious."

[177]

"That's my husband being protective of her. I was going to say she's divorced and that's a curse in this world. She might as well be a prostitute. I've never seen her react to a man before. She's scared shitless and so are you."

He reached for the shield rising inside him. He clamored for a response, not a reaction, steeped in some kind of logic, not based on fear, but found balled fists, visible to him inside his sacred place, ready to block and counter.

" You've just met me and yet you're acting as if you know a lot about me."

" I do know you Negro. I've seen those creative sensitive types all my life. It's what I'm most attracted to, let it be known. That's why you're so familiar. It's hard for you not to carry your feelings on your cuff. You cry easy, laugh easy, and will definitely fight if somebody crosses you. However, your anger is slow to burn. But when it does, you won't stop until whomever has hurt you is eliminated. It's all masked behind your pride. That's why you don't give a shit about what anyone says. You know exactly who you are and what you want. Your weakness though is your heart. You'll do anything for someone you love and it gets you in trouble because you're giving and trusting. Now have I or have I not described you."

His gulping and trying to drink from an empty teacup, answered her. Abdul called from the kitchen.

"Are you two going to be out there all day or do we have a basketball game to play?"

She patted her butt at him.

"He's also jealous. Don't jump in the water if you can't swim Lovell."

His finger mused the teacups lip as Aisha walked to the kitchen. She had a sister butt and was bow legged. Lovell, Matt, Jim and Abdul rode in Abdul's Benz to the American residence and school on the outskirts of Ripoli. During the

[178]

ride, they learned Abdul was from Philadelphia and Aisha
was from Florida. They had met as students at Florida
A&M in the business school, in the Muslim student's
association, which had five members. They had been
recruited by the Aybilian government, straight out of
college, by Khadijah's ex-husband, the fourth member, also
a student at the time, who still worked at the company.
They'd been in Aybil for seven years, and had two
children, who'd been on a sleepover in the American
quarters. Abdul and Aisha were both CPAs. She worked for
Al-Ma-Juwabi, from home, with her partner, Khadijah,
because after the divorce, her husband didn't want her to be
in the building. His family owned part of the land where oil
had been discovered and founded the company.   Entering
the machine gun armed guard gate, where they had to show
identification, ten guards, in plain clothes with bulges,
guarded the exterior of the twenty-foot high walled in area,
twenty yards from the entrance. Inside the wall, was track
homed suburbia, and stretched the length of a football field.
Children rode bikes through streets named for American
presidents and others had lemonade stands. Women, all
white, walked in jogging suits. They drove to the back of
the area to a large gymnasium.

Abdul opened the trunk and gave them all a gym bag.
Inside the gym smelled like human bodies in action. A
team circled, shooting lay ups at one end and a Masai
looking black man, bubbling with sweat, swooshed jump
shots at the other end. He walked over and introduced
himself as Phil Mendelson. The fifth person in the A&M
Muslim student's association. Matt immediately called him
Felix the cat. He played like a cat on the loose, being
everywhere on the court. Jim held down the middle, Abdul,
at six-four and had a heavyweight boxer's body, controlled
the boards on one side, Matt on the other, and Lovell fed

[179]

Phil, now called Felix. The American school team, made of teachers, and mostly ex college stars that didn't make it to the NBA and had joined DOD schools, couldn't match the speed and the power. The stands were full and only Abdul's two children, and an Olive Oyl looking woman, cheered for the brothers. When the game ended, the American school's players, all white, while shaking hands, said we now have our American team, and invited them all to lunch. It was like sitting in an upscale restaurant in the states with waitresses, A maître d piped disco, soft rock, pop and some R&B. It even served alcohol, homemade wine and beer. Lovell, Matt and Jim learned about flash, called Sadiqui, or friend, in Arabic, the restaurant used for spirits. The mixture was one bottle of water, or soda, to one glass of Sadiqui. A bottle cost two U.S. dollars, and the strength was determined by lighting it with a match, or lighter; blue, meant it was a good batch. They gave the three friends a twelve pack and invited them to a dance that night, wanting Lovell and Penny to join the band, comprised of some of the basketball players. People danced so all they played was dance music. They gave Lovell a book; it was all R&B, funk, pop, disco and soft rock. He said he didn't know about Penny, who played at the Hilton, but he'd come. They'd send a car for him. Farud and Jamilah, Abdul and Aisha's children, rode with their father and Jim. Matt and Lovell were taken to the university by Phil, who drove, but never spoke, the entire ride, until they passed the guard gate. He then asked about how late the guard was at the gate and if he was he a student. He wanted to help them carry the flash to their rooms. They all refused and carrying the cases, went to their rooms. Matt stopped before they separated.

"Isn't it strange he's been here all this time and has never been to the university?"

[180]

Jim also thought it strange. Lovell thought they were both paranoid and left them musing. They mused even more, when Phil was the driver, and took them to the American dance. Abdul, Aisha, Khadijah, Fuad, and Jamilah, met Lovell, Matt and Jim, at the dance. The American school had divided it into two separate parties one for the children, which played records, and the other for the adults, which had a live band. The children's dance ranged from six to seventeen years of age. The older kids controlled the younger ones. Phil was the announcer for the adult dance, and they discovered he was the school's principal, and Olive Oyl was his wife. They were both from Atlanta. Lovell walked to Khadijah and extended his hand. She gave him hers without looking up. Using his fingertips, he raised her face.

"How can I talk to you if I can't see you?"

She reddened.

"Seeing you makes me uncomfortable."

"Am I that bad?"

"Not bad. I feel as if you're looking right through me."

"And what am I seeing?"

"A woman who's uncomfortable with a man looking into her."

"That's not what I see. I see a pearl sitting on a petal."

Tears rose in her eyes.

"Poets use words, like others use eating utensils. It is their gift from God. Sometimes they use them to camouflage their true selves".

"He took a step backwards.

"Is that what you think I'm doing?"

"I have just met you Lovell and I don't know you. How can I say what you're doing? Whatever it is, I feel it."

[181]

Using the end of her purple sash, which matched the purple ankle length dress, revealing one shoulder, she patted her eyes at the tip. The musicians called Lovell's name.

"I'm not one to try and prove anything to anyone. If you listen closely tonight, you'll know what I'm doing because it's what also has disturbed me in meeting you."

He bowed and went to the bandstand. The American school band had bass, two guitars, drums and a piano with no player. Lovell sat at the piano, after setting up his horn, then went to the microphone, as they called Junior Walkers "What Does It Take". He played Honky Tonk saxophone and switched between piano and horn, all night, while watching Aisha, Abdul and Khadijah dance together. She wouldn't dance with anyone else, and in between sets, gave him water and light snacks to eat. She could gig like a sister. Jim and Matt had somehow gotten news to two Korean nurses, who drank and partied all night. The night ended, he'd made two hundred dollars, and horn in hand walked with Khadijah to Abdul's car. Phil had offered Matt and Jim a vacant house on the school premises for the night. He and Khadijah's hands brushed several times.

"You're Khadijah. I have a few loose ends to tie up in my life. I'd enjoy seeing you again though."

She squeezed his hand.

"My strings are also in knots Lovell. We'll see what happens after both ours are untangled. I'll see you at Aisha's in the interim."

She got into the car and Lovell headed for Phil who waited to drive him to the university. The guard at the gate wouldn't allow Phil to enter. Before Lovell exited, he tapped him on the shoulder.

"You've already managed to make inroads into Aybil and move on various levels in this society. What do you do in your free time?"

[182]

Lovell was puzzled by the question because he didn't think he'd have any free time.

*****

He awoke at his usual time shortly before the call to prayer and meditated. He managed, by following this routine, to do his TM and prostrate himself before the forces, in humility, then begin his day with a jog and exercises, and afterwards school, on the day he had classes. Dressed and ready for his run, he walked to the men's bathroom and heard adult voices coming from Jerzy and Anna's room. Leaving, whimpers drew him to the cracked door. He pushed it open slightly, looked in and asked if everything was okay. Jerzy, Anna and Danuta sat in front of a small television, each with a tissue in hand. Jerzy pointed to the television. Lovell entered and sat down. Two women, with shaved heads, drawn faces and hollowed sleepless eyes, wearing burlap dresses sat at a table being talked to by a man in a head wrap. Jerzy referred to him as a Mullah, a religious leader. They were the two Polish doctors from Al-Fateh.

Jerzy translated, saying they were admitting to having illegal drugs and to having illicit sexual activities in their room. However, they refused to name the men involved and therefore had agreed to accept punishment. They were then led in chains from the table and taken to a bare room, which had hooks on the wall. Their tops were then rolled down to their waists, hands extended and tied to the hooks. The Mullah, accompanied by another, took what Jerzy said was a camel's tail, and began to lash them. The Poles counted each lash out loud. The lashes made dark, dripping blood lines across the woman's back. After twenty lashes for each woman, who never uttered a sound, crumpled like

[183]

a wet sock, when untied. Then four women, covered in black, entered, lifted them and carried both women off camera. The screen went black, and the same Major from Al-Fateh came on and gave a speech about the purity of Sharia, respect for Aybilian law, and how no one, neither foreigners, nor Aybilians, were exempt from the law. Jerzy cursed when the Major stopped and spit on the television screen. Anna, scowling, wiped the saliva off with her tissue and flung it out the window, where smoke could be seen coming from a building. Danuta rose, walked to the open window, held out her hand, and then pulled it back rubbing soot-covered fingers together. "Anna, the furnaces are burning again. They're burning again Anna, just like before. Just like before Anna, they're burning. They're burning! They're burning! They're burning. They're burning again Anna. Look! See!"

She held out her soiled hand to Anna, who stood and walked to Danuta with measured steps.

"It is not the same Danuta. We are not there anymore. We are in Aybil now. That was twenty-six years ago. Come Nuta. Sit down and have some Brandy. Do not do this. It is not healthy."

She reached for Danuta, who fell to the floor and began to writhe and jerk as if given electric shocks. Slobber gurgled in her throat and spurted from both nostrils and the corners of her mouth. She then stopped, spittum still bubbling, crossed her arms over her breast, spread her legs and froze, mouth open and eyes rolling to the top of her head, with only the whites showing. Anna fell to her knees and began to shake Danuta, screaming her name. She turned a vanilla colored face to Jerzy.

"Holy mother of Christ Jerzy, what are we going to do? There are no doctors or nurses here anymore and Danuta has gone catatonic. I have seen her do this before. Only a

[184]

doctor or someone with medical experience can help. She can die. She has heart trouble. Jerzy please, think of something?"

Jerzy's hands covered his head, and he began to rock and weep. Lovell catapulted to his feet.

"I know someone. Keep her warm. I'll be right back."

He took off running towards Haba Shangira. His feet seemed to not touch the ground. A group of wild dogs snarled and approached him but he swooped up a big rock, still in stride, and tagged the biggest dog in the head, felling him. The other dogs began to fight each other. Jumping over bushes, holes, rabbit traps, he ran straight to R. S.'s garage, his breath fluttering. R.S. and Ali, whirled around.

"Mr. R. S. I have a medical emergency at the university and I need Mrs. R.S.'s help. It's a matter of life and death."

Mr. R.S. pulled off his surgical gloves and took a huge stride into his house. Ali ran from the garage and pulled a black Mercedes in front of the house. Lovell jumped into the back seat. Mrs. R.S. leapt into the back seat, covering her head with a black shawl, asking Lovell what happened while Mr. R.S. hopped into the front. Lovell explained and watched as she prepared hypodermic needles and cleaned her hands with alcohol. Ali wheeled his way to the faculty dorm and all four left running, Lovell leading and Mrs. R.S. matching him step for step. They entered Jerzy and Anna's room and found Danuta, covered in a blanket, on the floor, breathing in slight rises, blinking. Anna wiped the steady stream of dribble from her mouth and patted Danuta's sweat covered forehead. The room stank of urine, which had leaked from under the blanket and was around Danuta's feet. Mrs. R.S. knelt to Danuta, examining both eyes, removed a stethoscope from her bag and pointed to the door. "All of you men out. We'll handle this."

[185]

Jerzy, sniffling rose and followed Lovell, Mr. R.S. and Ali to Lovell's room. Lovell took four bottles of Sadiqui from his balcony, mixed them with fresh squeezed orange juice and handed the men a drink. Jerzy downed his drink and watched the Aybilian sun, lift like a tossed object, into the ashened sky. "They were thirteen and fourteen. They were thirteen and fourteen Lovell when they were put into the concentration camp. I was there too but I was sick with tuberculosis. They used to bring me food and candy. Good food. German food. Yes, good German food and medicine. Big Polish farm girls who looked years older than what they were. Healthy fully developed farm girls whose fathers, like mine, had been killed in the Polish uprising against the fucking Nazi's Lovell. They took them both and used them for their pleasure. It is a story, which has been told many times by the Jews Lovell. But they were not Jews. They were and are Catholic. A German Colonel and a German Major fathered their first children. If it were not for them I would not be alive today. I have known both of them all my life. We are from the same village and our families had farms. The Germans took them and they used them to keep me alive. And now this, we have come this far to this. First the Germans, then the Russians, and now the Aybilians, they are all the same Lovell, and the lesson to be learned is the same. It is the strong on top of the weak. And we must keep the military and all those who think they are the secretaries to God and therefore have access to his thoughts and wisdom, in the barracks, a church, mosque, or synagogue, where they belong and only let them out for religious activities, or holidays."

The grunts in the room showed agreement. Lovell, who had now bought his own burners and refrigerators from the Tunisian kitchen workers, prepared a breakfast of kippers, shrimp, scramble eggs and sautéed mushrooms for his visitors. Their shared silence was not from the alcohol, nor the severity of the situation. It was when men realize they are in a position where their lives and those they love, are in peril, and everything and anything they do must reflect the realization that an unthoughtful action can cause the loss of those they love and their life.   The meal finished, and hands washed from Lovell's fresh water supply, Lovell gave each man a pipe, which each smoked, staring inward. Mr. R.S., smoke coming from his nose, sipped his Sadiqui. "Son, I think we must move our plans forward. I feel a strange wind blowing. This man also feels the wind. Otherwise he would not be so bold as to have a foreign women flogged on T.V."

Jerzy raised his glass for a refill. Lovell poured him another.

"Iran is close and the Shah is on his way out because the Americans have misjudged the winds again. If that towel headed wearing Ayatollah comes to power. This entire region will change. This boy ruler knows this and is already stacking his cards."

Mr. R.S. gave his son a short knowing look. "Father, our only worry is Jamilah. Females."   Jerzy belched and Mr. R.S. farted. The men laughed for the first time. Jerzy opened his wallet. Lovell assumed he was looking at a picture of Kasha.

"I once read an African proverb. It didn't say which culture or country. But, it said, When a man is educated, you educate a family. When a woman is educated, you educate a nation. I don't know what your plans are R.S. I do know the Nazi's thought one of the ways to control the people, their people, and those they conquered, was to get to the women first. If it is your daughter you worry about. Place her in a school, which teaches her to think, not to follow. I didn't send my daughter to the French school, though I love

[187]

French, because I didn't want her to think like the agnostic French. I didn't allow her to go to the British institute because I never want her to have the superiority they exude. I liked the liberal education of the Americans and how they encourage freethinking, but their history and education is full of lies, deceit and its distorted, to make the whites seem noble. I don't have the time to be re-teaching history. That is why we formed the Polish school and Kasha goes there. The Polish women here are educated and can't work so they teach in the Polish school. Their presence gives our children a better education than what they'd get at home under the son of a bitching Soviet Union. Their minds are fresh, alive, and we must protect them. I don't want to insult you brother R.S., but I have lived under occupation since I was a child and I know its effects on children first. If you want your daughter's mind to be open, either educate her yourself, or send her to a school where you can have some influence. I'm drunk!"

He'd finished his drink and pulling out a scratch pad, began doodling, staring out the open balcony. Lovell followed Jerzy's eyes and saw four three foot black birds, hoisted on the edge of the porch guardrail. Ali stirred the Sadiqui with his finger. "Look Baba, nature has acknowledged our power. I think it's a sign."

Mr. R.S. walked over and scraping the leftover food from the plates into his hand, threw the food onto the balcony floor. The birds hopped down, ate everything and flew into the air and circled above the landing. Mr. R.S. whistled and they flew away. "I will try and get Fuad and Jamilah into the American school. It won't be easy. I know no one there."

Lovell took all the men's glasses and placed them into his dirty dishes bucket.

"I do. I met the principal last night when I played there. He's a brother and roped me off at the gate after I finished."

Mr. R.S. and Ali kissed him. Soon the four men were asleep. A three-knock pattern at the door startled them. Lovell began to scamper around. Each man put gum in his mouths. Mr. R.S. raised his hand.

"It's my wife's knock. Relax."

Lovell opened the door. It was Mrs. R.S., Anna and a clear-eyed, closed mouthed Danuta, who took Lovell's hand.

"Thank you for helping me and providing me with a new doctor."

Lovell welcomed all three women into his room. Mrs. R.S. looked around.

"You're an artist Lovell. It shows in your room." He glanced at the material hung from the ceiling, the canopy he'd made above his bed, the palms and flowers in wicker baskets and the purple, green and yellow paper with poems written on them stuck to the walls. He rarely viewed himself through others eyes and chuckled watching five people check him out. Hearing fluttering he turned to see the birds again resting on the railing. Mrs. R.S. strode to the balcony's edge and extended her arm. The tallest bird rose, swiveling its head. Mrs. R.S. muttered a few words and the bird flew in and sat in Danuta's lap cooing. Danuta stroked its head with her fingertips until it hopped down and walked to the balcony, then turning around, looked at all of them and led the others away. Jerzy crossed himself.

"My god, what kind of sorcery was that?"

Mrs. R.S. walked to the door and opened it. "There's no sorcery, just listening. Come Lovell I am going to make you a wonderful Nubian breakfast."

Jerzy stood and stared where the bird had been.

"It is going to take some sorcery or whatever you did to get the Aybilians to let you work with Danuta."

Danuta gave him a kiss on the cheek.

"It won't take a lot Jerzy. I handled the Germans and kept you alive. These people are amateurs compared to the Third Reich."

They all left Lovell's room and watching to see who was watching them, did a group hug. Outside, riding with the R.S. family, Lovell marveled at the Aybilian sun, massive fire engine red, which covered the entire sky. Mrs. R.S. sang with a honeyed voice, while Ali tapped a rhythm on the back seat. She stopped mid phrase and Mr. R.S. slowed the car. Lovell leaned out the window and saw a crowd formed in the distance. It formed a semi-circle. Mr. R.S. stopped the car and Mrs. R.S. bolted from it her black shawl and scarf making an arrow as she ran. Lovell, Ali and Mr. R.S. followed. Two girls stood in the opening of the circle. One, five ten, around sixteen, with waist length black hair, a plum colored swollen left eye, wearing a bloody Abiyah. Blood was dribbling from her nose and down her lip, she held a soot faced little girl with pigtails, but the same height, in black silk, the same face as Mrs. R.S., around the waist. She screamed at the crowd, and both wept. Mrs. R.S. threw people aside and ran to the two girls. The soot colored little girl let go of the other girl and clung to Mrs. R.S. who pulled her away. Ali and Mr. R.S. faced the crowd, until Mrs. R.S. reached them. The little girl fell to the ground, howling at Mr. R.S.'s feet. Ali turned to Lovell.

"She's my little sister, Jamila. That's her best friend Noor."

The girl Noor, looked at Jamilah and began to shout. Ali translated for Lovell.

"Jamila, I want you to look at all of them here who are about to kill me. See them clearly my little sister and never

[190]

believe a word they have to say. They are all liars and bad men who hide behind this religion because it helps them to hide what they really do. One of them is the father of my child. He told me he was going to marry me and it was okay for us to make love. Now that I am pregnant and he will have to face his wife and the men in this village, he has turned me in. My father, being the good Muslim he is, took me himself last night. Yes he took me the way he takes my mother Jamila, and then asked me the way I want to die. You know what I said little sister. They teach you lies in the school Jamila. Believe nothing of what they say my little sister. Your parents are good people. They are whom you should listen to. Not these liars and hypocrites who sleep with prostitutes, each other's wives, animals and drink more than any infidel. They are worse than the infidel because at least The infidel does not pretend to be something he is not. They do. They all do Jamila. Don't trust them and don't believe anything they say. They are the devil. Kill me now father. I am ready to meet Allah. I will see you in heaven Jamila."

Lovell heard an engine roar and then a Mercedes, at full acceleration, head straight for the girl, hitting her and propelling her body over the roof of the car. She landed on her head, blood coming from both ears and her neck twisted into a figure eight. The car then backed up. Lovell turned his head. A woman, in a white Abiyah, ran from the crowd and covered the body with a sheet. Red splotches dotted it. Mr. R.S. scooped up Jamila, who'd fainted, and walked with her toward the house. She awakened, turned her head towards her now dead friend and seeing the mother trying to scoop up her daughter, began to shout, "Mommy, mommy!" and reach for Mrs. R.S, who took her away from Mr. R.S. and placing her cheek against his face, went into their house and closed the door. The crowd

[191]

turned away, leaving the woman, alone, stroking the sheet, her head on what remained of the girl. She tried to lift the body and a lump fell off. He realized it was her head and walked over to assist her, by bending down. Mr. R.S. called his name. Lovell looked at him as something hit him in the right shoulder. He turned in the direction of the pain, and saw a group of men, some picking up rocks, and others arms in motion aimed at him. Ducking, he covered his head, as the stones hit his arms and hands. Mr. R.S. screamed "lah", no in English, and ran between them and Lovell, moving his hands. They stopped. The woman, snot covering her mouth, said "shocran", thank you in English, and wrapping her daughter's head in another sheet, grunting, hoisted the body onto her shoulder and wobbled toward the desert. Mr. R.S. lifted Lovell from his crouched position, and arm around his shoulder walked with him toward his car.

"No one except a mother can touch the body of anyone who has defied the religion and the family. Doing so is immediate death by stoning. I told them you were an American. Otherwise they would have killed you. Learn the customs here before you act, Lovell. It could mean your life. Sometimes your kindness can be deadly here."

Lovell rubbed his stinging shoulder and hands, as they entered the car. They drove toward downtown Ripoli, each man shrouded in his personal catacomb. Lovell's was textured with his first taste of death. It was when he saw Big Sarah, the prostitute, shoot Little Willie, the cocaine man, in the back of the head for selling her son, Wendell some heroin. Wendell was Lovell's best friend and he and Big Sarah, had placed Wendell in a bathtub of ice to revive him. Wendell had vomited for six hours and finally told his mom where he'd gotten the smack. She'd first collared Lovell, holding a razor to his throat, threatening to kill him

[192]

if he ever did drugs, then had lit out, gun in her purse, looking for Willie. Lovell had left Wendell alone, against Big Sarah's instructions, following her at a distance, then had seen her walk up on Willie in an alle. He was outside his house, where he smoked cigarettes because his wife wouldn't let him smoke inside. Tiptoeing barefoot, Big Sarah had pulled her pistol, silencer intact, and fired into the back of his head, which jerked, as blood splattered from his forehead, in the air. She had turned and finger across her lips, had beckoned Lovell to come. He'd run to her, and looked down at Willie, one shoe off, a trickle of blood oozing from a small hole in his skull. Lovell had peed in his pants. He and Big Sarah had put Willie's shitty and pissy body in a trashcan, and she holding his hand had walked to her apartment, where she cradled Wendell's head and sang "summertime". Lovell's nose itched remembering the stench of death, released through Willie and how the same odor, had hung over Noor.

"You must tell the world about this Lovell. I know you can find a way to do it. You have to son. Otherwise people will never know."

Lovell watched Mr. R.S.'s liver sausage lips quivering, after he spoke. They turned onto embassy row and Lovell saw the Italian Ambassador pointing at the engine of a grey Mercedes, gesticulating at an Aybilian, dressed in traditional loose baggy pants, knee length long sleeved shirt, and Kufi with one eye. Mr. R.S. pulled his car to the curb. Lovell thanked god. Mr. R.S., Lovell and Ali, exited the car and walked to the Ambassador, now within inches of the Aybilian's face. Mr. R.S. asked what was the problem in Italian. The Ambassador, after kissing Lovell on both cheeks, called his driver a dumb jackass, and explained something was wrong with the car. The driver couldn't repair it, and he had an important meeting in half

[193]

an hour. Ali went to the trunk of their car and returned with a tool kit and two pairs of surgeon gloves. They looked into the car. Mr. R.S. leaned out and said something to the driver in Arabic. The driver shook his head and Mr. R.S. spoke to the Ambassador in English, saying this man was a driver, but not a mechanic, like his regular driver. Ali said Baba, father and Mr. R.S. leaned back under the hood, and then stepped away from the car. "Lovell, soc dajah do da okie doke on the dego in da crib, scope it. (They did something to the Italian. Go inside his house and see what it is.)" Lovell asked the Ambassador if he could use the toilet. As they went inside, he told him something had been done to his car, and it was connected inside. Lovell heard a beeping and together, they walked from room to room, marking with a pen, where the sound originated. The Ambassador went outside and returned with Mr. R.S. and Ali, they told Lovell he'd told the driver to go home. Mr. R.S. used a crowbar to remove the plaster, in each room, where they discovered microphones and listening devices. The residency had been bugged, as had been his car. Somehow, the wires had gotten crossed. Mr. R.S. and Ali, ripped out all the bugs. Lovell, Mr. R.S. and the ambassador went into another shelf lined room, while Ali went to turn off the car. When he returned, the ambassador himself poured them all a glass of brandy.

"I knew these worms were capable of surveillance. However, I didn't think they'd be so bold. How naïve I've been. After all it has only been twelve years since they were our subjects."

He started to lift his snifter, but stopped, his arm frozen.

"I don't believe I said that in front of you Mr. Sulieman. You are also Aybilian and you've just saved my position, maybe my life. If a top secret had been leaked, Italy's secret service would have my head. Please forgive me."

Mr. R.S. inhaled and twisted his glass.

"I accept your apology. However, it isn't necessary. You've only spoken the truth. There is something, though, I want to make you aware of, Mr. Ambassador. There is no one an Aybilian hates more than the Italians, or loves more than the Italians. It is the classic master slave dynamic. I was spared and had very little contact with your people. Others were not so fortunate. Including our current ruler."

The Ambassador nodded in agreement, then looked at his watch. "How funny it is we men delight in the chase of the opposite sex. I have a lovely wife, my son, and my daughter upstairs, and I fumed because the car prevented me from dabbling in the Yugoslavian ambassador's wife's flesh. I think god may be trying to tell me something."

He stared at his brandy and then turned to Lovell. "And what brought the three of you down embassy row? Some Ambassador's wife?"

The four men clinked glasses.

"No sir. We just witnessed the killing of a young girl who'd been impregnated by a married villager. The man informed on her once she became pregnant and we watched while her father ran over her with his car. She was decapitated. I was searching for a way to inform the world about what actually occurs in Aybil, when we encountered you. I wonder if you could be of some help to me."

The Ambassador stood. "Follow me."

He led the three men into a room and closed the door. Two desks sat against opposite walls and a red velvet curtain hung on the back wall. The ambassador pushed a screw on a light fixture. The curtain separated, revealing a door. He then pushed a button on his keychain and the door opened. Inside a bare room with a huge computer was a red phone. "Any time you want to make a call and file your stories, come to me. You can call from here. It's untraceable. The

Countess has the utmost trust in you and her husband is responsible for me being here. She's even shrewder than her devious husband. Did you know she was here last week? Probably not. She spent quite a bit of time putting things in order to protect you. Is she your family?"

Lovell refused to answer. The Ambassador sat down.

"Now who is it you wish to call?"

Lovell called Eduardo's number at the television station and filed a report about the death in Haba Shangira. When he'd finished the Ambassador ushered them out of the room and into his private office.

"Mr. Sulieman, could I possibly make use of your services?"

His round fish eyes studied Mr. R.S, who chuckled. "Not me, but my son may be willing."

The Italian leaned toward Ali.

"May I interest you, young Mr. Sulieman?"

Ali cleared his throat.

"Yes. But you must do better than my Aybilian salary and all the benefits."

The Ambassador laughed.

"I'll triple your salary and give you access to my personal physician. However, you must be discreet in watching your countryman, who is still my driver."

Ali smiled for the first time.

"That will be easy."

The two men shook hands, as the phone rang. The Ambassador answered it and looked at his watch, before ending the call.

"You wouldn't mind giving me a lift to the Yugoslavian embassy would you?"

The four men left together. Ali drove the Ambassador's car and he and Mr. R.S. followed them to the Yugoslavian embassy, where Ali handed his new employer the keys and rejoined Lovell and his father.

"Baba, he gave me a one hundred dollar bill."

Ali held the bill up to his father. Mr. R.S. rubbed his hairless chin.

"There's a way you can do both jobs, you know."

Ali leaned forward from the back seat.

"How can I do that?"

"Give the Hajj that bill and he'll switch you to nights."

Ali patted his father on the shoulder, and then winked at Lovell. "And now where to, my brother? The house of delights?"

Lovell rubbed his thighs.

"No, to the American school and afterwards to the House of Delights."

They drove to the American school, listening to Jr. Walker and bobbing. Lovell called Phil from the gate at the American compound. The guard gave him the phone and Phil instructed him to meet him at the restaurant. The three men entered and the conversation stopped. Lovell watched the people, all white, stare at Mr. R.S., he was not only so tall he had to bend upon entering the door and black as tar, he was dressed in traditional Aybilian clothes. Phil entered from a private dining room and shook hands with them all, then the conversation resumed, but not the stares. Phil took them to a room near the back, where he sat alone, eating lobster and drinking white wine.

"They've never seen a Black Man as big as you and especially dressed like that. They're scared shitless."

Mr. R.S. laughed.

"I know and all those white women were fidgeting. They love some soul pole don't they?"

Phil slapped the table.

[197]

"Once they go black, they never go back. I'm married to one and I know a peckerwood will never touch her again. Even if she marries one, she'll have some soul pole on the side. Let me order you all some lobster and some wine. I hate eating alone."

Ali looked toward the outer dining room.

"Then why aren't you out there?"

He rolled his eyes.

"Because they're a bunch of damn bores. I prefer to be here when my family's gone."

Lovell watched Phil drink his wine.

"Excuse me for asking, but didn't I just meet your family?"

Phil acknowledged the comment while cracking a lobster shell.

"Yes you did. There's something I sense about to happen and I want to make sure my family's gone before it gets going."

"What's that?"

Phil waited until the waitress had left to answer Mr. R.S.

"Have you been following Iran? The Shah's going to fall and that creep the Ayatollah's no joke. This rum drinking fake ruler here's going to react and it's going to get very hot for Americans here because he'll want the orthodox Muslims to think he's on their side. He's a political gadfly."

They all drank a toast to the Colonel as the BBC came on the television. Mr. R.S. was impressed. "How do you get the BBC here and no one else can?"

Phil looked around.

"We have an educational satellite that gets everything. The Colonel's boys turn their head for a nice monthly fee."

The lead story came on and Phil stopped. It was about the killing in Haba Shangira. Mr. R.S. and Ali continued to eat, their faces showing sadness. Lovell could see Phil watching him in his peripheral vision. When the story changed, he gave Lovell a full all teeth smile.

"Isn't Haba Shangira behind the university?"

Mr. R.S. rubbed the upper half of his first finger. "Yes, it's right in back. My auto shop is there."

Phil's head snapped toward Mr. R.S.

"You speak with an American accent, not British."

"I learned American, not English."

Phil then turned to Ali.

"And what do you speak?

Ali washed the lobster off his hands in a finger bowl.

"Both, and Italian, French, Spanish, Berber, Nubian and of course Arabic."

Phil didn't blink.

"And what brings you gentlemen to the American quarters."

Lovell spoke before Mr. R.S.

"Mr. Suliemen has a daughter and a son, elementary age and they're fluent in American, I thought there might be a place for them in the school."

Phil gave him a closed mouth smile.

"Of course there's a place. Can they start Sunday? Good. After you finish eating, I'll show you the campus."

They finished the lobster, and leaving through the back door, walked into the jacket weather Aybilian night and star blanketed sky. Mr. R.S. waved his arm upward.

"And the night has a thousand eyes."

He stretched as if attempting to poke out an eye. "The desert is beginning to shed its clothes."

As he and Ali walked, Phil moved close to Lovell and whispered.

"I see you've found something to do with your free time."

He trotted over to Mr. R.S. and Ali, explaining to them where and what was in each building. Later, as Mr. R.S.

[199]

and Ali dropped Lovell off at the front gate, Mr. R.S. held Lovell's arm.

"Son, I have seen many men in my life. I must tell you this. We have a saying from Fezan. The man, who wears many hats, has many faces too. That man Phil, wears many hats." He and Ali kissed Lovell on both cheeks and left him walking to his room, pondering Phil.

CHAPTER SIX

Lovell glanced at the Aybilian student's paper on his desk about Dubois's loss of his child from being denied medical attention by a southern hospital. There were tear smears on the paper, where she'd cried, while recounting her mother's story, of an older brother, lost from a lack of medical attention because he was Aybilian, and the Italian hospital refusing to admit him. Her anger rose from the page, and he pressed it to his chest, sealing the needling rage, ever present and peeking out at different times. He felt its strength in the weekly basketball games played against the all Aybilian team. He, Mr. R.S., Ali, Phil, Abdul, Madusun, Ahmed, Jim, Matt, they had a full team and played with suppressed venom, which shocked the Aybilians ten to fifteen years younger than the university team. The Aybilians had brought in their national players, who took unsuccessful turns trying to hurt Ali and Mr. R.S, but ended each flurry holding a bloody mouth, nose, purple eye, or bruised ribs. Lovell, Mr. R.S., and Ali, after each game went to the Suliemen's home to eat, be soothed with Mrs. R.S.'s camel dung soothing patches for bruises, or cuts, and jokes to her husband about trying to revive his long ago ended basketball career. She served them hot turtle soup, greens, rice, goat to her son and husband and fish to Lovell, who never understood how they managed to have fish when no one else in the city had it. Going to their house had become part of Lovell's life pattern, not routine he called it. He was again up at four thirty, meditating for twenty minutes, then eating a cup of yogurt and trotting to the field behind the university where he met Ali and Mr. R.S. for a three-mile jog. He then returned to his room, showered, ate some fruit and either went to class or worked on the new novel he'd begun about black expatriates in

[201]

Africa. He ate every dinner at Mrs. R.S.'s assistance with the Sulieman's and taught Jamilah and Fuad, English afterwards and was taught Arabic by them, then watched, with the Sulieman's, Ahmed's live show on Aybilian television, which each week became bolder and more satirical of the military's taking all the fish, best vegetables. Doing as they pleased and the joys of, and contradictions of living in a country where all the basic needs were provided, but freedom of speech was controlled through disappearances before going home. Each night he returned to his room with something Mrs. R.S had given him in preparation for Nidia's arrival, which had been arranged through Faturi. Expecting twins, he had a twin carriage, bassinet, boxes of pampers, herbs hidden in several parts of the room to ward away bad spirits and to protect against what Mrs. Sulieman called desert sickness, which killed thousands of children every year, and for which they, not she, had not found a cure. She'd given him bottles of some black creamy paste to be mixed in the baby's food and smeared over the body every night. Mrs. Sulieman had given the formula to Danuta and they used it in the clinic on all the university professor's children. Danuta often remarked how Soheyla (Mrs. R.S., or Sulieman), though technically a nurse, was a better doctor than she, who actually functioned as Mrs. Sulieman's assistant. Lovell spoke weekly with Nidia, and their marriage was planned for the first vacation, in a couple of weeks, in Italy at Miss Marguerite's house. The gang of five would all be there. He, Jim and Matt lifted weights in the afternoons, three times a week, did karate every afternoon, and he and Penny practiced every night until twelve-thirty a.m., playing jazz, blues, classical and different Arabic and North African musical duets. Lovell then went to his room and Penny rushed home to some mysterious nightly visitor he refused to discuss or disclose. This was unusual for them, who'd adopted the Aybilian custom of good male friends holding hands when walking and kissing on both cheeks. Outside of Mr. R.S. and Ali, only Penny knew about the reports to the T.V. station in San Antonio. Lovell stored the hidden camera, disguised as a briefcase in Penny's room. He carried it with him and filmed all the beatings, then sent the film, by Italian diplomatic pouch, to Eduardo, who aired it in his reporting. Lovell had Penny arrange it so Penny was never near the event, and always with Faturi when anything occurred, to avoid suspicion. Penny called it his brunch because he and Faturi fondled each other and occasionally made love in Faturi's office during that time. Lovell suspected Faturi was Penny's secret lover. Penny never said. Lovell always went to his room alone and gave it to the sheets as he called it, having regular wet dreams. Danuta often came and slept with him, their bodies wrapped and melted together, and come morning, her white passion painted his thigh, and his her chest. They never made love, understanding Lovell's commitment to Nidia and Danuta saying he didn't want to face Nidia, after having been his lover. Once had been enough. Lovell and Penny also played together at Abdul and Aisha's every Friday, where all the Afro Americans joined together for what they called "church". Ambassador Daphne delivered the sermon each week. Khadijah, Aisha, and Lovell, with Penny on piano, were the choir, and Abdul, Matt and Phil sat in the congregation. The religious section was readings from the Koran, Torah, Bible, Bhagavad-Gita and any other text Mr. Daphne saw fit. The music though, was strictly black gospel and everyone made a joyful noise. Lovell felt soothed after each morning ceremony. It was as if some weight were lifted off him and in doing so, he was prepared for the week ahead.

[203]

The group after the service, then ate grits, sausage, pancakes, and eggs together, while drinking mimosas. Mr. Daphne held court at this time, talking about events in the world, the state of Black America, and the soon ousting of the Shah, whom he liked, from Iran. Lovell and Khadijah always sat together at the table, their legs touching, hands on thighs, and crawled inside each other's eyes, traveling roads of tenderness together. Their fork in the road was Nidia, holding the twins, and they separated, she walking alone, and he carrying his children. Coming back to reality, Khadijah and Lovell did kitchen duty together, brushing past each other as they handled dishes and washed pots. Leaving those mornings, he sat in his room alone, and prayed for strength, guidance, and a sign to direct him in love. The sound of Jami-Al Fateh, Jami -Al Fateh, Jami -Al Fateh, brought another reality to him. The chant stiffened the backs of all the professors in the faculty of education and made the university office workers scurry to corners to conceal themselves. Last week it had been Ibn Mustapha, an Aybilian accountant, who'd been pounded with fists to the ground by a group of janitors. One, who said he'd insulted the common workers, then was stomped until his nose flattened against his face, and his lips receded because they'd stomped his teeth in, then bashed his hands with small hammers until the bones made no crunching sounds. He'd laid on the ground making muffling sounds for help, spitting pieces of teeth onto his face, blood oozing from his eyes, nose, ears and the front of his pants. No one would touch him and crawling on his elbows, blood stained the back of his pants. He maneuvered, like a reptile down the center of the street, being spit on by every student who passed. He was finally shown mercy by one of the Tunisian cooks who picked him up outside his car and drove away from the university. The Tunisian had returned an hour

[204]

later driving the car and had been pulled from it, by the same janitors and dragged by his ankles down the university main street. Each student who passed the cook kicked him in the side until they reached the cafeteria where they turned him over and poured salt on his raw back, laughing as he howled. They had then forced the other Tunisian workers to pack his belongings and had taken Ibn's car, driving the Tunisian to the Tunisian Aybilian border, and pushed him from the car. Lovell's stomach gurgled and a stream of acidic orange juice tasting bile from last night's drinking session of Sadiqui flooded his throat. He swallowed it and his bowels loosened. Tightening them, his stomach cramped, he doubled over, gripping the desk, trying not to fart. As the chanting became more audible, the Indian women stared out the office back windows, their shoulders hunched and touching, pulling their sari's round them, trying to cover any exposed skin, while the men, backs to the women, watched the door, their fists balled ready to defend. The Aybilian professors sat erect but massaged their paper ends with twists and curls. The Egyptians, who'd armed themselves after the first student Thursday punishments, fondled their pocket knives, while the whites, American and Canadian, paced, ate, and pretended to correct their papers, but had never gone beyond the first page. Lovell smiled at watching how fear paralyzed people. Even him. Even though he had been told it would not happen to him. Had been told. Had been told. He repeated it over and over. He'd been told because he'd paid. One thousand U.S. and a bottle of cognac every month for a year, one thousand counterfeit dollars paid to the Major's son. He'd paid because Yusef, Doris's boyfriend, had warned him that the young man had organized the students against him because Lovell had made him go outside and smoke, instead of

[205]

letting him smoke in class. Lovell had gotten the money from Jim in exchange for an arrangement of continuous food cooked by the Tunisian cook because Jim had also noticed everyone being sick except Penny, Doris and Yusef. Lovell had gotten the case of cognac from the Italian ambassador in exchange for his son's piano lessons. Exchange. He had learned how the system of bartering worked here, outside the States, from these experiences and from Mr. and Mrs. R.S. They had shown him. Shown him how she saved Danuta and Danuta gave her a job. Their children went to the American school in exchange for Mr. R.S. teaching a class in auto mechanics. It was the way of the world but more pronounced in Aybil because the trappings of western civility, hypocrisy Mr. R.S. said, had been stripped away. Lovell's exchange had stripped away his coveted position in the prized faculty of medicine. One thousand U.S., twelve bottles of cognac, and being moved to the faculty of education for Lovell it was a treat because he'd be able to teach literature and writing. The other faculty members saw it as a demotion, gossiping it was because of incompetence. Faturi, who knew everything as the new president of the university, had called Lovell into his office and told him to ignore the rumors, saying as long as they knew, ignore what people said. Faturi knew, as did Lovell, the talking had been instigated by the Major's son, who organized all the punishments as the university student representative. Castigating anyone who committed crimes against Islam, the university and the country, the People's Republic, which were one in the same, and was part of the deal, though it was never said.

"What's not said is what you have to worry about here, Lovell."

Mr. R.S.'s words stung his ears, eyes, crept down his throat and threw three left hooks to his ribs. He gasped, doubled

over again, this time allowing the pain to escape from his backside, a then lit an incense to conceal the smell.
"What's not said is what you have to worry about here Lovell."
Putting a book in front of his face, he hid the loss of those words, which were insistent on dangling from his eyes. Though the loss, he knew was temporary, still, he wouldn't be able to hear, if not those words, some words from Mr. R.S., Zoraida, Mrs. R.S., Ali and even the children, who had become not only his mentors, but his family. Jami Al-Fateh, Jami Al- Fateh, Jami Al -Fateh, the chant, outside the building, demanded he remember its true significance. The First. That all knowing. Those whom God has blessed. His father had always warned him about those believers who think they sit at the right of hand of God and therefore have the right to do anything in God's name. Christians, Jews, Muslims, Buddhists, TM practitioners, Catholics, judging and maligning in the name of God and using religion as a frame of reference. Two weeks ago, he, Mr. R.S., and Ali had been in their garage talking after Ali and Mr. R.S. had finished tuning up the Ambassador's mercedes. The smell of whisky reached them before the voice. As they turned, the father of Noor, the girl who'd been run over, stood in the garage doorway. Mr. R.S., and Ali, with Lovell behind, had walked to the door. A discussion, in Arabic, which Lovell had learned due to classes with the children, ensued and the man had insisted Mr. R.S. repair his car, still bloody and bent from the killing. Mr. R.S. refused, saying he was over loaded and pointed to the cars waiting outside his shop. The man became belligerent, called Mr. R.S. gary-gary, (nigger), and cursed his entire family calling them Egyptian niggers, in English. Mr. R.S. had grabbed the man, thrown him into the street, then turned his car around and removed it from

[207]

his shop's door. He'd then closed business for the day and they returned the Ambassador's car and picked up the children. The next morning, Lovell, Ali, and Mr. R.S. who jogged together every morning at five before the first prayer, finished their jog at their house, and were stretching, when the chant began, Jami Al-Fateh, Jami Al-Fateh, Jami Al- Fateh. The three saw a crowd led by Noor's father. They carried axes, shovels, sticks and even torches. Mr. R.S. stood his ground and listened to the shouts and curses. He accused the R.S. family of being non-believers, Mrs. R.S. of being a whore, Ali of being a spy for the Italians, and the family of being disloyal for having a friendship with an American. They stepped toward Mr. R.S. and he stepped to them. They stopped and he advanced. The crowd moved back. Mr. R.S. stood over Khadijah's father, snatched the shovel from his hands, and tossed it away.

"I see you all at the mosque every week. My wife is either at home with my children or at work. My son works like all of your sons for this country and plays basketball for this country and your children idolize him. He helps them all with basketball. My friend is a distinguished professor at the university and you have all seen him on television. If you try and hurt my family, you must kill me, but I swear to Allah, many of you will die doing so."

Ali and I stood by his side. The men, led by Noor's father, backed up. Before they left, the father blew his nose at Mr. R.S.

"The next sun will not find you in this village, Ramadan Sulieman. My son is in the military and they will help us drive you and your infidel family from this village."

They all turned and walked down into the village, then entered the main teashop. Lovell walked into the R.S.'s house and found Mrs. R.S. sitting with a pistol and the two

[208]

children, holding knives. Five large suitcases sat in the
floor. Mr. R.S. glanced around his house and took one step.
Mrs. R.S. stepped in front of him.

"I have taken everything we need to carry Ramadan. There
is nothing else."

The family and Lovell sat in the living room while Mr. R.S.
looked out the window. They then got into their Mercedes
and drove to the Ambassador's residence. He met them at
the door, stepped outside, and the seven people rode to the
airport. Exiting the car, Mr. R.S. handed Lovell the keys to
the Mercedes.

"This is your car now Negro. Don't go back to the village.
My house is probably on fire now and they've destroyed
my shop. Listen to me! They don't forget and will find any
excuse they can to harm you, trying to get back at me. They
won't come on the university campus though. We'll all see
you soon. Italy's not far and the first break is very soon.
We can't hug you but you know we all love you. We'll
check you later."

Lovell kissed Mr. R.S., Ali and Farad on both cheeks and
nodded to Mrs. R.S. and Jamilah.

"Tell Danuta what happened Lovell and tell her I apologize
for not saying goodbye."

Mrs. R.S. blew Lovell a kiss and they walked into the
airport, through a private gate, to the Ambassador's private
plane. Lovell had covered his face that morning, the same
as he did, sitting in the office of the Department of
Education, crying and having seen, what Jami Al-Fateh
meant. When the chanting students, led by the Major's
son, walked past dragging Dr. Mohammed, Head of the
Music Department, who'd insisted on teaching western
classical music, along with Arabic classical music, Lovell
vomited in the center of the room, then walked, briefcase
with camera in hand, and followed them filming, as the

[209]

Indian female professors fainted and the other faculty members crumpled in their seats, relieved. Dr. Faturi, flush faced, smelling of peppermint, emerged afterwards, looking over his shoulder. The other faculty members had begun to chatter. He surveyed the room. The whites were in one corner, the Indians in a cluster, the Aybilians and Egyptians together and Lovell, who'd poured baking soda on the vomit to kill the smell, covered it with paper towels, sat alone. Penny, red lipped and smiling, followed Faturi and sat with Lovell, who looked at Penny's hand to see if the swelling had subsided from the fight he'd had when Dan, from New York, seeing Penny, Lovell and Matt together, collecting their mail, and laughing, had made the comment you can dress them up but you can't take them out. Penny had hit him first before anyone else could respond. The Canadian, English and Americans had pulled together and there had been a face off in the faculty office. Dan, six one, had been dropped to his knees, by Penny's front kick, then crumpled over, when the little man's roundhouse connected his temple. Dr. Faturi, who'd just happened to be passing, sided with the African Americans, and fired Dan on the spot. Dan had disappeared the same night, his clothes and belongings still in his room. The Aybilian's had begun calling Penny, Mohammed Ali. Penny sat down and kissed Lovell on the cheek. His hand was its normal tiny size. Faturi stood over the vomit.

"There's going to be a few more changes in the department now that we're short staffed. And to answer your question, no one has seen or heard from Dan. It's being investigated. All the English professor's mail will be brought to this department, that's from all faculties, and Penny Marshall will be joining our department. The lab is now ready and we need the native speakers to make tapes for the students."

[210]

The white corner began to murmur. A Scottish woman named Eileen Dwyer, cleared her throat.

"Are we going to get paid for making these tapes? I don't remember that as part of my contract?"

Faturi devoured another peppermint stick. "Yes, you'll get paid."

"And will this be English, Canadian, or American English, or now that we have two, whatever they speak?"

Only her group laughed. Faturi's face puffed and his nose flared.

"Miss Dwyer, you've been here a long time and I would expect more from you. I fired Dan for those kinds of comments and unless you apologize, you'll be next."

"I was only joking Dr. Faturi. It's my Scottish humor. I apologize."

Faturi's expression didn't change.

"I don't think the two Afro-Americans here will find humor in your comment, especially since they're the most qualified in the entire department and the only faculty members who've been published."

Reddened faces greeted his words.

"On that note, and speaking of our esteemed colleagues, I'd also like to announce they'd be doubling in the Music and Department of Education."

Eileen placed her hands on both hips.

"I also play piano." Faturi mocked her stance. "You play piano, but you can't teach it. They both have degrees."

"I thought there was to be no teaching of western music, Dr. Faturi. Look what happened a short while ago."

Faturi dropped his head.

"There was more to what happened than just western music. They're also both familiar with eastern music. As a matter of fact, Professor Pendleton has a minor degree in ethnomusicology, and has played with Arabic musicians."

[211]

Eileen patted her foot.

"Will they get paid double salaries?" Faturi flexed again.

"Why are you so worried about how these men are being compensated?"

Eileen sat on the desk where the group stood.

"I'm not concerned about them per se. I'm concerned that you're showing favoritism because of some political agenda."

Faturi stomped his foot.

"Who are you to question my decisions and whatever political agenda which implies favoritism is all in your prejudiced mind."

Eileen stood again. "What are you implying Dr. Faturi?"

"I'm not implying anything. I'm making a statement. You, Dan and the rest of you reflect some very colonial ideas, which we, as educated Aybilians do not adhere to in anyway. That's what I'm saying. I'll make it clearer, Miss. Dwyer. Racism. That is why you question me and my decision about these professors. Racism!"

Eileen's face turned crimson and she covered it. Faturi nodded to Lovell, Penny, the Aybilians, and left the room. Eileen wiped her eyes.

"I'm not a racist! I'm not a racist! I'm Scottish and I've grown up with the English. I'm not a racist!"

She strode over and stood in front of Penny and Lovell. "I'm not a racist. I'm not a racist. I was only joking."

   Lovell, taking Penny's hand, strode from the room and walked down the hall almost dragging Penny. He had merely nodded at Eileen before. She and the other English, British and Canadian professors, who dropped comments about the blackouts, backed up toilets, the Arab custom of getting close to someone when speaking, and the Aybilian smell of spices, which to them was repulsive. He had told Penny how they never realized their smell, likened to wet dogs, was offensive to him and other non-whites, and how they were too full of themselves to even consider this. They, who reached out to Penny, he said because he was light skinned, had told him they thought Lovell was unfriendly, because he refused to socialize with them and was cordial and silent with them, not participating in any of their discussions, or jokes, which were always at the expense of some other group. Penny and Matt were more tolerant, especially Matt who used the opportunity to discern who was lonely, or unhappy in their marriage. Taking advantage of the information and using chess, checkers, backgammon, or cards, as an excuse to get inside their rooms, and befriend their husbands, then sleeping with their wives, calling it payback, when the Korean women were unavailable. None of the Fab Five judged or criticized him, but did warn him to be careful. Those same women often came to Lovell's room, alone, when their husbands taught classes, but he refused to let them inside. Penny dug his nail in the inside of Lovell's hand, forcing him to let go of his, and walked with Eileen. Lovell stopped, bending to tie his shoe, as Penny and Eileen passed. Looking up, he noticed her fleshy thighs, melon butt, and midnight curly pubic hair. She wore no panties. He thought about football, his usual distraction, to stop his rising erection. As she and Penny stopped, and he felt her green-eyed gaze, slight smile, giving him a still view. Pulling out his shirt to cover the pole protruding from the side of his pants, and dropping his head, he walked past them, shouting over his shoulder he'd see Penny later. Hurrying to his room, he lie on his bed, penis to bedspread, groaning, and wishing for some relief. The closer his reunion with Nidia, the more difficult his nights. Sometimes he'd awaken, dry humping Danuta, she biting into his shoulder, his semen having launched to her chin, dripping. They'd

[213]

then both wept and would lie awake afterwards, listening to
Miles Davis "Sketches of Spain", discussing existentialism,
or Danuta would sing "My Funny Valentine", trying to
sound like Sarah Vaughan, her Polish accent making Lovell
laugh. She'd then wash him, and herself, with steaming
towels, and creep back to her room before the sun rose.
Rolling onto his stomach, and dropping his pants, he held
his throbbing member, his thoughts and breath coming in
arpeggio bursts. He didn't want to masturbate. Didn't want
to tear at himself because, in his mind, everything was for
Nidia. He and Danuta had decided not to sleep together,
agreeing the temptation was too strong and the frustration
was overbearing. He rolled onto the floor and began doing
sit ups. Reaching five hundred and perspiring, he rose and
remembering to take his keys, went to the shower. The
shined faucets, sinks, toilets and spotless walls of their
bathroom never seemed to amaze him. He often contrasted
the sanitized disinfectant smell with the Europeans who
cleaned them by his and Penny's standards, were funky, he
thought, because they only washed up in the mornings and
didn't seem to bathe very often. They'd complained that he,
Penny, Doris, Matt and Jim, smelled like soap, cologne or
perfume, not like a human beings, and they covered their
noses when around the Sudanese women, who carried
enticing oil aromas with them. Lovell often felt
uncomfortable in their presence, not wanting to look at
them, afraid his Sudanese comrades would notice his
arousal. They thought he was being respectful, by looking
down, whenever their wives were around, and patted him
on the back, telling him not to worry. He did respect them,
but was more worried about himself. Pampering himself
with a long shower, he noticed a bottle of palm oil, given to
him by Mrs. Sulieman's, so he oiled his body, feeling the
tingle of being in shape, then left, walking with only a

[214]

towel around his waist, not wanting to get the oil on his bathrobe. Opening his door, Penny and Eileen sat in his room drinking wine, their eyes glazed from hashish. Penny winked at Lovell and pointed to the towel.

"You're starting to slip. First you left your door open and second, you're not covered. If you'd run into an Aybilian, your muscular ass would be in jail."

Eileen crossed and uncrossed her legs.

"In jail or bending over for one of them."

Lovell stepped behind his partition and slipped on a mint green silk Nubian caftan, another gift from the Sulieman's.

"I'd do my time. I'm not bending over for anyone."

She put her bare feet up on his chair, her legs open, hair and moist vagina lips greeted him.

"If you went to their jail, you might not have a choice."

"I'd have a choice Miss Eileen. They'd have to kill me first and I'd die fighting before I got fucked. You saw what Penny did to Dan. Triple it with me." He sat down thinking about football and trying not to look between her legs. Penny saw Lovell lean forward trying to cover himself, and got up pretending to get another drink, then sat down after two steps, seeing what was in front of Lovell.

"Eileen has something to say and I think we need to know it. Then she'll have to get home to her husband and child, we have dinner with the Feiner's tonight, or did you forget?"

Lovell sighed and smiled, knowing his friend was trying to calm the fires burning within him. He'd often told Lovell, there was no question Nidia was waiting for him. Eileen swallowed her drink, and placed her feet on the floor.

"All the whites had dinner with Faturi last night. His wife didn't even show her face. That's unusual because she loves to entertain and sometimes feels more comfortable around westerners than Aybilians. I've known her for eight

[215]

years. Instead of her, there was this creepy Iraqi guy, who was the deputy head of Saddam Hussein's secret police, and is now working for the Albanians trying to solve the death of president Abubakar and Dan. He listened, asked us some questions about Dan, who'd not had any problems with either of them, then watched while Faturi tried to get us drunk. I said tried because I didn't get drunk but everybody else did, including Faturi. I got the feeling he wanted to see how people were once they got loose."
Lovell and Penny exchanged knowing looks. He stood ready for her to leave.
"What does that have to do with us?"
"Most of the answers everyone gave pointed to you and Penny because both of you had a conflict with Dan and you had a serious problem with Abubakar. He hated you. Faturi pretends to like you but I don't think so. In private he refers to you as our illustrious professor but it's always with sarcasm. I can understand how he feels about you. Think about it. Even if he did get an offer to teach somewhere else, this country wouldn't let him leave. He's the head of the university now, but that's as far as he's going in life. He knows this is just a stopping off point for both of you; especially you Lovell. They also know about your friendship with the Italian ambassador. Those reports to the BBC about what's happening at the university has the government furious and if they continue, Faturi's head's going to fly and he knows it. The Iraqi asked which of us speak romance languages and was a journalist. The only two people on the staff who were former journalist were you and Dan, and he's disappeared.
Lovell poured Penny another drink. "How do you know about the Iraqi guy?"
She didn't hesitate.

[216]

"My hubby's a geologist and worked in Iraq. He recognized him because the guy was in charge of oil security when he was there."

Lovell then poured her a drink.

"And you're telling us this because you don't want us to think you're a racist?"

Eileen's alabaster colored face darkened.

"I don't need to prove a fuckin thing to you mate. I'm Scottish and I know how the sting of someone standing over you feels. I'm also built like no other Scottish or English girl because I've got a big round bum and my hair's curly. As a matter of fact, it's kinkier than yours mate, and I've been teased about it all my life. They teased me at school calling me spadie, and saying my father, an American G.I., was a spade, that means black like an ace of spades. I'm telling you this because I've seen people disappear here before and I've never liked seeing their families live with not knowing what happened. I wouldn't wish that on anyone. Once they become suspicious of someone, they don't stop until they get them! Mate! And the two of you better watch your asses because they're watching you." Standing, she downed her drink and walked to the door.

"And by the way. You look like lime sherbet, or as your "Colonel" would say, "Finger lickin' good." Come out to my farm sometime and see another part of Aybil, now that your Nubian family has been run out of Haba Shangira. They know about that too. Faturi told the Iraqi last night in a drunken stupor. I heard him, and one more thing mate this will interest you Penny. My hubby says the Iraqi's a closet pufter. To you that's a fag, queer, ankle grabber. Penny just taught me those words. Good night mates. I have to go before it gets dark. A woman can't be on the roads here at night."

She winked at Lovell, nodded to Penny, and closed the door. Lovell and Penny, both inhaling deeply, sat in silence, until someone knocked on the door. Concealing the alcohol, Lovell opened it and found Dr. Faturi standing there. He invited him inside but Faturi refused, and spoke loudly.

"I forgot to tell you two I'm having some people over for dinner. I'd like for you, Matt, Penny and Jim to meet tonight. I'll send someone to pick you up in about three hours. You will make it won't you?"

Lovell agreed and closed the door. Penny poured them both a drink.

"Lovey, this is more than we imagined."

Lovell studied his lip.

"More, but less. If they really knew something, they'd have picked us up. Who knows what Eileen wants and it's rather peculiar she leaves and a few minutes later Faturi arrives. And did you notice how loud he was talking. It was as if he wanted someone to hear."

"Either that or he was speaking into a microphone."

Lovell looked around his room.

"I'll get Jim and I'll sweep the room for bugs. This we'll talk about, how we're going to play this at our gathering."

Penny stood and wobbled.

"Tell me what they say. You know I can't be at the gathering."

Lovell played with his friend's shoulder.

"This is different, the Sudanese won't be here."

"That's not true and you know it."

He sat down coughing gasps into those tiny palms. Lovell knew the truth. He knew what Penny said was correct and it burned his stomach lining. The men on the floor had gotten together to have what they called they called gash sessions. They sat in Lovell's room and talked about their sexual

[218]

experiences. There was a rule though; no masturbating in the room. This had developed after Yusef, Doris's boyfriend had come and brought what he considered to be a progressive Aybilian on the first day. Lovell had begun with Miss Marguerite. He was eleven and she lived across the street, alone. She had asked his mother if he could do some work in her backyard. Lovell had chopped wood, stacked it, and then raked the yard. It was hot, and he'd worked without his shirt. He still had to trim the shrubbery, saw the tree branches, and stack them, when she called him inside for a break. She wore a thigh length aqua robe with burgundy and white flowers drawn at the shoulders and where the breasts stood. Lovell entered her house and heard bath water running. She gave him a glass of sweet lemonade and as he'd lifted it to drink she'd taken a towel and wiped the sweat from his chest, then rubbed it across his stomach in circles, making him quiver. She stepped back, glancing down at what had risen, then taking his hand, had led him into the bathroom.

"Let me wash some of the sweat off you. Sit on the tub."

He'd obeyed and dipping her hand into the steaming water, she soaped his chest, stomach, then opened his pants and pulled them down. Lovell had shuddered, standing bare, trousers around his ankles, as she kneeled, helping him step out of them, then sat him in the tub, washing his entire body, stroking his member until his arms spread, he'd flattened out, closing his eyes. Miss Marguerite had stood and called his name. Opening his eyes, she stood, her peach colored skin, glowing with sparkle. She put one foot on the tub, pulling back the hood of her straight haired private.

"Lean over here and smell this Lovell. It smells like candy doesn't it?"

He'd nodded, unable to get his breath.

[219]

"Do you see this little dick here like yours? It's candy and I want you to lick it real slow, on the tip, with the tip of your tongue. Go round and round."

Lovell had complied and was amazed at how she arched her back, eyes closed, mouth open and moaned aloud, rubbing his neck, then pulled his head hard against her. A cherry liquid had flowed into his mouth and she'd then laid him back, moving her hand up and down until he began to gasp, then had covered his penis with her mouth as, what he thought was a gallon of juice spurted from him. She'd swallowed, then laughed.

"You're full mon cherie. This will be our secret. You're physically a man already. I'll teach you how to be a man in every other way."

After that, he'd worked for her daily, and she'd introduced and taught him about making love to a woman. The Aybilian had taken out his penis, masturbating, but Yusef had grabbed his hand, screaming at him in Arabic. Embarrassed, the Aybilian had left. Penny had then began his story. Living in his friend's house and being seduced by the mother with a dildo and wine. Her rubbing it all over his body, the husband kissing him at the same time, then the wife undressing him, inserting it in his anus, while the husband gave him head, then the wife taking over, while the husband entered him from the back. Madusun had jumped to his feet.

"I don't want to hear this disgusting stuff, Lovell. This is not natural. "

Penny had laughed.

"If it's not natural then why is your dick hard and standing at attention?'"

He pointed to the tent in Madusun's Jalabia. Madusun covered it.

"You're a disgusting little sodomite."

[220]

"I must not be too disgusting. You're hard. I guess you don't go up your beautiful wife's ass. I know about you Arabs. Black and brown."

"Don't you ever call my wife beautiful. It's not allowed in Islam."

Penny stood, his chest out.

"Oh and you're a good Muslim aren't you? How many drinks have you had this evening? How much dope have you smoked, Mr. Muslim man? And why should you care what I say about your wife anyway? I'm a filthy sodomite and a faggot at that?"

Madusun had reached for Penny but Matt had grabbed his hand. Madusun had jerked away and he, accompanied by Ahmed, had gone to the door.

"I'll no longer sit with the brothers as long as that half man, half woman is here."

They'd both left. Matt had scowled at Penny.

"You didn't have to bring your shit in here. You know it's not appropriate. We accept you for what you are, but you don't have to flaunt it Penny. Nobody wants to hear about you getting fucked in the ass. Give us a break."

Penny had given them the finger.

"My sexual experiences are just as valid as yours. Don't tell me your dick wasn't hard, Matt."

Matt rose to leave. Jim also stood.

"Well we don't want to hear about no ass fucking. You've fucked up everything. You should tell him Lovell. It's not cool here. We're men."

Lovell had cleared his throat.

"He's a man too guys and he's my friend. This is a gash session, so everything goes except jerking off. I'm the houseman so I set the rules. I was digging it and so was everyone. I think that's the problem. Everybody's

[221]

embarrassed his story turned him or her on. Everybody except me and Yusef."

Yusef sipped his drink. "I enjoy some good bottom. It's just another hole to explore."

They'd both laughed as Matt and Jim left. Penny had wept, unable to speak until the screams from next door jolted them. Running next door, Yusef used his key and opening it found the Aybilian trying to penetrate Doris with legs up, pushing him away. Yusef, leapt on him and with a choke hold, rustled the Aybilian to the floor and grabbed him by the testicles. The Aybilian howled as Yusef screamed in Arabic. The Aybilian, hands between his legs, writhed on the floor and spoke in English. "She likes sex. What did I do wrong? You have sex with her and she's not your wife. Why can't I?"

Yusef grabbed him by the collar lifting him up.

"It's a harem, that's why. If you did that here they'd hang you. Even if she is a foreigner, she's a Muslim woman." The Aybilian stopped moving. Yusef dragged him to the door.

"If you say anything about us drinking I'll report you to the mullahs. They can deport me but you they'll flog. Now get the hell out."

Lovell, Penny and Yusef all kicked him. Doris whimpered. Lovell and Penny had left Yusef and Doris alone, closing the door. Sitting in Lovell's room again Penny blew his nose.

"Thank you for being on my side but I don't want you to get into this. It's my fight. I've had to deal with this all my life. They're all the same Lovey. They only tolerate me because of you. Come and get me when it's over."

He had kissed Lovell on both cheeks, as was their custom and left, walking with the same steps, measured and conscious not to swerve as he did this day. Lovell laughed

[222]

thinking how alcohol affected Penny's equilibrium. He could smoke hashish though and never stagger.

****

Lovell stood on his balcony looking in the direction of Haba Shangira. Every morning, since the Sulieman's had departed, he'd avoided it but still ran to the edge of the village where he could see the flattened ground where the Suleiman's house had been. Someone had bulldozed it and the garage, and even dug up the concrete foundation. He longed for their company. Mr. R.S.'s words and knowledge about the workings of Aybil because, for the first time since arriving, fear stood in front of him, as a formidable foe. Mr. R.S.'s words did come to him though. His words and him holding the bottle of sand, with multi hues flowing like a prism through it.

"The people of this land are like the sand, Lovell. They seem simple on the surface, but actually they're multi-dimensional, like all these colors beneath a simple tan surface. Never forget that when you're dealing with them."

Lovell found himself holding that bottle of sand, not realizing he'd picked it up, until another knock, vibrated throughout his room. He opened the door to Doris, head hanging to her chest, fists opening and closing. She collapsed into his chest, hurting his back with her grasp. Lovell sat with her on his bed, kissing the top of her head, rocking her, as his caftan moistened in the chest. She groaned for a few minutes, then limped to a chair easing into it. Lovell's neck began to heat.

"Faturi paid you a visit?"

She bobbed her head.

"And he sodomized you roughly."

She looked up and Lovell saw a red hickey on the left side of her neck.

[223]

"He marked me so that Yusef would know, the muthafucka. But that's not the worst of it. He told me if I don't help him get some information about who's sending the news reports to the states and England, he's going to turn me over to the mullahs for adultery and make Yusef leave the country. I told him I don't know anything but he wouldn't believe me. He said it has to be either you, or Dan, because you're the only two with contacts to news agencies. And the son of a bitch won't let me leave during the Eed so I won't be able to go to your wedding."

She leaned over and rocked, pulling her hair.

"I've got to get out of this fucking country Lovell! I've got to get out of here if I ever want to be happy. I know you have Miss Marguerite. Please help me. Please, I can't take this anymore."

Lovell paced, swinging his fists in the air.

"Don't worry sister. We'll get you out of here. You and Yusef."

She sat up.

"Lovell, I'm pregnant. If I start showing, they'll surely kill me."

He sat and held her hands.

"I have to ask you this as your friend. Faturi, or Yusef?"

Doris patted his cheek.

"It's Yusef's. All Faturi likes is my ass. It's funny. I thought once he'd tasted Penny, he wouldn't want anymore of me. Penny says he acts like he's famished with him. I think it's because he's scared of that switching guy who was with him and watching while he fucked me."

Lovell leaned back, still holding her hands.

"What'd he look like?"

"He's dark skinned with one glass eye, and a pony tail. The guy's thin but fit. I noticed the veins stood out in his arms so he works out. He's a fucking freak though because he

[224]

stood trembling while watching Faturi then he came in his pants. I saw the spot. What a scary fuck Lovell"

He'd never seen her afraid before. She always seemed ready for anything. He pulled her ear.

"I said I got it."

Helping her up, he closed his door and plotted a strategy. Leaving his room, Lovell rounded the hall corner heading towards Matt and Jim's rooms. He'd seen very little of them since the argument between Penny and Madusun, and often sensed them steering clear of him. Once, he'd walked by Jim's room and heard Madusun, Jim, Matt, Ahmed and a voice he didn't recognize, laughing and talking. Feeling excluded, he hadn't knocked because a small voice, inside a crevice close to his heart, told him, his friendship with Penny, including the kiss and their nights practicing, made them wonder about him and feel uncomfortable. He'd notice little actions. A pause when he'd come into the bathroom if they were peeing. A halt when he'd come into the shower after a game. Them watching the way he walked, or a knock on his door and peeking into see who was inside. If Penny were there, they'd glance at each other and wouldn't enter. He stopped and listened before knocking and entering Matt's room. Entering, Jim and Matt jumped and sat on some papers they'd been viewing. They exhaled when realizing it was Lovell.

"You guys are slipping. The door was open."

Matt glanced at Jim.

 "Yea, we are, anybody could have walked in here."

Lovell stared at the papers Jim had sat on.

"And they'd see whatever you're trying to hide."

Jim pulled out a heap of counterfeit twenty dollar bills.

"It's just my new shipment. You want some?"

He held a wad of bills to Lovell, who opened the pack and held a bill up to the light.

[225]

"Man, you can't tell the difference."

Jim gave a throaty laugh.

"You can't, but any bank in the states would spot them immediately. I'm glad we're over here. Before I leave I'll be a rich man. I should say we. That includes you, or are you puritan about that too?"

Jim and Matt slapped fives.

"What the hell is that supposed to mean?"

Lovell pocketed the bills, as Matt handed him a joint they'd just lit.

"You have every chance in the world to get some pussy and you pass it up being loyal to a woman thousands of miles away. That's what he means. Or maybe you're not being so loyal, considering the company you've been keeping."

Lovell held the pipe and studied them. They sat, waiting for his response, their mouth's pulled tight in seriousness.

"You mean Penny. I'd think you two would be cooler about him. He's my friend, we play music together and he's real. Have you two ever thought the same might be thought about the two of you? You're always together."

Jim reddened.

"Nobody'd ever think that about us. We're both men. Penny's flaming."

Lovell lit the joint and took a long hit. His throat burned and he coughed. A chemical smell filled the air. Matt immediately lit a pile of incense.

"Put that out. It's the wrong one."

Lovell staggered, then caught himself.

"What's in this shit, Matt?"

Matt helped him sit down. "Cocaine."

He poured a glass of ice water over Lovell's head. "It's some new shit we're trying. There's a market here."

Lovell's head cleared.

[226]

"I don't want to know about it. But I need to say this. What you're doing to Penny and the shit you're trying to dump on me's not cool. There's too few of us here to be trippin', and you know it. And to respond to what you said Jim, who'd know Faturi was such an ass lover? You can't tell from looking at him. Penny's gay. But like they say at home. He's probably one of the baddest faggots you ever met. So leave him alone and cut him some slack."
They spoke in unison.
"He is bad, but we don't want to hear about his sex life in the gash sessions."
Lovell watched their eyes drop. They both knew they were wrong.
"You don't have to worry. Even if we invited him, he wouldn't come. You Both know you're wrong! You never know when the way he is will come in handy. People underestimate him because he's effeminate and they open up to him in ways they'd never do with us. Look at the situation we're in now. He has Faturi's ear and Faturi's trying to save his ass and pin Dan's murder on me or Penny. He won't touch Penny so that leaves me. Penny can keep me informed of his every move. His and this Iraqi guy they've brought here to solve the case. I guess Faturi didn't talk to you guys?"
They shook their heads in unison. Matt looked worried, chewing on his lip.
"What Iraqi guy? And who said you're being investigated?"
Lovell noticed Jim's face twitch.
"I have my sources just like you have yours. This is serious though. Faturi's invited all the Afro-Americans to his house tonight. I'm sure the Iraqi guys are going to be there. Faturi's threatened Doris telling her she better give him some information on us or they're going to punish her. I

[227]

thought it'd be good for Jim to sweep the rooms, they might have planted bugs."

Jim stood and stretched.

"I'll do more than that. Give me your keys and I'll set up Faturi's house. I'll be able to listen to everything he says."

Lovell tossed Jim his keys.

"He's sending a car for us soon. You better hurry."

Jim picked up his black suitcase of tools.

"You'll have time. I'll cause a blackout. I know just where the grid is and the Aybilians love this weed and coke mixture. They won't even realize what's happened they'll be so high."

He took two steps toward the door and turned around.

"Be careful Lovell. We're at war and you don't understand this shit. I can't cover your back all the time. Keep your mouth shut and your ears open. Trust only me and Matt. We've been through the fire before and won't crack. The others will to save their ass."

Closing the door, Lovell heard the slight patter of his canvas shoes. A snarl turned him around. It was Matt.

"It's the glory of war I live for Lovell, the thrill of combat. These muthafucka's don't know who they're fucking with. We some educated American niggers use to surviving in the briar patch. They have no idea."

Seeing Matt's snarl, with a bit of saliva forming at the corner of his mouth caused a knot to form in Lovell's stomach. He backed toward the door, wishing to escape. Matt blinked, wiped his mouth, and smiled at Lovell.

"Don't worry nigger, I'm not at war with you. They are! I'm trying to protect your ass. Now tonight, drink nothing at Faturi's house except water. Drop one of these pills inside it before you drink. If it turns red, don't drink it. Knock the plate on the floor and act embarrassed so you won't have to eat. Make sure they can smell alcohol on you

[228]

and act tipsy. That'll make them relax and think you're
drunk. Faturi will get his wife away from you immediately
and I'll handle the situation. Don't even tell Penny you're
not drunk. You got to act so we can fade these
muthafucka's hand. You got me?"
They slapped fives and Lovell turned to leave.
"One more thing, bro. You're right. We haven't been cool
to Penny. The little brother doesn't deserve that. I'll
apologize to him. I worry though man. I don't know how
tough he is and I think he'll crack under pressure. We know
you won't. Don't let him know too much of your business.
It might work against you. Now close the goddam door and
wear black tonight. It'll hide the microphone."
Lovell closed the door, dismissing Matt's warning. He
saw Jim leaving his room. Jim gave him the thumbs down
sign indicating the room hadn't been bugged, and knocked
on Doris's door. She peeked out her head and let Jim enter.
Lovell passed his room and headed towards Jerzy and
Anna's. He had longed to see them since the Ramadan's
had left and had missed wallowing in the warmth which
generated from family, the breath of familiarity. The subtle
knowing which only comes from time spent together and
the knowledge of small intimacies, only shared by those
who love, unconditionally. That was family. That was what
he longed for in the midst of this desert world which
constantly demanded watching every move for an
indication of something he either didn't understand, didn't
know about, needed an explanation, or demanded he
investigate for clarity. The unspoken understanding existed
with family and he cherished it, wanted it, and even though
they were not his family, felt more secure being around it.
Knocking on the door, Anna answered in her bathrobe and
a white towel wrapped around her head. She allowed him
to enter and went behind the partition.

[229]

"Jerzy took Kasha to the Polish school. She's having a play tonight. When Danuta gets off work we'll be going. Would you like to come?"

 Lovell allowed himself to breathe in the pepper spices of fresh Polish sausage, Drambuie, boiled potatoes, and spinach. Anna's black silk dress was draped across a chair, her make up on a small table next to the glass of Drambuie and an unsmoked cigarette. Jerzy's house shoes sat under his easel, with the unfinished painting of Lovell, showing only his face, and a bouquet of flowers over rode the tang of oil paint. He sat on the water, bubbling embers spilling from his heart and into his eyes. They'd made a home. A home. A place to lay love with Kasha's poems on the walls, Jerzy's paintings with love hanging infinite particles in the air. Wiping his eyes and rocking to control the over flow, the scent of sandalwood raised his head. Anna stroked his chin.

"Sweet sensitive man. You were whimpering. Come stretch out and have some liquor, it will help your throbbing heart. Danuta has told me about your wife to be coming and your twins. I know you are trying to be true, but it is unnatural Lovell. Love is all over you. We are not like Americans. We Poles, and Europeans, who experienced the war, for us, My English fails me here. For us, Lovell, what is, is what it is, and no more. Whatever life gives us at the time is what we partake in. Nothing more. Danuta understands more than what you think. She agrees with you because of how you are, not how she is. I know she says things about not seeing your wife after sleeping with you. That is only for the moment. We have shared the same men before and never been bothered Lovell, that is truly us."   Giving Lovell a small snifter of Drambuie, she massaged his temples until his shoulders sagged. Anna lay on the couch and pressed her full breasts to Lovell's chest. He tried to

rise but she pushed him back and began to unbuckle his
pants.

"Don't Danuta, I mean Anna! This isn't right. Jerzy's my
friend."

"Don't worry Lovell. Jerzy has already suggested we do
this. He thinks it will help you because Danuta has not been
able to reach you. Now close your eyes and let me give
you pleasure. Your speaking will slice my flow. Sh-h-h-h-
h."

Her mouth was hot and mounting him she began to pour
over him, moving in a circle and sucking his breasts. He
exploded and wept, again covering the tears. Anna washed
his body with a hot wet towel, until he slept. A familiar soft
lipped kiss awakened him. It was Danuta, kissing him on
the forehead. She pinched his nose.

"I see Anna was able to get through to you in a way I
wasn't. Do you feel better?"

Lovell nodded affirmatively.

"Then get up because we must leave. I will see you later
and hopefully you will be more open."

He rose and was kissed by both Danuta and Anna. Going
to his room, he sat watching the daylight and night share
the sky and pouring himself a drink, waiting for the knock
on his door, signaling the driver had arrived. He thought
about the rules he'd learned from his dad and uncle. They
called them the lines. The first line was never run when a
friend was having a fight and judge your friends by those
who stayed with you when a fight occurred. The second
was never sleep with someone a family member had been
involved with, or your friends wife or girlfriend because it
showed no loyalty. The third was never rat on a friend, or
anyone. You could always remain silent, but never give
someone up. The others were more Colonel. If you don't
have something good to say, keep quiet, and the final line,

[231]

the best way to get along with someone you don't like, is to stay away from him or her. Sipping his third drink, he churned inside knowing, no matter what Anna had said, he'd violated a rule; he'd slept with his friend's wife. Looking down at himself, he wanted to bathe again, to wash the muck he'd wallowed in. Emptying his glass, and grabbing a towel, he opened the door to find Jerzy, ready to knock. Embracing Lovell, he back walked him into his room, pushing Lovell into a chair. Lovell looked at the floor but Jerzy's fingertip lifted his head and kissed him on both cheeks.

"My friend and brother. It is from women we came and it is through women we are given life. We are healed through women Lovell and they have a mystery we, as men will never fathom. I, long ago gave up trying to understand their depth. I do understand this though. They are not ours. They belong to something higher, and therefore it is not our place to try and possess them, my young brother. Your tears tell me how sad you feel. But they are not for me. They are for you. I have sat for nights and listened to Anna and Danuta discuss you. I have heard them speak of your brilliance, your beauty, your sincerity, and your attempts to stay true to someone you love. For us, this is noble but not real Lovell. Who I share myself with does not mean I love Anna any less. I've just shared with someone, that's all. My love and the love between Anna and I will remain untarnished. They have, she has tried to relax and heal you, in there, in her own way Lovell. Don't make it into something wrong and dirty. I love you as my friend, as do Anna, Danuta, and Kasha. Nothing can change that. Especially not sex."
Kissing Lovell again, he rose, leaving Lovell wiping his face. "Jerzy!"
Lovell watched him inhale, his hand on the doorknob.

[232]

"I lost friendship with someone for sleeping with my girlfriend. Where I come from that's a line you don't cross. It's considered betrayal."

Jerzy's fingers played with the curled hair on his shoulders. Lovell noticed red paint around Jerzy's cuticles.

"That was deceit. I would feel offended if Anna had not discussed it with me. This is different. It was my idea Lovell. No one gets hurt when you're honest. It's when lies are told that people get hurt."

He opened the door and exited, his back straight.

CHAPTER SEVEN

The knock on the door was light. Lovell opened it to a copper colored, string bean bodied man with a left glass eye, scars down the left side of his face, a straight but flared nose and full lips.

" Professor Pendleton, I've come to drive you to Dr. Faturi's house."

As he turned, Lovell saw the ponytail and as they passed Doris' room, from her door, her finger pointed toward the man who'd walked ahead, then spun his entire body around to face Lovell. He then looked towards Doris's ajar door, his lips twitching. Doris' finger had vanished. Looking forward, Lovell walked past him, and was surprised when the man, walking backwards, trotted in front of him, the one eye darting from Lovell's face to Doris' door. He continued to walk backwards, down the steps, but turned to face the street, once they'd gotten outside. Lovell glanced up at Doris' door and saw a thumbs up coming from her door. The Iraqi swiveled back around. Lovell noticed he always moved to the right because of the blind eye. He switched to a limousine and got into the front seat, closing the window between them, the black driver wearing a white turban. Lovell closed his eyes but was awakened by the door opening. Stars blanketed the sky, lighting the area, and Lovell's finger opened his knife, still pocketed, barely able to see the Iraqi and only the driver's cigarette tip. He eased out his knife, feeling the Iraqi near him, then slid it back into his pocket, as candles came alive, like street lamps in a neighborhood, from a house to his left. He saw Faturi, carrying a candle, emerge from a door, motioning for them to come towards him and he double-timed it to the house. The Iraqi followed him, almost running to enter before Lovell, whispering something to Faturi. Penny and Matt sat

[234]

at a table, drinks in hand. Matt blinked twice, which Lovell interpreted as everything was fine. The Iraqi pulled Faturi to the telephone, pushing the receiver into his chest. Faturi dialed a number, but the lights came on before he could speak. Lovell asked for the toilet and was led to it by Faturi. Closing the door, and turning on the light, he smiled seeing the white marble floors and walls with gold fixtures everywhere, including the bidet. The one window opened from the outside and Lovell heard Jim's voice.

"Everything's set. Touch the Iraqi with this little patch on his bare arm or anywhere. It's a microphone. Later!" Jim's bloody hand held a dime sized clear flimsy piece of material, which he dropped into Lovell's hand.

"Wash the wall with some alcohol in case any blood got on it. It's under Faturi's sink."

Lovell relieved himself and taking toilet paper, wiped the wall, holding the device in his left hand. He placed the toilet paper in his pocket.   Entering the living room where Matt, Penny, the Iraqi and Faturi sat, he paused seeing all four men, tuned towards the Faturi's stereo, as if seeing the speaker. "The black man is our brother. He has not brought pain to us, as Muslims and as a people. Instead, he has suffered from the same imperialism we have, in the United States. Unta Ikwo. We are the same. And as he works and lives among us, we must not forget this. We must not treat him as if he is the symbol of United States tyranny, good night."

Faturi stood, strode to the stereo, and turning it off, turned around, dabbing at his eyes. The Iraqi back wiped the streams of tears, and standing, reached out his arms to Lovell, who embracing him, stuck the membrane inside his shirt, on the left shoulder blade and then pretended to shake with sobs. The Iraqi wept, patting Lovell on the back. Opening his eyes, Lovell saw Matt, Penny and Faturi all embracing. Faturi sniffled, Penny was dry eyed and Matt, who'd summoned tears, winked at Lovell. A bell ringing broke their embraces and Lovell saw a female figure, body covered in black, and veiled, leave a dining area, ripe with cooked food. Lovell, Penny and Matt sat facing the Iraqi and Faturi, who poured brandy into snifters and reached for the piles of fish, chicken, beef, lamb and vegetables, piled on platters. The Iraqi, between downing brandy, ate, ambidextrously. He explained he was actually a Palestinian, who'd lost his eye fighting against Israel in the 1967 war. He'd been imprisoned and finally deported, never able to return to Palestine, as he called it, again. He'd met the leader when he was still a soldier, they'd become friends, and after living in Iraq for years had been offered a position at the university in criminology and internal security. He admitted he'd been investigating the white American's death, as he referred to him. He paused and glanced around the table.

"Do any of you, my brothers, know anything about the man's death?"

Penny belched.

"I do. I saw him several times at an illegal club for homosexuals in Ripoli dancing with the same man. He was an Arab, but he had blond hair."

The Iraqi finished his drink and held his glass out to Faturi.

"And where is this club, Ibn Jamin? I promise you I will not have it closed. I do though want to find this man. It will be good for both of us."

Matt inhaled placing his hand on Penny's.

"You must trust him Penny. Remember, we're all brothers and they've given us refuge."

Penny sipped brandy and reddened.

"It's the first blue door next to the last material shop at the end of the souk. The password to enter is Village People in

[236]

English. You walk down a hallway, which has private rooms and leads to the dance floor. They always went into the last room on the left hand side. It has a coiled snake on the door. I saw him there last night wearing that white boy's watch."

The Iraqi jumped to attention from his chair and leaning across the table, knocking over platters, kissed Penny and ran to the phone, without staggering. He dialed, shouted into the phone and hurried out the door, shouting something to Faturi. Matt placed his arm around a trembling Penny.

"I just ratted on someone Matt. I just ratted on someone. I just ratted on someone!"

Covering his face, he went to Faturi's toilet. Hearing the toilet door close, Faturi poured them more brandy and raised his glass.

"He just saved all our lives."

Lovell turned hearing a door open and a six foot pale woman, with sparkling blue eyes and midnight hair, hour glass body, in a sheer gold caftan with matching heels, tiptoed into the room.

"Has that heathen left?"

Faturi pursed his lips.

"Fatima, I have told you not to speak like that."

Lighting a Virginia Slim cigarette, she blew smoke at Faturi.

"He is a heathen and you know it Abubakar. You're afraid of what he can do. I'm not!"

She looked at the table.

"Look what a mess he made and all the alcohol he drank. I'll get us some of the real brandy. Penny come help me."

Lovell hadn't heard Penny come in, but noticed Mrs. Faturi holding his hand as they walked. Faturi shook his head, said "damn women" in German and watched Penny's swaying walk. Mrs. Faturi and Penny returned each

[237]

carrying two decanters of dark brandy. They sat one in front of Lovell and Matt. Penny sat one in front of himself. Faturi and Mrs. Faturi had one in front of them. Mrs. Faturi, after pouring herself and Faturi a drink, raised her glass. "I'm Fatima Aisha Imelda Gaddafi Faturi and I welcome you to our home."

They all bottoms up their drinks. Faturi poured another and as he sat down, Fatima grabbed Penny's decanter and ran from the room. Faturi, picked up her glass with lipstick on the rim and followed her. Penny removed the new decanters and hurried into the other room. He and Faturi had just returned when the door opened. It was the Iraqi, smiling. "Gentlemen, the driver will return you to your living quarters."

Moving to the side he allowed Matt, Penny and Lovell to pass and as they exited Faturi's home, Lovell turned to see the Iraqi guzzling a decanter of brandy. Riding in the car Penny covered his face with his handkerchief. Lovell held his head back, sometimes letting it roll to the side, as if he were drunk. He'd open his eyes periodically, looking in the car's mirror and noticed the driver watching him. The car stopped in front of the faculty dorms and Lovell pretended to not be able to get out of the car. Penny and Matt supported him as he staggered until the car pulled off and was no longer visible. The three men laughed until Matt blew his nose on the sidewalk and Penny gagged.

"You two acted your asses off. That driver's going back to Faturi's and report to him and that Cyclops Iraqi. We have to watch that muthafucka though. He's dangerous. Let's go upstairs and get high."

Penny looked up at his room.

"I'm going to my room. I have company."

Matt slapped Penny on the back.

[238]

"Man, Penny, I'm sorry about what I said. I was wrong. Your sex life is nobody's business. I guess I was embarrassed about it turning me on. Come on back to the session. I'll deal with Madusun. I hope you don't mind but I'm going to call you half a dollar because you're the only one getting some steady sex. What I want to know is, who is it?"

Penny shook his butt at Matt and winked.

"Only the shadow knows Matt. Only the shadow knows." He switched away from them.   Lovell and Matt chuckled walking upstairs to Doris' room and knocked on the door. Jim's voice said come in. Matt entered first, still chuckling, as Lovell followed. Jim rushed him, grabbing him by the collar slamming Lovell's back against the door, which sounded as if a cannon had gone off.

"You almost fucked up the plan by not doing what you were supposed to do. Penny's job was plan b. Don't you know we're at war!"

Lovell, his head hitting the door saw black spots, then instinctively, he slammed his right foot onto Jim's instep, and using his left leg, swept Jim's left ankle, knocking his feet from under him. Jim hit the floor on his right arm and Lovell dropped onto Jim's throat with his knee. Raising his right arm, ready to strike, Doris screamed, and Matt grabbing his arm, stopped him. Doris stood to the side.

"Look at the two of you fighting. That's just what they want you to do, get at each other. Jim, I told you it was nothing because they bought everything."

She stopped looking down at Jim whose eyes were closed. He was pale and unconscious. Lovell and Matt lifted Jim from the floor and placed him on Doris' bed. A trail of blood made a small puddle on Doris spread. Doris got some ice, placed some on the back of Jim's head and rubbed the rest on his forehead and temple. Jim opened his eyes.

[239]

"What the"

Doris placed her hand over Jim's mouth.

"Take it easy big boy. You hit your head and got knocked out."

Jim blinked.

"What happened?"

Doris, still rubbing the ice on his head, pinched his nose.

"You flew at Lovell and got leveled."

Jim sat up, holding the back of his head.

"What'd the fuck I do that for?"

Before Doris could answer, he lifted his right foot, examining his ankle. A blue knot had formed. Jim winked at Lovell.

"You ankle slipped me."

Lovell's head movement said yes. Jim rubbed his eyes.

"I must have deserved it."

The four friends, plus Yusef who'd been sitting in a corner, laughed and said in unison

"Yes, you did."

Penny knocked on the door and entered wearing a lavender silk robe. Yusef shushed the group as he turned up the speaker on the short wave radio. They could hear the shouts and people screaming. Lovell recognized the Iraqi's voice and someone was screaming. Yusef held up his hand.

"He has the guy now and is questioning him. He's asking him what he was doing and every time he doesn't give him the correct answer, he hits him with the camel tale. The guy is denying he knew the American. Now he's saying he did."

Yusef leaned back, then turned to them.

"Someone just got stabbed. It must have been the Iraqi because the sound broke off. He got it in the arm where you put the microphone."

[240]

They all sat trying to visualize the scene at the nightspot in downtown Ripoli. Penny's sniffles forced reality upon them.

"What have I done? What have I done? I'm responsible for someone dying and they're innocent."

Matt snarled.

"It was either he or you. That's the war Penny and I are fighting. Get used to it."

Penny stood, fists balled, and approached Matt.

"To you everything is war and you or them. I slept with him and got to know him. How can I be unfeeling about betraying him!"

Matt snickered.

"You can have all the feelings you want. But, tell me Mr. Marshall, how long do you think it would take him to turn you if he could save his ass? Don't blame me because you stick your dick in any ass you can. And if you don't watch out, it's going to get you in some shit so deep, none of us will be able to help you."

Penny stood in the middle of the floor, clenching and unclenching his fists. Matt, and Jim walked past him, leaving Lovell staring at Penny's convulsing body and Yusef and Doris, sitting on Doris' bed, whispering.

[241]

CHAPTER EIGHT

Lovell watched the clock in his classroom, hoping it would move fast so he could dismiss the class. He always had a problem letting his students go early. He was the only professor with this dilemma. His colleagues never held class the correct amount of time and their students never complained. His students, though accustomed to his keeping them in class, crossed and uncrossed their legs, glanced out the windows at the other students passing by, waving, and watched him unsuccessfully willing the clock to move. The young men, on one side and the young ladies on the other, looked at each other, a rare occurrence. It was the last day of classes before the winter holiday. Lovell's time watching was interrupted by a cough. Turning to look in the sound's direction, a wave of stiffness struck each student's body, with each head focused on the door, where the Major and the Iraqi stood. Lovell, nor anyone he knew, had seen the Iraqi since Faturi's party, one week ago, and seeing him, his arm in a sling, brought stomach acid to his throat, and he coughed, spewing it across the room. The students covered their noses and Lovell wheezed out class dismissed, walking towards his discomfort, splattered against the wall. He poured his drinking water on it, covering it with paper towels, ignoring the Iraqi and the Major. Wiping it up with his foot, electricity zipped through both arms, as the sound echoed from outside. "Jami Al Fatah, Jami Al Fatah, Jami Al Fatah" It was the chant every student, professor and administrator feared, because it meant, the student leaders, the people's court, had found someone not obeying the law, and they were to be punished in public. The Iraqi took two steps toward Lovell and stopped.

[242]

"You need not worry Dr. Pendleton, it is not you. It is someone you know though, and you must come with us."
Lovell fingered his knife, coughed up a ball of spittle and hacked it onto the floor. The students, administrators, and other professors, plastered themselves against the walls, whispering to each other, then staying a few feet behind, followed the three men, towards the chanting. As Lovell and his escorts turned a corner of the hallway, Penny, Matt and Jim, two soldiers in front and back, waited for them. Once they reached Matt and the others, Matt whispered in French,
"Whatever happened, this shit is serious." Walking from the building, the entire university, it seemed to Lovell, stood waiting, smoking, whispering, pointing and watching as the Americans were led from the university, down the main street of the campus. Faturi, head down and moving his shoe in the dirt, waited at the corner, which turned into an open field, next to the economics building. The group of Americans, pausing, bumped into each other, seeing the gallows which had been built, next to the economics building, and Doris, dressed in a black Abiyah, with Yusef, in black filthy pajamas, heads shaved, with two soldiers holding them at gunpoint, stood. Being led closer, they could see Yusef's right eye was closed, his nose twisted to the right and flies buzzed around what was once the top of one ear. Doris looked at Lovell and attempted a smile, but blood dribbled from a toothless mouth, and inhaling deeply, she spit a glob into the face of one of the soldiers who was guarding her. Penny collapsed. Lovell caught him. The Major growled at Lovell. "Take him to his room and come back immediately."
Hoisting Penny over his shoulder, Lovell carried Penny across the street to the faculty dorms. Penny patted Lovell on the back once they entered the building.

[243]

"I can't watch it Lovell, I can't. You have to document this though so the world can see. Take the camera. Get it all Lovell! Get it all! I'm so sorry. I'm so sorry."

Covering his face, he walked into his room, closing the door, then opening it with only his arm being visible, handed Lovell the briefcase with the camera inside, then slammed the door. Lovell thought he heard voices from Penny's room as ran down the hall. Three armed soldiers exiting the building met Lovell. The crowd parted as he was led to the front. Faturi, the Major, and the Iraqi were on the gallows. Lovell, standing next to Matt and Jim, their jaws working, briefcase in front of him, looking down into the lens which was viewable from a hole in the top of it, pushed a button which started the filming and the microphone.

"This woman, Doris Akbar and this man, Yusef Bahar, have been found guilty of thievery by The Aybil Socialist Republic, Jami Al-Fateh University, and of attempting to flee with the funds, plus spying for the Egyptian government and having illicit relations not condoned by the laws of the Koran. The punishment is death. Yusef Bahar, do you have anything to say?"

Yusef, straightened his shoulders.

"This is no Socialist Republic and you Major, are a hypocrite."

The gallows door screamed and Yusef jerked twice, his tongue twitching from the corners of his mouth, eyes bolting from his head and neck at a forty five degree angle, swung in circles, urine squirting from his pants legs. Doris, eyes on Lovell, spoke to him in Spanish.

"The money hidden at the bottom of my drawers in my room Negro, take it and live. Only one other person in our-"

The Iraqi backhanded her.

[244]

"English!"

Blood leaked from Doris' nose. "These men are not good men. They are non-believers and"

The door belched again and Doris dropped, blood shooting far, it splattered Matt, Jim and Lovell's shoes. Her eyes rolled up into her head and a mound of feces hit the ground, turd driblets falling with each twirl her body made. She made a gagging sound, her body spasmed, and her tongue twisting and moving from the left to the right, saliva dripping. The Iraqi and the Major shook hands. Faturi, head over the side of the gallows, heaved, as the crowd of students cheered and dispersed. Lovell, Matt and Jim stepped towards the bodies, wanting to cut them down, but the soldier pointed their rifles at them, as the Iraqi and the Major passed them. The Major paused, looking at the three friends.

"Let this be a lesson to you. You can't touch these bodies, we'll bury them. We should feed them to the dogs."

Lovell, Matt and Jim, refused to look at him. They watched Doris and Yusef, whose bodies now touched.

******

Lovell, Matt and Jim, holding hands, walked to the faculty dorms. The five o'clock call to prayer chilled Lovell, and leaning against Matt for warmth, he heard Jim mumbling he'd like to waste all of them at that moment. Matt squeezed Lovell's hand. "What'd she said in Spanish man?"

Lovell, a whisper from his throat wheezing past his lips, answered Matt in his ear.

"I don't know. She spoke too fast."

Matt flipped his elephant ear.

"I heard her say only one of us, then they pulled the lever. I wonder what she meant?"

[245]

Jim brushed a tear from his lip.

"I'm the only one of us probably knew something about her. One of the soldiers told me they caught them the same night as the incident with the Iraqi, on a caravan of Chadians before they could get to the desert. They were loaded with money but there's still a lot missing. Who knew she and Yusef were trying to escape? I know I didn't."

Lovell and Matt also said they didn't know. Jim belched out an answer.

"I know she wouldn't be stupid enough to tell Penny. He's vulnerable because he can't keep his ass in his pants and Doris knew it. It has to be someone else."

The infirmary car with Danuta in the passenger's seat, chugged past them. They didn't turn to see where it had gone. Matt motioned his head towards the car, which had just passed.

"Do you think it was Danuta? Doris always talked to her." Jim wiped his eyes and stammered an answer. "Impossible. She hates them worse than we do and with what she's doing."

Matt growled an answer.

"With what she's doing she'd have a reason to tell them. It'd divert attention from what she's doing."

They all tuned in time to see Danuta, carrying a sheet, exiting the car and walking towards the gallows, as Matt finished his own sentence.

"And we're at war, and people will do anything to save their ass. Lovell, you're close enough to feel her out. Let us know and we'll handle it. She'll probably come to your room wanting to console you. Keep her there while we check out her room." Matt and Jim crossed the street to the faculty dorms, not glancing back in Danuta's direction, and leaving Lovell, face flooded with tears, watching as Danuta

[246]

carried a body, wrapped in a sheet, to the back of the infirmary's car. He waited until she'd gone back for the other body, then jogged across the street and up the stairs to Doris' room. Checking the hall he turned the knob to her door, and finding it locked, used a small blade from his Swiss knife and opened her door. The room was bare with the scent of Jasmine incense, the only reminder Doris had lived in the room. Not turning on the light, he placed the briefcase with the camera in front of the door, crawled across the floor to the clothes cabinet, and opening the door wide enough for his shoulders, used his knife again to unscrew the bolts holding the board at the bottom of the cabinet. Removing it, he placed his hand inside, touching what he knew to be money. Scooting backwards, he felt the width of whatever held it and using both hands, pulled out a three foot wide and long cookie cutter sized tray, stacked with close to four inches of bills. Replacing the board and making sure no wood particles had fallen on the floor, he slid the tray across the floor to the door, then taking off his shirt wiped away any trail which might have been left. Cracking the door enough to peer both ways, he crawled backwards out the door and lifting the tray, went into his room.   Closing his drapes, Lovell turned on his light, and saw neat stacks of dollar bills. Examining them, they were all fifties and twenties. A small note was stuck between to the first stack. Opening it, Lovell read;

Hello Lovely, if you're reading this I'm either dead, or I've notified you from Italy. We couldn't take this with us and had planned to contact you when we reached Italy, so you could bring it to us. This is Aybil money, owed to Yusef and I. If you don't give it to us, use it and have yourself some fun, for once, when you see Nidia and your baby. Ahmed helped us get a taxi to the Chadians. He's the only one who knows we're getting a taxi but he thinks it's to

[247]

Tunis. Again, I'm dead, or enjoying myself. If I'm dead, find him and do what you have to do. Matt and Jim are right. We're at war Lovell. You can trust them because they'd die before they'd tell on anyone. Trust no one else. You were my first love, Lovely. Be good to yourself and that lucky woman who's waiting for you. Doris

He stared at the money, then crumbled the note into a ball, and set it on fire, in his trashcan. Watching it burn, and putting the money in his room, where Doris had hidden it in her room, someone knocked on his door. It was Danuta, who called his name. He opened the door to Danuta, stone faced, opened and closed her mouth. Then, mouth drawn into a line, she rubbed her fingertips.

"I have your friends. I know you'd like to put them away with dignity because the Aybilians will just throw them into a hole."

Lovell followed Danuta to her office in the infirmary. Closing her door, she placed a mirror on her desk and poured two long lines of cocaine. This is not pleasant Lovell. Hanging distorts the face." Lovell snorted the lines. Blinking his eyes, face numb, heart pounding, being led by Danuta, and entering a medical examiner's room with two metal tables, he saw Doris and Yusef's faces turned towards the other, smelling of feces and urine. Her left hand hung from beneath the sheet. He had always thought of elves when seeing her hands. The thumbs were larger than any other finger. Looking closer he could see it had been turned completely around and the thumb nail faced inward. Danuta removed Doris' clothing and Lovell removed Yusef's. There were long rope size purple welts across her breast and legs. He then looked at her feet. The toes were all the same size. He pulled the sprayer and began to spray her body, with a soft rain like stream. Turning Doris on her side and rinsing her back, blood came

[248]

from her buttocks. Lovell turned to Danuta who'd been watching him. Her face paled and eyes turned to glass.
"She's been sodomized Lovell. That's why there's the blood."
She turned Shariff to the side and the same blood came. Lovell looked at Yusef's fingers. They were bent backwards. Both arms were also twisted.
"Both his arms were broken and so were his fingers. He endured incredible pain. Both of them did. I'm sorry"
 Danuta, flattening Yusef, and using white sponges, patted his upper body, pulling the sheet over his lower parts and without looking washed his private parts. Lovell, also using a sponge, wiped around the damaged parts of Doris' body, then cradled her into the sheet as if she were a new baby. He and Danuta then wrapped them in heavier sheets, one atop the other, placing them on the bottom of a gurney. He started to push the gurney out the door, but having to turn it around, noticed a covered body in a corner. The foot, with the baby toe missing, looked familiar. He'd seen that foot before, and stepping towards it, Danuta grabbed his arm.
"You've seen enough today Lovell. Please don't look."
 Removing Danuta's hand he walked over to the body and pulled back the sheet. It was Ahmed; a purple slit exposed his Adam's apple. Lovell spit on his face and began to kick him until Danuta threw him to the floor, grunting, having to use all her strength.
"Don't deface the dead Lovell"
Lovell stood staring at Ahmed.
"When was he killed, Danuta?"
Danuta opened her arms to Lovell, who didn't move.
"Wasn't he also your friend?"
Lovell looked at Ahmed's face. The left side was flattened.
"You didn't answer the question."

[249]

"He was just brought in. The Sudanese mullah is on his way to care for his body and wrap it correctly."

"You mean he was killed after Doris and Yusef?"

"He wasn't killed Lovell. He was tortured to death. His fingernails and toenails have been pulled out. Now we must go before they arrive."

They pushed the gurney out to the car where three of the Tunisian cooks, friends of Shariff's waited. They loaded the bodies into the car and drove off, leaving Danuta and Lovell standing in the darkness. Danuta took Lovell to her room, and pouring him a glass of brandy, made finger size lines of cocaine on the mirror in her room. Matt and Jim soon joined them. Lovell, his mouth numb, slammed his fist on Danuta's table.

"It was Ahmed who told the Aybilians about Doris and Yusef. They tortured him until he gave in. I saw his body. His fingernails and toenails had been pulled out. They slit his throat after he squealed. His body's in the morgue."

Jim and Matt exchanged a glance.

"Are you sure it was him?"

Jim's eyebrow was raised.

"I'm sure. He helped them get a taxi to the Chadians. Doris left a note for me and explained everything. I found it in her room, on her balcony."

Matt cleared his throat.

"How'd you know where to look?"

"You know as well as I do that Doris and I almost had a thing, so don't play suspicious with me Matt. She told me a lot of things about herself. Especially where she liked to hide little messages."

"I meant no harm bro. We've seen a lot of shit today and I'm fried. Tell me bro, did she tell you where she hid the money? There must be more."

Lovell held out his empty glass to Danuta.

[250]

"I wish she had. I'm sure she and Yusef hit the Aybilians hard. He had access to everything."

Danuta placed a perfume-sized bottle full of cocaine in front of each of them.

"Let us celebrate the life of a wonderful woman, fellas, and the real beginning of our war with the Aybilians. Our enemy has made himself very clear. I want you all to enjoy yourself and try not to think about Doris' death. I know she wanted to be free of the prison she lived in, and she was successful. Drink and ingest."

Singing medleys of Miracles and Temptation songs, they drank, and snorted all night, until the five a.m. call to prayer ushered them to their rooms, to prepare for their trip to Italy. They left Danuta snoring in her bed.

CHAPTER NINE

Landing in Italy, Lovell, Matt, Jim and Penny staggered through customs and were met by a driver holding a sign with Lovell's name. They entered a limousine and each curled into a ball, eyes closed, for however long the ride would be. It was so short that they were unable to sleep, and were pulled up the stairs of Ms. Marguerite's private plane, one at a time, by Penny, who smelled of cognac, and who'd met them at the taxi, in front of their building, in the morning. Exiting the plane, they fell into the limousine and staggered from it, being led by servants, to the rooms Ms. Marguerite had for them.   Lovell, removed his shirt, leaving a trail of clothes to the shower and holding on to the walls, struggled from it to the bed. Closing his eyes, someone using their first fingers, massaged his temples, then using the Venus palms of her hands, rubbed his shoulders, the back of his neck, ears and forehead. He rolled over to see Ms. Marguerite, bare breasted, looking down at him. Smiling, she held him to her breast, rocking him, saying,
 "It's alright, you're safe now. It's alright", until he exploded in tears, his sobs echoing off the twenty foot ceilings.

*****

He awoke in the morning, pillow soggy, eyes cached together, sandpaper mouthed. The room was dark and he couldn't remember where he was. Looking up towards where he thought the ceiling should be, he recalled Marguerite's lavender soap and her cooing words. Then he remembered he was at her estate and they'd all come to Italy. Opening the curtains, night greeted him with fresh

[252]

echoes of crickets and fireflies illuminating the air. The TV in his room clicked on.

"Hello Lovely, you're finally awake."

Lovell saw Matt walking across the football field yard outside.

"Looks like it. What day is it?"

"It's two days after you arrived. And you've been out all that time."

'I've been asleep for two days?"

She chuckled, running her flat palm over her head. "Almost three. Are you hungry? Or you don't know yet?"

"I don't know. Let me shower first. You know how I am in the mornings.

Her cackle jerked his head up.

"Yes, I do. Spacey."

He showered with water as hot as he could stand it, then dressed in the gold and black evening clothes which hung in the closet. He knew that Marguerite had selected these for him. He'd brought no clothes and his bags were full of money. Ms. Marguerite embraced Lovell as he opened the door.

"I see you've stayed in shape as usual, Lovely. I told you you'd be a handsome man. I didn't realize how handsome, though. Now come, guests are waiting. "

They wore the same colors and he measured his steps, keeping pace with hers, as she'd taught him years ago. The guests were the Suliemans, along with his friends from Aybil, Matt and Jim with curly haired Italian women on both arms and Penny, with a younger version of the dead Count. It was obvious to Lovell that it was the Count's son, or some close relative. Everyone sat at a table fashioned from a door. Mr. and Mrs. R.S ran to Lovell. Mr. R.S. lifted Lovell off the floor.

"I'm glad you're here. We missed you."

[253]

Lovell held onto Mr. R.S., struggling with the cavalcade of tears waiting to flood his suit. Mrs. R.S. guided him to his chair beside them and next to Ms. Marguerite, who sat at the head.   They were aware of everything which had occurred in Aybil. Marguerite was most interested in the tape of the hanging, which Lovell had brought. He left the table and giving his grief full reign, moistened the front of his shirt, walking to his room. "But I was cool", mimicking Oscar Brown Jr., upon returning to the table. Giving the tape to Marguerite, his shoulders relaxed, and he spoke of Doris to Ms.Marguerite and the Suliemans. Mrs. Sulieman, held Lovell's hand.

"I was raised by the Christians, on a farm, near a leper colony. I know that if you want to get an enemy, there are several ways. It depends on how long you want them to suffer. One way is to brush, or what we call curry a horse, then comb the hair from the horse into someone's food for several days, and they will become violently ill. The hair punctures their intestines and they die a violent death from vomiting. Another way is to get the dirt from someone who has died of a very serious disease, and put the dirt in your enemy's food. He, or she, will die from that same disease. Or, you can get the hair of a leper, mix it in their food and condemn them to life, having them live as a leper. You don't have to strike your enemy directly Lovell, there are other ways."

He sat, thinking of the Major, the Iraqi, Faturi and how close the farm was to the school. The night ended with everyone dancing to Motown and Ms. Marguerite reminding Lovell that Nidia would be flying in tomorrow. Sitting in his room, sleep refused to visit him, until the sun, peeked its head above the Ischia Porte Hills.

*****

[254]

Lovell had the chauffeur carry the four-dozen roses he'd bought for Nidia. His three friends laughed, watching him pace in the airport. Ms. Marguerite had made arrangements for Nidia to be met at the foot of the plane's stairs, with the roses, and Lovell, hiding, would surprise her at the door. He watched as she waddled down the steps. Her two pumpkin size stomach, dwarfing the rest of her body, and he was surprised to see Ann accompanying her, carrying some bags. Nidia's eyes misted, her smile spreading across the walkway to the terminal, as she was pushed, in a wheelchair, inside. Ms. Marguerite had taken care of customs, and as they wheeled Nidia around the last corner, after customs, Lovell stepped out. She stood, opening her arms, and Lovell moved to the side unable to hug her from the front. She whispered in his ear.

"There are two big babies inside me."

He fell to his knees, kissing her stomach, feet, legs, and wept at her feet, unable to rise until Matt and Jim lifted him from the floor. Ann, once Lovell had managed to stand, gave him a one-shoulder hug. Penny stood away from the scene, watching everything, then sat in the corner of the plane, saying he had a hangover. Lovell held Nidia's hand the entire trip, kissed her stomach, face, fingers, played with her hair, and tongue in her ear, told her how much he'd missed her, and loved her. Matt and Jim sat with Ann, who, face flushed, drank shots of tequila, one after the other, through the short flight. She sat on one side of Nidia in the limousine, with Lovell on the other, spoke to Matt and Jim, and tried to have a conversation with Penny, who turned his back to her. Ms. Marguerite met them at the door, kissing Nidia on both cheeks. She insisted Nidia sit in a wheelchair and be pushed around because her feet were swollen. She told one of the servants to take Nidia's bags to

Lovell's room. Nidia, showing all her teeth, smiled. Ann overcome by a coughing fit heaved on the marble floors. Marguerite, her eyebrows pulling together, motioned with her head for the servants to clean up the mess and to escort Ann to her room. The servants wheeled Nidia to Lovell's room, and they were alone. Lovell removed his clothes and stood in front of Nidia, ready.

"Let's take a shower. I want to look at you Nidia." She sat on the bed, not moving, studying the floor. Then sighing pushed herself up. "Help me take off my shoes and get out of these clothes." He eased off her shoes, then kissing each toe, ankle, knees, and thighs, removed her panties, dress, bra and stood back, marveling at her stomach and his two lives, his seed, which lived within her. He then helped her to the bath and washed her body. Listening, and talking to the children, he knew were inside. Drying Nidia's body, they stretched out on the bed, naked. Lovell kissed Nidia between her legs

"We can do this can't we?"

"We can, but it's been so long, and you're so big. I don't know if I can take it."

"I'll be gentle. But if you don't want to I'll understand, Nidia."

She turned on her side, facing him.

"I missed you. I missed you so much it became dangerous. The Longoria family won't speak to me if they see me in the street. My parents say they don't have a daughter. I don't know what I would have done without Ann. She's been more than a friend to me and she's become more than a friend to me."

Lovell stroked her stomach.

"That's what friends are for. She was there for me when that artsy fartsy crowd tried to ruin me and she always defended me to your primo and everyone. I know what

[256]

kind of friend she can be and even more so, the type of sister she is. That's why I call her homefolks. "

"Lovell, we've-"

"I don't want to talk about Ann. I haven't seen you in months."

Nidia stroked his beard, pulling him with open lips, tongue extended, to her, then moved her body around, placing her mouth on Lovell's organ and opened her legs beckoning him to eat from her valley. They tasted each other's love, then fell asleep. Awakening an hour later, Lovell pushed Nidia to the dining room, where Matt, Jim, Marguerite, Mr. and Mrs. R. S. and Penny waited. Champagne sat in ice beside each chair. Marguerite raised her glass. "This is a toast to the two new lives which are about to come into this world and the amazing people who are bringing them into it." Everyone clinked glasses, except Penny, who stood after everyone had sat. Penny pointed his glass at Nidia and Ann.

"What I want to know is how long have you two bitches been a couple?"

Nidia, hands to her face, squealed and screamed, while Ann, circled her glass's rim with her first finger, making a high-pitched sound. "I'm so sorry Lovell. It just happened. It just happened. I never meant to hurt you. I never want to hurt you. It just happened. I'm so sorry, but we're in love. We're in love. We both love you, but we love each other more."

Nidia, hands still covering her face, turned to face Lovell. Jim threw his champagne in Ann's face and left the table. All other eyes turned to Lovell, whose mouth hung like the trap doors of a gallow. He, using all his strength, stood, and walked towards his room. He heard Matt say as he left, "If you were a man I'd kill you." and Marguerite say "I want you two cunts out of my house in a half an hour."

[257]

Using both hands to steady himself against the wall for support, he made it to his room, and once inside, collapsed on the floor, crawling on hands and knees to his bed and pulled himself up. The room tilted, to the right, left, and he lay flat trying to keep everything from spinning.

"I tried to tell you Lovell."

Nidia's voice ended the merry go round in Lovell's head.

"Yes you did. But that was today. This didn't happen today. I should have known. An apple doesn't fall too far from the tree."

"What's that supposed to mean, Lovell?"

He walked over to the window and looking out, saw Matt and Jim standing below it, looking up at him. He gave them a thumbs up.

"I heard Marguerite give you a half an hour to leave, you'd better get packing."

"I'm not going to let you get off that easy Lovell."

He whirled around and walked towards her.

"You're not going to let me off that easy. I restrain my passion, sacrifice my heart, waiting for you and you betray me and have the nerve to say you're not going to let me off that easy? You have some nerve. You belittled your cousin for doing the same and you're just like him. I'll take care of my children if that's what you mean. But I want nothing to do with you and as far as I'm concerned, you're a hypocrite, just like the rest of the Longoria's."

Nidia ran at Lovell, pounding him first on the chest, then sinking, pounding each part of his body she encountered, until she fell at his feet.

"That's not true. That's not true. I'm no hypocrite. I'm a woman of honor and you know it! I didn't realize it was happening Lovell. All I know is every time I needed something, or someone, Ann was there. When she was down and hurt, I was there for her. We found ourselves

[258]

cooking together, shopping together, and staying up all night just talking. I never realized I had so much in common with someone until I started spending time with her. Then one day, and it was only a week ago Lovell, I realized, and she realized, we were in love and wanted to be together, and because of our love for you we'd been denying it. It almost ripped our hearts out Lovell because we both love and respect you and we know what you've been through. But you can't fight love Lovell, you can't. You can't fight love. Believe me, I've tried. I tried with you. I tried to love god more than my body and life but I lied to myself. Being with you and loving her would be a lie, mi amour, and I can't live a lie. I did that for ten years in the convent and you know it! You know it! You know I've been true to everything in my life. I'm no hypocrite mi amour and I never meant to hurt you. Love just happened Lovell. It just happened. And you have no right to say anything about my family because they love you and you know that."

She'd sunk to the floor, beating her head against it. Lovell lifted her onto the bed.

"Lovell, I swear, we still haven't consummated our love."

He watched her body heave.

"Stop, Nidia. What you feel, the babies feel. I understand. Things do happen in life. I see with my heart, and my heart has no eyes. Sightless heart, guiding me into pathways of love."

He handed Nidia a handkerchief and turned his head as she blew out her dilemma.

"That's one of your poems, Lovell. You read it to me the first time you told me you loved me over the phone, when I was in the monastery. I'm so sorry Lovell. Understanding doesn't eliminate hurt."

He strode to the window again. Matt and Jim were gone.

[259]

"No, it doesn't Nidia. No, it doesn't. I'd like to propose something to you. I hope it's not asking too much and may seem a bit cold."

"What's that?"

"When you have the babies. I'd like to take one and you take one. I'll always be in touch and we can make sure they know each other. I'm also sorry for what I said about your family. They were good to me and I know they love me as I love them".

"Lovell, you're asking me to give up my child."

"No, I'm not. I'm asking you to let me raise one of our children and you raise the other. I'll support both. You don't have to answer now, just think about it and let me know soon. They're due in three months so you have some time."

He heard Nidia inhale and watched the corners of her mouth quiver. He knew, if he were a woman, and a man, even the father of his children, had asked him to give up his child, he'd be torn, pained, reluctant, and damn near belligerent. Lovell saw all this in Nidia's face. Each emotion a quiver, the sigh an extinguisher to quell the embers of loss, being stoked.

"Okay, I'll think about it."

He continued to look out the window, watching the mansions of Ischia.

"Now I want you to go to Ann's room and get ready to leave. It will be better for both of us and the children."

The bed yawned with Nidia's rising.

"Lovell, I'll always love you. I'm sorry."

"I'm sorry too, Nidia."

The door closed and without removing his clothes, Lovell climbed into bed....

It, the bed, down covered and silk sheeted, changed daily by a raven-haired maid who delivered and removed food, mostly untouched, was where he'd been for a week. When the door opened to Ms. Marguerite and Mrs. Sulieman's, holding towels, a bathrobe and clothes. Matt, Jim, Mr. Sulieman and Penny stood behind them. Raising his head from under the pillows, Lovell saw Matt step between the two women."Let me tell you there's a function at the Junction, and baby you better come on right now. We got ling ting tong from china, long tall sally from Carolina, we got 007, private eye, he's bringin' all the guys, from eye spy."

Matt stood next to the bed and stopped singing. "There's function at the junction and brother you better come on, right now. It's time to get up blackman. You can't go to the function at the junction, smelling like you do."

He pulled the covers off Lovell, who, naked, was curled into a fetal position. Matt motioned to Mr. Sulieman, Jim and Penny.

"Come on, let's get him up. Ladies, please leave the robe and clothes on the bed. We'll take over from here."

Each grabbing a limb, they lifted Lovell's listless body and carried it to the bathroom. Inside the bathroom, Penny held up Lovell's back and head while Mr. Sulieman shaved him, leaving the washing to Jim and Matt. Lovell remained silent during the bath and Matt, seeing the despondency, slapped him with an open palm, snapping his head back.

"Damn Matt, that hurt."

Matt tapped him on the chin. "I knew that'd wake you up. That left hook has dropped many a fool. The next one will be for real."

"Jigaboo, you hit me with a left hook and we'll be fighting until one of us is dead."

Matt raised his hands, taking a fighting stance. "Well, I've never been afraid of dying. Get up, or it's coming.

[261]

Lovell climbed out of the bathtub and into a bathrobe, held by Penny.

"Okay, I'm up and functioning. I don't know about some function at the junction though."

Mr. Sulieman, arm around Lovell's shoulders, walked him to the bed and the clothes.

"The function, young brother, is my son's game. He's playing the final game of the European championship and though he doesn't know it, there'll be six NBA scouts there."

Lovell glanced at himself in the mirror.

"I've lost a lot of weight."

Penny, standing by the window and controlling his tears, lit an incense.

"You haven't eaten for week."

Lovell touched his ribs.

"Is that how long I've been down?"

Jim, pacing, paused.

"A week and counting. You okay man?"

Lovell surveyed himself again.

"I got up on the eight count."

Jim raised his hands, elbows tucked in, covering his sides.

"I always knew you could take a punch."

Lovell bent over in a jackknife position.

"Well, brother Jim, this one was below the belt."

None of the men laughed. Penny cut through the moment by kissing Lovell as he walked to the door. "We'll see you downstairs for dinner in five minutes.

"Mr. Sulieman cuffed Lovell's ear.

"And he means five and no longer!"

They left Lovell pulling on his underwear.

He sat at the dinner table, his mouth feeling as if he'd eaten sand. Relief visited him in glasses of Merlot and mixtures of amaretto and brandy. His throat finally opened after the

[262]

sixth glass of wine. He tasted Calamari sauce, the raw
Octopus, fresh squid and the avocados, floating in
vinaigrette. He watched Ms. Marguerite tell the maid to
bring him more and he devoured it all, his taste buds
suddenly coming alive. Matt, who sat next to him, his left
arm around a flame haired Sicilian, leaned toward him.
"I'm glad to see you're eating. It took you two bottles of
wine and three Zorba's to get going. How's your hammer
hanging?"
Lovell felt his private under the table.
"I can't find it. I think it died."
Matt didn't laugh.
"Don't worry. It's only whiskey dick."
The dinner ended when Mr. Sulieman rose and urged
everyone to get ready because it was time to go to the
basketball game. Lovell stood without difficulty. Miss
Marguerite came to his side. "Lovely, you're scary.
Lovell pulled his mouth open and widened his eyes. She
held his forearm.
"I'm serious Lovely. You've drunk three bottles of wine,
almost a bottle of brandy and you're still not drunk. Tell me
the truth, are you taking drugs?"
"No, I'm not. I've built up a tolerance to alcohol from
drinking that pure stuff in Aybil."
She brushed her lips against his.
"I hope that's it Lovely. I watched alcohol kill the Count.
He started drinking as a young man and never stopped.
There were many of nights I slept with a wet noodle. He
finally had this special operation where they put in a pump.
Then it never went down unless he deflated it. You have to
take care of yourself, Lovely. You won't be young
forever."
He placed his hand on her basketball bottom.
"A word to the wise, from the wise, is sufficient. Let"

She covered his mouth with her fingertips and stuck her middle finger in his mouth.

"You don't have to say it. Let me grieve a bit. I know this Lovely. I know. But baby, don't let alcohol become your confidant. Especially when you have me. Now go and watch that game. I can't stand being around all those screaming Italians. The directions to my room will be on your screen when you come back."

Lovell felt his hammer rising, watching the double dribbling on her backside.

******

The game was a man playing with boys. The Americans were amazed how Ali had grown five inches since he'd left Aybil, and was now 6'11, 250, with a young Jim Brown, sculpted obsidian body. Lovell had asked Ali's mother, Mrs. Sulieman about the growth spurt and she'd told him it happened over six months and they'd monitored his growth with Nubian herbs, not wanting him to die like the Chinese player. The NBA scouts were pushing to talk to Fuad, who carried the European MVP trophy with him, referred them to Miss Marguerite, who would act as his agent and was waiting for the entire team, at her villa. Everyone knew it would be a long night of partying. Riding in the limousine with Matt and Jim, a tan Italian woman plastered against them, pouring driblets of champagne into the women's full mouths and Penny, who fed the Tony Curtis faced Counts nephew, their hands in each other's pants, Lovell watched the caravan of limousines shimmying its way to Ms. Marguerite's estate. Each car contained members of the basketball team, trainers and coaches. He could see champagne bottles being thrown from the car windows along with some clothes. Some players were puking and

[264]

occasionally someone urinating. The city, a collage of the team's flags echoed with triumph and loud speakers barked Martha and the Vandellas song, "Heat Wave," the Italian team's theme song. He moved his arms as if pulling something, doing the heat wave, while marveling at how the two women with Matt and Jim, sausage lips and ringlet hair, ham hock thighs, small waists, medium breasts with round sunshine behinds, spread against the limousine seat, looked like light skinned black women. Sitting in the corner facing them, he snickered at how, the more they drank, the wider their legs opened, giving him a clear view. Seeing the imprint of hair and the v, between their thighs, Lovell turned to watch the sprouting fireworks, signaling victory, and the familiar scenery of Ms. Marguerite's estate, unfolding.

*****

Martha and the Vandellas *"Heat Wave"* singed the air and the limousine belched out everyone who had been invited to the celebration. Ali started the dancing line, moving to the music and everyone else, hands on each other's hips, moved to the music. They stopped, upon entering Ms. Marguerite's hall, when seeing Martha Reeves, with some new Vandellas, singing live with a band. The live band set the party off. People screamed and danced everywhere. Lovell moved to the bar and watched people dancing and drinking. Matt, his lady with legs wrapped around him, staggered over to Lovell and handing him an envelope, both hands cradling the woman's butt, moved towards his room. Opening the envelope, Lovell saw it was full of cocaine. Walking towards the toilet, he saw Ms. Marguerite leading a six foot nine inch Ethiopian power forward down the hall. She looked over her shoulder, winked, waved at

[265]

him and continued with the young man in tow. He watched
the basketball on her back jiggling, noticed how, upon
seeing him she drew the Ethiopian closer, rubbing his
private area, kept winking at Lovell over her shoulder.
Lovell, envelope in hand, fast paced it to his room and
turned on the television. Snorting and drinking amaretto
with brandy and ice. He sat in his room watching Ms.
Marguerite and the power forward pivot, dribble, do lay
ups, pass the ball and slam dunk, until sleep overcame him.
He awoke at midday to voices coming from the courtyard.
Looking out, banquet tables had been arranged in triangles
and the overnight guests, talking in loud voices, hands
gastrulating, feasted. Lovell showered and walked across
the football-sized green, to the festivities.   Penny, Matt,
Jim and their mates sat together, wearing sunglasses. Ms.
Marguerite sat and the head of one triangle, the power
forward at her side. Lovell sat at the table with his friends
from Aybil.
"Long night, huh Lovell."
Matt raised his Bloody Mary in salute to Lovell. The others
joined in.
"No, it was a short night but a good show."
They all ceased to move. Penny's mouth twitched. "What
did you see? You turned in before anyone."
Lovell asked the waiter for a big bowl of fruit salad. "The
queen and one of her entourage in the fourth quarter of the
game."
All heads turned in unison to look at Ms. Marguerite, who
raised her glass to them. Jim cleared his throat.
"That's cold. She's supposed to be"
Lovell cut Jim's comments with a wave of his hand. "She's
not cold. I am and she knows it."
Penny, lifting his lover's hand like a mother raising her
child, walked over and embraced Lovell, who noticed Ms.

[266]

Marguerite motioning him over to her. Approaching her and watching her rise, resplendent in fuchsia, hair pulled into a bun, he saw a pleading look, below the surface of her eyes and he reassured her, by winking, everything was fine. Ms. Marguerite, took Lovell's hand, kissed him on the cheek, and led him to a small chapel, where entering he saw Mr. And Mrs. Sulieman with their son Ali and a white gentleman, in his forties, gray haired with a receding hairline and pop eyes, sitting at a table. Ms. Marguerite sat down, pointing to a chair next to her for Lovell.

"Well, Mr. Nelson, have you considered my offer?"

"Yes I have, and we're willing to accept everything just as you've stipulated."

Mrs. Marguerite snapped her fingers and a waiter appeared with a tray of champagne glasses.

"Then we'll sign the contract and drink to the success of your franchise, now that you've secured the best player in Europe."

Mr. Nelson opened his briefcase and placed the contract on the table. Everyone except Lovell signed.

"Lovell, darling, I want you to sign as my personal assistant and future representative."

Lovell signed, noticing the glances and smiles from the Suliemans. Mr. Nelson, having left and the festivities in the courtyard in full swing with people dancing and eating, Lovell sat watching his friends and the glory of Ms. Marguerite's estate. The power forward licked on Ms. Marguerite's arm. Penny sat on his lover's lap and Matt and Jim had disappeared. Rising, an anchored heaviness about his shoulders, Vichy water in hand, he maneuvered through the mauve, tan and cream stylish robed people, and headed towards his room. Entering the corridor, a whippoorwill whistle-stopped him. He knew it was Ms. Marguerite because the whistle had become their signal,

[267]

years ago. She placed her arms around his neck, pressing her body against him.

"I am who I am Lovell. And, as you know well, I like them as I like them."

Lovell, arms around her waist, kissed the beehive, atop her head.

"Yes, you like them young, dumb and full of cum."

She pinched his ear.

"Not dumb. But, Lovey, so much has changed now. My desire for you has turned to something else. I guess it has something to do with seeing you smitten with pain. It's brought out the mother in me. I want to hold you and console you. That's why I haven't come to you, and why, I guess, I took on this new lover. A mother doesn't sleep with her son."

Lovell, lowered his head and holding his lips against her forehead, spoke into it.

"You've always been my mother. You've taught me the erotic aspect of love and the filial segment of love, which is unconditional, and something you told me a long time ago. There's nothing anyone can do to make you stop loving someone if you truly love him or her, because your love for him or her is not based on him or her, it's melded inside of you. You may stop liking them, but you'll never stop loving them."

She placed a moist face against his chest, rubbing his back.

"And do you still like me Lovey?"

He patted her on the firm soccer ball under her dress.

"More than before. Now dry your eyes, go back to your lover and let me sleep. I do have one question though."

She stepped back, frowning.

"Mommy, can I watch?"

Lightly patting him on the cheek, she turned and walked away, the soccer ball jiggling, then looking over her

[268]

shoulder, she winked at him and flipped up her dress, exposing her pantiless bottom, and shouted.

"Mommy's a bad girl."

Lovell sat on the windowsill and watched as the festivities continued. He could see all his people dancing, drinking, and laughing, as couples. Opening the liquor cabinet in his room, he cradled a bottle of wine close to his heart and danced around the room, spinning it and chuckling as he did every old dance from his childhood. He'd finished four partners by nightfall and noticed, as the Suliemans left, how people removed their clothes and ran through the courtyard shouting and jumping. Ms. Marguerite gyrated her bottom atop the long dinner table and Penny did cartwheels down the center of it, his penis standing at attention as he twirled. Lovell stroked himself as an orgy pursued, holding his wine lover in front of him, and shrieked as he exploded into the air. He awoke the next morning, naked, on the windowsill, seven lovers laid flat, as the sun welcomed him.

*****

The dining area was silent, but gasps and sniffles drew Lovell to a room not far from it. Entering, Ms. Marguerite, The Suliemans and a small group of Italians, men dressed in suits and women looking officious, all watched a twenty-foot television screen, built into the wall. The hangings were being shown on Italian television. Ms. Marguerite tried to halt him with a raised hand, but he entered and sat on the floor, close to the door. Italian subtitles translated Doris and Yusef's words. When the bodies actually dropped, the Italian women cried out and the men, in unison, lit cigarettes.

The commentator then began to discuss what he called the savagery, before the Aybilian ambassador to Italy, who

[269]

was involved in a discussion concerning the tape. Unable to deny the hangings, he focused his commentary on the crimes committed by Doris and Yusef and then proceeded to discuss the humanitarian aspect of instant death, as opposed to the bestiality of people spending their lives in prison. An Italian Bishop, and two politicians, also on the panel, defended the sanctity of life and the conversation turned completely away from the hanging. Ms. Marguerite, sniffling, turned off the television and speaking in Italian, told her guests, the Aybilian ambassador had been successful in diverting the conversation from the hanging. They, like the Bishop and the politicians, began to discuss morality. Lovell, attempted to rise, but his head spun, and he was unable to move. The images of Doris' body dropping, whirled in his head and closing his eyes, while holding his legs, which shook, and leaning his head against the wall, sat until the images stopped, and he no longer needed to secure his legs.

Lovely, are you alright?"
He rubbed both legs for assurance.
"Yes, why?"
"This gentleman asked you a question and you didn't answer".
Lovell faced a red-eyed gentleman who dabbed at each eye.
"I'm sorry. I dozed off. What was the question?"
The man spoke in Italian.
"I wanted to know, since you work in that ghastly country. Did you witness the hangings and what do you think will happen to whomever sneaked them out of the country?"
Lovell calmed his voice.
"Yes, I witnessed the hangings and if the person who sneaked out the tape is caught, he, or she, will also be hanged."

[270]

He could tell the matter-of-factness, in his voice, alarmed them. Both men and women crossed themselves.

"We pray to god, whomever this brave person is, will never be caught."

Ms. Marguerite, her eyes full of tears, enveloped Lovell with her gaze.

"I also pray this person will never be caught because they are of great value to the world and a phenomenal individual. Shall we have cocktails?

Her standing moved the group to a larger lounge where Penny, Matt, Jim, and their companions waited. Matt, head down, spoke as they entered. "Homeboy, I hope you didn't watch it again."

Lovell, now next to him, patted Matt's shoulder.

"I did, but I'm okay."

Penny sobbed into his handkerchief.

"We're not and I'm afraid when-"

"There's nothing to be afraid of. We had nothing to do with it."

The Italians had stopped and were looking at them. The man, who'd asked Lovell the question, lit a cigarette.

"I feel for all of you. I was ambassador to Aybil for two years. The Aybilians will first start with theirs. They'll persecute any Aybilian who've had contact with the Italians, and were at the hangings, then move on to everyone who was there. They will do this slowly and methodically. They will watch everyone who was there for any outside contact, and then pounce, when they think they know. They will stop at nothing and make life for all foreigners' hell to discourage any more such slip-ups. If any of you know who did this, tell them to do nothing more."

Ms. Marguerite motioned for the butler, drinks on a tray, who stood at the door, to enter.

[271]

"Let us leave all this sadness behind and enjoy food and drink. Tonight is these young men's last night in paradise and we must help them enjoy it."

She led everyone, drinks in hand, to an outside patio and walking close to Lovell, whispered.

"Penny is the weak link in your chain. He can't control his emotions. Keep whatever you're doing away from him and leave any drugs you have here!"

Smiling, she joined her guests, who requested a waltz. Ms. Marguerite pointed to another room and whispering to the butler who'd brought the drinks and taking the outspoken Italian's hands, maneuvered the group to another room where a waltz, played by a string quartet, began as they entered.   Lovell, after watching the couple's dance for an hour, went to his room, and finding the envelope with the cocaine, sat watching the Italian landscape, from his window, until the birds informed him a new day had arrived. It was time to shower, and prepare to return to Aybil. Ms. Marguerite, the Suliemans, Penny, Matt, Jim and their mates stood at the foot of the steps as Lovell descended. Matt scratched his head and blew through his nose.

"Did you sleep, Negro?"

Ms. Marguerite lightly tapped him upside the head. "His eyes will give you the answer. Sleep on the plane and get some rest when you get back to Aybil"

She kissed Lovell on the mouth. Mr. Sulieman stepped in front of Marguerite and took both his hands.

"A wise man knows when to be cautious. A fool acts, before he thinks. You are very wise.

Mrs. Sulieman took Lovell's face in both her hands.

"Remember the horses son. Remember the horses. Patience is what you must exercise to make it out son. Don't forget that."

[272]

Ali Suleiman embraced Lovell.

"Go to the room to the right, before you go through customs and find my friend Ramadan. He will guide you through without any problems. I also have a Chadian friend named Muhktar. He is always at the far end of the souk, where the garbage is. He stays there because he knows the Aybilians won't come near the filth. Plus, he has some mean mules. Stay in contact with him. He can move anything and anyone through and out of the city. Anything!"

Ms. Marguerite clapped her hands.

"Okay, let's break this up. These young men have to get their heads ready to step into the lion's mouth. They need to focus."

Penny, Jim, Matt and Lovell entered the limousine, which took them to the private airport and directly to the Aybilian airplane. They entered and all immediately went to sleep.

****

Machine gun barrels nudging them in the face awakened them. Penny put his hands in the air. Matt and Jim stood with arms folded, looking eye to eye at the soldiers. Lovell, making sure his hands were visible, spoke in his childish Arabic.

"Is there something wrong soldiers?"

One answered in perfect British English.

"Come with us gents."

Lovell touched his shoulder.

"I see you studied in England. Was it Cambridge or Oxford?"

The young soldier beamed.

"Oxford, of course."

"And you've chosen the life of a soldier? That's very noble."

[273]

The young man looked at his fellow soldiers.
"I haven't chosen anything. I have to do my military requirement before I can work. Thank God I'm part of the Royal Guard. I loathe this uniform. I'm a barrister and a criminologist."
Lovell looked at the uniforms closely. There were gold leafs on the red berets, red and gold stripes down the sides of the pants and sleeves with a gold leaf symbol on their red ascots. They were all off the plane and walking towards a limousine.
"Why is the royal guard taking us somewhere?"
The young man slowed his pace and whispered.
"I can't speak English to you anymore. You're going to the Colonel."
The Sahara desert clogged Lovell's mouth. Trying to gulp, his saliva stuck in his throat and he gagged. The soldiers stopped and allowed him to spit. As his friends walked over, Lovell whispered to them. "They're taking us to the Colonel."
 Matt and Jim said
"Oh shit".
Penny looked at his clothes.
"I wish I'd dressed differently. I don't want to die looking like this."
Lovell kissed Penny on the cheek and took his hand. "If they were going to kill us, they wouldn't be driving us in a limousine".
The soldiers sat next to the friends with their guns between their knees. They tried to speak English. One kept speaking in Italian, but Matt, Jim, Lovell and Penny, pretended they didn't understand.

[274]

CHAPTER TEN

The Colonel's palace was marble and gold, with pictures of him, on every wall. The ceilings were domed and the sun shone through in long rays and sometimes in arks. Lovell realized this was Jerzy's work and wondered if he'd ever see him again. They reached twenty foot solid gold doors, which were opened by four soldiers. A long marble table with gold legs outlined in gold sat in the middle of a ballroom. The Colonel sat at the head of the table, his afro picked out, medals on both breasts, his bushy eyebrows pulled together. The friends, Lovell, Matt, Jim and Penny were seated across from seven soldiers whose decorations demonstrated they were high ranking. The Colonel spoke in American English.

"I've heard a lot about you gentlemen and I wanted to meet you. We welcome Black Americans because your struggles are our struggles. We are both under the watchful eye of the U.S. government and it means us both no good. That is why we open our doors and treat you like a brother. Brothers must respect each other and be loyal to the family. Brothers must appreciate what the family does for them and show loyalty and obedience. When loyalty is not shown, betrayal raises its ugly head. And when betrayal raises its ugly head, people, outside the family learn the family's secrets and embarrassment occurs. Embarrassment can't be tolerated because the family unit must be maintained at all times. From family, a nation is built. When the family is betrayed, the nation is betrayed. Betrayal can't be tolerated. Enough of my words. Let us eat together."

The military men had nodded while the Colonel was speaking. No other conversation occurred. Penny whispered,

"Is this our last supper?"

[275]

The Colonel heartily ate with his hands. The other military men also ate a lot. Lovell, Matt, penny and Jim, picked at their food, unable to swallow. They drank a lot of the fresh watermelon juice, which was refilled by other soldiers whenever their glasses were empty. Lovell noticed each of the military men, after eating, left the room. Soon, there was only the Colonel, Lovell, Matt, Penny and Jim at the table. The Colonel looked at each one, while washing his hands.

"I have a special Aybilian treat for you gentlemen. Soldiers brought in seven platters and placed them on the table. They stood waiting for the Colonel's orders. He nodded his head and they lifted the tops off the platters, and then exited. On each platter was the head of each military officer who had been at the table. Penny heaved, and then fainted. Lovell gagged, and then spewed the table with his splatter. Matt and Jim sat like statues. The Colonel rose. His eyebrows were pulled together in a straight line.

"Unappreciation will not be tolerated."

He left leaving them at the table, alone with the heads. Matt lifted Penny effortlessly. Lovell and Matt trailed behind him. The palace halls were empty. Jim, with Penny on his right shoulder, walked in a crouch, his left hand holding his knife. Lovell, following Matt's movements, turned facing the opposite direction, his knife extended, so no one could get behind them. They walked in this manner until they were outside the palace doors, which they had to push open. The air woke Penny, who Jim lowered to the ground.

"Jim, are we in heaven?"

Jim's head moved back and forth, surveying the environment.

"No, we're outside the palace and very vulnerable. Get up, we have to move."

He gave Penny his hand, pulling him up. Penny, seeing the other three with their knives out, pulled his. They walked down a hill, which they hadn't noticed before, with Penny and Jim in the front and Matt and Lovell in the back. Trees secluded the land on both sides. Though they saw no one, they heard the click of rifles, and deep breathing. The palace gates opened as they reached the bottom of the hill and closed behind them. They turned around and saw the royal guard posted on both sides of the path they'd just walked and in front of the palace doors. Matt blew his nose towards the gate.

"These muthafuckas play some real mind games". Lovell shushed him, pointing to a camera, on a pole, pointed towards them. They walked about a mile of sand and called a taxi. Inside they spoke in Spanish. Jim, white knuckles showing, punched a fist in the air.

"These rag head muthafuckas want to go to war. Then war it is."

He and Matt slapped fives.

"How in the hell can you go to war against an army in someone else's country?"

Matt, eyebrow raised, chuckled.

"You tell me. You've been doing it ever since we got here, by sending those tapes. Or have you forgotten?"

Penny slapped the back of the taxi seat.

"That has to stop or we'll all end up dead. Are you all crazy? Did we not just see seven heads which had just been chopped off?"

Matt and Jim only looked at Lovell, before Matt answered.

"There're many ways to fight a war. I don't know about you Penny, but I'll never forget little Doris and Yusef swinging from those gallows."

"They shouldn't have put themselves in that position and you know it!"

[277]

Penny turned away from him, and then looked at each man. "Leave me out of whatever you're doing. It's crazy and I value my life."

He rode with his back to them to the university and walked towards his room without saying a word. Jim watched Penny swish away.

"Do you think we'll have to?"

Matt touched his arm.

"He's harmless. Don't even think about it."

They turned to Lovell. Only Matt spoke.

"And what about you?"

Lovell stared in Penny's direction.

"If you have to ask me that, you'll never know."

They parted and went to their rooms. Watching until they disappeared, he headed to the back of the cafeteria and found the Tunisians huddled together. They jumped when they saw him. Lovell saw a seven-foot shadow standing to the side and heard a mule snort.

"Muhktar, Ali sends his greetings from Italy."

The shadow didn't move. Then a graveled voice spoke in perfect Spanish.

"If you know Ali, what has he done recently?"

"He won the most valuable player award in Europe, led his team to a championship and signed a NBA contract at Ms. Marguerite's in Italy."

"What can I do for you Lovell?"

Hearing Muhktar say Lovell's name, though in another language, relaxed the Tunisians who began to take cases from the mules. Lovell could now see in the darkness. Lovell thought he heard at knife click.

"I want five pounds of smoke and three cases of drink."

Muhktar stepped into the partial light. Lovell looked up to see two white eyes, shoulders that spread like two men and a long stick coming from a mouth. It was too dark to recognize the features. The smell of sheep stung Lovell's nose. A hand, twice the size of Lovell's took his shoulder, guided him behind the mules who turned their heads, following Muhktar.

"You pay me for the drink, not for the smoke, always in dollars and never in front of these Tunisians. I came here tonight because I knew I'd meet you. You know where to find me from now on. Don't bring that white man, that he/she neither nor the other black man with you and only come once a month. This is the best clear drink you can drink. Don't drink the dark, I pee in it."

Lovell put his hand in his pocket. Muhktar held his arm. "Come to the back of the International hotel, in the garbage cans tomorrow and pay me. Now, hold out your hand. This is the smoke and the horsehair you'll need. Only work with the Tunisian with the scar. He's the only one that doesn't drink. The cases will be on your balcony tonight. Now go." Lovell left, watching the Tunisians pass a water bottle with dark drink between them. Leaning his head against the door, listening for any activity, Lovell raised his hand to knock, but held it mid air. The nerves in his hand twitched and moving to the side, placed his forehead against the wall, his hand still suspended.

"You don't have to knock, Lovely, I'm here." Danuta's voice, which he likened to the sound inside a massive tree, brought his hand to his side. She had come from the bathroom, her blond hair wet and hanging beneath her shoulders. She had on her white terry cloth robe, ankle length, pulled tightly about her, showing no skin, which she knew, could get her arrested if an Aybilian were to see her. Walking past him, she took his now limp hand and led him into her room, after glancing down the hall. Using both hands, palms spread on his chest, then pushing him with her fingertips onto her bed. She removed her robe, letting it

[279]

fall to the floor, squeezed the water from her hair onto mango sized breasts. Climbing onto the bed, and straddling Lovell, she lowered herself down on his face, moving side to side.

"It's fresh and clean for you Lovely. I've been waiting for this moment."

He ate from her fruit tree, for an extended period, then waited as she removed his clothes. Mounting her, he rode her hard, raising his body into the air and slamming into her, then wept. His cries muffled between her breasts as his seed exploded inside her. She stroked his head, whispering it's okay, I understand, until he slept, and was awakened by Danuta, telling him he had to leave. The call to prayer would be soon and people would be walking the halls. He walked to his room, face puffy with grief, until he was awakened by a knock at his door. Opening his door, Penny stood in grey sweat pants and sneakers.

"I thought you'd like to go for a walk. I know you stay in shape and I need to smooth this alcohol gut." He waited for Lovell to return from the toilet, dressed in sweats. Passing droopy-eyed Aybilians going to the first prayer, Lovell looked at the orange outlined tips of the sun.

"You thought it was earlier didn't you?"

Penny had intercepted his thoughts.

"I saw you coming from the doctor's building. How are you?"

Lovell focused his eyes on the sun's first crescent and half unzipped his sweat jacket.

"And what were you doing up so early?"

Penny punched Lovell on the shoulder.

"He was leaving the same time you were."

Looking at Penny, he could see Penny's moist hairline and smelled a slight whiff of vodka.

"He likes vodka, doesn't he?"

[280]

Penny covered his mouth.

"That's why I need to walk. I'd rather sweat it out now, than in those unairconditioned classrooms. Plus, I don't want the student cadre coming to my class chanting Jama Al- Fateh."

"Is he anyone I know?"

Penny unzipped his jacket. His white basketball shirt showing round moist pockets. The sun, vibrated in the sky and waves snaked across the air. "You have enough business of your own instead of getting into mine, Lovell Pendleton."

Lovell faked a blow at Penny. "Well excuse the hell out of me."

"You're excused. Now answer my question, Lovell. How are you doing? Your face is puffy."

Lovell took Penny's hand and they walked this way until their palm's moistness made it impossible. Lovell wiped the perspiration on his pants.

"There's no rest for the weary, Penny. No rest for the weary.

They had walked around the campus and were back at the dorms. Their shirts and pants, ready to be wrung out and both in need of a shower. Penny kissed Lovell on the cheek.

"When the weary needs someone to talk to, I hope he knows he has a friend. I'll see you when I see you, friend. I got me a high-ranking non-military government rep. Now stay out of my business."

Lovell walked to his room humming the song, *"You've Got A Friend."* After showering, Lovell smoked two bowls of hashish, made hot tea, which he poured into a thermos, filling it halfway with tea and the other half with flash, drank a half a glass of orange juice, half flash, went to class and returned to his room with an empty thermos and no

[281]

recollection of what he'd taught. Three weeks had passed
since Italy and Lovell's morning ritual had remained the
same. Jog in the mornings, smoke and drink before class,
drink during class, smoke at lunch, smoke at home, practice
his horn, practice with Penny and search. His searching
took him to Danuta's bed, the young Indian women married
to old professors and married Pakistani Muslim women
who asked Allah for forgiveness. He had seen her on the
campus walking behind her husband, a balding science
professor, slumped shoulders, whose arms and legs
dragged. Lovell had walked by their room and had seen
him on top of her, grunting and she, with eyes open, had
seen him watching her.

Later, during the day, he'd seen her in the hall, by herself.
Lovell had walked by her, then backtracked and walking
by, had touched her on the arm. He felt her shudder. He
looked up her husband's schedule and hers and discovered
she was home during the same hours and the same days as
he. Lovell had walked by her room and had not heard
anything. Looking down the hall, he'd checked to see if
anyone was coming, then had opened her door and gone
inside. She was sitting on the bed, combing her hair, only in
a robe. He'd walked to her saying,
"I know you're lonely and this older man doesn't
appreciate you. I do. I've seen you around. Seen you
watching me and I know your heart because mine is the
same."
 She'd smiled and he'd moved towards her.
" God blesses those who find love and cherish it. I have
found you, you have found me and we shall cherish it."
 Before he slid himself into her, she'd asked god to forgive
her lonely heart and welcomed him inside her.

He paid attention to the students admiring him and one,
six foot one, Fatima, had asked for help. Lovell had rubbed

[282]

his leg against hers under the table as they talked. She drew
an orange tree with a question mark. Lovell wrote 11
o'clock and she nodded yes. The girl's dorms were right
next to the orange groves and students. Dressed in his
jogging suit, he went to the orange grove and waited at the
farthest end. He saw a flame flicker in the distance. It was
from a lighter. Walking towards the light he heard whispers
and moaning. The light flickered again and Lovell walked
faster. It flickered twice and he was there. Hands touched
his face, arms, hair, and lips formed around his, the tongue
darting. Lovell felt firm breasts, a round bottom and
wetness covered his hand, which he placed between her
thighs. She grabbed his hand when he tried to put his
fingers inside her. Feeling a skirt rise, she bent over,
offering a watery anus.   Lovell studied the schedules of all
the married wives. Knew when their husbands would be
teaching, when they'd return and visited each of them
whenever their schedules permitted. Daily he saw Mrs.
Faturi on campus. She visited a friend who directed the
women's studies. Lovell noticed, instead of going towards
their home, she turned towards downtown. On his off day,
he went to the taxi stop off campus, where taxi's picked up
those going downtown. Mrs. Faturi passed in her black
Mercedes with tinted windows. She opened the door and
Lovell got in the back seat and laid down.
"You've learned how it works here, haven't you Lovell?"
"I have to learn to survive."
She looked back at him, eyeing him up and down. "Where
are you going?"
Lovell cleared his throat.
"Wherever you are."
She veered to the right then straightened out the car. "You
think I'm that kind of woman?"

[283]

"I think you're a lovely, intelligent woman who's very lonely."
He watched her sigh deeply and wiped a tear from her eye.
"How can you be so perceptive?"
"When is the last time your husband licked your valley?"
She sighed again
"And the last time you had an orgasm?"
He reached up and touched the back of her neck, then massaged it touching her hair with his fingertips. She sighed again.
"I often go to the western hotel for tea and get an Asian massage."
Lovell rubbed the back of the driver's seat before speaking.
"Go to the back by the trash cans and let me out. What room do you usually get?"
"333."
"Go to the room and go out on the balcony. I'll see you and come up."
He stood behind the trash bins until he saw
Mrs. Faturi, and then walked up the emergency stairs. Mrs. Faturi opened the door quickly and took him into the bathroom. Penny, Matt and Jim had nicknamed him sleepy because of his eyes and the Aybilian and Sudanese called him the fighter because of how he played basketball three times a week. Words fled from him, his journal dry and he and Penny's Friday gig at the American residence was wild and raucous, with him falling on his knees, screeching and honking, like Illinois Jacquet. He gyrated, licked his tongue out at women, grinded, humped his horn like Jimi Hendrix, drank on the stage and snorted cocaine between every set. The Americans loved it and every performance was packed. He watched Phil, checking him, checking Phil, checking them and Phil out. Phil standing at the corner of the bar, near the men's bathroom, never clapped, smiled,

[284]

nor said a word to him. The band members, including Penny, collapsed in their chairs after every set. Lovell had set his mind to have sex with one teacher, married, or unmarried, every Friday, Saturday and Sunday they played, before leaving the American compound and going back to the university. He'd meet them in the storage room, which also served as the band's room with sofa, tables, and chairs and had a private entrance. Matt and Jim, pretending to be smoking, stood watch while he performed with the women. They were also his drivers. Alternating Friday and Saturday, and an Aybilian drove on Sunday. Sundays, during the day, continued to be fellowship day, as they called it. Mr. Daphne gave his sermon and they all ate together. Lovell and Penny played. Brother Bibbs and Phil talked business with Matt and Jim. Lovell high, moved from conversation to conversation, moving to another side of the room whenever Khadijah approached him. Aisha was outside the bathroom as Lovell emerged, having snorted three lines of cocaine. Neck moving from side to side, hands on her hips, lips pulled together in a line, she collared Lovell, dragging him into she and Abdul's bedroom, slamming the door. He heard footsteps outside the door and stopped.

"I feel like slapping the taste out of your mouth and if I was a man and I'd knock you out. I could do it with as high as you are but I need you to hear what I have to say. How long are you going to keep doing this Lovell? How long? Huh? How long are you going to keep running from your hurt by hiding in drugs and fucking? You think staying loaded is going to wipe away your hurt? You think fucking everything moving, even other men's wives and taking out your anger on women is going to wipe away what Nidia and Ann did? Well it's not! It's not! It's not! It's not Lovell! You've been blasted every day since you've been

[285]

back. Yea, I know what you're thinking. Who told me? It doesn't matter. What matters is we love you and refuse to see you kill yourself or get killed by some jealous husband. We know it hurts and it was chicken shit. But you can't stop love and you know it. Yes, if it were me, I would have told you before. But she handled it the way she could and it's over. It's over Lovell. It's over! You have everything in the world going for you. Don't blow it by dying running. I know you hurting baby, but you have to pull it together. Accept what is Lovell. Accept it and know every woman isn't her and you're a good man, a fine, good, talented brother. Don't do this to yourself! Don't do it! You have a child on the way. Don't you want to see your child grow up? You'll be a fine father and any woman would be proud to have you. But not like you've been. You've been a low life gash man who'll stick his dick in anything and is always high. It's not you Lovell. It's not you! It's not!" Her last sentence wasn't completed because she caught him falling into her arms, wailing. His wails echoed throughout the house stopping all conversation. Khadijah, standing outside the room, stuffed her fist into her mouth, fell to her knees rocking, then opened the door and rushing to Aisha, took her place, patting his back, wiping his nose with the other end of her skirt, because where his head lay, had soaked through to her skin. He had no idea how long he'd wept. The hammers pounding in his head, his mouth cached, told him his reservoir had emptied. Khadijah sat, back straight, hair loose and hanging to her elbows, some strands on the bed, with moistened eyes, watching him. He tried to move quickly, but she steadied him, raising him slowly to a sitting position. He looked down and saw the dried, hard snot on her skirt. She covered it with the other end of her skirt, revealing a tan knee, calf and feet. Lovell stared at her leg, which she lifted up and sat on.

[286]

"I'm sorry, Khadijah."

"There is no reason to be sorry."

"I ruined your skirt and I still-"

She placed her fingers over his lips and rubbed her first finger over his top lip then across her own mouth.

"You're not alone in what you feel. I want you to heal first, and then come to me. I'll wait for you."

Lovell looked in the mirror in front of Aisha and Abdul's bed.

"I hope you're patient because right now I'm a mess."

Khadijah moved close to Lovell, pulling him to her and spoke in his ear.

"The valley of hurt is very deep Habibi (love). Sometimes when we fall into it, the rocks and thorns inside it cut deep and stick. What's important is that we realize we're in it and are willing to fight our way out. I know you are a fighter and will come out stronger than before."

She took his hand and placed it on her heart.

"Every beat is for you, Habibi. Every beat is for you."

Lovell stood, bringing Khadijah with him. Their bodies touched and she shuddered. She opened her mouth, giving her lips and tongue to him. A knock on the door pulled them apart.

"Before you answer, Habibi, I want you to know, you are the only man, besides my ex-husband, who has tasted my lips. Please cherish them. I am yours, when you're ready and you may do with me as you wish."

Someone knocked again at the door. Khadijah wiped her eyes as she and Lovell walked to it. Aisha stood outside.

"You alright, brother?"

He held up he and Khadijah's hand.

"I'll be alright.

"Well, good brother. You've got people waiting for you. It's about that time."

They had walked while speaking and were now in the living room. Everyone sat on the edges of the couch.
"Rise up Lazarus. Rise up and go forth singing the praises of the Temps, J.B., brother Charles, Ronnie Laws, Smokey, Bill and all the soul brothers from them there United States of America. Now Negro, now that you done laid your blues down, it's time for you to go blow so we can get on the good foot." Mr. Daphne did a quick turn. Lovell slapped hands with everyone and led them out the door singing "My Girl", to their cars, the American quarters and their gig. It was the first time he'd played sober in three weeks.

Horns blowing and guns being shot woke Lovell. The chant Allah Akhbar and Jami Al-Fateh echoed throughout the faculty residence. Lovell grabbed his knife and went to the bathroom. Jerzy stood shaking.
"The Iranians have stormed the American embassy and taken the diplomatic staff as hostages. The Shah is gone and Khomeini has taken control. Washing his face, Lovell noticed the date, Nov 5th, 1979. "I'm going to my room to guard my family."
Jerzy trotted to his rooms. Lovell washed, went to his room, dressed and walked towards the campus. Penny, Matt and Jim met him enroute.
"You might as well turn around. It's a holiday, the Islamic revolution has started."
They all spoke in unison.
"Let's go downtown and see the fireworks." Arriving downtown, they watched groups of Aybilians chanting and talking. Others marched, fists in the air. Whites ran and were chased by groups of Aybilians. A group approached them, pointing at Jim. Penny, Lovell and Matt formed a circle around Jim and walked him to a taxi, which had stopped. It was a Sudanese driver. They put Jim inside and the taxi sped away. The group moved on, looking for other

[288]

whites. Smoke attracted their attention because it came from the Daphne's residence. Running they saw and heard a group of Aybilian's chanting, "down with America, the great Satan", throwing rocks at the embassy. Others tried to break down the doors and a few tried to pull the bars from the broken windows. The three Americans pushed through the crowd and went towards the back entrance, which the Daphne's had told them was secret. The Aybilians were too busy to notice. They called to the Daphne's but heard nothing. Walking closer to the building they called out their names again.

"Mr. and Mrs. Daphne?"

"We're here and we're okay. We can't come out. Go get Phil and he'll know what to do."

The three looked at each other.

"Phil?"

"Yes, get Phil and he'll know what to do."

"Act like an Aybilian and you won't be noticed when you go back out."

Shouting Allah Akhbar and down with the great Satan America, they went to Abdul and Aisha's house. Abdul peeked out the window when they knocked and opened the door. He held a 45. Aisha and the kids came from different rooms where they'd been hiding.

"We have to get Phil to help the Daphnes."

Abdul got into his car with Aisha and the children and placing an Aybilian flag on the antennae, drove to the American quarters. Phil met them at the gate. The Aybilian guard had been replaced by an American they called Tex who held a shotgun. Phil hopped into the car after telling Tex to take Aisha and her children inside the compound.

"Step on it."

Abdul floored the car. Arriving at the embassy, the crowd had left. Phil, his head scanning the scene, exited the car.

"Don't let anyone come around."

They stood in front of the embassy, hands in their pockets. Voices were heard from the inside and the Daphnes called out for them to enter. Phil came out and opened the front door. The Daphne's could see the questions in their eyes. "Phil is the associate consul here. He has a contact to assist us if any real emergency occurs. This isn't a real emergency. It's a reaction to Jimmy Carter saying even the Colonel condemned the taking of the hostages. That smiling jackass should have kept his mouth shut."

He looked at them raising his eyebrows.

"I guess being black is an advantage isn't it. They've attacked all the white Americans and left you all alone. It's because of the Colonel's policies."

Matt snorted.

"Do you think they knew we were Americans?"

Mr. Daphne rubbed his baldhead.

"They knew."

Lovell kept staring at Phil who was expressionless. "We had to get Jim out of here."

"I think he'd better stay away from downtown for a while. It won't be safe for whites until this calms down."

Mr. Daphne rubbed his wife's hands.

"My love here will be out on the next thing smoking Mr. Bibbs. I'd suggest you do the same for your family.

Lovell still watched Phil. Mrs. Daphne moved to stand as Phil moved to help her, his jacket pulled open. Lovell saw a pistol.

"You all had better get back to campus. We're all right now. Abdul will take Phil back to the school."

Kissing Mrs. Daphne and shaking hands with Mr. Daphne they left the quarters and met another Sudanese cab driver who told them three Swedes, mistaken for Americans, had been hung. Reaching the campus, the chanting and marching was still going on. The taxi stopped at the gate and as they walked in, an Egyptian gardener swung from a lamppost. Friend of the Shah was written on a sign stuck to his chest. They quickened their pace, but stopped when seeing Howard, a biology professor, from Connecticut, who'd quarreled with the students about coming late, hanging from another lamppost. They ran to the dorms and Jim's room. Knocking loudly, Jim asked who was there. Identifying themselves, they heard furniture being moved before Jim opened the door. He was armed with a pistol and knives stuck into an army belt. "All hell is breaking loose. I heard them drag Howard from his room. He squealed like a pig."

Matt paced back and forth.

"Brothers we're truly at war."

Penny bit his lip. Matt and Jim took ammunition from hidden places in Jim's room. Penny touched Lovell on the arm, and spoke too loudly.

"We don't have to worry about anything. They're not bothering black people."

Matt whirled around.

"How long do think that's going to last. That brother shit is only a front. We're Americans first and black second. Don't let the propaganda fool you."

Penny stood.

"That's not what Mr. Daphne just said. I'm going to my room. I'm not at war with anyone."

"You're not but we are. And as soon as the shit hit's the fan, you'll come running to us for help, Mr. Penny Marshall. Mark my words."

Penny walked to the door.

"I don't think so. I think we're alright."

Matt and Jim looked at Lovell.

"And once again brother?"

[291]

Lovell rubbed his hands together.

"I don't trust the propaganda either. So, I'll keep my guard up and give you all the support I can. We're all Americans."

The statement made his heart race. He'd never thought of himself as an American. Being an American meant identifying with its crimes. Jim offered Lovell a gun. He refused and slapping fives walked towards his room. Jerzy waited for him outside his door, eyes sunk into his face, nose red, and hands shaking. He fell into Lovell's arms.

"The fucking Aybilians got to Kasha."

Lovell took Jerzy inside and locking his door, poured him a drink. Jerzy drank it down and held his glass out for another.

"We went out to see what was going on and left Kasha in her room. One of the Aybilians, who had a key, went into her room and raped her. She said it was the Major's son. The son of a bitch, I'm going to kill him! He's ruined her life!"

Jerzy fell to the floor weeping and slamming his head against it.

"I want to kill Lovell! I want to kill! You must help me kill him!"

Lovell helped Jerzy up and back into his chair. "Where is she now?"

"She's in Danuta's room. They've bathed her and tried to ease the pain. She's pretty torn up. She's only thirteen Lovell. Only thirteen."

His floodgates opened again.

"Jerzy, please go back to your room. I'll be there shortly."

Hugging Jerzy before he left, Lovell watched him drag himself down the hall. When Jerzy was out of sight, Lovell went to Jim's room, entered and hit the wall.

"I'm in the war. They raped Kasha, Jerzy's daughter."

Matt and Jim cursed and threw Lovell a gun. He threw it back.

"We'll never win with these. We have to use other tactics. Let's go see about Kasha and work with Danuta. You've already started fighting. I think that's the way to go."

Walking to Danuta's room, they held hands. Upon entering, Lovell noticed Kasha's bloody clothes in a corner. She was asleep on Danuta's bed. Anna sat on the bed, stroking her hair. Danuta, steel eyed, sat at her table, smoking. She motioned for them to go outside.

"Do you see what animals they are? Do you see what they did? Let's squash them in every way we can."

They all placed their hands on top of each other's.

*****

Jerzy, Anna, and their children returned to Poland two days later. Danuta made mounds of cocaine, which she gave to Matt and Jim to distribute. Lovell met Mukhtar at the western hotel and gave him bags of the drug to sell and distribute. White Americans were harassed at the university daily. Jim stayed in his room, only emerging to eat, and teach. However, his classes were empty. Lovell gave the horsehair to the Tunisians, who fed it to the Major. Danuta reported the Major was in her infirmary. His stomach, beach ball size, feet like an elephant, his throat so swollen he couldn't eat. She had inserted a tube to assist his breathing and to feed him. He suffered for two weeks, and then died. The Aybilian flag flew at half-mast and classes were cancelled.

*****

[293]

Lovell, Matt and Jim sat outside the faculty dorms, within
the courtyard; watching the Aybilian sun descend.   They
turned, hearing a car roar, stop and the sound of boots
running in their direction. Soldiers rounded the corner and
stopped pointing their guns at them. The Major's son, snot
running from his nose, reeking of whiskey, teary eyed,
moved between the soldiers and pointed a pistol at Lovell.
"I know you had something to do with my father's death
and I'm going to kill you. Not now, but soon I will get
you."
He turned and the soldiers followed him. Jim nudged
Lovell.
"You have to watch that mutha fucka, he's serious."
*****

The Sudanese taxi drivers reported strange behavior and
deaths in the city. The men walked around like zombies,
shot each other, fought and many died. Whorehouses were
raided and the secret police were employed to discover
what had taken over the young people. Lovell noticed the
Iraqi around the dorms more and more. Every morning
Lovell looked out at the village, Haba Shangira. He awoke
with the call to prayer and jogged past it. He could see
green tents now dotted the outskirts and people gathered in
them nightly.   One morning he turned towards the village
and stopped outside. People were just beginning to walk
towards the stores. The smell of fresh bread hung in the air.
He walked into the village, staying in the middle of the
street. The villagers stopped. They looked at each other,
nudging one another. Some pointed and said Haram (bad).
Lovell continued to walk. A group of men gathered,
whispering. He'd seen them in the teahouse with Mr.
Sulieman. They followed him down the street, blocking his
exit. From a photographer shop, a man emerged with his
arms open and spoke in Arabic. "My friend I see you

[294]

accepted my invitation. I didn't think you'd come so early from your English class. Come in and have some tea." Putting his arm around Lovell, he pulled him into his shop and closed the door.

"You are a fool. With the city and country the way it is, those men will kill you. My name is Basam and I was a friend of Sulieman. I saw you many times. He was going to introduce us but you know what happened."

Basam walked to the door and looked out.

"They're still out there. One will come in very soon to see what we're doing. Here are my English books. Let's pretend to study."

Lovell took the books and opened them. They were advanced grammar and composition. Words were underlined and Arabic was written on the side. He asked Basam to explain a paragraph to him in English. Basam faltered a first, but slowly explained what the paragraph said.

"You really do want to study English, don't you?"

Basam nodded as the door opened and one of the men entered. Basam poured him some tea and began to read a paragraph aloud. The man sat for a minute, looked at the book, drank his tea and left. Basam went to the window to watch.

"They're leaving. You should stay for a while and then I'll walk you back to the university. Why are you here?"

Lovell stammered.

"I don't know. I was here before and I wanted to see it again. I'm trying to face-"

"These aren't times to be sightseeing. Fathers don't trust sons and Mothers don't trust daughters. The green guards guard every village and they convince the young to tell on the old if they don't do as the Colonel's book said. Everyone is afraid."

[295]

"And what about you. Aren't you afraid?"
Basam looked out the window again.
"I'm a comedian and I have a license to say what I want sometimes. No, I'm not afraid because I know a lot and they know it. No one will bother me because I have the radio and television on my side." Basam took his book and placed it back in a drawer. He then reached under his stove and pulled out another book, covered in a brown paper bag. "This is what I really want to read but it's not allowed." He handed Lovell the novel. Opening it, the novel was the "Invisible Man" by Ralph Ellison.
"This is a great book Basam. Why can't you read it?"
"It's on a list of books which encourage heresy and bad religious practices."
"I teach this book at the university."
Basam put the book under his table.
"You do now but you won't be able to tomorrow. You stay in the dorms at the Jamahariya, don't you?"
Lovell nodded.
"I'll come and see you every day and we will be friends. I'll show you the real Aybil. Now come with me. I'll walk you out of the village and to the university. You know it's that close to us and no one in this village has ever been there. They're afraid."
"Afraid of what, Basam?"
"They're afraid of learning something different which might change them from what they think is right."
They left the shop and walked down the middle of the Haba Shangira Street. Basam held Lovell's hand and talked to him, staying very close to him, as they walked through the village. Once out of the village, he stepped back, only a bit, but continued to hold Lovell's hand as they walked to the university. Entering the faculty dorm, foreign professor's eyed Basam as if he smelled. Lovell wrapped his arm in

Basam's and walked up the stairs to his room. Jim and Matt met him coming up the stairs. They gave him a what the hell is this look as they passed. Lovell took Basam to his room and offered him some mint tea. Basam drank a sip and handing it back asked for more sugar. Basam put four teaspoons of sugar in his tea and looked out the window at his village.

"You can see my village clearly from your room. Is that one reason you came?"

"It could be. I also want to know the people."

"You knew the Suliemans, they were Aybilians, but very different."

"I love them. They were very kind to me."

"Sulieman was a good man. He didn't deserve what happened. But then again, life isn't fair."

"Did he take you downtown to the resting places?

"No."

"Do you want to go?"

Lovell looked at his clothes.

"I think I need to change clothes. I've been running."

Basam asked for more tea.

"Change and we will go."

Lovell showered and changed into street clothes.

Downtown had changed since the attack on the American embassy. Soldiers were on every corner. Only a few men sat in cafes. Those who did, sat with soldiers. No westerners were on the street.   Lovell and Basam passed the souk market and turned to the right, walking towards the ocean. He looked over his shoulder, both ways, and went into an alley that Lovell hadn't noticed. A brick building with tall blue doors stood in front of them. Basam knocked three times and the door opened. Red lights hung in rows from the ceiling, as did colored material. Music could be heard coming from different rooms and cushions flat with backs, covered the floors. Basam sat on the cushions and a black woman prepared them tea. As she placed the tea on the table and turned to leave, a group of women, all black, slim, tall, wearing see through veils and pants with a string of pearls around the middle, came out dancing. They moved their bodies in front of Basam and Lovell. Laughter came from another room as a door opened. Men came from other rooms and sat around drinking tea and whiskey, as the women danced. Lovell recognized some of the men from Haba Shangira. Basam touched Lovell on the arm.

"These are women from Somalia and Ethiopia. Their country is very poor and they come here to work. This is the only work they can find. You see these men, they are all good Muslims. They pray, go to the mosque five times a day, and give to the poor what they can. However, they're still men. One of these women is for you if you want them. I must tell you though, refusing will insult the owner who knows you're here and a new guest."

Lovell watched the parade of dancing women and chose an almond colored Somalian with green eyes. Walking to her room, she told him her name was Sophia. Lovell emerged from the room satisfied. Basam waited for him and they went to have tea afterwards. Sitting in the outside café, people approached Basam and shook his hand. He took Lovell by the hand and they walked the streets until reaching a building with antennas. It was the television station where Lovell had been when he first arrived. Entering, he and Basam went to a smaller studio. Lovell watched as Basam was made up, given a costume wear, half a clown and half a person, and a bag, which he carried, in front of the camera. Basam's skit, recorded live, was about people having a lot of money, and acting like a clown as a result. The studio technicians applauded when he finished. Leaving the studio, Lovell had to say, "You're famous."

Basam patted Lovell on the back.

"Not as famous as you."

Riding back to the university, Basam looked out the window.

"You see this beautiful country. Look at the orange trees, the grapes, the corn, the sorghum, the farmers and the sheepherders with their looks. This is my country and it is beautiful. We have the ocean, but there is no fish in the city. It's given to the soldiers. I swear, they should put the military in the barracks and keep them there. They are good to fight, but not to rule."

Lovell looked at the taxi driver and wondered if he spoke English. Basam continued to watch his country. When they got to the university, Lovell went to his room. He watched Basam walk across the field and disappear into Haba Shangira.

*****

Matt and Jim left Lovell after class the next day. "Why did you bring an Aybilian into the faculty dorms? He could be a spy."

Lovell looked from Matt to Jim, their faces were twitching.

"He saved my life in Haba Shangira. I think I can read people as well as anyone. He's no spy. He's on television and is quite progressive. I spent the day with him."

Matt's lips curled.

"You got to be careful man. We're at war."

Lovell stared straight ahead.

"I know what we're at. Trust me."

Jim patted Lovell on the shoulder.

[299]

"We're not worried about you. It's the company you may keep."

"I told you to trust me."

They parted at the dorms, Matt and Jim walking towards the orange fields. Lovell went to Danuta's room and knocked on the door. One of the Polish professors sat drinking a beer. Lovell started to back away but Danuta pulled him inside.

"This is professor Griory and this is Professor Pendleton." The Polish professor drank his beer in one gulp and left the room. Danuta raised an eyebrow and chuckled.

"He thinks because I'm here alone he can come by, drink and have something on the side different from his wife. What a fool. He won't come back now that he's seen you. Where have you been Lovely and how are you?"

Lovell flexed his arm, showing a muscle.

"I'm strong, clear, ready and determined."

"And how is your lovely heart?"

"My heart is healing and getting stronger every day."

"And is there a place for a Polish doctor in your heart?"

Lovell acted as if he were taking his heart from his chest and offering it to Danuta.

"What part do you want?"

Danuta changed from her floor length dress, in front of Lovell and put on her long, full bathrobe.

"I'll return shortly and carve a piece of your heart."

Lovell went to the men's bathroom and using his shirt, washed his upper body, genitals, feet and returned to Danuta's room, where she awaited him with pieces of fruit on different parts of her body. He awoke to Danuta's hands.

"Lovell, you have to go. Someone has stopped outside my door, three times. I'm afraid."

[300]

He went to the door and listened. Peering out, the hall was empty. He went into the men's room and walked down the hall, leaving her building and entering his. Matt and Jim stood outside his door. "They've been in every room. They were in yours too. We don't know what they were looking for, but it was serious. How's the doctor? We keep our eyes on our brother. We wouldn't want anything to happen to you."

Jim paced.

"What's wrong with you?"

Jim stopped and made circles on the floor.

"That damn Iraqi is leading this search. He's onto something."

Lovell opened his door and looking inside, saw his room had been turned upside down. He showed it to Matt and Jim.

"They didn't do this to anyone else's room. It's you they're after."

Lovell's stomach churned.

The next day Dr. Faturi called him into his office. "Sit down Lovell."

Lovell studied Faturi's face. The lines around his eyes had grown deeper.

"You know these are bad times and there is a lot happening in the country. You were at the television station with Basam Akbar. He's been arrested for subversiveness and they might want to talk to you."

Faturi shuffled some papers.

"I wouldn't leave the campus if I were you."

Faturi's silence and downcast eyes, signaled to Lovell he could leave. Leaving, he again marveled at the Aybilian sunset, which covered the entire sky.

*****

[301]

They came in the morning, opening his door and pulling him out of bed. The soldier's allowed him to get dressed, but he couldn't take anything with him. Entering the police vehicle, he saw that Penny sat in the back, his right eye closed and lips swollen. He began to cry as soon as he saw Lovell.

"I didn't do it. I didn't do it."

Lovell looked back at the soldiers who sat in the front seat of the vehicle, leaving Penny and Lovell alone.

"Didn't do what?"

"I didn't kill Ahmed. They found him hacked to death and because we were lovers they think I did it. I didn't. They beat me trying to make me confess."

Lovell noticed the soldiers had opened the window. He covered his mouth signaling Penny to be quiet. Penny continued to cry and repeated I didn't do it. The van stopped and the soldier's opened the door, motioning Lovell and Penny to come out. They were taken into a military barracks. The soldier sitting behind the desk was the Major's son. He stood upon seeing Lovell and Penny.

"I told you I'd get you for killing my father."

Penny's body shook and urine wet the front of his pants. Falling to his knees, Penny covered himself. The Major's son jerked his head and the soldier's dragged Penny away, screaming.

"Your friend screams like a woman. Pretty soon you'll be able to hear a different kind of scream coming from him."

Lovell heard Penny call his name.

"He's done nothing. Why do you torture him? I think it's me you want."

The Major's son licked his lips.

"What are you saying?"

Lovell looked towards where Penny had been dragged.

[302]

"I'm saying take me and let him go."

His teeth showing, the Major's son shouted something in Arabic Lovell didn't understand. Penny was brought from the back, naked. The soldiers took him to the door, threw him outside and flung his clothes at him. Grabbing Lovell by both arms and twisting them back, they took him to a room with chains hanging from the ceiling. He was hoisted up by his wrists and stripped naked. The soldiers then hooked sand bags to the chains and slammed them against his sides until he felt something wet on his thighs. Looking down, Lovell saw blood running in streams, from his penis. More slams and it ran from his anus. Turning him upside down they beat him on the bottoms of his feet. Lovell chanted his mantra until red flashes appeared before his eyes and blackness swallowed his mind. He awoke to Mahalia Jackson singing and Khadijah sitting next to him on a bed. He couldn't lift his arms, his feet were bandaged, he was unable to sit up and both hands were three times their normal size. Khadijah called out, he's awake. Mr. Daphne walked into the room. "Rise up Lazarus." he roared, his face covered in tears.

*****

Lovell, wincing as he sat up, couldn't grasp the clips, which held the bandages on his feet. He thought this must be how boxers felt when trying to grab something with their gloves. Khadijah spread her hands against his chest, guiding him back to the bed and undid the wraps. Knife thrusting pain grasped his breath as he lifted his right arm, for support, placing it around Khadijah's neck. Watching Mr. Daphne's soaked face, he stood as electric needles pricked first the bottoms of his feet, then spread up his calves. Mr. Daphne touched Khadijah on the shoulder.

[303]

"Remove his arm."

Khadijah squeezed Lovell's hand, and he bit his lips.

"No, I won't. His feet are the size of an elephant's and you want to act manly. I won't do it. No disrespect intended sir."

Lovell kissed her on the cheek. His jaw made a clicking sound and he spoke through his teeth because he was unable to open his mouth.

"Let me go."

Khadijah covered her face and stepped away, watching him teeter. Jaws flexing, pucker mouthed, Lovell slowly walked to Mr. Daphne, who took one hand, as Khadijah took another. They walked into the Daphne's living room, where Matt, Abdul, Jim, Penny and Aisha, awaited him. Penny ran to Lovell, grabbing him around the waist, weeping. Lovell let go of Mr. Daphne's hand and touched Penny on the head.

"You're hurting my ribs you little muthafucka."

Holding Lovell's hand he and Khadijah guided Lovell to a chair.

"He's going to be alright. Did you hear what he said?"

Penny used his silk handkerchief to wipe his eyes. Jim, red eyed, raised a clenched fist.

"I knew you'd make it back."

Lovell looked around at the group gazing at him and looking away. He spoke through his teeth.

"Do I look that bad?"

There was a collective dropping of heads. Aisha ran from the room into the kitchen followed by Khadijah. He heard the two women weeping. "What happened to my mouth?" Mr. Daphne had walked to the window and stood with his back to Lovell, while speaking.

"They broke your jaw son."

Lovell turned to Matt.

[304]

"Give it to me straight, Matt. How do I look?"

Matt clasped his hands.

"Do you remember Anthony Quinn in Requiem for a Heavyweight, when he looks in the mirror?"

Lovell inhaled and exhaled, pain throbbing in his sides. "Yes."

Matt winked at Lovell.

"Negro, you look worse."

Lovell tried to smile, but the stinging in his lips, prevented him. Touching his lips, he felt stitches. "They busted up my mouth too?"

Matt's blink answered the question.

"You have four broken ribs, a broken jaw, busted lips, a severe concussion, a ruptured eardrum and your eyes look like purple plums with slits in the middle. Your nose has also been reset because they broke it. Therefore, my brother, you won't be playing basketball for a while."

Lovell pointed to the kitchen door.

"Close it. I need to ask you men a question."

Abdul closed the kitchen door. Mr. Daphne sat next to Lovell.

"Did they sodomize me?"

All the men laughed to tears, and then, all cried, except Penny, who spoke with flexing jaws.

"They would have except I teased them into taking me instead. I was through with all of them in minutes. What a bunch of deprived animals."

Jim slammed his fist into his open palm.

"Yea, and I bet you enjoyed every minute of it. It was because of you-"

Mr. Daphne stood, interrupting.

"I told you two we've had enough of that. There is no blame."

[305]

Jim sucked his teeth, then stopped, seeing Lovell staring at his hands.

"They held you up by your wrists and the Major's son stomped your hands. Pussy here watched while they went up his dirt road.

Lovell threw Penny a kiss.

"Thanks Penny. I love you."

Penny spoke through hands covering his face. "It was the least I could do."

Jim's mouth opened and closed. Lovell felt something trickle from his eye. Touching it and looking at his fingers, he saw blood.

"Abdul, would you get me mirror?"

Matt stood over Lovell.

"Man, you don't want to do that."

Lovell faked a blow at Matt.

"I can't look that much worse than Anthony Quinn."

Abdul left and returned with the mirror. Handing it to Lovell, he left the room. Looking at himself, a muffled quick shriek escaped from him. Purple welts covered his forehead, jaws, silver wire guarded his teeth, beneath jumbo sized lips and cotton protruded from his left ear. Placing the mirror face down, he saluted Matt.

"Damn, man, if I didn't know myself, I wouldn't recognize myself. I look like a damn monster."

Matt handed him a handkerchief to wipe away the blood, mixed with the tears.

"I told you that, Negro. Don't worry, we got some real ghetto shit for their asses."

Mr. Daphne's fist pounded the couch.

"It's just that kind of attitude and behavior that created this situation. You think you're fighting against a few individuals when you're actually fighting a regime. Believe me sons, you'll only end up dead. Especially now with this

[306]

religious fervor about to take over this entire area. Lovell
was rescued only because his death would have created an
international incident. He was lucky. You've all been
lucky. You know, they know one of you, or all of you are
responsible for that hanging and all that footage being
aired. It took place at the university and you were the only
ones with the Italian contact. Don't write yourselves a
ticket your ass can't cash. You're all on lockdown now. Do
anything else and you'll disappear. Believe me sons, the
next time I won't be able to help you."
Nostrils aflame, he gave each man in the room an I'll kick
your ass look.
"Sons, you have forty five minutes to get Lovell back to the
campus. Bibbs, I'd suggest you get your wife and her friend
home. And Mr. Marshall, I'd suggest a little discretion on
your part. Your lifestyle has become hazardous to your
health. Good night all. I'll see you again next Friday. You
can show yourselves out."
 Aisha and Khadijah came from the kitchen, with Khadijah
pushing a wheelchair. She kissed Lovell on the mouth, in
front of everyone before she, Aisha and Abdul, left. Lovell
was forced to ride in the wheelchair, then loaded into a
university car. He was told on the ride to the campus, he'd
been in and out of consciousness for a week. Matt and Jim
had gone to Mr. Daphne's residence and told him about
him about Penny's arrest. Mr. Daphne had appealed
directly to the Colonel, who'd called and stopped his being
tortured. During the week he'd been unconscious, the
embassy had been attacked again. All American families
had been evacuated, the school emptied, closed, and all
western professors had been confined to the campus six
days a week. They were allowed to shop, in town, one day
a week, under guard, until further notice. However, only
they had come to town to see Lovell, who'd been taken to

[307]

the Daphne's residence, though the Mrs. had been evacuated with the other Americans. Lovell also learned the Colonel has issued a special apology to Mr. Daphne, for what had happened to Lovell and assured him Lovell would be paid for the days he missed at school and those who'd tortured him would be disciplined. Mr. Daphne hadn't believed a word because nothing happened to any American, without the Colonel being informed first. Lovell had been stretched out in the back of the university van. Looking up, he saw the university arch.

"Hey brothers, when I get out of this van, I'll walk to my room. I don't care how much pain I have to endure. I never want them to have the satisfaction of seeing me disabled."

An "I hear you" echoed throughout the van as it stopped, but Penny interrupted.

"You he men can pat each other on the back all you want. However, he can't get any shoes on those feet and you know how filthy the ground is here." "We'd thought about that already Miss Penny. There are crutches in the back seat where he is. All he has to do is get them and hoist himself up." Penny gave Matt the finger.

"You're so smart I can't stand you.

Lovell looked at his puffy hands, then opened and closed them, feeling the sting with each movement.   Opening the door Matt, Jim and Penny stood guard while Lovell, grunting, crawled on his elbows to the open car door, then sitting up and bringing his legs around, grabbed the crutches from Matt and growling, stood on them without his feet touching the ground.

"Let's move brothers."

Breathing through his nose, ears hot and his shirt plastered to him, he made it to the stairs without resting, but biting his inner lip. He pulled himself up each stair, being flanked by his three buddies. Resting at the top of the stairs, Penny wiped his forehead.

"You look like you just stepped out of the shower, Lovely."

"I feel like I need one, Pen Pen."

Rubbing their hands together, Matt and Jim's heads, swiveled around.

"I got it from here, brothers."

"You got what fool? You're defenseless."

Jim's fist made a popping sound in his palm.

"I can make it on my own from here. I appreciate your help. Now go to your rooms. I'll make it."

A heavy sigh circled through Matt, Jim and Penny, then turning on their heels, they left him alone, maneuvering down the hall to his room. Opening his door, Lovell smelled sheep.

"Close the door black man and don't turn on the light."

Lovell sat on his bed and lit a candle. Muhktar squatted in a corner, concealed in a black caftan and head wrap, with only his mooneyes showing surveying the room.

"Are you one of those turn the cheek Negroes or do I see an African man poised for battle."

Lovell's oversized hands covered the bottom half of his face.

"I was born a warrior, and you have yet to see me fight."

Mukhtar reached across the table from the corner and extinguished the candle with his fingers.

"Then know this African warrior. The man who flogged you, stole your friend's daughter's treasure and back humped your friend in Fazan. He favors an emerald-eyed Ethiopian named Celie and he will come to take her from the blue door house tonight because he can't live without her. She tells me he belongs among my sheep and she will gladly offer him as a sacrifice. However, she wants three thousand U.S. dollars for travel to get out of Aybil. The

[309]

price is right. I gave it to her. Give me the money for her and they will only find his face and skin. It will be a pleasure to treat him as he treated that young girl and skin him like I skin my sheep."

Lovell went to his incense holder and took the money from the bottom. He added another thousand.

"Thank you brother. This is only one battle in a shameful war."

Lovell heard the rustle of bills and an exhale.

"I only asked you for three thousand African American warrior. This will be part of your reserves. I have a feeling you will need it for the future."

A fist touched Lovell's heart twice, something dropped in his lap and then he saw a long figure slide across the floor, open the balcony door and go out. Closing the door with his foot, Lovell saw Mukhtar's shadow take something from his pocket and heard a rubber band pop, the breaking of glass, darkness in the dorm's courtyard, then heard movement down the dorm's wall. Lovell waited until doors were opened. He heard voices asking what happened. Turning on his light, he fingered a freezer-sized packet of white powder. Opening it, he tasted Epsom salt. Taking three of his cooking pots, then lifting a bottle of water with his arms, filled them with water to be warmed, for his feet and hands. Three taps awakened Lovell. Darkness had still spread its wings across Aybil. After knocking over the now cold water in the pots, knife in hand, Lovell, making sure the double chain was across the door, eased the door open. Danuta, red eyed, stood, opening and closing her fists.

"Please let me in Lovely. I can't sleep."

Removing the latches he allowed her to enter.

"I couldn't sleep and went to my office. I called Poland. Kasha was pregnant and killed herself. She jumped off

Jerzy and Anna's roof. She was only a child, Lovely. Only a child."

She laid beside Lovell. Her body spasmed. Her grief splattered his left shoulder as his pillow caught the pain pouring from both their eyes. She cried until she finally exhausted, fell asleep. The call to prayer startled them.

"I'm sorry about what they did to you Lovely. I see the swelling in your hands and feet have gone down. I am angry about what they did to Kasha and you. I will make them pay."

"Is it they, or he, Danuta?"

She wiped the sleep from lined eyes.

"It's them Lovely. She told me, and only me, the others held her down while he took her. They would all do it if they could, to any woman who is not like they want. Don't defend them because you know one who has shown some humanity."

Danuta stormed out causing the room to shake as she slammed the door.

******

Feet wrapped in towels, Lovell slid to the communal bathroom, showered, shaved and returned to his room before anyone could see him. Drinking tea through a straw, and listening to the hacking of faculty going to the bathroom, he exercised his hands, feet, and mouth, by opening and closing them quickly, then soaked his face in warm water and Epsom salt to ease the swelling. Danuta's three-knock signal moved him to open his door again, without being armed. She and Penny carried baskets of fruit and vegetables. Danuta sat him down and examined the wires holding his mouth together, while Penny placed the fruit in his blender, and spoke before grinding it.

[311]

"Here's your breakfast, lunch and dinner. You won't be having Danuta for a snack with your mouth like that."
Danuta gave Penny the finger.
"No, but I can have him, even though I now have to share him with that Arab woman."
Penny turned on the blender, giving Lovell a quick glance. Lovell and Penny understood the salt inside her words. Khadijah, also a doctor, had maneuvered her way into working in the university medical clinic with Danuta during the day as her assistant for a couple of hours, and at night as the emergency doctor for the university and Haba Shangira, along with a gay Moroccan doctor. He recalled when she came to his room first with Danuta. Walking behind Danuta, Lovell saw her, and she mouthed, "I'd do anything to be with you." Danuta's body had stiffened, then turned to Khadijah, and back to Lovell. She allowed Khadijah to bathe him, change his bandages, and after asking Khadijah to leave, sucked in air and staccato bursts, her bottom lip quivering, imprisoning her tears.
"So this Arab woman has now captured your heart, Lovell? You don't have to answer. A woman knows when another woman has the man's heart she loves because she's in touch with that feeling when she's around him. I'll not stand in her way Lovely."
Khadijah came alone or with the Moroccan doctor after that, and was allowed to do so because she was a doctor, and not an Aybilian. Bribing the Moroccan doctor at night by staying silent about the boyfriends who visited him. They partied, staying high on Danuta's cocaine. She would sometimes dress as a man, or pretend to make her rounds. They laid naked together, drinking from each other's mouths, finger tasting the fruit from each other's bodies, reading Neruda poems out loud, discussing the future and having hushed conversations about the world and beyond.

[312]

Hands aflame, he once tried to pull her on top him, but she held his arms.

"Not like this Habibi. Not until you're well, and we're not in this situation where we're watching the door, afraid someone will enter and flog us."

She used her hands to release his seed, letting it escape into her mouth. He learned of her wish to heal during this time. Her love of children, boxing, soccer, and basketball. How there was a competitive side to her nature, and how she would hold her point, defending it with solid logic and support. He grew to love the sister in her as he called it. The stand up for yourself and willingness to sacrifice, and stand beside her man. She attributed this to spending a lot of time with her paternal grandmother, who made her fight back when girls attacked her for having what they said was good hair, being light skinned and the professor's daughter.

Danuta whispered into Lovell's ear, while darting her tongue in and out of it.

"I'll remove these in two weeks. You don't have to wear them as long as they say. The body will heal itself. I have to get to the clinic. The unwashed Arab and Indian women will be waiting. I have something for them."

Kissing Lovell she left, leaving him alone with Penny.

"Did you hear that Lovely? She knows about Khadijah. Our secretive, militaristic comrades have loose lips."

He handed Lovell the blended fruit drink.

"She knew before they told her because Khadijah has been taking care of me. It's good she knows where she stands."

Penny tapped Lovell on the chin with his pinky. "First there was Nidia, and now Khadijah. Do you really think she hasn't always known where she stands with you? Don't be naïve. I thought you knew more about women than what you're showing. Even Khadijah knows her place with you. Third fiddle. And now, with your babies en route, maybe

[313]

fourth. Now drink your juice, I have to go teach. I'll see you later."

A kiss between them ended the conversation. Lovell sipped his drink, thinking of the twins. One for me, and one for her, he said aloud, and gasped thinking about raising a child, either a boy, or girl, by himself. Texas was out of the question. The Harbor, a thriving graveyard was so small you could do something on one side of town and before you got to the other side, everyone already knew was not even a consideration. Aybil was a stone to step on passing through Africa. Italy? Well, it was Miss Marguerite, her opulence, and the Suliemans, who now represented family. Looking at his calendar he noted Nidia was six months pregnant now. Six months. Three more and he'd be simmering in the nectar of fatherhood. Even more so if Nidia agreed to give him one of the twins. He remembered reading about how twins, separated at birth, always felt the presence of the other, and longed for them. He wondered how Khadijah would feel raising another woman's child. He knew she would accept his child. She would want one of her own with him. He imagined a child with her would have fifty cent size curls on his head, and a full mouth. He would be hairy, like her, with mahogany skin. Someone trying his door, severed his thought. They tried again, turning the doorknob. Lovell, easing the latch across the door, opened it stepping back. He was able to see, Faturi, Mrs. Faturi and Eileen Dwyer.

"We're the welcoming back committee. Here to hail the fallen hero."

Lovell opened his door, knife behind him, backpedaling to the couch. Groaning, for emphasis, he stretched out on the couch. Mrs. Faturi and Eileen's eyes misted. Faturi's Adam's apple bobbed up and down.

"I want to insure you there's no pressure for you to return until your face, I mean, until you begin to look, uh, until you're able to teach. You'll be paid as if you're teaching. One of the teaching assistant's will be teaching your classes."

Faturi extended his hand. Eileen stared out Lovell's window, tears dripping from her chin. Mrs. Faturi rose, covered her face and ran from Lovell's room. Faturi inhaled, his shoulders rising.

"I'm very sorry Lovell. I'm sorry this was done to you. That boy is cruel and dangerous."

He looked at Lovell's floor.

"Can you speak?"

Nodding, Lovell watched Eileen go to his window, turning her back to them.

"I can speak. I just don't know if you understand me."

He had to repeat his words. Eileen began to sob. Faturi stood.

"I'm sorry Lovell. I'm so sorry. We have had our differences, but no one deserves to be treated like you have. I am ashamed people have treated you this way. You are doing us a great service and we have maligned you. I want you to know this is not indicative of the Aybilian people. This is the military and whenever they pull a string, we all jump. Eileen?"

Eileen now sat on Lovell's bed.

"I'm going to stay and help Lovell a bit. I'll be there directly. My class isn't for another hour." Back stiff and head raised, Faturi stepped towards Eileen.

"I suggest you come with me. You are a married woman and it would not be proper for anyone to see you leaving a single man's room. Your rep."

"You can shove all that Aybilian crap, Abubakar. You know I don't buy it and I could give a good fuck about my

[315]

reputation. I've been here for eleven years and you know, I know how things work. I'll come when I'm damn ready." Faturi's thumb and first finger made circles against each other.

"You knew how things worked, Eileen Dwyer. You don't know how they're going to work from now on. Neither do I. A revolution has taken place in Iran and life for all of us, will never be the same. I will leave you here now. But if I were you, I'd not dally here. It could be hazardous to your health."

He looked from Eileen, to Lovell and exited Lovell's room. "Did he just threaten me?"

Eileen put the latch across Lovell's door.

"I've been here eleven years and in Algeria for five years. I know these Arabs like I know the back of my hand. It'd take a lot more than sniveling Abubakar Faturi to scare me. "She sat on Lovell's bed and lifted his feet.

"Well mate, you look a lot better than the pictures I saw." Lovell pulled his feet away from her. Eileen put them back, this time in her lap.

"You saw a picture of me?"

"I've been here eleven years Lovell. I know the people able to pull a coup de tat. I saw a picture of you laying on the barracks floor before you were rescued. Bloody mess you were. Not as bloody as he is."

Eileen took an eight and a half by eleven photograph and handed it to Lovell. It was the severed head of the Major's son with a pained expression on his face.

"Here's another one."

The man's headless body lay sprawled out in a street. It had been skinned showing the bloody epidermis layer, the first layer under the skin. A dark purple pool of blood from the pit of its back to the mid-thigh, covered the ground and attracted his attention.

[316]

"That blood you see is from someone having driven their long rod up his arse while he was still alive. They skinned him alive too."

He handed her the pictures.

"They beat me too it."

Eileen massaged Lovell's feet.

"Your feet are still swollen, Lovell. Lay back and relax."

Closing his eyes, her velvet fingers brought sleep. Hands raised his robe and the tip of a tongue, teased the big vein of his member.

"Stop."

He spoke through his throat and sitting up, lifted Eileen's head.

"What's the matter Lovell? Don't you like it?"

"I like it, but I'm not into it."

"Into what? Sex?"

The left side of her mouth twitched and she sucked her teeth.

"No, I'm not into married women, and my heart is somewhere else."

Eileen wrapped a curl around her finger.

"Oh, I guess you believe in fidelity and your heart's between that forty something Polish doctor and that Arab woman you've yet to fuck. That's some kind of fidelity. Two women."

She stood and backed to his door.

"It's more about respecting myself and karma."

She stood at the door, facing him, her hand behind her back, touching the doorknob.

"Karma? You mean that what goes around comes around crap? I don't believe in it."

Lovell picked up his pots and approached the door. "I do. Whenever I've been involved with a married woman, nothing ever turns out right."

[317]

Chuckling, the left side of her mouth and left eyebrow raised, she opened the door.

"That's guilt mate. I don't believe in it. It's usually about something you can do nothing about."

Making sure he had his keys, he ushered Eileen from his room.

"This I can. You're beautiful and I love that midnight hair and those almond eyes. And for a white girl, you've got booty for days. If we were both free, we'd dance. But pretty lady, both our dance cards are full."

Eileen walked ahead of him, and didn't look back.

"Not mine."

He heard her footsteps clacking down the steps as he pushed open the bathroom door, which was normally left open. Entering, he encountered Rhineheart, kicking and punching two young Aybilians, whose backs were against the wall. Lovell dropped his pots, and stepped forward, with bawled fists. The Aybilians, taking their eyes off Rhineheart, looked towards Lovell. Rhineheart, seeing their distraction, leaped forward, arms straight and extended, simultaneously catching both on the jaw. Knees buckling, they crumbled to the floor, and Rhineheart, stepping back, used their heads for footballs and kicked extra points, causing their heads to bounce off the walls, blood and teeth splattering. Lovell pulled Rhineheart away.

"We've worked hard to keep this bathroom clean and they keep coming in here and using it. They leave their shoe prints on top of the toilet, don't flush it and use our shower because we always have hot water, then leave it dirty. Fucking disgusting filthy Arabs, I hate them. They blow their noses on the floor, spit everywhere and never clean up after themselves. You better get your water and leave Lovell, because I have to drag theses scum bags out of here

[318]

and I don't want anyone to see you. That's all they need to come after you again."

Lovell filled his pots. Leaving the bathroom, he watched Rhineheart grab both young men by the collars and drag their limp bodies down the hall. Before entering his room, he saw Rhineheart lift each Aybilian, carry them through the door, then return to the bathroom. After soaking his feet and hands, and drinking the blended fruit from his fruit basket, he stretched out to read Auto De Fe, a new novel Penny had left for him. Having dozed, he was awakened by the chant, Jami Al Fateh, Jami Al Fateh, Jami Al Fateh. He grabbed two knives and placing a chair in front of his door, opened his balcony windows to insure an escape route. The chanting grew louder, closer, entered the courtyard and came up the steps. He heard pounding on a door, shrieks, the thuds of blows being thrown, then the chanting again and shouting in Arabic and German. Doors and windows opened on balconies in the faculty dorms. Lovell, still armed, crawled onto his balcony and watched a crowd of Aybilians, led by the mangled faced Aybilians Rhineheart had fought, put a noose around Rhineheart's neck, secure the rope onto the lamppost, and together pull Rhineheart into the air. Feet twitching and jerking, hands tied behind his back, blood spurted from his nose, ears, and only the whites of his eyes showed. Urine squirted down his pants legs, while the crowd chanted. Joan, his wife, stood outside the crowd, her arms in a v shape, head looking to the sky, mouth opening and closing. Rhineheart ceased to move. The Aybilians, letting the rope go, turned in formation, still chanting Jami Al Fateh, Jamil Al Fateh, Jamil Al Fateh, letting Rhineheart's body plummet to the ground. Balcony doors closed, and Joan was left standing in the same position, her hands now opening and closing. Lovell stood after the crowd had disappeared. The chanting was fading

[319]

in the distance. About to re enter his room, he saw Danuta pull Joan's arms down, give her an injection and help her into the building. Rhineheart's soiled body, one shoe now off, lay in the courtyard. Lovell sat on the balcony drinking tea and watching the flies swarm around Rhineheart's body and the rope, which had hung him. It had been three hours. Faculty members had come from their classes and no one had touched the body, except Lovell who had struggled down the steps and had covered the body with a sheet, after removing the rope from around Rhineheart's neck and carried it to his room. Still not full strength, he was unable to move Rhinehart's corpse by himself. Still watching his colleagues corpse, he ignored the knock on his door until it turned into pounds. Opening it, Faturi, brandy coming from his nose and saliva dripping from the corners of his mouth, handed him a packet.

"You've been given a brief leave of absence to Egypt. Here's your ticket. You heard me say this morning life was changing. Now you see. You can leave whenever you want. I'd suggest tomorrow."

Taking the ticket Lovell pointed to his balcony, then going back to it and retrieving the rope, handed it to Faturi, who stepped back, refusing to touch it. "And what about Rhineheart?"

"You westerners will have to handle that yourself. I've spoken to your friends. They should be here soon."

Lovell couldn't feel his legs walking back to the balcony. Perspiration trickled from his hairline. He watched Matt and Jim tie a cord around the body, hoist it onto their shoulders and carry it out of the courtyard. He heard their unison steps approaching his door and a knock. Opening the door, he handed Matt the rope.

"I saw the whole thing. He beat two of their asses for using the toilet and they retaliated."

[320]

Jim uncoiled the rope and wrapped it around his arm.
"This is another declaration of war and they've drawn
blood again. First with you and now Rhinehart. From now
on, like in a war, anything goes. They don't know who
they're dealing with but they'll soon find out".
He and Matt pumped fists. Matt looked at Lovell's feet.
"Did you get your exit stamps?"
Lovell opened his packet and found the five pieces of paper
with the stamps from each ministry, allowing him to leave
the country.
"Yea, I got them."
He could feel Matt's question.
"Don't worry, I'll be able to walk. I'm going to get a
massage and soak these monsters all night. What time do
we leave tomorrow?"
Matt and Jim extended closed fists to him.
"We'll be here at the first call to prayer."
Lovell touched their fist with his.
"I need you guys to do me a favor and get Danuta to come
here."
They made humping motions and laughing left his room.
He soaked his feet in Epsom salt until Danuta knocked on
the door and entered without waiting for him to say
anything. She lifted his feet and winked at him.
"You heal very fast. Your feet have gone down a great deal
and they're almost normal size. Are they painful?"
Lovell stood then squatted.
"Only a little at the ankle when I bend."
"Try walking barefoot."
The first step smarted, but the more he moved, though his
soles stung, he could walk with a slight limp. Danuta
rubbed ointment which smelled like eucalyptus on his feet
and her hands made the muscles in his legs relax. His head
began to jerk when the door opened. It was Matt and Jim

[321]

again. "We've got to get him up and rush to the export ministry. Drunk ass Faturi forgot to get the final stamp. Bring some dollars, you know how it goes. Let's go."

Danuta held Matt's arm. "I've just given him a muscle relaxer and some ointment to ease the pain. Walking too soon could reverse everything."

"That's a chance we'll have to take Danuta. He has to get this stamp in person."

Danuta gave Lovell two pain pills. The four walked slowly, and Danuta didn't assist him. Penny waited in the taxi and Lovell sat in the front seat, his legs extended. The ministry was dark, with only a one eyed, Kufi and Jalabia wearing guard with a cloud of cigarette smoke around watching the front door. They each gave him a thousand dinar bill, and he ushered them to the elevator. Stopping on the second floor the door opened and stepping out, Penny extended his arms for them to stop and turning, silenced them with his finger. Inside the office, through the glass, they watched an Aybilian with only his white long sleeve shirt and hairy legs showing, making rapid dog like humps on someone they couldn't see. Smoke rose from the floor beneath him. Penny made a sucking sound and faced Matt, Jim and Lovell.

"He doesn't have very much technique."

Hands covering their mouths, they watched until his back arched, and he sat on the desk behind him. They glimpsed something in black go to the floor, then watched as the Aybilian's shirt was lifted and water was heard being squeezed from something. The Aybilian stood, stooped, and pulled up his pants, his back still to the door. The something in black stood, veil up, showing a crimson faced woman with a flood flowing from both eyes; it was Khadijah. The warmth of hands on his shoulders forced the blood into his upper body, but Lovell couldn't feel his legs. Matt and Jim pushed him forward, then arms under his armpits, caught him as his knees folded inward. Penny cupped his face, kissing both cheeks.

"Breathe Lovell. Breathe damn it. We're trying to get out of here and you knew she was married. If he suspects anything we're not only not getting out of here. We're all dead. Now pull your shit together Lovely."

He pimp slapped Lovell, who tasted blood inside his right cheek.

"I got it together brothers. Let me go."

Penny moved to the side, allowing Lovell to see the Aybilian sitting at his desk, a cloud of cigarette smoke concealing his features. Khadijah, her head dangling downward and hands folded in front, had moved into a corner. The four of them moved through the smoke and faced a cream colored Bill Withers. Penny hummed the first few notes of "*Ain't No Sunshine When She's Gone*," and the Aybilian sang, "Only darkness everyday", and lifted the wet blanket vibe in the room.

"That's one of my favorite songs and when I was in the states studying, people told me I looked like Bill Withers all the time."

"You could be his twin."

Penny laid his papers on the desk and the Aybilian rested his hand on top of Penny's.

"And whose twin are you. If I may ask?"

He spoke to Penny in French, and Penny checked to see if Khadijah was looking.

"I'm not sure. It depends on who's asking and what part of me they're looking at."

The Aybilian, hand atop Penny's, patted his desk with his other hand. "I assume you gentlemen want to travel and needs stamps. May I have your documents please?"

Lovell, Matt, and Jim placed their documents on the desk.

[323]

He opened them, eyeing the dollars, then stood, pulling Penny with him as he left the room. "I'll return in one minute gentlemen. My stamps are in the back."

Penny winked at them as he followed the Aybilian. Khadijah shook, and sniffled. Matt punched Lovell in the back.

"Be cool niggah."

Penny and his new friend emerged from the room, their excitement protruding from their pants.

"I'm told you gentlemen are traveling to Egypt. It's the land of freedom and fun. The Cairo Hilton is lovely. I always stay in the third floor suites. Ask for Jamal and tell him Tarek from Ripoli sent you. He'll take care of you. I promise. Here are your documents. Have a good trip."

He ordered Khadijah to make him some tea, speaking in Arabic, and as she left, so did Penny, Jim and Matt. As the elevator door closed, Penny wrapped his arm through Lovell's.

"He's shameless."

Matt's middle finger expressed his thought, and Penny tried to bite it.

"You do what you have to do Matt, and I'll do what I have to do to survive. We got our stamps didn't we?"

The doors opened and the Aybilian night silenced their conversation until they reached the campus and each man walked in a different direction. Lovell heard someone shout from behind him.

"Nothing is ever as it appears good brother. Never as it appears."

He waved, allowing the desert night to wash the sand from his lungs and escape through both eyes. He sang Smokey Robinson's "Don't Look Back," "If it's love that you're running from, there's no hiding place. For love has problems, I know, but they're problems we'll just have to face. So if you just put your hand in mine, we're gonna leave all our problems behind, keep on walking don't look back," over and over, as loud as possible, until he reached his building, then hummed to his floor, which was dark. Pulling out his knife, back to the wall, he moved along it until a match was struck and he saw Danuta's face. The light was blown out. "Come to your room quickly Lovely. I unscrewed the bulbs because I didn't want them to see me." Knife in his pocket, they entered his room and closing the doors to the balcony, Lovell lit candles. Danuta wore a trench coat and carried her doctor's bag. She was pale and her eyes darted around the room.

"I've come to remove those wires because you really don't need them. I want you to open and close your mouth 100 times three times a day and stay on liquids or soft food for another two weeks. Slice your fruit, or anything else you eat, very finely and stay away from nuts".

She opened Lovell's mouth and began to twist and clip the wires holding his jaw in place.

"Don't try to talk until I finish. I may not be here when you get back, so I want you to know I love you Lovell Pendleton and if you ever tire of your Arab princess, come to Poland and I'll be there. If I'm not, Jerzy and Anna will know how to find me." Holding his chin with her hand, she removed the braces/wires from Lovell's mouth. She fingertip massaged his jaw, then opened and closed it one hundred times before cleaning her hands and pulling Lovell to her breast. She smelled of lilacs, and he closed his eyes, inhaling her fragrance and feeling comforted by the fullness of both breasts, cupping his face. Wetness dripped onto his scalp, and wet her bosom.

"Where are you going Danuta?"

"I'm not sure, but it's no longer safe for me here."

[325]

He tried to pull away from her but she held him with both arms. Feeling her melon bottom, and putting his hand beneath her dress, he touched hot flesh.

"Will you make love to me one last time Lovely?"

Pushing him backwards, she wept while straddling him, and afterwards, trying to wipe her face, she pushed his hand away.

"Listen Lovely. We have been at war since Kasha was violated. I have killed many Aybilian babies and made sure many of these women will never have children. They will never be able to bring more filthy monsters on this earth. I have to leave because I sense they're onto me. That is why I came to you tonight. All of you will leave tomorrow and I will be right behind you. Don't speak to me if you see me in the airport. Just smile and blink. Now I must go. Remember to exercise your mouth."

Slipping on her trench coat, the shadows showing her thick figure, she left without looking back. Lovell placed his back against the cement wall and sang, "The sun is shining, there's plenty of lieing. Anew is dawning, sunny and bright. But after I've been crying all night. The sun is cold, and the new day seems old. Since I lost my baby."

Placing his face against the pillow, lavender smothering his nostrils, he called Khadijah's name into the pillow, mouthing her name through his mouth exercises, until darkness overwhelmed him, and three knocks signaled it was time to leave for Egypt.

Humming, he met his three friends at the taxi and hugging Penny, he heard him groan.

"What's up with you sweet cakes?"

Penny thumped him upside the head, and opened his shirt, displaying blue hickies on each nipple. Matt pushed Penny's nipple with his finger and Penny gasped.

"You're an animal Matt."

[326]

"From what he did to you, he must be an animal too."
Penny protected his chest with crossed arms and sang Little
Anthony's Hurt So Bad.
"You should have been singing, "Stop In The Name of
Love," before you break my nipples."
Penny pinched Matt on the nipple and held it until Matt
twisted his wrist, forcing him to let go. "There'll be a
limousine waiting for us at the airport, courtesy of Dracula.
Now how do you like that? Mr. Matt Johnson?"
Matt raised his hands and acted as if he were bowing to
Penny as they rode to the airport, watching the empty dark
streets of Ripoli. Arriving at the airport, they were taken
by a military officer through customs, without their
passports being checked. They boarded a plane with the
official Aybilian symbol. A redhead in pink raised her
purse while boarding a Polish Air flight. It was Danuta.
They all searched their papers, until they heard a voice
which made them turn around.
"Gentlemen, you're official guests on the Aybilian airlines.
Once we're out of Aybilian airspace, drinks will be
served."
It was the Aybilian from yesterday, dressed in a white suit
with tie and shoes. He closed a door separating them from
anyone else entering the plane. The plane ascended and
after a few minutes, someone knocked at the door and
handed them a tray of martinis.
"Welcome to the real world gentlemen, and turn your
clocks ahead 20 years. We're free in the friendly skies."
Penny and the Aybilian Ramadan snorted cocaine and
drank martinis the entire flight. They landed in Cairo, and
exiting the plane, they saw Khadijah and her little girl
Rahima, entering one of the waiting three limousines.
Penny and Ramadan rode in one, with Matt, Lovell and Jim
occupied the other. The Cairo Hilton glimmered in the

[327]

morning sunshine, with its fountains spouting gold streams of water. They were guided into the hotel and taken to the front desk. There was no Penny though. Lovell opened his mouth to ask Matt and Jim about him, but closed it, seeing their backs harden; Phil was checking in at the same time. Phil slid down the counter, his eyes honed in on Lovell.

"I see you're wearing sandals and your wires have been removed. Egypt's a good place for R&R."

"How did you know I had wires and something wrong with my feet Phil?"

Phil turned his back to the counter and surveyed Matt and Jim, standing on both sides of him. Matt gave him a wide grin.

"Damn, everywhere we go we see you. What's up my niggah?"

Phil's mouth puckered.

"Matt, Jim. I didn't know they let coons out the cage."

The concierge told Phil there would be a short delay in him going to his room. Phil nodded and walked towards the bar. Matt, Jim and Lovell checked into the third floor suites. Getting off the elevator, Matt grabbed Lovell by the shoulders and spun him around.

"No matter what you hear coming from my room, don't knock on the door. Do you understand me? Listen to me clearly Lovell and for once do as I say. Promise me."

Lovell gave his word and entered his room. He peeked out and saw Matt and Jim running to the elevator. Resting on the chaise lounge facing the balcony, the aqua Egyptian sky slowed his pulse, and the hum of Cairo's traffic made his fingers tingle. He tapped out a rhythm to its sounds. Closing his eyes, he heard its world in time with his heartbeat, thoughts, and the footsteps approaching his door. The three knocks accented the rhythm and opening it, Penny pushed him aside and slammed the door.

"You'll have forty five minutes to be with her and that's it. Take advantage of it. Forty-five minutes Lovell. I'm out of here."

Kissing Lovell on the cheek he scurried out the door.

Lovell took a quick shower and while drying himself, heard three knocks again. Opening the door, it was Khadijah, and pulling the towel from his waist, she led him to the bed, discarding her dress as she moved. They lay together after their scorching love making. Lovell blew the curls on Khadijah's head.

"Lovely, Habibi. Aisha wanted to see the pyramids and the only way I could get him to allow us to come here was to let him do that to me. I'm sorry you witnessed it. I want you to know this because I want to be with you, and I'd do anything to make it happen."

Lovell massaged the top of her head with his lips, then lifted her head, his tongue showing his appreciation in her mouth.

"He's a back door man isn't he?"

She nodded her head against his chest.

"And he likes boys."

Khadijah kissed his nipple.

"He likes both. But always from the back. He likes me to put my finger in his."

Lovell patted the smooth roundness of her butt. "You've never told me about him."

"There's not much to tell. I graduated from high school at fourteen, and at 15 I was at the university, then to medical school at Drew. He was older, handsome, athletic, and a connection to a memory I had of Africa from my childhood. We were married in Chicago and then returned to Aybil. The man I married became someone I didn't know. Once he changed, or I saw whom he was. I wouldn't

[329]

bathe and I just laid there when he took me. He can't stand filth, and soon left me alone."

She kissed his navel.

"Are you still married?"

"We had two ceremonies. One in Chicago and there in Aybil. We divorced in Chicago, but there isn't any divorce in Aybil. So, I'm his."

"But you don't live together, Khadijah. And what's all the intrigue going on? Why do you have only a few minutes here? I can understand in Aybil. But here?"

She ran her finger across his top lip and placed it in her mouth.

"No man wants someone to have his possession. Plus, my parents live here Lovell, and he wants to make sure I don't take Aisha away from him. He's having me watched and followed at all times. It cost me two thousand dollars to get these forty minutes with you. He has my passport Habibi. I have to go."

She dressed and stood at the door listening. Hearing footsteps and an owl's call, she opened the door.

"I don't know if I'll see you again. I love you Habibi."

She exited before Lovell could speak. Staying in bed, he recalled her father was the president of Cairo University and was from Chicago. He decided then, he wanted to meet this man and after showering again, dressed to do so.

Leaving his room, he saw Matt and Jim with Phil between them, his feet dragging, head sitting on his chest.

"Back to your barracks soldier."

Matt pointed to Lovell's room and he ran back inside. Standing at the door, three quick knocks startled him, and barely able to open it, Matt's derby cologne reached him.

"Wait fifteen minutes before you come outside and don't look at my door."

[330]

The door was pulled shut and Lovell waited. Reaching the lobby, he headed to the outside café where Egyptian music in 6/8, had heads bobbing and the waiters moving to the rhythm. Ordering tea and a large bowl of fresh strawberries with sliced oranges and Egyptian melon, he breathed in the tangy scent of fragrant tobacco.

"I see from that look on your face you enjoyed yourself."

It was Penny, easing himself into a chair. He ordered a mimosa, and falafel.

"And I see by the way you sat down, you enjoyed yourself."

Penny snapped his fingers.

"Lovely man, but his technique leaves a lot to be desired. I'll have to train him."

His head snapped up and he nudged Lovell under the table. Khadijah and her daughter Aisha sat at the table next to them. Aisha came over and hugged Penny.

"This is daddy's new friend. He and Daddy were holding hands, and they kissed."

Penny studied the ground. Khadijah looking pensive in white, with her head wrapped, pulled Aisha into a chair. Laughter echoed through the patio and they turned to see two dogs engaged in sex, one from the back. Aisha's mouth formed into an Oh.

"Mommy, is that what daddy was doing to you before we came down here. You two thought I was sleep but I wasn't."

The waiters threw hot water on the dogs and beating them with brooms, drove them from the outside café. Khadijah stood and moving Aisha's chair closer to the table, turned her back to Penny and Lovell, displaying a red spot below the melon Lovell loved to eat. Penny tapped her arm.

[331]

"Khadijah, there's a blood spot on the back of your dress darling. I'd suggest you never wear white after him. He's not the most gentle man with his tastes."

Khadijah took off her sweater and wrapping it around her waist, returned to her seat, covering her face. Her hairy arms teased the hair on Lovell's and he thought of the baldness above her valley, under her arms and on her legs. Rising, she lifted Aisha from the chair. Three men Lovell hadn't noticed, came to the table. Khadijah, sitting down, covered her face with a serviette, and Penny lifted Aisha onto his lap.

"And what will you have to eat princess?"

She told him she also wanted Falafel and Penny ordered another plate. Lovell told Penny to turn around and look in French. They watched Matt and Jim, walking behind Phil, wearing sunglasses and a trench coat, to a taxi. They watched him get into it alone while Matt and Jim entered a taxi behind it. Lovell ran to a taxi, telling Penny to hold his seat and food. Getting into the taxi and telling the driver to follow the one with the two men, he watched as the two taxis stopped in front of the American embassy, and Phil get out, remove his trench coat, leaving him naked, and holding his hands in the air with his passport, begin turning in circles. "I'm a CIA agent and I work for the American government. I spy on my friends and I'm a piece of shit. My name's doctor Phil Mendleson and my badge number is 558079294.558079294. I'm reporting for duty."

He walked to the embassy gate, handed a soldier his passport, saluted, and stood his hand in the salute position. Horns blew and people watched, women covering their mouths. The soldier took Phil's passport, and removing his jacket and placing it around Phil, opened the gate and pushed Phil inside. Three men in suits ran from the embassy and took Phil into the embassy. Jim and Matt's taxi turned around, as did Lovell's and returned the way they'd come, though Lovell lost them in traffic .The taxi driver laughed and almost lost control of the taxi. When Lovell arrived at the hotel, Matt and Jim weren't there. Penny sat alone with three empty glasses where mimosas had been.

"What happened?"

Lovell explained to Penny what he'd seen. Penny slapped the table.

"Lovely, this is where you and I part on this trip. I'm sorry, but this is more serious than I can handle. Have a good trip."

A chill spread from Lovell's ankles to below his chin. Phil, the CIA, employed by the U.S. government. Matt and Jim said they were at war with the Aybilians, but the U.S. government was another step. Watching everyone in the café, the chill numbed his feet, and he rubbed them, attempting to bring them to life. Rising and walking towards the hotel entrance, he saw Matt and Jim sitting at the bar, touching glasses. Jim moved his head in Lovell's direction.

"Don't start Lovell. This has nothing to do with you."

"I didn't say it did. But they know we got on the same plane, they saw us arrive together and that puts me in the mix."

Matt raised his drink to Lovell.

"You sound like sweety Penny who just blew past here. We didn't do anything. The acid did and you were nowhere near him. Now stop being paranoid. After all we've been through do you really think I'd put you in danger. You my boy, and you should know me better."

Jim snorted.

"Ditto Lovell. You, if anybody should know we wouldn't put you at risk. Penny's putting himself at risk because of

[333]

who goes up his ass, and that's not our problem. Lovell, that guy he's with is the Minister of the Interior for Aybil. He's got bodyguards around him everywhere to protect him. Now what kind of heat has Penny brought on himself, and what's going to happen when that minister tires of him? Be for real."

The whites showed in his knuckles. "But guys?"

Matt stopped Lovell's words with a raised hand. "Khadijah went to the university to see her old man. Why don't you go and see if she can help us get a job once we leave Aybil? You've got the reputation. Now buy us a drink."

Lovell paid for five rounds and took a taxi to The American University at Cairo. Dome shaped buildings, others in red brick with swooping sword designs and some with gold murals depicting ancient battles and the dynasty of Upper Egypt contrasted with the plain white buildings of Jami Al Fateh. Students dressed differently, walked, holding hands, and young men and women laughed and met in groups. He asked for the administration building in English and a female student guided him to it. She would glance at him periodically until they reached the building. "Excuse me sir. Aren't you Lovell Pendleton?"

Lovell stepped back in surprise.

"Yes, I am."

"We read your play and your book in our contemporary American literature class. Will you sign my book, sir?"

Lovell signed her book on the page his story appeared below his picture and walked up the stairs to the second floor. The three men in black he'd seen at the hotel stood at the top of the stairs smoking and drinking tea. He passed them, thinking they'd probably be in Jalabias in Ripoli, entered the president's office, and was greeted by a Diana Ross look alike in a yellow dress. Miles Davis "Sketches of Spain" played over an office speaker, and Romare Beardon and Charles White mosaics covered the walls. Lovell held his arm out mimicking the Supremes and she mouthed stop in the name of love. Before he could ask for the president, the inner door opened and Khadijah, with Aisha in hand, exited followed by a white haired man Lovell thought resembled Pops Staples of the Staple singers. He extended his hand.

"The incredible Lovell Pendleton. I've heard a lot about you and I'm an admirer of your work. I must say though, your broadcast on Aybilian T.V. made you sound like a sniveling dog."

"Daddy. You know that was dubbed."

Khadijah faced her father, who rubbed his palms together.

"I didn't say I believed it baby .I just told him how it sounded."

"I've heard it before sir. It's my pleasure. Your granddaughter looks just like you."

Khadijah's father squatted and kissed his granddaughter.

"You should see her grandmother. She looks like she spit her out."

He shifted his eyes behind Lovell. The cigarette smoke told Lovell the bodyguards were in the office. Khadijah's dad mouthed muthafuckas and extended his hand.

"I forgot to introduce myself and my daughter didn't do it. I'm Tom Freeman. You can call me Bigger."

They laughed, knowing the reference to Bigger Thomas from Richard Wright's book Native Son. Khadijah kissed her father, whispering something in his ear, and passing Lovell, squeezed his hand. Little Aisha spun around.

"Bye Baba, we'll see you later. Tell Nana I look forward to making falafel tonight. Bye Mr. Pendleton."

The cigarette smoke guided them from the office, as Mr. Freeman moved aside allowing Lovell to enter his office, closing the door.

[335]

"It's a goddam shame that muthafucka treats her like a prisoner when she's here and they don't even live together. He'd never get away with that shit in the states."

His fist shook the desk.

"Excuse me Mr. Pendleton. I shouldn't speak like that in front of you. But this shit burns my ass. Treating my daughter like that. I'm like Richard Pryor though. We got something for his ass."

He lit his pipe.

"Mr. Pendleton, excuse my frankness, but my daughter's in love with you. Do you love her, and what are your plans for her and her daughter? It's a package you know."

Lovell noticed the veins pulsating in Mr. Freeman's hands as he fingered a statue of Imhotep. His office had pictures of the black Pharaohs of Egypt.

"I want to spend my life with her, sir. This is the first time I've verbalized it."

"Then you have to get her out of Aybil and it won't be easy. He'd let her go easily. It's his daughter he wants, and he's serious as a heart attack." Eyebrows pulled together showed Lovell his seriousness. "I know he is sir. But my momma gave me something that's going to carry me through this world."

"I got your back."

They slapped five's and Mr. Freeman stirred his pipe, keeping the smoke in a slender line.

"I guess that nullifies your wanting to teach here."

"How'd you know sir?"

"Why else would you come and see me on your vacation?"

A knock on the door sliced through their thoughts and Mr. Freeman said "futha", enter in Arabic. Lovell stood, knowing it was Khadijah's mother, because the face was like little Aisha's, and identical to Francis Davis, Miles Davis first wife who adorned the cover of Miles "Someday

[336]

My Prince Will Come." Hair covered her folded and locked arms, like Khadijah. She gave Lovell a teeth clenched smile after introducing herself as Fatima, and didn't sit down. Lovell excused himself and left after doing a Supreme's move with the secretary who played Baby Love on a small recorde. He was greeted by a group of students waiting outside the building. After signing books, he was escorted to a taxi, and returned to the hotel, thinking of Mr. Freeman's words. A hog call directed him to the patio, where Matt and Jim sat with two blonds with hairy legs, wearing clogged sandals.

"Where you been boy?"

Lovell grabbed his privates.

"Here's your boy Matt."

The women giggled.

"I see you two have been enjoying yourselves."

Jim flexed his muscles.

"Not yet, we just met Ulla, and Hanna. They're Danes."

"Obviously."

Lovell's lips pointed to their legs.

"Your buddy and his new lover just left for a ride down the Nile. They're in love."

"May!"

Khadijah and little Aisha, flanked on both sides by a man in black, with one following, entered the open café. When they were close to Lovell, Matt and Jim's table, the Swedish woman jumped from the table.

"How dare you put your hand under my dress you fucking nigger."

She slapped Matt so hard that his head turned. Matt stood and raised his hand.

"You white fucking hoe, don't you ever-"

He couldn't finish the sentence because the other Dane attacked him, kicking over the table and knocking Matt into

[337]

Khadijah and Aisha. The bodyguards moved forward and Matt, Jim, and the two Danes attacked them, though they pretended to be fighting each other, and knocked them to the ground. They fell on top of them, and Lovell could see the four of them punching the bodyguards. Aisha shouted to her Nana and Lovell saw Khadijah's mother scoop Aisha up and she and Khadijah trotted out of the patio. Khadijah looked back at Lovell and waved before they were out of sight. Whistles blew drawing Lovell's attention. Four Egyptian policemen, batons drawn, separated Matt, Jim and the women, three more rushed in, picked up the body guards who lay on the ground unconscious and carried them away. He could hear police sirens making whirling sounds and getting fainter. A concierge appeared and told the women they had to leave, while waiters sat up the tables. Jim and Matt returned to the table.

"I hope you said your goodbyes because you won't see her for a while."

Both their faces had scratches and marks. Lovell froze, the image of Khadijah, dressed in purple with a pink scarf wrapped around her head, eyes brimming with love, waving to him.

"We're checking into the Four Seasons. You stay here. And bro, they'll be watching us so you'll have to spend this break alone. Watch your back and we'll see you back at the Jamahariya."

They left Lovell sitting with Khadijah's image fresh and flowing, until the concierge touched his shoulder and handed him a box.

"This was left on the ground. I think it belonged to one of your friends."

He winked at Lovell. Opening the box, Lovell smelled Khadijah's lilac lotion on a pink silk scarf with thin purple stripes. Wiping the love oozing from his eyes, he smelled

[338]

it, placed it back in the box, and ordered falafel with humus, and a Zorba; Amaretto DiSardonia, and brandy. Dusk was dawning when, on the third try, he was able to rise from his chair, making sure one foot was in front of the other and made it to the elevator. Seeing he was alone in the elevator, and no one was on his floor, he crawled to his room, opened the door from his knees, and scooted to the bed. Pounding awakened him on his door. The room swirled momentarily, he cleared his head by slapping himself, and shouted wait a minute. After washing his face with cold water, he opened the window, birds greeted him and a trickle of light peeked from the horizon's edge. Opening the door, Penny blue faced with rage, stomped into the room.

"Did you have anything to do with it?"

He turned on a light and covered his nose. The room reeked of stale vomit.

"Do with what?"

Penny called room service.

"Khadijah and Aisha got away. Ramadan's in a rage. Matt and Jim were fighting with some bitches and they got away from the bodyguards who've disappeared. You didn't answer my question."

Lovell moved close enough so Penny could see his eyes in the lamplight.

"No, I didn't. I wish I had though."

Penny backed away from Lovell, and the room brightened from the sun revealing its first stretches. "I'm glad you didn't. Someone's going to pay and I'm glad it's not you. I'll see you in Aybil Lovely. Be careful."

Lovell spent his time in Egypt riding down the calm blue Nile, smoking hookah and hashish with Nubians and Sudanese. He visited the pyramids, avoiding loud North Americans in groups, and dancing in Cairo's clubs,

frequented by Europeans on vacations. He saw Matt and
Jim in the clubs with the Danes, and they danced together,
shared the same tables, laughing about the men in grey
suits following them, but went to their own hotels when the
nights ended. He saw Penny, sour faced, at a hotel in
Aswan with Ramada, who had a tall blonde on each knee,
sucking their breasts, while Penny watched. They all
noticed bearded men in grey suits wearing Fezs following
them. Mr. Freeman called the hotel and invited him to
lecture at the university on contemporary American
literature and to read from his work. He gave Lovell a note
when they shook hands. Lovell placed it inside one of the
student's books he'd been given to read his work from, and
read it before he began to read; she's safe and at home with
Chess Records. Acknowledging the note with a nod, Mr.
Freeman raised his eyebrows and in the direction of the
men in grey, standing against the wall. Mr. Freeman
accompanied Lovell to his taxi.
"These sock dodgers can't see the forest for the trees. They
think the blind is blind and don't know they just can't see.
Little do they know my momma gave me something gone
carry me through this world. Them wearing tar and it be
sticking when them running through the briar patch."
"Stickin' and stinkin' Mr. Freeman. Tell sistah rabbit I be
in her patch soon. And I be's joining you and hanging my
hat there soon cause I come to da end of dah road."
Giving Lovell a fatherly pat on the back, he turned and
head towards the men in grey, now standing together.
"Fuck you, you dumb muthafuckas. Don't you know, I
know you following me? Tell Ramadan to suck my big
black sausage and leave my family alone."
His middle finger almost touched their stone faces, but they
stood like stone behind dark glasses. Facing them, he
walked towards his office building. Returning to the hotel,

[340]

the front desk gave Lovell a message stating he'd been booked on a first class flight to Ripoli tomorrow morning at 7 a.m., Egyptian air. A flower drawn on the bottom of the typed note identified it as being from Penny. He called Mr. Freeman in his office at the university. "This is Lovell sir."
"You don't have to say it to me son. I know I'm not being cool. But there's something from home they don't understand."
They spoke in unison.
"You don't mess with a man's family, his money, and his home."
He heard Mr. Freeman light his pipe.
"These people think just because I'm in this position, and I wear this tie, I won't go street on them. I've already shown them something and if they keep fucking with my family there'll be more. And I hope they're listening."
Lovell took deep breaths which he sent to Mr. Freeman in his mind.
"Watch your back and be cool Mr. Freeman."
"I will son, and you do the same. How much more time do you have in that hell hole you're working in?"
"Eight months, sir."
"Stay in touch and I'll see you state side. I'll be out of here in three."
They hung up and he showered, then rested.   Later, sitting on the balcony of his room, watching the Cairo traffic. One knock on his door alerted him and grabbing his knife, he stood beside the door and asked who was there. It was the front desk saying they had a message for him. Lovell told them to slide the message under the door but they said they couldn't. He opened the door enough to see someone, standing to the side with his knife ready. The hotel clerk slipped the message through the slim opening and Lovell handed him some money. The message read "let

[341]

the phone ring twice, pick it up, and hang up. Then answer when it rings again." He followed the directions and picked up the phone on the third ring.

"Hello Habibi. I only wanted to tell you we're safe and I miss you."

Her voice was distant and he could hear the sounds of trains moving.

"I spoke to your dad today and he told me. We're being followed here."

She held her breath.

"They're here too. My mother thinks we're safe but I don't. I know him Habibi. He won't stop until he gets Aisha back. Even if he has to kill someone."

Lovell changed his tone to iron.

"Then you'll have to get some ruthless brothers to protect you because his people won't stop until they succeed, unless they realize you have power too and you'll use it."

"But I don't know anyone like that Lovely, and my dad's in Egypt."

Her voice cracked.

"He'll be there soon and until then, I'll help you. I promise Habibi. Now go to your mother's house and wait for someone to call you. Give me your mom's number."

She gave him the number and hung up. Leaving the hotel in a taxi, he instructed the driver to take him to the souk where he knew he'd find prostitutes. Watching a man in grey get into a taxi and follow him, he kept the taxi waiting, entered the souk and found a six foot one Sudanese prostitute sitting in a teashop. Leaving the souk with her, he checked into a four star hotel, instructed her to take a shower, and while the water was running, he pulled the phone as close to the bathroom as possible, and called his uncle.

[342]

"Unc, it's Lo. Take the horse and turn him around cause wolf's be barking at the door."

He gave his uncle the number backwards and hung up. The Sudanese woman came out of the shower, covered in a towel that he pulled off her. He enjoyed himself with her for an hour. The man in grey sat in the lobby smoking as Lovell and the prostitute left. She walked away, after winking, and he returned to the hotel. Dark glasses and cologne couldn't conceal the alcohol escaping from Jim and Matt's pores in the Cairo heat. Jim placed his head on Lovell's shoulder.

"Can you help me Bro? I think I'm going to lose it."

Lovell put his arm under Jim and propped him up. Matt rocked. The Aybilians choked down their smiles and smoked, concealing the alcohol coming from them. Getting to the check in counter, the male attendant checked their passports and laughed.

"I see you've numbed yourselves like all the other foreigners returning to Aybil. We understand. Thank God we're stationed here and we don't have to live there. I wish you luck."

Lovell steadied his two buddies and walked slowly to the plane. They slept through the 2 hour and twenty-five minute flight, snoring freely.

CHAPTER ELEVEN

The smell of gasoline, fried peppers and raw meat signaled they were in Ripoli. Jim held his head out the window.

"Nothing like that smell to sober you up. We've only been gone two weeks but it feels like years."

"There are years differences between the two countries." Matt spit.

"Back to the war zone."

They pumped fists, then froze. Lovell, who'd been looking down and writing in his notebook, felt their energy and followed their eyes. Green tents had been placed in all the empty spaces of land with people entering and leaving them. The road to the university had green flags and the taxi stopped at the gate, took the money and sped off, covering them in dust. Walking down university lane, which led to the faculty housing, green flags hung from every post and tree, and a banner hung from the lamp posts outside the residence; LET US TURN THE DESERT GREEN! Hands in pockets fingering their knives, the three men entered the faculty residential gates, and forming a circle, looked up at the flags hanging from the roofs of all the buildings. A Palestinian from the agricultural department chuckled as he passed them.

"While you were gone the tyrant ordered all the ex-patriots home and now has a new slogan. It means use the fertile minds which have come home to make the country better. What the idiot doesn't realize is none of them wanted to come home and they can't do anything because they haven't finished their studies. I pray to god these last few months go quickly."

Breathing easier, Matt and Jim went to the building. Lovell, reaching his floor, entered his room, found his mattress

[344]

slashed, the bedding thrown everywhere and his pictures ripped into small pieces. Opening the closet, his pants had all the pockets turned inside out and the drawers were open. Removing the piece of wood at the closet's base, he exhaled realizing they hadn't found his stash. People walked in and out of the green tents in the once vacant lot separating Haba Shangira from the university. Children and adults entered different tents and the teenagers weren't around. Lovell assumed they were in school. Walking to school alone, the Sudanese stood in a group whispering. He crossed the street not wanting to pass them and they followed him. Hand in pocket, his knife was ready, but they parted allowing Madusun, their leader to step forward. Removing his sunglasses, Lovell was greeted by cut lips, cached with purple dried blood, and two barely opened eyes.

"We forgive you for kicking Ahmed in death brother Lovell because we found one among us and in our rage we did the same. There is no need for you to handle your knife. We come in peace".

One ham hock sized hand was extended. The other was wrapped in a cast. Lovell shook the hand. "What happened to you?"

"The same which has happened to many professors since the students took over the university. They beat me because I refused to allow them to teach my class."

The other Sudanese mumbled their agreements. "And if you're not careful, they'll beat you and all the other westerners. This is the new green power Lovell. The ruler calls it the youth revolution. Be careful. We have all sent our wives and children home because it's no longer safe."

Heat rose from his chest and he exhaled while watching the Sudanese walk towards the faculty dorms, all over six five and carry sticks.

[345]

"What do I do Madusun?"

Madusun swung his stick in the air.

"Do whatever they say and stay ready to defend yourself."
The other Sudanese also held their sticks in the air before
turning and leaving Lovell searching the ground for a stick.
Reaching the university, groups of young uniformed
women sat together talking in hushed voices. The young
men stood in circles, watching a group of about five young
women dressed in blue jeans, shouting back at three young
men in Jalabias with beards and Kufis. One of the young
men put his finger in their faces, shouted something and the
students conversations stopped. The girls dropped their
heads and walked away, and the young men screamed one
sentence Lovell didn't understand to all the students before
leaving. Someone pushed Lovell inside the university. It
was Faturi.

"Pendleton, you haven't been here so there are some things
you need to learn quickly if you want to survive. Number
one, if you see young men dressed like that speaking, don't
listen. Walk away because they think westerners shouldn't
listen to Aybilian conversations. Number two, if they walk
into your classroom, sit down and let them do what they
want. Number three, you have an Aybilian teaching
assistant who'll be doing most of the work. You give some
instructions the first five minutes of your class, then let him
do the rest. Anything you want done with your class, you
tell me and I'll tell your assistant."

Lovell waited for more instructions, and when none came,
Faturi tried to leave but Lovell held his elbow.

"What was that about?"

Faturi bit his bottom lip.

"They told them if they didn't stop wearing western
clothes, they'd send them to Allah."

"And what were the girls saying?"

"They're good Muslims. It's 110 degrees and too hot to be dressed in those dark uniforms. You stay out of it. Now go to class."

Lovell went to class, reintroduced himself and listened while his teaching assistant taught The Souls of Black Folk in English with frequent phrases in Arabic. The class was ending when someone pleading was heard in the hall. The class stayed in their seats but Lovell went to the door. A female Indian music professor was being beaten in the hall. "I'm sorry, I'm sorry! I won't wear my sari again. I'm sorry."

Three female students beat her with camel tails across her hands covering her head and her back. She lay on the floor moaning until blood squirted into the air and urine ran from under her clothes. Her attackers shouted Jami al Fateh and left the hallway, blood dripping from their weapons. Faturi peeked from his office and seeing the women had left, placed a blanket over the now unconscious professor and returned to his office, closing the door. A voice behind Lovell told him not to touch her. The students and Lovell left the classroom. Leaving the professor in the hallway, Lovell was walking towards home when he saw her husband, an Englishman and three other British professors from the science faculty run towards the university carrying a stretcher. He'd taken a couple of steps when a sky blue Mercedes pulled beside him with Penny driving, and Matt, and Jim, inside.

"Come Lovely!"

He sat in the passenger's seat, facing Penny. He was also able to see his two friends in the back seat. Matt raised bruised knuckles and showed them to Lovell. Jim did the same and they pointed at Penny. Lovell touched the right side of Penny's face and Penny winced, blood trickling from his swollen temple and darkening puffed jaw. Blood

[347]

dripped from his nose and Lovell wiped it with his handkerchief and held it there until Penny took it with his left hand, steering with his right. "He ran into our classrooms. They were chasing him and whipping his ass. We had to knock a couple of muthafucka's out for them to back off." Penny whimpered as he drove and adjusted his body, wincing each time he moved. Penny drove to the Ambassador's residence and parked. Moaning each time he moved, he finally grabbed the top of the door and pulled himself up. Blood covered the seat of his pants, and red welts showed through the jagged torn strips on his legs where the camel tails had cut through. He took two steps and collapsed face first, a cracking sound coming from his face as hit the ground. Lifting him, his head turned to the side and pieces of teeth, and blood, fell from his mouth. They rang the Ambassador's bell and the housekeeper answered. Lovell identified himself, saying it was an emergency, and Mrs. Dupree, his secretary came from their residence. Seeing Matt and Jim holding Penny between them, they opened the gate and allowed them inside. Mrs. Daphne, ran and returned with a blanket, which she placed on the carpet and told Matt and Jim to lay Penny on his stomach. Leaving again, she returned with a medical kit. Penny moved when she put something under his nose. Seeing her, he started to wail. Shushing him by rubbing his head, she cleaned his mouth, and asked me to get some ice from the kitchen. Opening the refrigerator door, he heard Mr. Daphne.

"Matt, and Jim, the two of you have done something that has more far reaching effects than you can ever imagine. My assistant will patch up Mr. Marshall and then all of you will leave my residence and never come here again. Do I make myself clear?"

[348]

Matt grunted and Lovell heard Jim's heavy strides move towards the door and open it.

"I'm ashamed me and my friends got shot and died for assholes like you and this government. We're fighting another war and you're hanging us out to dry again. You take care of your own faggot friend, and the next time they come after him I'll let them beat him to death."

Entering the living room, Mr. Daphne stood wide legged with his arms crossed while Matt watched Mrs. Dupree wrap Penny's legs with gauze. She then she put Penny's hand on the ice pack she'd placed on his jaw.

"Get up Penny Marshall, and walk out of my residence. I told you once before about your choices and now your mouth has written a ticket your ass can't cash. Please leave. Pendleton, be careful. I wish you all the best."

Penny limped, Matt swore and Lovell felt as if he'd been thrown out of his own father's house as they left. Penny stopped before he reached his car.

"You two will have to take a taxi. Thank you for helping me Matt. You'll never have to do it again. I can take care of myself."

Matt gave Penny the finger and headed towards the street. Penny hugged Lovell.

"Take care Lovely. I've made my bed and now I have to sleep in it. Watch for the flowers. You'll always know it's me. Goodbye."

Spinning Lovell around, he pushed him towards the street, and Lovell heard Penny sing, "keep on walking don't look back." Matt, Jim and Lovell rode in silence back to the university and walked together to the faculty dorms. Matt and Jim accompanied Lovell to his room and stepped close enough so he could smell the spearmint gum they chewed.

"We're at war bro. We're at war and don't you ever forget it. They've shown you what they'll do and now you need to

[349]

keep your antennas up. And stay away from Penny. He's now one of them."

They marched away, and Lovell entered his room closed the shutters, placed a chair in front of the door, and practiced his saxophone throughout the night until his lips gave out.

CHAPTER TWELVE

The University was silent. The classes were silent. Professors taught classes in monotone voices, avoiding any mention of the men and women together and skipped passages in books displaying intimacy. Lovell sat in the back of his class, writing letters to his uncle in code for Khadijah and Nidia, while listening to the teaching assistant twist everything to fit the Colonel's new philosophy; "unta ikwo"; we're one. A bearded observer sat in the class sipping tea, sometimes sleeping, the students never asked questions. Lovell nodded from listening to the students read from Dubois, when someone pushed his head back. It was the bearded dark glass-wearing observer.

"Come outside professor."

Lovell was the only person in the class. Following the beard, he stood at the back of the crowd, and saw three other beards, white head wraps and Jalabias standing on the back of a truck. The truck moved until it was under the lamppost. One threw a robe over the lamppost until it hook and knotted. The part hanging down had a noose. One of the young women he saw was wearing western clothes, her arms tied behind her back, was lifted into the truck, and the noose placed around her neck. Some female students started to cry but were shushed. Faturi's voice came from behind Lovell.

"Close your eyes unless you want to see something gruesome." Lovell knew he shouldn't turn around. "It can't be any worse than before."

A beard with a bull horn spoke into it and Faturi translated. "We warned this girl to respect the Koran and the new revolution which teaches modesty and obedience. She continued to disobey and be an unrighteous woman and now she must pay. Jump!" The young woman didn't move. Three other beards lifted her until she stood on the edge of the truck's side and pushed her. He turned his head and heard screams and groans as some students fainted. "Return to your classroom. Unlike Doris, they will cut her body down."

Lovell almost made it to the building before his lunch spewed onto the ground. Others did the same. A few of the young men accompanied him to the bathroom. Hearing someone move, one student bent down and looked beneath a stall, then motioned to everyone a beard sat there pretending to read a book in the toilet. Lovell looked down and saw his pants were up. They cleaned their mouths and each returned to their classroom. Inside his classroom, the students and the teaching assistant stared, wordless at the beard. He stood to say something as the class ended, but they walked past him, leaving him standing in front of the classroom. Not wanting to return to his room, Lovell crossed the open space before getting to the green tents and was approaching Haba Shangira, when a cloud of dust behind a car came towards him. He measured the distance to the dorms, and calculated the car would reach him before he got there. Both hands holding knives, he readied himself for battle, when the car stopped, blinding him with dust. He backpedaled, knives raised, and tried to clear the air.

"If I had wanted to kill you I would have run you over. You crazy American. What can knives do against a car?"

It was Basam, his friend from Haba Shangira.

"I've been looking for you for some time. I'm glad I caught you before you reached the village. Don't you see those tents and don't you know what's going on?"

Putting his knives away, they kissed on both cheeks. "Brian washing for betrayal."
Basam stopped him.
"I know. And I know what happened to you. It's everywhere and it could be you if you entered the village. Fathers don't trust sons, mothers don't trust daughters, adults don't trust children and everyone's afraid of each other. These are the new plants which have grown in the Colonel's garden."
Looking over his shoulder, men emerged from a tent and watched Lovell and Basam talking.
"Put on your sunglasses and turn your head when you see me throw the dirt. I'll see you at the yellow door at nine." He threw dirt in Lovell's face, pushed him to the ground and pretended to kick him. Lovell heard cheers and he crawled, then getting up, ran towards the faculty living quarters. The souk echoed with six eight rhythms, with the smell of ground garlic, peppers, kabob, barbecued fish with saffron, garlic, baked chicken and perfumes, seasoning the air. Exiting the taxi, he bopped and two stepped, then entered the shopping area, where stores touched and merchants sat around smoking hookah, drinking tea, or black coffee from half finger sized cups. Dresses and pieces of material hung from extended wires, and he moved his head to the music, while pretending to avoid touching something with his face. He knew better than to dance inside the souk. Buying two bags of oranges, some figs, candles, and three twenty four carat gold bangles, which he didn't have to bargain for, merchants he'd usually joked with, or had seen in the blue or green door clubs, avoided his eyes and only nodded. Walking through the lane which couldn't have more than three people stand together, and staring into a mirror he picked up to make sure he wasn't followed, he slipped between a row of dresses and walked

[353]

down the lane with the different colored doors. Night was spreading its cloak of darkness, he slowed again and seeing no one behind him, opened the yellow door and eased inside. Teddy Pendergrass *"Turn Out The Lights"* played and black beads hung from the ceilings, with black and yellow Pappagallo birds in cages. Yellow cushions sat on the floor and inhaling Egyptian Musk incense mixed with hashish, he relaxed and went to the fourth door, where he knew he'd find Basam. Basam greeted him by raising his pipe, which he gave to Lovell as he sat. Red eyes and a flushed face, plus a dry lip kiss on both cheeks, told Lovell his buddy had been here for a while.

"Always the brother. I say nine, and you get here at ten." Lovell laughed and coughed at the same time, the hashish being strong.

"CP time."

They slapped fives.

"I'd have gotten here at ten too, but I have a show tonight, and I needed to gas up before I went on."

Lovell's raised eyebrows spoke to Basam.

"Don't be surprised. A lot has changed since I last saw you."

Two tanned skinned women, full lipped, and hipped with Cleopatra haircuts, the bangs just above the eyebrows. They were naked except for a red string of jewels around their waists with one string hanging down the crotch, between the legs entered the room and sat beside them. Basam bit the one beside him on the nipple and she jumped, then pinched his ear. The other rested her hand on Lovell's thigh and pointing to herself, said Anise. Lovell said his name and she repeated it.

"For one thing. Look around you. There's hardly anyone here, and the music's being piped in. Men are afraid to play live instruments and get caught here."

[354]

Lovell remembered how the few times he'd been to any of the clubs, girls and men bumped shoulders. "You're here." Basam drank from a glass of gin.

"I'm Basam and I know my way around. I know when they're coming and if they're coming. Being on television helps me know a lot."

A wave of blood moved through Lovell's head and he leaned back against the pillow the keep from falling forward.

"Many have died Bilal. And mostly young people. Its white powder. Something new here and only found in the west, or Afghanistan."

His upper body angled towards Lovell.

"If my children die Bilal, then your children have no right to live."

The hashish dissipated.

"What do my children have to do with this?"

"What do mine Bilal? They're innocent and someone is taking advantage of their misery and killing them. The same should be done to their children."

Lovell thought of the pictures he'd shown Basam of his family. He thought of the money he'd let Basam have, the nights they'd spent partying together, the homes they'd entered and the risk Basam had taken just this afternoon. Basam's wife Mar, had even walked around the house without her veil when he was there.

"I thought you were my friend Basam."

"I am. But someone is killing our children, and their, or your children are not more important than mine. This white powder comes from one of you. And, none of the women in the village can get pregnant, or carry a child full term. The only doctor they've seen is the one in the clinic at the school. We aren't stupid Bilal."

[355]

Getting to his feet, Lovell threw a pile of money in Anisa's lap. Her eyes opened and she muttered shokran (thank you). Basam rubbed the glass of gin between his palms. "She'll show you how to leave through the back way. Don't come here again unless I tell you Bilal." Reclining, the woman unbuttoned his shirt and licked Basam's nipples. Anisa took Lovell's hand and guided him through candle lit hallways to a door which she opened, letting in the night.

"Hada ques" (you're good). Then in English with a mush mouthed accent.

"Go hotel. Chaddy there."

He side stepped into the darkness, heading for the western hotel.

*****

The smell of clove cigarettes guided him to the trash cans, and wrapping his handkerchief over his nose, bowing, he moved towards Mukhtar, arms wide for an embrace. Mukhtar, using the cigarette to display cloud white eyes and teeth.

"Ah, my African American brother. You have returned to me. I-"

Four streams of light flashed behind Mukhtar, then stopped on he and Lovell's faces, blinding them. They were from flashlights. Someone spoke in Arabic, Lovell couldn't understand. Mukhtar threw his cigarette in the voice's direction and moved Lovell so his back was against the wall. Lovell felt Mukhtar dive to the ground, heard him rolling, then grunt and heard the garbage container being thrust towards the lights. Two fell, the light showed two Arabs, dressed in army fatigues, one on top of the other with his arms spread, and a gun on the ground in front of him, trying to get up. Knives in both hands, Lovell

[356]

attacked, striking the one on top in the back of the neck. Lovell felt his body spasm, and saw a white flash coming from the muffled sound of a silencer. The body on top jerked, the head hitting something making a crunching sound, and the flashlight which rolled, revealed the face of the soldier on the bottom, contorted, with blood squirting from his nose. Lovell rolled to the side and swung his knife towards one of the eyes. Hitting it, a hand clawed at his, and he continued to stab with his other hand, hitting hard and soft flesh, until the body stopped moving. Looking to his left, the other two flashlights rolled on the ground, making crossed lines. One clicked off, and the other was turned face down, showing a circle on the ground.

"We need to put them in the bins."

He and Mukhtar lifted the four soldiers and threw them into the trash bin. Mukhtar climbed in and Lovell heard him moving the trash, covering the bodies, and smelled him as he climbed out. Using the flashlight on the ground, he pulled Lovell with him behind the bins, concealing the light with some piece of cloth, shine it over Lovell's clothes. No blood showed on his clothes, but it covered his hands, up to his forearms. Mukhtar, using a clean knife, cut off the sleeves to the elbow, and placed them in his pockets. He clicked off the flashlight.

"We'll have to scale this wall."

The light flashed again, giving Lovell the fence's height, both squatting, they leaped high enough to reach the top and pull themselves up. Feeling Mukhtar's head moving from side to side, he swung his legs over and hit the ground, squatting like Mukhtar.

"What happened? Why did they try to kill us?"

A calloused, garbage-smelling hand covered his mouth.

"Tuaregs, dressed as Aybilians. They want to take my trade."

Lovell pulled Mukhtar's hand from his mouth and spit. Mukhtar chuckled, and threw water in Lovell's face.

"That should make you feel cleaner. I see you still haven't learned to carry water with you."

Lovell felt the small water bottle in his chest. Taking it, he washed out his mouth.

"Don't wash the blood off here brother. They'll check this side of the wall."

"Mukhtar!"

"Yes my brother."

"What are you trading?"

Mukhtar drew something in the ground. "Everything except people. Including what your friends need to continue the war the Polish doctor prepared in her lab."

Lovell heard a low whistle, and a taxi with no lights slowly stopped about fifteen feet in front of him.

"Stay low and lie flat in the back seat until you can't see the city lights. Then you'll be safe to sit up. Come downtown every day and look for the Fezzan butcher shop where the Fezzani's work. When you see two chickens hanging outside, cross the street and walk down the narrow lane. The fifth door will have a rose on it. Knock four times and Anisa will open it. She will give you a message from me. And you can tell her how I can reach you. You must take her like a man African American warrior, or she will feel bad you have given her money for nothing. Now go! You can trust this driver. He's my cousin, and he has something for your friends. They'll be in the veterinary school." Reclining on his back, and listening to James Brown's, "The Big Payback" on the taxi's speakers, he closed his eyes and saw the soldier's squinting eyed, pained face flashed in his head. One second the face would have one eye dripping with blood, then the mouth would curl, and the teeth would drop out. Opening his eyes and sitting up because the city lights had ended and the featureless night surrounded him, he said "self-defense" out loud. The taxi driver looked in the mirror, his face carved from an oak tree, favoring Sidney Poitier, and spoke to Lovell in French.

"There's a war going on my brother, and we all want to return to our families."

Slowing the taxi, he handed Lovell a shoebox and a wet rag that smelled of chemicals and washed the blood from his hands. Stopping outside the university gate, he mouthed to Lovell in French, remember your family. Lovell entered the university, and passing the portrait of the Colonel, he bent down, pretending to tie his shoe and spit on a red light bulb at the bottom of it. The Aybilian sky was a blanket of stars, close enough to touch. He cradled the box for warmth, until the veterinary building came into view. Walking to the back, the Hausa professor, Abdulai, surrounded by students, bent over a horse, giving birth. He opened the door and was pulled into a dark room.

"Give me the box, go outside and watch the birth, then go to your room. We'll talk later."

It was Jim's voice, and he doing as he was told, watched a horse come into the world. Unafraid, he sat on his balcony, watching the lighters flicker in the orange field, and mouthing Khadijah's name for his jaw exercises, until three knocks called him to his door. As he was lost in his thoughts, Jim and Matt entered, smelling of orange soda and Siddiqui. They sat on his balcony, smoking weed mixed with a sweet tobacco to disguise the smell. He passed the joint to Matt, and turning up Stan Getz and Astrid Gilberto's "Corcovado," spoke from inside his room.

"I killed a man tonight."

[359]

Matt and Jim whirled around. Matt skipped into the room and made the volume louder. He moved his hands in the air as if he were dancing.

"Are you crazy? Saying that out loud."

Lovell returned to his seat and they huddled. "Mukhtar and I were attacked behind the hotel and I stabbed a Tuareg to death. I keep seeing his face." Matt rubbed his shoulder.

"It's always like that the first time you do it face to face. It will be gone by the time you go to bed."

"And you're all dealing something to the Aybilians. I know about the coke, but this feels like something else. What is it?"

The candles from his room gave shimmering glimpses of his friend's faces.

"Speedballs. They kill faster. The more the Colonel represses, the more we sell, and the more bodies we drop. We're at war."

"And what if?"

Matt tapped Lovell on the jaw with his fingertips, and Jim clinked Lovell's glass.

"We've got it covered. You just watch your ass because this shit's about to get crazy. And one more thing Lovell, just because you've taken out two men, doesn't mean you're in this fight. Your visibility's too high and you're an easy target. You got me?"

Jim's white fist touched Lovell's before he and Matt left. Lovell sat on the balcony, his head bobbing up and down until the first call to prayer drove him to bed, without seeing the soldier's face.

CHAPTER THIRTEEN

Lovell sat in his classroom smiling at the pictures Nidia sent of her watermelon stomach. Two melons he said aloud and looked to see if anyone had heard him. He counted ten of the fifteen heads in his class, down on the desk sleeping, the others writing, or he assumed, drawing on their paper. The beard sat with his back to Lovell, a soft snore coming from his rising and falling head. The student directly in back of the beard, mimicked his head movement and the teaching assistant stifled a smile. Instead of reading Linsay Barret's "*Song For Mumu*," the beard had the class reading the poems of Omar Mukhtar, "The Revolutionary," but not a poet. Looking out the window to his left, Sharif, Ashraf, and Sakel saw the Tunisian cooks bodies swing like washed clothes on a clothesline. Flies buzzed around their feet and below, where their waste hung. Fishing deaths is what he called them. Fishing deaths because someone needed to answer for the deaths on campus and throughout the city. Four on the soccer team, two on the basketball team, six returning students from overseas, and countless deaths throughout the city. The Tunisians were being blamed for the deaths.

Matt and Jim sat in their classes like all the other professors, watching the Abeyant teaching assistants teach the classes according to the student cadres wishes. Lovell rubbed his fingers over Nidia's two fingers held in the air, signaling twins, and though Lovell's hurt had been stored in an alcove in the reservoir of his heart, he knew what had happened between she and Ann happened, and that was it. Marguerite had told him so and looking at how sometimes the heart leads with sightless eyes, he knew it to be true. From Nidia's letter, he knew the censors had taken the

[361]

picture she sent of her naked stomach, and he cursed them, and almost said aloud "keep on kicking their asses Matt and Jim." His uncle's letters, written in code, said Khadijah and Aisha had settled in Chicago. He had a team of bad mamatapping Vietnam Vets watching her every move, and they'd thwarted three attempts by Ramadan's men to capture Aisha. Their bodies had been sent back to Ramadan with messages in their mouths. Disappearances had become normal now, and the knot in his stomach no longer rose up, when he heard the chant, Jami-al-Fateh, because students and faculty were beaten now, not killed now. Even the raid he witnessed from his balcony in the orange fields last night, with flashlights darting, and students being dragged into the headlights of cars, stripped naked and flogged on the spot, hadn't bothered him. It was the life he now knew, and expected.   Seeing the white layer of something on Faturi's nose, and his half drooped eyes standing above him, wasn't what he expected. Faturi motioned for him to follow him, and heads snapped up as they passed. The beard's smile exploded across his face, and three female students dabbed at their eyes. Entering Faturi's office, Lovell stopped in front of Ramadan, Khadijah's husband/ex-husband, and the Iraqi. Faturi began an introduction, but Ramadan stopped him.
"I've met the professor before. How are you professor?" Neither Lovell, nor Ramadan extended their hands. Faturi rubbed his nose and sat down as if waiting for a show to begin. The Iraqi moved his head forward from the neck, peering into Lovell with his good eye.
"I'm fine sir, and you?"
Ramadan and the Iraqi sat, but Lovell stood over them, making them look up. He knew this game. "I'm taking over the investigation of the deaths on campus and I'm talking to all the foreign professors."

[362]

Lovell thought only the foreign professors, but kept his tongue.

"Does that include Professor Marshall?"

Ramadan reached for a smoking cup of tea sitting on the desk, and drank from it. His eyes misting, and lip quivering from the heat of the tea Lovell knew, had scorched his tongue. Ramadan sat the cup down quickly and ran his tongue across his lips. "I said all professors."

"Then I hope your investigation will be successful. Children being taken away from their parents must truly hurt the parents."

The Iraqi looked from Ramadan to Lovell, then to Faturi, whose middle finger twitched. Lovell knew the coke was now streaming through his blood, now that the heroine down had passed.

"Hurt it does. Thank you, Professor Pendleton. That will be all."

Lovell turned to leave, then stepped so close to Ramadan, his head looked up at a sharp angle.

"I hope your investigation won't interfere with the foreign professor's spring break since we'll all be traveling. I'm told Egypt's a nice place to visit. What do you think sir?"

The veins in Ramadan's hands stood at attention as he grasped the arm of the chair.

"I think like any other place, it's nice, but it can be dangerous, professor."

"I'll keep that in mind when I visit there again, Mister Minister."

He left the university, taking a taxi, went downtown to the back of the Fezzanese butcher's shop. Seeing Lovell standing by the garbage bins, flies buzzing and the air ripe and full of the foul putrid smell of blood, the owner, with a Joe Frazier face, came outside. Lovell made a smoking a cigarette motion with his fingers and Joe Frazier, eyes

[363]

looking in all directions, opened a trash can, lifting a bag of entrails, handed him a rectangular plastic bag with a brown bag inside. He pointed north towards the university and told Lovell to take the black taxi at the corner. Tearing off the stinking plastic as he walked to the corner, he entered the taxi and recognized the driver from before, who asked him in French, how was his family, and gave him a card with a number on it. They rode to the university listening to James Brown again. Getting out of the taxi, the flame from a cigarette flashed three times in front of him, and he heard his name called. It was Faturi. He walked to Faturi's Mercedes and stood with his back against the car.

"I don't know what was going on today Pendleton. But the minister isn't someone you want to cross, and you've angered him. That was very unwise."

Lovell hummed Donny Hathaway's The Ghetto. "The ghetto will do you no good here Pendleton. You are very crazy. Move!"

Faturi allowed Lovell to move away, and spinning his car around without lights, sped away. Opening his door, he stepped on an envelope with a flower drawn on it, and on the inside flap was written,

"you made a stupid mistake today." Lovell burned the envelope and after washing his hands and opening the brick of compacted weed, rolled himself a joint, lighting ten sticks of incense to conceal the smell. He stored the rest of the weed in his hiding place, smoked and listened to Sonny Stitt play, "My Mom." He awoke coughing, struggled to breathe, and heard the fire alarm. Opening his balcony door, he realized there was no smoke outside, but it came from under his door. Voices yelled fire and opening his door, smoke covered his room. Screaming came from the hall and holding onto the walls, he moved along, avoiding the people running past him, and found his way to the

[364]

stairs, where there was very little smoke. He eased down the stairs and stood outside along with the other professors from his floor. They stood outside in the numbing desert air for an hour, until Hajj, the building custodian, told everyone it was okay to enter.

The air was clear, but upon entering their hallway, they all saw their mattresses, cushions and some clothes, had been slashed and thrown into the hallway. Lovell's room hadn't been touched by fire, but all his clothes had been shredded, and left in the middle of his floor. Wrapping them into a ball, and waiting until the halls were quiet again, he went to the basement where the pipes and heaters were, and stepping behind a water heater, squatted and found the key Rhinehart had hidden there. The key opened a door three steps beneath the ground. Rhinehart had found the opening by buying the only blue prints from the head engineer, an Egyptian, and had showed Lovell how it led to a tunnel running under each building, ending with a trap door, which opened up into the highway leading south to downtown, and north to the mountains. The pathway had an opening to the mechanical floor of each building, and anyone who knew about it only had to step onto a small footstool, to enter the room. Rhinehart thought it was there because they'd built the buildings on top of existing structures.

Carrying his clothes and counting to make sure he was at Penny's building, he climbed into the basement where the pipes were, and using an inflammable lubricant Rhinehart had left, set fire to his clothes beneath the pipes, and scurried away from the building. Back in his room, he listened as the fire alarm sounded, and watched as people ran from the smoking building before the explosions started. He sang Edwin Starr's "War", but changed the words from absolutely nothing, to absolute revenge. Sleep

[365]

finally caught up to him but he was awakened by the Aybilian national anthem, Allah Akbar, Allah Akbar, instead of the call to prayer. Hearing footsteps, he reached for his baseball bat until they passed his door. It was still dark outside and again hearing voices, this time coming from the courtyard, he crawled between his doors and looking out, saw the soldiers dragging an Indian doctor and his wife, both in their night clothes across the courtyard, their mouths bound. The woman struggled and one of the soldiers knocked her out by slamming his rifle butt against her temple. She crumpled and he pulled her across the cement by her hair. Dressing and cleaning his mouth inside his room, he left for his morning run, heading north, away from the university. The desert air showed itself in soft gusts, and the limestone houses stood out like white pins on a tan board with splashes of cumquat and orange trees. Running about a mile, the smell of barbecued lamb caught his attention, and signaled a market was near. Stopping at the market, he bought bags of vegetables, fruit, dried fish, and bottles of water.

 "You jogged here, but with that load, you'll be walking back slowly."

Eileen gave him an alligator grin. He could count all her teeth.

"Aren't you a bit far from home?"

"Here, home is where the hatred is."

"Are you talking about Aybil, or America."

"I'm talking about Haba Shangira. It's a green fortress."

He searched the fields behind the market for green tents. Eileen followed his gaze.

"This is the area where the ones who tell them to set up the tents live, and they won't have them here. Come I'll give you a ride."

They got into her white Volvo with the Jami Al Fateh sticker on the bumper.

"You don't mind if I stop by my house do you? I have to tell my partner I'll be gone for a few minutes."

Riding north, the two and three story homes were made of multi colored bricks, with many shaped like castles from Europe. Eileen read his thoughts. "They copy what they say they hate. Sick isn't it?"

Eileen's ranch style brick home sat back about fifty yards from the road. Vineyards covered both sides of the narrow lane and rows of orange trees were in back of the house, along with two other homes. Eileen gave him some bags of supplies and following her, they entered a room with children sitting, running, playing games and eating. They stopped and stood silently when seeing her. Books, chalk boards, games and supplies were stacked against the walls and Eileen nodding her head, signaled the children to sit down. They remained silent until Eileen jumped in the air. "Play children. School hasn't started yet."

Lovell carried the supplies into a kitchen where a dough bodied woman with three heads of hair cooked at a stove. Turning and seeing him, she pulled the scarf from around her neck and placed it over her head, and faced the stove. "It's okay Fatima. He's an American."

Fatima wouldn't turn around, so Eileen turned off the stove and turned her to Lovell. She studied her pudgy feet. She and Aretha Franklin could be sisters, except for the weight. "Fatima, this is Professor Pendleton."

She extended a covered hand and narrowed eyes. Lovell thought she was beautiful, felt a trickle flow through his loins, and held her hand a bit too long because she trembled and dropping his hand, again turned to the stove. Eileen, hands in a prayer position to her face, went to Fatima and whispered something to her. Fatima nodded, they giggled,

[367]

and Eileen smacked her on the butt before she and Lovell exited. The children stood again as they entered, then sat down when Eileen acted as if she were lassoing something. Getting in the car, he saw Fatima at the window, she smiled, and waved. Pulling out into the street, he turned to look at Eileen's spread.

"How long have you had a school?"

Eileen concentrated on the road.

"Eleven years. Keep your eyes straight ahead when you talk to me Lovell. We don't want them stopping us."

His frown spoke to her.

"I'm a western woman driving a car with a man who could easily be an Aybilian. Though we're in this area, you never know when the guards who protect him will act like a dick."

Lovell kept his eyes looking forward, until they reached the university gate. She parked in the blind spot, like Faturi before, where the guard couldn't see her.

"My school is for the farmers and poor children around me who work for them. They're what you'd call guest workers and they can't go to Aybilian schools. The farmer's children don't go to school because they have to help their parents. That's where I come in. They test into schools once they finish primary school."

"And who's Fatima?"

She watched the rear view mirror.

"A western educated widow whose husband was killed by the Colonel five years ago. The farm is in her name because westerners can't own land. Her husband was my husband's friend at the University of Edinborough. That's how we got here. I have to go Lovely. It's not good to be out here talking too long. You never know who's watching these days."

Thanking her, he carried his supplies into the residence and

[368]

saw Matt standing outside his door. Matt's eyes burned
with hatred and a sliver of saliva escaped from the corner
of his mouth. He followed Lovell inside, closed the door,
and sat in front of it. "They got Jim last night."
He sniffled, and ground his teeth.
"Jim's too smart for them to get him Matt. What
happened?"
"I don't know but I'll find out. This was in his mouth. He
must have put it there before he died. They knifed him in
the back behind the veterinary building."
He handed Lovell a bloodied piece of paper he didn't read
because he recognized the flower on the bottom left. Matt
pried the paper from Lovell's hand. "I know. It's hard to
believe. That's not my handwriting. Somebody's good
because they fooled him."
Lovell went to his desk and studied a note from Penny. It
was the same stationary. He looked at Haba Shangira.
"Where's his body, Matt."
Matt covered his face and banged his head against the door.
"I'm a get these muthafucka's. I'm a get these mutha
fucka's."
Lovell reached for Matt, trying to catch him before he hit
the floor, but only managed to break his fall. They landed
on top of his table, which splintered. Matt rolled off Lovell
and sat up, pulling his hair.
"I burned his body in the incinerator for the animals. Many
will die."
A knock on the door startled them and they grabbed pieces
of the table. Armed with table legs and knives, Lovell
shouted for the person to identify themselves.
There was a pause.
"It's Eileen. Please open the door. There's trouble."
Lovell, standing to the side, opened the door enough for
Matt to pull Eileen inside by the collar. He threw her on the

bed and they both stood over her, knives raised. Urine squirted from beneath her long skirt and dripped onto the floor.

"Please, please, don't. I'm here to help. I just saw you Lovell. How could I have done something so quickly? One of my former students is part of the green guard and I saw him on my way home. I doubled back Matt. They're on their way."

Matt lowered his knife.

"What's the plan?"

"I have no idea, Matt. Lovell?"

"Follow me. You got your passport."

Matt patted his chest and his waist. Lovell knew he carried his money in a money belt at all times and the rest was in a belt. Going down the stairs and to the boiler room, Lovell used the key to the passageway beneath the dorms. He'd told Eileen to meet him at the north end of the campus where the orange orchards ended. They ran through the underground tunnel, their hands against the wall guiding them, until it came to an end. Lighting a match, a rickety ladder was against the wall. Matt and Lovell wrapped their arms around each other. "I'll see you when I see you black man. And you take this spring break and don't come back to this muthafucka. You hear me Pendleton."

Matt climbed up the ladder, pushed open the door and was covered with brown dirt. The door closed, and in the darkness, he heard Eileen's trunk close, and her car turn in the direction of downtown. He knew, if they made it, Muhktar would take care of Matt. Running as he never had before, he reached the door behind the door, peeked out making sure the Hajj wasn't there and taking the stairs three at a time reached the top, and walked to his room. Picking up the destroyed table and placing the pieces in a pile, he carried them outside and placed them in the trash

[370]

can that was down the hall. Using turpentine, he washed the floor, and was still cleaning up the pee when the banging started. Cleaning rag in hand, he opened the door and the green guards entered, followed by wide-eyed Faturi. Rifles in his face, they looked under the bed and opened the closet. Faturi spread his arms and told them in Arabic he knew Matt wouldn't be here because we weren't friends anymore. Placing Faturi in front of them, Lovell watched them march down the hall. Knives in both sleeves, he went to Penny's room. No answer. He went to his classroom. No students, no Penny. The practice rooms. The recital halls. The cafeteria. The showers. Basketball court. No Penny. Going into the English Administration Building and opening the door without making a sound, he heard someone snorting something and then turn in the stall, and peek out. It was Faturi. Wiping his nose and the snot which dripped from it with a handkerchief. Droop eyed, he washed his hands.

"What are you doing here? Classes are over for the day. They're over period. It's almost spring break."

He rocked and held onto the sink for support. "Where's Professor Marshall?"

Faturi adjusted his tie.

"Professor Marshall's already left for vacation. Destination unknown."

Lovell crossed his arms and Faturi, seeing the knives, pushed himself against the mirror.

"I only work here Lovell. I had nothing to do with Jim or Matt's death. I'm a victim like you."

Lovell breathed through his nose to calm himself. "Matt's dead?"

Faturi took a baby food bottle from his jacket pocket and using a small spoon, took a one on one. "I'm not sure, but he's nowhere to be found."

[371]

"And Jim?"

Faturi checked the mirror to see if his nose was clean.

"The greens killed him on Ramadan's orders."

Bending his knees for leverage, Lovell left hooked Faturi knocking him against the wall. A goose egg rose on the left temple.

"I guess you're in trouble now that your suppliers are gone."

Faturi didn't attempt to get up.

"You can't beat me or punish me any more than I've punish myself. So hit me again if you want. I deserve it."

Lovell moved towards the door.

"Pendleton, they're not going to let you leave until the end of next week, so don't even ask. And you better go to class or he'll doc you."

"You, he and the rest of this fucking country can kiss my black ass Faturi."

An hour later, sitting in the Hilton lobby, he watched Billy Carter drinking whiskey shots, which he chased with beer. Head swimming, he wanted to ask him what the hell he was doing here, now that his brother was out of office, but kept his mouth shut. Instead he went to the piano, and readied himself to play "Satin Doll," "The A Train," "Creole Love Call," "Sophisticated Lady," all Ellington tunes. He was about to begin tenderly, when a tap upside the head made him stop. Fists ready for a fight, he turned to see Aisha, Abdul's wife and Khadijah's friend, with a sour mouth pinched look on her face.

"Now you know you're not supposed to be playing no music at this time. Do you want to get beat again, you crazy mutha fucka."

Taking him by the ear, she led him from the dining room and outside.

"Get in the car."

[372]

Aisha placed her hand atop his, as the driver, a charcoal skinned Chadian, drove them to Abdul and Aisha's house. Aisha studied the second floor of their house.

"I need you this time sweet brother. I need you to go up there and get my children's baby pictures and the family album. I know they're still sitting on the table because that's where I left them. I don't care about anything else. Okay brother?"

The Chadian drummed the steering wheel. Lovell exited the car, went up the stairs, and knocked on the door. A voice said "Futha," Come in."

Lovell entered the home, seeing a surprised family of three children, all wearing Abdul and Aisha's children clothing, with the father sporting Abdul's grey velvet smoking jacket and even smoking one of Abdul's pipes. Lovell picked up the family album from the table, and left. Aisha kissed him as he handed it to her, and the driver drove them back to the hotel, where Abdul and Aisha had a suite. Lovell saw a white Volvo with the Jami Al-Fateh sticker on the back fender. She fixed Lovell a gin and tonic, and sat across from him.

"Take a drink."

He guzzled his gin.

"I'm sorry about Jim."

Lovell held out his glass for more.

"I know you're wondering what I'm doing here, and it's simple. I can't be without my husband. I'm not some suffering, abstaining, dutiful wife Lovell. I'm a black woman, and wherever my man is, that's where I should be, as long as our children are safe."

Lovell studied his drink. She sat beside him and hugging him, spoke close to his face.

"And Khadijah's fine, and on fire waiting for you so when you leave here, you better get your ass to Chicago."

[373]

They high fived and she walked to the kitchen. "Now tell me what's been going on, while I fix you some grits with that funny Chinese stuff that tastes like eggs I found in the Chinese market."

Lovell explained to Aisha about Jim, Matt, the university, Danuta, and then Penny. Placing his plate on the table, she sat across from him, and passing Lovell the hot sauce, rubbed his face with the back of her hand.

"Don't fret sweet brother. God don't like ugly and Penny's gone get his."

They sat talking until Abdul arrived while Aisha was in the restroom. His hair had greyed and dark craters lived under both eyes. Abdul shook Lovell's hand and as they embraced, Lovell pushed Abdul back.

"Your mouth and your hands smell like pussy. You better do something before Aisha comes out."

Abdul hurried to the kitchen and after washing his hands and face with salt, skipped to the table and sprinkled hot sauce on his hands. He was eating from Lovell's plate when Aisha walked towards the table.

"What the hell has gotten into you? There's more in the kitchen. You don't have to eat from the homey's plate. Country Negro."

Abdul gave Aisha a guilty look and she went to the kitchen to prepare her husband a plate. He and Abdul smoked until Aisha's head dipped in sleep, then he left, and checked into a room at the hotel and slept until the main desk called him with his six a.m. wake up call. Leaving the hotel, he noticed a white Volvo with the Jami Al-Fateh university sticker on the bumper. Walking towards the main street, two chickens hung outside the butcher shop, and heading towards it, a horn blowing spun him around. It was Eileen and her husband Jim, driving towards the airport.

Downtown Ripoli was alive with shop owners opening

[374]

their windows, hanging clothes outside, containers being filled with fresh vegetables, fruit, and the tangy aroma of fresh coffee. Aybilian policemen, starched and pressed in white, smoked and sipped steaming cups of coffee. Lovell hummed James Brown's "This is A Man's World," and entering the butcher's shop, asked for two chickens, from the same Fezzani he'd seen before. The Fezzani butcher moved his mouth, motioning towards the back, and as Lovell walked towards the garbage bins, he was yanked inside the toilet, smelling of Pine sol.

"Matt is safe and away, but you must be very careful." Coffee came from Muskrat's mouth, and he slid the licorice stick to the side.

"The man woman is in Malta. Shall I have my brother's there slice him like a fresh fish?"

He lowered his neck so their eyes met.

"No, let me handle him. I want him to see me before I do whatever I have to do to him."

Muhktar stood to his full height.

"He deserves a slow death. The Aybilians will be confused because the deaths will continue, so they will be looking for someone to blame. That's why you must be careful. That, and the man who blames you for the loss of his child. He's weak and I will enjoy killing him, like we do all those he sends to follow you. More will die this morning."

Someone coughed outside the door. Muhktar flushed the toilet and turned on the water faucet. "Leave here and walk across the street and into the alley. Whenever you see a door with a flower on it, take the flower and enter the door. You'll have a bouquet to give to Anisa before you take her. She will get you home."

He put Lovell's hands into the running water and pushed him outside. Lovell dropped his bankroll on the floor as he exited and heard Muhktar. Getting paper towels to dry his

[375]

hands and carrying the wrapped chicken, he crossed the street and entered the alley, taking the red roses and entering the doors, Anisa sat waiting inside the last door, simmering in candle light. Giving her the roses, and the chicken, which she opened, removing the chickens wrapped in one pack and something else wrapped in another, Lovell sat on her cushions, and allowed Anisa to spread her appreciation through him. He handed her the reserve Aybilian dinars he kept inside his belt.

"Take the package and put it inside the trash can in the infirmary. The man woman will get it. Now go through that door, a taxi is outside. And American, please come more. I am here alone and I need your offerings. I am not greedy."

Leaving, he took the black taxi with the same driver to the university. Walking through the campus, bearded youth in their black Jalabias and turbans walked in threes around the campus and a sprinkling of students, heads lowered scuttled to class. Going into the infirmary, he encountered red nosed Faturi exiting a toilet.

"Abubakar."

"Pendleton."

Standing at the counter, Faturi standing behind him, he waited for the Moroccan doctor to come to the front desk. Dressed in a sky blue uniform, he opened the gate.

"Come in Professor Pendleton. I need to check your jaw."

Lovell entered and followed him to the examining room noticing the doctor left the door open. Lovell sat his bag on a chair behind the door then bending down emptied the package into the waste basket. Sitting on the examining table, Faturi walked into the examining room. The Moroccan had Lovell open and close his mouth.

"Your jaw has healed perfectly. Any pain when you chew?"

[376]

"No."

"Then you can go on your vacation and eat hardy."

Faturi followed Lovell and handed him a small stack of papers.

"Here are all your stamps. You've been cleared to leave. Go to the financier's office and get your money. I pulled some strings and paid you for the rest of the year, and gave you your severance pay. They'll never discover it. I wouldn't come back if I were you."

He opened his arms to embrace Lovell, but was met with an extended hand to shake.

"Take care of yourself Abubakar."

Abubakar Faturi returned to the examination room and closed the door. Lovell heard the trash can being moved as he exited the infirmary. Waving his papers, he jumped in the air, did the long jump, skipped and danced his way to the faculty residence. Leaping up three stairs at a time and reaching his floor, he did two cartwheels and reached his door. Entering and looking at the room with only the bed, couch, blenders, lamps, and table, Lovell opened the door to his balcony and shouted,

"Fuck you. I'm out of here."

Closing the doors, he lit every candle he owned. He opened his closet finding the two suits he'd had made since he returned, and taking them down, he retrieved his stash, and placing the suits in his suitcase, the money and passport in his bag, and preparing to leave, realized he'd left his letters. Opening the bottom of one blender, Lovell discovered his letters were missing. He opened the bottom of the other blender. No letters, no pictures, and no notes from the book he'd outlined about Aybil. His mind jumped into third gear with images of everyone who'd been in his room. No one had ever seen him place the letters in the blender bottom. He shouted at the ceiling. Fuck it. They can have them.

[377]

They'll never be able to decipher the code from his uncle
and Miss Marguerite and Nidia were safe. Closing the door
to the candle brightened room, he strode through the
building, spitting and farting as he left. The campus moved
like a snail through land, and head raised, Lovell sniffed the
air, savoring the desert freshness. He stopped in the open
lot where Doris had been hung and patted her passport.
 "We got some of them back sister. Only some but we put
up a good scrap."
 A whirlwind of dust swirled around him and he embraced
it, feeling Doris' essence. Throwing a kiss into the air at
Doris, he did the jerk from 1966 through the dirt paths to
the financier's office and encountered a line of professor's
waiting for their checks. The Sudanese, together as usual,
stood at the back of the line. Greeting them with a nod, he
walked to the front of the line, hearing the Indians mumble
as he passed and entered the office where other professors
stood waiting. Passing them and going to the financier's
desk, a German professor told him to go to the back of the
line. Lovell gave him the finger and heard fucking
American as he stood in front of the Pakistani Saied's desk.
Saied opened a drawer and handed him an envelope.
"I envy you escaping hell."
Lovell gave a small salute.
"I need you to take all my Sudanese brothers now because
we're together."
Saied studied the line of professors.
 "Go get them. These Europeans can feel what we feel
when we're in their countries."
Lovell told Madusun and the group of Sudanese to come to
the front of the line, ignoring the mostly German, English
and Australian professors who'd gotten there early. Turning
to leave, Madusun, held his arm.

[378]

"If you're ever in Khartoum, look me up Lovell. My family is well known. Just ask for the Akbar family. They will know us."

Pulling Lovell to him, they kissed on both cheeks, as did the other Sudanese as he passed them. Heading towards the front gate, he turned, hearing running behind him. Madusun led the Sudanese in a full trot, reaching Lovell, they stopped, not even breathing hard.

"The Paki gave us cash to not take up so much time. We need to get cashiers checks from the bank. Can you help us again?"

Holding hands, they walked to the bank. The tellers, headlight eyes with red noses, fidgeted in their chairs. One, Ashraf, had visited Penny's room when Lovell was there. He winked at Lovell.

"My friends need cashiers checks. Will you help them?"

Ashraf inhaled from his inhaler in both nostrils, his eyes going back into his head.

"Yes, professor."

Two Sudanese stood in front of each teller. Lovell was leaving the bank when a group of Aybilians came into the bank and pushing the Sudanese to the side, stepped in front of them to the tellers. The tellers took their inhalers from in front of them and placed them in their pockets. The other Sudanese looked at Madusun who, face puffed like a snake, grabbed the Aybilian in front of him and threw him across the room, and the fight was on. The tellers pulled down their window curtains. Lovell could hear them taking hits from their inhalers and laughing, as Aybilians were pounded to the ground amidst shouts of gary-gary (nigger). Madusun stopped one Sudanese from kicking an Aybilian he'd knocked out.

"Is anyone coming Lovell?"

[379]

Lovell searched the area. No one moved. The tellers chewing their lips, fingers buzzed as they typed the cashier's checks. Whenever an Aybilian would move, a Sudanese would swing and knock him unconscious.
"Go Lovell!"
Madusun waved to Lovell, who trotted to the taxi stop, and left Jami Al Fateh University, and getting into the taxi, the Sudanese, led by Madusun, sprinted towards the highway in a formed unit. The hotel lobby was empty and Lovell sipped his Zorba again and waited for Abdul and Aisha. The piano called to him and he crossed his legs to restrain his desire to play. Entering the hotel he searched the lobby and the bar for Eileen, who's Volvo was again parked in the lot. But she hadn't appeared. Having made his reservations on Air Alitalia or his flight home in three hours, he wanted to feel family, and especially Aisha's closed mouth smile, her taps upside his head when he was out of line, and the head moving, hand on her hips, wide legged stance she took, when serious. Missing Aisha, Matt, Jim, and even Penny, leaving the double zorba sitting on the table, he left the hotel, entered the souk, and went into the blue door. Miles Davis', "He Loved Him Madly" played and following the Egyptian musk incense, he found Basam alone, smoking from a water pipe.
"The sweet pain Bilal. I knew you couldn't leave without tasting the sweet pain. Sit down."
Basam held Lovell's hand, clasping the thumb.
"First, I would never kill your children Bilal. Anger is a monster which eats at one's heart and mine had been devoured that day. Second, I am sorry you are leaving. And third, you are my friend."
They embraced and wet each other's shoulders. "Now go Bilal. This is now a place for politicians and soldiers. And

[380]

oh yes. That Nubian you enjoyed is now gone. Ma salama (Goodbye)."

Turning his head from Lovell, he pointed to the pathway to the street. Lovell exited the souk and circling back around to the alley in front of the butcher's shop, now closed, collected the roses and entered the last door. Anisa sat fully clothed, a backpack next to her, with Muhktar sitting in front of her. Muhktar stood keeping his head bent to not hit the ceiling.

"Your trust in that Aybilian has kept him alive African American warrior. I hope it is warranted."

Anisa took Lovell's hand and kissed it.

"I think so Muhktar. I read people very well."

"Did you read the man/woman?"

"I knew what he was about. No, he fooled me."

"We can all be fooled by love, warrior. But war brings out the best and the worst in all of us."

"Anisa must go. Her job here is over."

Lovell took the Aybilian dinars he had left from his pockets and gave them to Anisa. She said something in Arabic and Muhktar translated.

"When I see you again I will speak to you in English."

Placing her head against his chest, and Muhktar leading her by the hand with Lovell holding the other hand, they walked to the last door before the street. Muhktar placed both hands on Lovell's shoulders.

"I know you've wondered why I fight them my brother. The answer is very simple. I do not want to be an Arab and have them destroy what is mine because it is different from them. I am different from them and they want to destroy me and you, African man".

The three hugged as a group, and moved to the street, Muhktar and Anisa entering a black cab and Lovell heading back to the hotel. A napkin had been placed over his drink and he knew Aisha had done it. It was that sister thang he liked. Taking the stairs, he stopped on the second floor and watched the Tunisian workers emptying the trash into the garbage bins. I put bodies in there he thought to himself. Following the smell of chicken being fried, he stopped at Aisha and Abdul's door, trying to grip the reservoir of emotion trying to overflow. The door opened and Aisha in an apron sucked in her breath.

"Well you've been standing out there long enough. What are you listening for? Now give me a hug." Flour covered her hands and she closed the door with her butt.

"Get a paper towel and wipe off that door knob. Do you know Eileen?"

He noticed her right eyebrow was raised. Eileen sat in the living room, the sun showing the touches of red in her twilight hair. Her dress, made her alabaster skin look translucent. He couldn't count the teeth in her smile. Aisha returned to the kitchen, moving to Teddy Bear lead "The Love I Lost," with Harold Melvin and The Blue Notes. Eileen poured Lovell a drink from a wine bottle. Aisha shook her shoulders.

"I made you a Zorba. It's in the refrigerator." Lovell and Eileen got up at the same time and went into the kitchen. Abdul emerged from the back in a black caftan and sat at the table as Lovell poured himself a drink and returned to the couch. Aisha continued to cook and Abdul and Aisha sat across from each other. The song changed to Teddy's *"Turn Out The Light"*, and Aisha swayed. Abdul and Eileen also swayed. Lovell could see Abdul his eyes steady in Eileen's direction. Aisha stopped swaying. She cleared her throat and placed her hands in a prayer position in front of her face. Abdul and Eileen continued to sway. Aisha turned off the stove, and Lovell watched as she grabbed another skillet and spun around swinging. Abdul's head snapped

[382]

backwards and he fell backwards in the chair, his feet knocking the table backwards, hitting Eileen who fell with the table on top of her. "Muthafucka. You gone bring this bitch in my house after you been fucking her and then sit at my table and send her love vibes while my back is turned. Don't you think I can feel it? And you bitch. Get up, because I'm gone kick your ass. Not for fucking him, but for having the nerve to come into my house and disrespecting me."

Aisha rushed Eileen swinging but the Scottish girl was ready and sidestepping knocked Aisha down. Aisha rolled on the floor laughing and jumped up. "Is that all you got bitch?"

Eileen charged forward swinging but a kick to the private doubled her over, her mouth opening in a grimace as she reached between her legs. Aisha was on her with a knee to Eileen's stomach, bringing the wine up and shooting across the room, then pulling Eileen's head down to meet her knee. Aisha knee kicked Eileen in the chin four times and as Eileen's body went limp, she stepped back and threw a right uppercut, snapping Eileen's head back and sending a stream of blood across the room. Eileen's head made a loud crack on the carpet and as she lay flat, Aisha kicked her in the crotch three times. She stood over Eileen her chest expanding and deflating. "Lovell, do you think I killed her?"

Lovell helped Aisha turn Eileen on her stomach. She was still breathing, blood bubbled from her mouth and nose. Lovell stepped on something. It was a piece of Eileen's tongue she'd bitten off. Aisha took ice from the freezer and rubbed it along Eileen's neck, temple, and using her fingers, pushed the blood from the back of her neck upward. Lovell applied ice to Abdul's temple and face, until he sat up.

[383]

"What happened man?"

Eileen started to cough, blood spewing from her nose and mouth. She sat up and touched between her legs.

"Oh my pussy."

She touched her mouth.

"And my teeth and my tongue. What happened?"

Lovell righted the table and put the chairs back. Aisha held ice to her swelling jaw.

"You two got into a fight."

Daggers shot from Aisha's eyes toward Lovell. "Don't lie to them. I kicked both your asses. Now get the fuck out of my house."

Eileen tried to get up, but kneeled over one hand between her legs.

"I don't think I can walk. Would you help me Lovell?"

Her words were unclear.

"Help her to her car and come right back here Lovell. Do you hear me?"

"Yes ma'am."

Taking Eileen's arm he helped her rise. She tried to walk, but collapsed into an "s" figure on the floor. Aisha stood over her. Eileen pulled on Lovell's arm to help her stand up. Taking slow baby steps, holding onto Lovell's arm, they eased out the door and to the elevator. She crumbled again in the elevator, urine running down her legs. Lovell carried her to her car and helped her get inside. She groaned when sitting.

"If I were you, I'd go straight to the infirmary at the university. I think it might me something serious."

"Did we really fight?"

"You tried."

Eileen started her Volvo and pulled away, leaning over the steering wheel. Lovell looked down as she drove away. Globs of blood dotted the asphalt. Upstairs again, he knocked on Abdul and Aisha's door, but there was no answer. Opening the door, and entering, he went to get his suitcase

"Don't touch me Abdul. Get your hands off me. Sorry isn't enough."

She emerged from the back carrying her suitcase.

"Let's go Lovell. I'm going to get on that plane with you and we're going home."

Abdul, with a baseball size knot on the right side of his head, fell to his knees.

"Baby please don't leave me. I know I was wrong."

Aisha opened the door allowing Lovell to leave first.

"No baby. I was wrong for coming back here. You don't deserve me."

Slamming the door, she held onto Lovell's arm and walked to the elevator. She didn't break until they were in the air, where she covered her head, which almost touched her knees, and convulsed with muffled sobs. Marguerite's limousine met them at the airport. Observing Aisha, she wrapped her arms around her, allowing Aisha's head to rest on her shoulder as they rode to Marguerite's estate. Lovell thought how women support each other even though they've never met. Marguerite walked with Aisha like a mother does with her daughter after her first heartbreak and sat with her in her room, shutting Lovell out. He wandered through the castle's halls, looking at the Giuseppe family's crests and crowns. The portraits of he and Marguerite showed a regal couple clad in pink and burgundy. Walking the grounds, the late winter, early spring coolness made his bones tingle. He rushed back to the house, and his room, looking in the closet for a winter coat. Marguerite opened the door, entered and sat on the bed.

"If you men want to get some pussy on the side, you should leave it on the side and outside. How stupid."

[385]

She moved her fingers, beckoning him to come close, and sitting next to her, he relayed what had happened since he was there. She ran the back of her hand across his chin.

"You never cried once when you told me what happened. You're different now. I see the full man in you. What's your next move?"

"I'm going to get my baby, and Khadijah and her baby. Then I don't know."

Miss Marguerite ran her fingers along the lines of the bedspread.

"You don't want to live in the states, and you don't want to go back to Africa. Why don't you bring your new family here until you make up your mind? You can have the south wing."

He watched the sway of her hips as she left the room, and thought about Khadijah, little Aisha, and his newborn child. Whatever it might be. A light knock on the wooden castle door awakened him. He couldn't remember where he was and reached for his pants where he knew his knife was. Someone was calling his name.

"Lovell, baby open the door."

He rose, naked as usual and opened the door. Ms. Marguerite thumped him on his rod.

"I haven't seen that in a long time. You have a call from the states. Plug in the phone that's next to the bed."

He returned to the bed and after plugging in the phone, heard his cousin's voice.

"Lovell, Papa died in his sleep last night. When are you coming?"

It took him a few seconds to grasp the words. Papa, was his uncle Mack.

"Did you hear me Lovell? Papa died last night. I found him. I need you here to take care of all this shit. Are you coming?"

[386]

"Yea, I'll be right there."
Placing the phone on his bed. Images of his uncle throwing him in the air, showing him how to skin animals, clean fish, and taking him shopping ran across his mind. Marguerite came into the room and climbing into the bed, rocked him, his head on her chest.

CHAPTER FOURTEEN

Watching the red stream of landing lights, Lovell
fingered his initials LP, on the embroidered handkerchief
Uncle Mack had made for him. His actual name was Mack
Lovell Pendleton and Lovell had been named after him.
 "If I don't see you no more in this, I'll see you in the next
one so don't be late", the lyrics from Jimi Hendrix's
"Voodoo Child" came to him, and he sang them out loud.
"Excusa me senori. We're here."
The attendant from Marguerite's private plane stood over
him, with a closed fist to his mouth.
"Does the senori need some Kleenex?"
Wiping his eyes with the handkerchief and putting on his
winter coat, he walked down the aisle preparing to meet the
windy city hawk. Exiting the plane, and feeling his pants to
make sure they were on because the hawk had pecked
through them, he saw the white stretch limousine with
Pendleton Enterprises at the bottom of the stairs. The door
opened as soon as he reached the bottom stairs. "Get in
before you freeze to death Birdy."
There was only one person in the world who called him
that; Little Mackie, Uncle Mack's son. Lovell got in and
was handed a mimosa. Little Mackie, six foot five, two
forty, with a David Ruffin looking man on one side, and a
Lena Horne look alike model on the other, both with their
hands on his ham hock thighs, raised his glass and clinked
Lovell's.
"Welcome back. It's too bad you're greeted with this, but it
be's like that."
They clinked glasses. Little Mackie, face like the Indian on
the nickel coin, with a grapefruit forehead and hair like

[388]

ringlets, was a replica of Uncle Mack, except for the size. Lovell pointed his glass at his cousin's companions.

"Aren't they drinking?"

Mackie kissed both on the mouth.

"This is Margaret and Micheal. We've been at it since we left the harbor. Let's all toast to my daddy. He could be a real asshole, but he was a good man."

They all touched glasses and Lovell closed his eyes, and was awakened by a hand on his shoulder. "We're here."

The Harbor City chill made his lips purse and leaving the car with Margaret and Micheal staying inside, his shoulders spasmed when seeing the Pendleton Rest services sign on the white stucco building loom above him. It was the crematorium. Mackie took Lovell's hands.

"I don't think I can get through without holding onto you."

Lovell squeezed the hand swallowing his, and together they entered the building, walking through a stark-lit hallway until they reached a door to their right. Mackie gripped Lovell's hand until he winced. Prying loose Mackie's grip, and entering the room, Uncle Mack lay on a table, a sheet to his chest, and a slight grin on his face. Mackie crumbled, taking Lovell with him. Mr. Mays, in a white apron and gloves, and two other men dressed the same, rushed from the back and carried Mackie to a chair. Mr. Mays woke Mackie with smelling salt. Lovell stood over Uncle Mack, smoothing the few strands of remaining silver hair.

"He looks peaceful."

Mackie placed his chin on Lovell's shoulder, and Mr. Mays stood behind Uncle Mack's head.

"Are you two ready for this? It was his wish. You'll have to step into this room."

Mr. Mays wheeled Uncle Mack's body into the next room, then he and the other men lifted the gurney after opening

[389]

the incinerator door, and slid his uncle's body inside. Mackie dropped to the floor on his knees.

"Dad?"

He held Lovell around the legs as the incinerator begin to hum. Hearing a loud popping sound, he joined Mackie, until Mr. Mays comforted their shoulders.

"It's done sons."

They rose and supporting each other, left, and rode to Lovell's old home. Two manila envelopes with their names distinctly written, sat on the kitchen table. Mackie's companions sat in the living room. Opening the envelopes, they discovered Uncle Mack had liquidated everything, splitting the money between them. A handwritten note was in Lovell's folder, giving him the numbers for the men guarding Khadijah, and Aisha, and saying

"These boys are serious."

Mackie read the papers again, and pushed them into the center of the table.

"We've spoken everyday since you've left and I saw him every other week. If I didn't come here, he'd come to me. He was ok with me being as I am, as long as he didn't see it. He wasn't ok with Margaret though. Birdy, I'm outta here. No, we're outta here. This is no longer our house, and the Harbor has nothing for us anymore. You going to Texas?"

Lovell ran his hands along the kitchen floor's carpet, thinking of his mother walking barefoot across it and saying datnammit, every time she dropped something.

"First Chi-town, and then down there. I got-"

Mackie pushed him outside, closed the door, and threw the key in the air.

"You have twins on the way, a woman in Chi-town you're trying to protect from her powerful husband trying to kidnap her daughter, and you've just come back from North

[390]

Africa where you feared for your life everyday. Cuzzo, I'd say your life is in disarray."

They were on the highway enroute to Chicago, drinking mimosas, and recalling Uncle Mack. Arriving in Chicago they sat in the limousine, observing the family lines in each other's face. Mackie heaved and held Lovell's hand between his.

"We only have each other in this world Birdie, and I don't want to lose you. Please stay in touch. Let's talk each week like me and the old man did."

Lovell cleaned his face and stood outside the limousine, until the window rolled down.

"Yo Mack, when does spring training start?"

Mackie touched both his companion's thighs.

"I'm on my way there now. With both of them."

The window rolled up, Lovell entered the Chicago Hilton and checked into a suite. He dialed the number Uncle Mack had given him, ordered a limousine, showered, and waited for the knock on his door. Fully dressed, he opened the door after the knock, and was pushed backwards by someone dressed in a full-length black cashmere coat, with the head wrapped and dark glasses. Stumbling backwards, keeping his eyes on the person who pushed him, he felt the table next to the bed where he left the knives. He lifted one and advanced. "Habibi."

Khadijah unwrapped the head and face scarf and flipped the dark glasses into the air. She threw each piece of clothing she wore at him, moving her hands as if unscrewing a lightbulb, and swiveling her hips, she went to Lovell. They lay amidst soaked sheets and watched the snow flurries blanket the Chicago skyline. Khadijah nibbled on Lovell's nipple and ran her first finger down the hairline starting at his navel down to where his forest grew.

[391]

"I long for the day when there won't be guards outside our doors and we can walk anywhere and feel safe."

He played with a lamb's wool curl.

"I know what you mean. We still have work to do."

Sitting up, piano fingers cradled his chin, and she delved into his eyes.

"I'm sorry about your uncle. He was a wonderful man and we all loved him. How are you?"

Lovell opened the expressway to his heart and she strode down it, inspecting each memory of Uncle Mack.

"I'm complete with it as much as I can be. That's the way he'd want it."

Rising from the bed, she removed the sheets, rolling them into a ball and carrying them into the bathroom, returned with towels, which she placed on the bed.

"He welcomed us into your family and we welcomed him into ours. He and Baba were like old buddies who hadn't seen each other for a long time. Without him, they would have taken Aisha." Sitting cross legged in front of Lovell, she told him how Ramadan's men had first come to the house dressed as city inspectors and had tried to take Aisha from the back yard and escape through their neighbor's home, but Uncle Mack's men had subdued them and driven them away somewhere. Another group of Aybilian women who had worked in Aybil that Aisha knew from visiting their home in Aybil had attempted to kidnap the child inside a toy store, had actually gotten outside the store with Aisha. Luckily, the brothers outside were waiting for them. Aisha was carried back inside and the women disappeared. The last time two women had snatched the little girl during a fire alarm at school, and were running with her but the guards were waiting in their car, and when they entered the men took Aisha from them and drove away with the Aybilian women. Aisha started to wet the bed after this

[392]

incident and hadn't stopped yet. Khadijah showed him the pistol she now carried and Lovell noticed her feet and hands had tightened and her eyes had become glassy. "We have to put a stop to it, Khadijah. I'm here now and I'll help."

After showering together, they left the hotel with the four brothers in suits, Khadijah called them. What Lovell noticed was they wore dark glasses even at night and didn't speak. Two walked in front, two in the back, and their heads moved all the time. He couldn't see any bulges for guns, and as soon as he and Khadijah stepped out of the hotel a car door opened and they were ushered inside. Two brothers rode in the front seat and two sat in the back with them. Arriving at Khadijah's parents' home and parking in back of the house, two men met them at the door and entering the house, he saw two more at the front door. Aisha ran to Khadijah and leapt into her arms.

"Mommy you look very happy. I haven't seen you smile like this since we left Aybil."

Turning her head to the side, she touched Lovell's shoulder.

"I think you're why my mommy's smiling."

Fatima, Khadijah's mom hugged Lovell and took Aisha. "Come Sha, we're going to cook for everyone." Looking over her shoulder, she winked at Lovell and Khadijah. "You can't fool kids can you?"

Mr. Freeman greeted Lovell with a high five, a low five and a deacon Jones tackle embrace and condolences about his uncle. Large splotches of white were now visible in his hair. Seeing Lovell looking at it, he pointed to the guards. "Guess the price we pay for freedom is high isn't it."

Sitting in the Freeman living room, they discussed the new young guard for the Lakers, Magic Johnson, and "The Great White Hope," Larry Bird from the Boston Celtics,

[393]

"The Deer Hunter" and the shifting change in the world, and the U.S., after Reagan. Finishing the conversation, and being called to dinner, Mr. Freeman, squared Lovell.

"We got to get this muthafucka because he's not going to stop. We keep killing his men and the women he sends, but he keeps coming. This is a nonstop situation, son."

Dinner was joyful, and Mr. Freeman and Lovell played together; Freeman on piano and Lovell on saxophone. Mrs. Freeman held Khadijah and Lovell together as they were about to return to the hotel. "You two belong together. Let nothing come between you."

They rode back to the hotel, wrapped in a bouquet of love, watching the now silent city pass in front of them. Waiting for the car door to open, they tasted each other's love again until being surrounded and moved inside the hotel, where they were stopped and Lovell was given a note; call Ann. Rushing to his room, and dialing the number, his legs jerked and Ann answered

"Nidia went into labor. You better come."

Khadijah took the phone form Lovell and dialed. "Mommy, you and Baba will have to watch Aisha for a few days. We're going to San Antonio to get our baby."

They left the hotel and called the airport, getting a flight to Houston, then to San Antonio. The window in the town car separating the passengers from the driver opened and a dark glass wearing red haired man with a scar across his jugular vein turned his body to Lovell. His neck didn't move.

"Do you want some company on your trip? Your Uncle asked us to protect you."

"No, I'm good."

Flying to Texas, Lovell felt Khadijah making circles on the top of his hand.

[394]

"You'll have a ready-made family Khadijah. Are you sure this is what you want?"

She ran her first finger up and down his lips. "Didn't you hear what I said on the phone? This is our baby because I'm going to raise it, and then we'll have one more for us. I knew what came with you, and I told you I'd do anything to be with you. Don't you know that yet?"

His lips answered her. San Antonio was heavy jacket cool and they felt warm, but overdressed. Pulling into the parking lot in the Benz they'd rented, Lovell turned off the ignition cupped Khadijah's face.

"I don't know what's going to happen in here. It could be weird. I mean a woman's giving up her baby. At least she said she would. She might change her mind."

Khadijah removed his hands, kissing the palms. "We can only go inside and see."

Riding to the maternity ward on the second floor, prickly pulses shot through his hands which Khadijah eliminated by kissing his fingers. The door opened and turning to the right, Ann sat by herself. She sprinted to Lovell, vice gripped him and spoke into his chest.

"I'm glad you could make it. They just came. A boy and a girl, like Nidia said. The Longoria's have disowned her, and I think they'll try and kill you if they see you because they think you betrayed them."

Khadijah tapped her on the shoulder.

"I'm Khadijah. I need to speak to Nidia alone."

Ann welcomed Khadijah with a one armed hug. "It's nice to meet you. I've heard a lot about you. She's in there."

Khadijah went into Nidia's room and closed the door. Lovell walked Ann to her chair and sat holding her hands.

"How'd you know about Khadijah?"

Ann's eyebrows pulled together.

"Penny told me. We've been communicating for the last month and he just left here."

She dropped Lovell's hands.

"What's going on?"

"Did he show you the pictures of Nidia?"

Ann leaned toward Lovell who'd rested his against the chair.

"Yes he did. I thought it was weird he'd have them. He asked us a lot of questions about when you were coming. Nidia opened up because he asked for forgiveness. You know how Catholics are."

Lovell stood to go see Nidia, but Khadijah stepped in front of him.

"Let's go Lovell. They're waiting with the baby."

He tried to push past Khadijah but she put her body in front of his.

"This is the way she wants it, Habibi. She doesn't want to see you or the baby. There's only one inside. The girl."

Lovell turned towards Ann, who studied the floor, and nodded yes, anticipating Lovell's question. Ice flowed through him as Khadijah led the way to the office. Time moved as if he were in a vortex with the hospital official's voice echoing and real time didn't reach him until she stood above him with a baby and he heard a voice.

"Here's your son Mr. Pendleton, he's a beautiful healthy boy."

Khadijah took the baby and they walked to the elevator. Feeling Nidia, he turned towards where he and Ann had sat, and heard a door close.

"Let's hurry Habibi. We don't want the baby to be in the night air."

Rushing to the car, he heard the baby murmuring and his head swiveled searching for anyone in the parking lot. He opened the door for Khadijah, his son, and got into the driver's seat.

"What's his name?"

Khadijah turned the heat on low and the blast of hot air pushed Lovell back against the seat.

"You didn't hear and word she said did you? His name's Primavero Love Longoria Pendleton. Look at him Habibi. He's copper skinned like her, but he has your face. Look at his hands, they're massive like yours."

Lovell peered into a face like his, and the boy smiled, then reached out a pudgy hand with long fingers. Those were his mother's fingers and he'd be able to reach more than an octave on the piano. "One life gets lost and another is born. I lose one and gain another. I wish my parents and Uncle Mack could see them Khadijah."

She rocked the baby and placed her fingers to his lips.

"I'm sure they can. Now drive Habibi. We have a plane to catch."

He waited until they were on the private plane Khadijah had rented. The baby fell fell asleep holding onto Khadijah's finger

"What did Nidia say to you in the room?"

Khadijah pulled back the blanket and studied Primavero's face.

"She made me swear I'd take care of her son. I swore and I meant it."

A hard iron edge creeped into her face. He'd seen his mother look like that when she'd watched him playing sports or in a fight. It was protection and his mind eased seeing the mother instinct in her. "Khadijah, I think trouble awaits us when we get back to Chi-town."

Her head bobbed like a buoy in water.

"Is it Aisha?"

Trying to stop her lips from trembling, he placed his fingers to her lips but she grabbed them.

"What do you know Habibi? Tell me!"

"Penny stole my letters from my room, and he was in San Antonio before we got there. I think he's been helping Ramadan and they'll probably plan to strike while you're away."

Khadijah rose and walking with her back straight went into the pilot's cabin. He heard her talking, then emerge flushed, but smiling.

"Everyone's ok, but I put them on high alert. They'll meet us at the airport."

Khadijah sang lullabies and patted the baby as they returned to Chicago.

CHAPTER FIFTEEN

The limousine met them at the airport and took Lovell to the hotel, where he checked out and went to the Freeman's home. Mr. and Mrs. Freeman, she in white Terry cloth and he in burgundy silk pajamas, robe and slippers, met them at the door. Mrs. Freeman, wiping the joy from her eyes, helped Khadijah, as if she'd given birth, up the stairs, chattering in Arabic. Mr. Freeman took Lovell into the kitchen and sat him down at the kitchen table. "You know you can't sleep with my daughter under my roof unless you're married. Right?"

"Yes sir."

Mr. Freeman lit a long pipe and passed it to Lovell. "Don't worry. I mixed it with something. They won't smell it."

They finished the bowl in silence and ate sherbet ice cream. "Khakha told me about your friend. We have to stay on top of them, son. I can feel the danger heightening. We own a place in Puerto Rico and our plan has always been to retire there. It's time. What are you going to do?"

Lovell finished his bowl of orange sherbet, scooped out some more and put the rest in Mr. Freeman's bowl. They'd eaten a pound of ice cream. Looking into the empty carton, they laughed until the tension hanging between them ran from their noses and mouths. Mr. Freeman wiped his mouth and nose. "That was some mean green. I brought it back from Egypt and I've got pounds of it. We can kick back and enjoy it when we get to Puerto Rico."

Mr. Freeman nervously tapped the table with his fingers. "If I was Ramadan, I'd strike now because we're all distracted with my son."

Mr. Freeman pulled out his pipe again, but Lovell waved him off.

[399]

"Kha Kha told her mother, his mother's a lesbian and she gave up one of her twins. I can only imagine how she must feel."

Lovell opened his mouth to speak, but the plates shattering and windows breaking made him lurch. Mr. Freeman grabbed his arm, tumbled to the floor, and Lovell pulled the table on top of them. Bullets thudded against the walls, and he heard the snort of silencers, and people running. Mr. Freeman lifted his twitching arm.

"Fati, Kha, you are you all alright. Is the baby ok?"

"We're all ok. Daddy. Are you and Lovell alright?"

"We're alright."

Lovell could see Mr. Freeman's arm flapping like a wing, and he was reaching for him, when the table was turned over. Three black men with dark glasses stood over them, and seeing Mr. Freeman's arm, lifted his legs, grabbing him under the arms, ran with him outside, pulling Lovell with them. Being pushed into the town car, Lovell saw Khadijah carrying his son, and Mrs. Freeman with Aisha jumping into a car behind. They tied Mr. Freeman's arm to his side, tore open his sleeve and stuck needles in his arm as the car moved. Arriving at a hospital, they scooped up Mr. Freeman and dragging Lovell with them, entered the emergency room. Nurses placed the now unconscious Freeman on a gurney and rushed him into a room, closing the door. Khadijah and Aisha wept aloud, but Mrs. Freeman, eyes closed, placed her hands on their shoulders.

"Be quiet. Just sit here in silence, and know that he's going to be alright. It's only his arm."

The guards stood at the door where they'd taken Mr. Freeman. Lovell, his son and Khadijah, who holding the baby, had her head on Lovell, until a doctor came from the room where they'd taken Mr. Freeman.

[400]

"He's fine but we'll have to operate immediately because the bullet hit some nerves."

Aisha held onto her grandmother.

"Can I see him?"

The doctor touched her cheek.

"Not now because he's sleeping. He'll be out in a little while and you can talk to him. Ok?"

The child sat down and glued herself to her grandmother. Lovell pried himself from Khadijah, and went to the red beard he'd seen in the car.

"How many did you get?"

Red beard lifted his glasses, displaying one glass eye.

"All except one. The driver."

"They're not going to stop are they?"

He looked at Aisha.

"Not from what I've seen. They don't care nothing about dying because they jumped out of their vehicle firing and there's no way they could have thought they weren't going down. They serious as a heart attack. We got you covered though."

They slapped fives and Lovell returned to Khadijah. Looking at his son, smoothed the night black hair and marveled at how he smiled when Lovell made a funny face, and gripped the finger he extended with long thick fingers.

"Those are my father's hands", he said aloud.

"And his hair's a combination of the two of you. Look at those curls. He's a quiet baby. I have to change him."

A guard accompanied her to the bathroom and stood outside. Lovell straightened Aisha's sweater, which had risen as she stretched out across her grandmother.

Returning, she sat next to him and surveyed the hospital floor.

"It's something we have to live like this now. My parents are old and they don't deserve this. I need to do something

[401]

about this. I-"

Lovell sealed her mouth with his fingers.

"You don't need to do anything. I'm going to handle it."

A nurse came to them and offered Khadijah, Mrs. Freeman and Aisha a room to lie down with the baby. They walked together, accompanied by two guards. Two hours later, red beard fisted Lovell's shoulder.

"Mr. Freeman wants to talk to you."

Lovell took the stairs to the third floor with Red Beard, who nodded to the guard outside Mr. Freeman's door. They entered and found Mr. Freeman sitting up.

"As soon as this medicine wears off I'm outta here and we're off to get this muthafucka. I could have lost my arm. Rodgers, can you get into Aybil?"

"I can get into anywhere sir."

"Then let's do it."

Lovell sat on the chair facing the bed.

"Mr. Freeman, you're the man I'd like to be, but I need to handle this. Khadi-"

"Khakha's my daughter and that's why I need to handle it."

Red Beard cleared his throat.

"Why don't we all do it together? This is a serious operation. Didn't you tell me this Ramadan was a high official in his country? That being the case, it will take some major planning to take him out. Mr. Pendleton you're the only one who's been there, so we'll need your expertise. We need to get Mr. Freeman out of the hospital before we do anything."

Mr. Freeman tried to get up, then grabbed his head. "I need about an hour to rest and I'll be ready. Keep my wife and daughter occupied until I'm ready." Lovell and Red Beard left him closing his eyes and using the stairs again, returned to the second floor. They met Mrs. Freeman and Aisha coming out of the room where they'd been resting.

"This child has gotten very restless. I had to take her out of the room because Kha Kha and the baby are sleeping."
They were passing by the nurse's station.
"There's a playroom down the hall where she can play. I'll call Marcus to open it because it needed to be clean. A child got ill in there."
She made a phone call and in a few minutes a charcoal skinned, snow headed woman and bearded black man came along pushing a big toy box. The nurse smiled and winked at him.
"I see you're still playing Santa Claus."
Marcus winked back at her.
"Yes, I'm the bearer of gifts for the little ones. You don't need to ask me about the room because I already cleaned it. I just need to put these new toys in there and take the old ones out."
His keys jingled as he passed them. Red Beard watched his slow movements and following him, stopped him outside the kids playroom as Marcus put the keys in the lock and turned it.
"Could you please open the box?"
Marcus stiffened.
"Who are you?"
"I'm working with internal security here. Please open the box."
Marcus sucked his lips, which disappeared in the beard.
"I'm not opening nothing for you sock dodger. I don't know who you are and you can't ask me to do a damn thing."
His voice carried down the hall and the nurse came from behind the nurses' station counter.
"It's ok Marcus. Please open the box for him and let him check the room."

[403]

Marcus, mumbling, opened the box and Red Beard looked inside, then went inside the room and inspected it. He motioned for a guard to stand outside the door. Aisha skipped down the hall and she and Mrs. Freeman entered the room with Marcus. The guard watched them go inside, and closed the door. Lovell could hear Aisha's tiny voice singing Stevie Wonder's *Isn't she lovely*, but she'd changed the words to Isn't he lovely. Red Beard walked with Lovell to check on Khadijah who slept on her side towards the baby who slept in a hamper. Lovell left them there and sitting down dozed, until a knee nudged him.
"You ready son?"

It was Mr. Freeman dressed, with his arm in a sling. He and Lovell went to the playroom, hearing Aisha's singing the same song as they approached. Inside, Mrs. Freeman sat in a chair with her back to the door. They could hear Aisha's voice, but they couldn't see her. Mr. Freeman touched Mrs. Freeman and she toppled over, almost hitting the floor before Mr. Freeman caught her. Lovell ran around the room looking for Aisha and opening a cabinet, found a tape recorder playing Aisha singing. Mr. Freeman tried to wake Mrs. Freeman, but she lay in his arms, with her mouth open. Lovell opened the door.
"Aisha's gone and Mrs. Freeman is unconscious."
Red Beard ran to the guard outside the door. "How in the hell did they get her soldier?"
The guard banged his head against the door.
"They didn't sir. Only the janitor left here."
He stopped, his head slumped, but he straightened himself.
"He left here with the toy box about an hour ago. I saw him leave by himself. I heard the child's voice. I thought she was still inside. I accept full responsibility sir, and I want to help find her."

[404]

Red Beard opened his mouth, then shut it, his jaws making the red beard move in and out.

"Go to the cars. He spoke into his walkie-talkie. Red alert! Red alert!"

Opening the door, he ran down the steps followed by Lovell. Marcus, blood on his mouth, was propped against the wall next to the toy box. Moving him, they opened the door to the janitor's room, which led to outside. The Chicago night looked like a frozen desert. Riding the elevator upstairs Lovell could see Red Beard's eyes moving from side to side.

I'm sorry Mr. Pendleton. We failed you."

Lovell elbowed him in the chest.

"That could happen to anyone because their plan was tight. They won the battle, but not the war. I want that man who was guarding the door to continue to work for me. Get all your men to get ready to travel to Italy because we're taking the war to them. They ain't seen nothing yet."

Arriving on the third floor, Khadijah sat staring at the elevator holding Primavero. Mr. Freeman embraced Mrs. Freeman who shook, a handkerchief to her mouth.

Khadijah, dry eyed came to Lovell. "I'm going back to get my daughter."

She tried to hand Lovell his son, but his arms refused to take him.

"You promised Nidia to take care of him. You swore, and you can't go back on what you said. I need you to take care of him while I'm gone, so I'll be at peace knowing if anything happens to me, he'll be taken care of."

Khadijah looked through him with glass eyes.

"I'll take care of him, but wherever you're going, I'm going with you."

"And so are we."

[405]

Mr. and Mrs. Freeman, lead faced, were now behind their daughter, and Red Beard had assembled all his men who were on the third floor. Circling Khadijah, Primavero and the Freeman's, Red Beard led everyone to the elevators and once in the cars, they drove to the Freeman home, where Lovell called Marguerite.

CHAPTER SIXTEEN

Lovell checked the money in his money belt and secured
it around his waist. The military rolled clothes and shoes
he'd need, fit into a backpack. He would buy anything else
when he arrived in Aybil. Khadijah with his son, her
parents, Marguerite, and Red Beard watched him prepare to
board Marguerite's private plane for Aybil. Mr. Freeman
held his hands in the air for a high five.
"Ain't nothing to it, but to do it now son."
Clasping Lovell's hands in the air, he swung them down
into a hug.
"I'll see you in three days."
Hugging everyone except Red Beard, he took one step on
the stairs and turned, feeling Khadijah behind him. She
lifted Primavero for him to kiss.
"I don't want to raise him and Aisha by myself, so you
come back to me, Habibi."
Kissing his son and Khadijah, he walked up the stairs and
entered the plane without looking back and watched their
shapes diminish as the plane rose. Warm water calmed his
raging stomach and he urinated four times before the 90
minute flight landed. Wearing a hooded sweater, he walked
down the stairs and entered the Mercedes with the Al
Majuwabi, Aybil's national oil industry sign on the door.
Abdul sat in the back seat waiting for him. "You know you
crazy don't you niggah."
Lovell began to slide down in the seat, but stopped, seeing
the tinted windows.
"Did you take care of everything?"
Abdul faked a left hook at him.
"Is Muhammad Ali the baddest mutha fucka in the world?"
Chuckling at the question, Lovell watched the lights grow
denser and they headed into downtown Ripoli and pulled

[407]

into the alley behind the Fezzani butcher shop. Abdul held Lovell's shoulder.

"God be with you brother. God be with you." Lovell waited until no cars were passing and exiting the car, walked with slow easy strides down the alley until the smell of rotten flesh and garbage made the water in his stomach rise to his throat. Swallowing hard, he followed the glow from Muhktar's cigarette.

"So you came back African American warrior and this time you're willingly joining the battle."

He gave Lovell a joint and they smoked together before a black taxi backed down the alley, allowing Lovell to get in the back seat. Lying flat on the seat, he watched the lights fade until there was only darkness and the sound of cars passing. They turned right and drove down and road without bumps. He knew where he was and after waiting for 30 seconds, opened the door and ran to the second building on the property, which he entered because the door was unlocked. When his eyes adjusted, he recognized Eileen's figure sitting in the blackened room. She flicked a lighter, giving him a quick peek at her face.

"I see you made it mate. You're very lucky you picked a time when Jim's out in the field."

"That's a good sign."

He could make out a small table with plates and a bottle.

"I made some food for you and you'll be okay here for the night. Remember you have to get in my trunk before sunrise because Yasmin will be here very early."

Lovell sat next to Eileen and rubbed the pale hand he could see in the obscure night.

"I appreciate everything you're doing and the risk you're taking. And how's your health?"

Her swallow echoed around the nursery room.

"I'll never be able to have children again and as you can hear, my speech will always sound different because of my tongue. Other than that, I'm fine."

The hand he'd touched went to her eyes.

"People are unpredictable Lovell. You'd be surprised that Aisha and I have grown to respect each other, and one day we might be friends again." He thought about Aisha and the hollow dip in her jaw. She'd once told him they called her Olive Oyl in school because of her size, but when a girl had bothered her, the nickname had changed to Mighty Mouse. He hoped he'd see her, but doubted it. Eileen kissed Lovell on the mouth.

"I'm not sure what you're up to, but please be careful Lovell. The Aybilians can be ruthless." Listening to her footsteps fading, he finished eating, and slept, until the 5 a.m. call to prayer awakened him. Washing himself and the dishes in the preschool's bathroom, he covered his footsteps with a branch from an orange tree, eating the oranges from it, climbed into the trunk of Eileen's car. He could sense the sun rising and heard Yasmin's car stop. She grunted as she carried the supplies into the school. Eileen greeted Yasmin and got into her car. "I'll be back in a minute Lovely. She knows I have an eight o'clock class." He waited until Eileen returned and they drove until he heard cars, then reclined in the backseat. Eileen watched him from her rear view mirror.

"Are you sure you remember where Matt got into your car?"

Eileen winked at him.

"I'm a Scottish woman, not some spoiled English school marm. I'll take you right there and you'll be on your own then Lovely. I hope you don't get yourself killed. The Colonel will be on campus today and there'll be security everywhere."

[409]

A twitch of fear showed at the side of Eileen's mouth, and he held the image in his head, before pulling up the backseat. The car stopped and he waited until the trunk opened, then rolling out behind Eileen, he used his knife to open the door in the ground enough to slip in and heard Eileen pull off. The ladder was still there, and he felt along the walls, counting his steps until he came to the first building. Pausing, he listened for the Hajj, and not seeing him, moved on to the next building, where he knew Penny lived. Crawling along the floor, he stopped, hearing someone talking to the Hajj in Arabic.

"Our leader is coming today and you should go there to hear him."

"But my job is here in this building?"

"Your job is to honor our leader old man, now go. This building is empty because everyone's there so don't worry about it."

The splat of the Hajj blowing his nose on the floor echoed and Lovell heard four feet moving into the distance. Opening the concealed door with his knife, he stepped over the Hajj's splatter and went to the stairs. Turning off every light bulb he saw, he climbed to the fourth floor, opened the door enough to see out, then ran to Penny's room. Using his knife to pick the lock, he went inside and stretched out in the closet. His clothes were sticking to him and he heard the shots in the distance from Penny's open balcony. It was Penny's habit to never close it. He had peed into three of Penny's shoes and heard the evening call to prayer. Penny's door opened and one set of footsteps was heard. Knowing Penny would close his balcony before he stripped naked and changed, Lovell waited until the balcony doors closed. His clothes were laid across the chair. Lovell heard Penny inhale before he laid face down across the bed. Once he heard the bed creak, he opened the

[410]

door and taking out his knife, put it to Penny's throat, pulling his head back. Laying on top of Penny, he bit the top of Penny's ear.

"Don't shout, or say a word, or I'll open a new smile across your neck. You know what goes around comes around Penny Marshall."

He let go of his former friend's hair, but kept the knife to his throat. Penny peed.

"Please kill me Lovell. Do it. I deserve to die for everything I've done."

Lovell turned him over and placed the knife at the bottom of Penny's dribbling penis.

"That'd be too easy for you. You backstabbing piece of shit."

Using his left hand he pimp slapped Penny across the mouth sending blood across the room. Penny smiled.

"I've already tortured myself Lovely, so do as you please. I just want you to know I didn't hurt you and Khadijah willingly. Ramadan became cruel and he said he'd send me to prison if I didn't help him."

Penny sucked on his bottom lip, swallowing the blood, and hiccupped his words. Lovell backhanded him again, knocking Penny's head against the wall. "Where's Aisha?" Penny wiped the blood from his nose with the back of his hand.

"She's at Ramadan's sister's house about a mile from Eileen's place. You can't miss the house because it has stained glass windows and pieces of stained glass outside the house."

He reached down and touched Lovell's hand. Lovell snatched his hand from Penny's touch.

"If you're on the outs with your boy, how do you know where she is, and why should I trust what you're saying?"

"I told him they'd never suspect her there because nobody knows where she lives. Not even Khadijah. He trusts what I say because he knows I can think like you do and he can't. I orchestrated everything Lovell. I broke your code. Whenever you used a street with a number, you were talking about women and men. The last word at the end of the sentence was the subject. You got your baby and we shot Mr. Freeman to get you to the hospital where we kidnapped Aisha."

Lovell pressed the knife against Penny's now peanut sized organ. Penny eased his hand on top of Lovell's.

"You should know me well enough to know you don't have to threaten me Lovell. I know you'd cut me, but it won't be necessary."

Lovell moved the knife from Penny's organ, and sliced him across the leg. White showed, then blood bubbled up and dribbled down Penny's leg.

"I thought I knew you. But from what you've done, it shows I didn't know you at all."

Penny stood, his legs buckling, held his hands in the air.

"Would you open my closet and hand me that long chord on the floor?"

"No, Penny. You forget I know you're trained."

Penny stared at his pants.

"You can tie my hands with my belt."

Taking the belt from the pants on the chair, Lovell tied Penny's hands in front. Penny's hands reddened.

"I can smell you peed in here. Can I throw it out?"

Lovell looked at the left eye closing, the lip rising and the blood coming from both Penny's nostrils. Keeping his eyes on Penny, he bent down and taking the shoes, threw the urine in Penny's face and on his body.

"I know that's what you wanted to do."

[412]

Penny leaned his head back and laughing showed the roof of his mouth. There were white burns on it. "You see, you do know me somewhat, and you know what I want to do. But I want you to know they almost succeeded in assassinating the Colonel today and security is very tight. It will be difficult for you to get out of here. Now please give me the chord."

Penny's body spasmed and he fell against the wall for support. Lovell handed Penny the chord and watched while he tied four double knots on the balcony's railing, then looped the cord and tying a slipknot, placed it over his head, pulling the cord to his throat.

"You know how the electricity is here. If you take out my light switch cover and mess with the wires, you can short out the floor. I used to do it all the time so Ramadan could come here unseen. Do it now and go before I meet the devil I know is waiting for me. Lovell, I'm sorry, and I love you. You were always my friend. I need to tell you something else before you go."

He limped to the balcony dragging a chair. Lovell unscrewed the light switch cover and removing the cap, which held the wires together, pulled them apart. The room darkened and he could see Penny's silhouette climb on the chair, then onto the banister, rock, and jump. He heard a snap and saw Penny's body jerking. Opening the door and staying against the wall, he found the stairs and tiptoed down them, while using his open palm to clear the tears from his face.

Reaching the basement, he heard the Hazz snoring and smelled grain alcohol. The Hazz was drunk on Siddiqui. Slipping past the Hazz and into the pathway, he felt along the walls until he saw the ladder. The light was on, so he slowed, then saw a shadow projected across the floor. Taking off his jacket, he threw it forward and someone

[413]

swung down with a long knife and realizing he'd hit air, spun towards Lovell. It was the Iraqi. Lovell slid to his right, towards the Iraqi's glass eye. As the Iraqi turned his body to see him, Lovell stabbed him in the side. Unflinching, the Iraqi came at him, front kicking and swinging. Lovell rolled under the kick, extended his arm with all his power, sticking the Iraqi in the testicles. The Iraqi dropped his knife, screamed and doubled over. Lovell extracted his knife and moving to the side, sliced the jugular vein and blood squirted in a straight stream against the walls. The Iraqi fell backwards, his mouth and eyes still open.

Wiping the Iraqi's knife on his own shirt, he used the long blade to break the light bulb. Using the ladder to climb up, lifted the door, rolled into the darkness and used his jacket to cover the door with dirt again. He sat in the orange trees across from the university, watching the car lights shine on the feet hanging from the lamppost outside the university, which was never lit. He recognized the shoes. They were a pair of tan on the top and brown on the bottom, two tones Uncle Mack had made for him. He had traded them with Basam for a pair of hand sewn slippers with pointed toes which turned upwards, like elf slippers. A handkerchief stuffed in his mouth silenced the weeping springing from him, at seeing his friend swinging from the lamppost in front of Jami Al Fateh University. The lights from a car stopped in front of the university gate, and he watched a woman drag a ladder from the car's truck. Her cries bounced off his head, as she unsuccessfully tried to keep the ladder upright. Breaking the promise to not have contact with anyone except those they'd arranged, he bolted from the shadows.

"Karima, don't be afraid, it's Bilal."

She sunk to her knees with the ladder beside her, placing her face in the dirt.

"Bilal? Bilal? Where are you? They killed Basam Bilal. He killed Basam for making fun of him."

Lovell turned off the car's lights and knelt down next to Karima.

"You have to be quiet while we get him down."

He lifted the ladder, leaving Karima on the ground, and cut the noose holding Basam, whose lifeless weight overwhelmed Lovell, causing Basam to hit the ground. He heard Karima, who grabbed her dead husband and moaned. Three cigarette flashes came from across the road, and he struck a match-signaling wait.

"Come Karima, we have to get him in the car. Take your babies and go to the yellow house back from the road about two miles from here. There's a Scottish woman named Eileen who lives there. Tell her I sent you. I have to go."

They lifted Basam's body and placed it in the back of their car. Karima drove off in Eileen's direction and Lovell ran across the street and stretched across the taxi's back seat. A familiar voice came from the front seat.

"There's no time for sentimentality in war my brother, especially concerning women. Trying to help you, they hurt you."

Lovell grunted to let the driver know he understood, and listened as he was driven outside the city to where he could hear and smell water. Getting out of the taxi, he got in the boat waiting for him on the shore.

Day 2-

Lovell and Red Beard registered at the Hilton Hotel separately and two hours apart, in the early morning. The hotel staff was drinking coffee and they each ordered breakfast in their room. They'd agreed to not communicate until dark, when they'd meet on the stairs. Sitting in his

[415]

room, he turned to the channel where Basam had worked and watched him on the screen wearing makeup to make him look like the colonel, complete with uniform, marching across the stage carrying a net with bread, fish, and chicken in it, and giving all the food to slim, cardboard soldiers. Dropping the empty net, he slipped behind a partition and emerged as a common Aybilian carrying an armful of money to an empty store, and when he turned around, the paper soldiers were now fat. Exasperated, he threw the money in the air, left the stage and returned dressed as a soldier, patting his stomach and eyeing the food. The TV. then switched to Basam being hanged with something written below it in Arabic. "You were too brave for your own good my dear brother. Too brave for your own good." He flicked the tears from his face with his first finger, and gave the Colonel the middle finger, as pictures of him dressed in different clothing flashed across the screen. He stretched out on the bed, and waited until darkness crept across the Aybilian sky. Once the lights, like blinking eyes dotted the city were visible, and keeping the lights off, he left his room and met red beard on the stairs. Using his watch to guide them, they walked down the stairs, and opening the first floor door, saw Mukhtar's cigarette glow once, then go out. Mukhtar pulled Lovell by the collar away from red beard.

"You bring a "

Lovell stopped him by grabbing Mukhtar's collar. "I'm not a fool my brother and I wouldn't bring the enemy to you. He was part of my uncle's guard."

Releasing each other, they returned to red beard, who stood facing the hotel's entrance. Lovell tapped his shoulder. "Tell him."

Red beard's watch flashed on his face.

[416]

"I have men who need to get near where Ramadan's sister lives for the child, but we don't know where he is."
Mukhtar's teeth showed.
"I like that watch."
Lovell heard Red Beard unclasped his watch and flashed it long enough for a black hand to take it. Mukhtar's Brock Peter's face lit up and disappeared.
"Have three of them meet me in two hours outside this wall. The cars will be waiting. You'll need at least six to get him. They need to be in the water tomorrow at nine in the night because it will be the only chance you get. He swims in the sea with his men then".
Lovell lit a Camel cigarette without the filter and gave it to Mukhtar.
"Will there be room for another?"
"Ah black American warrior, you heart is too big. You want to save your Aybilian friend's family. He was a fool. They can go by water, but not by land".
Red beard inhaled.
"Land?"
Mukhtar moved to the fence and jumped.
"One of you will have to travel by land."
They heard his feet hit the ground on the other side of the wall, and they reentered the stairway. Lovell pulled red beard to him.
"I'll take land. You just get Aisha and the others to safety."
Lovell heard red beard's mouth open and close, as they separated and went to their floors. Sitting in the darkness in his room, Lovell showered and ordered the most expensive fish dinner in the hotel. Bribing the Tunisian bellhop with a fifty dollar bill, he bought two bottles of Courvoisier, placed them inside his small back pack, and rested until five to nine, when he went down the stairs, jumped the wall at the garbage cans, and landed on one of the three black

[417]

men lying flat on the ground. Two taxis' came to a halt at exactly nine and staying low to the ground they split with one joining Lovell in a taxi driven by Mukhtar, who pulled off slowly and drove until the Aybilian lights were no longer visible. He pulled off the road.

"My warrior brother, get in the front seat. I'm not sure where the road to the Scottish teacher's house is."

Lovell got into the front seat and placed the carton of Camel cigarettes, and the bottles of Courvoisier in Mukhtar's lap. He put a pack of Camel's in Mukhtar's shirt pocket and lighting a cigarette, put it in Mukhtar's mouth. Mukhtar blew the smoke through his nose.

"Ah, camels are very true animals, and they don't need much care. I hope your men don't mind sleeping with them. They can be very mean, but a tiny stick in the leg and they will do as you command. Your men will pose as camel and sheep herder's and get the child."

The cigarette had burned halfway when Lovell pointed out Eileen's road. Mukhtar slowed the car and holding his arm out the passenger's window, flashed the watch, and speeding up, turned off the main road and without lights drove down a road, the taxi rocking and lurching, until a fire could be seen in the distance. Reaching the fire, he got out of the car, and opened the doors for the other black man to exit. Mukhtar gave him the key.

"You should remember how to get back to where I got you. Get there with the child as soon as you can, and someone will guide you to safety. Remember black American warrior, here, women dressed in uniforms are soldiers, and if you hesitate, they will kill you. Come brother."

Lovell and Mukhtar walked to the other taxi and got inside. Mukhtar handed a bottle of Courvoisier to the driver before they pulled off, and they rode towards downtown, the two Chadians speaking in a language Lovell didn't understand.

[418]

The lights of downtown glistened like a circus awaiting customers but the taxi turned before they reached it and drove up a slight hill with rectangular three and four story homes. It stopped in front of the last house with metal gates and pulled inside after the driver opened it. Stopping, Mukhtar opened his door.

"Say your goodbye's warrior brother. Go to the back window."

Lovell knocked on the window and Aisha opened it. The room was dark, but the living room was lit. "Brother man, I knew I'd see you again. How you fairing good brother?" Kissing him on the cheek, after sliding it open, and holding his hand, she moved to the side allowing him to look into living room where Karima, with a three month old baby boy in her arms and Basam's two older children, Fuad, and Naznin sat with Abdul. Aisha called Karima, who rushed to Lovell and kissed his hand.

"Allah will bless you Bilal for saving us. Allah will bless you and Basam will watch out for you the rest of your life". The two older children sat like deer in front of headlights. Karima whispered to Lovell.

"They haven't spoken since they saw their father killed. They made them watch it".

Abdul came and they slapped fives. Abdul looked over Lovell's head into the obscure empty field behind his house.

"You got a lot of people praying for you sweet brother. Too bad there wasn't anybody looking out for Penny. He killed himself".

Karima kissed Lovell's hands again and returned to the living room.

"Nobody told me but I have an idea what you're doing. Your momma gave you something that's going to carry you through this world and you use it. You hear me Lovely".

[419]

"Yes, sister. Look out!"

She hushed him with a kiss on the lips. Abdul put his hand on Lovell's shoulder and kissed him on both cheeks.

"I'll see you in Italy homeboy".

They closed the window, and feeling a buzzing in his head, he returned to the taxi where he smelled Courvoisier. Mukhtar and the driver were drinking from the bottle's cap and passing a refer back and forth. They gave him a drink, and a hit of the refer, which smelled like cloves. Sealing the bottles, they backed out of the driveway.

"Tomorrow, when you start your journey, keep this under your tongue at all times. It will keep you from getting very thirsty. If you finish your water. Drink your pee, it won't hurt you."

He handed Lovell a flat black stone.

"Never drink anything the Berber offers you and if he tries to insist, give him a bottle of your American drink and tell him you're unworthy to drink with him. Keep a roll of dollars on your wrist where he can see them at all times and don't sleep. Chew this cot whenever you find yourself getting tired. Take this and put it around the donkey's hind legs and feed him these nuggets. You'll know when it's time to make your move and when you do, keep the moon on your right and keep lighting the flares. I will find you".

They had driven into the desert and stopped at an oval shaped building.

"Rest easy until we come for you tomorrow African American warrior".

DAY 3

He awoke before the call to prayer, not knowing where he was, and then remembered he'd been in the desert all night. Shooting stars arched themselves above him, and his teeth shuddered at the desert air on his body in the outside shower with the wooden walls he could see the desert's

[420]

loping hills through, and touchable sky through. Eating the dried dates and apricots left for him, he placed his head on the sand, and said the Lord's Prayer. Pushing the light on his watch, he understood why; it was 4:30 in the morning. The sound of a car coming in his direction, a puff of dust behind it, forced him to stand, and it skidded to a stop, sand covering his face.

"Get in warrior. The time is now!"

The driver from last night floored the car as Lovell jumped in and drove towards Abdul and Aisha's house. Halfway there, Karima and the children stood in the road and barely stopping to pick them up, the car hummed as he drove toward the water, slowing in the darkness as they neared the docks. Two of red beard's men grabbed a child and ran with them to a waiting boat and four others carried Karima and the baby to it. It's back dipped and the front rose as it moved out of site and Lovell ran to a speedboat, which sliced through the water. Red Beard sat in front, his machine gun ready. He noticed the engine barely made a sound though the throttle was pushed forward. Slowing to middle speed, Red Beard handed him a rifle as they approached the laughter coming from the water. The boat moved at a crawl's pace and when the voices were loud, and in Arabic, a wide ray of light flashed displaying the startled eyes and faces of the men and women in the water. Lovell spotted Ramadan and fired along with red beard the other soldiers who then jumped in the water firing. The spotlight had been turned off as the men hit the water, he could hear short staccato burst of gunfire and the yellow blasts of fire coming from the shore and answered the shots coming from the shore. Then there was silence and jumping back into the boat, they turned around and moved full throttle back in the direction they'd come. They sat in the boat, off the shore and he covered his watch to see the face

[421]

illuminated. Fifteen minutes later he heard a car coming and felt Red Beard's fist in his back. "You're on Mr. Pendleton. Good luck and may God be with you."

Lovell passed a group of soldiers running towards the boat, carrying Aisha. He waved to her and touching the shore ran to the awaiting taxi with the door open. Inside, he saw a child with a hood over its head and realized from the nightgown, it was a girl. Her hands opened and closed, and he smelled feces, along with Courvoisier. He picked up three bottles from the floor and pushed them into his backpack. The driver looked in the mirror, round blotches of sweat on his face, and spoke in French. "The Colonel's niece."

Sirens sounded in the city and he slid the taxi around a corner and stopped.

"Go warrior!"

Lovell rolled from the car and hopped into the back of a pickup truck. Moving his upper body back against the rail the mules kick missed him. He took the rolled rubber from his backpack and tied it around the mules back legs. The animal tried to kick, but he couldn't and turned its head downward trying to bite him. He eased back and pulling the guardrail up rested his back against it. The mule made a sound and Lovell saw the round eyes and three quarter beard of a turbaned face in the mirror. He inched over and keeping his hand open, offered the mule the sweet smelling nuggets. His slimy tongue slurped them up and he chewed, his tail moving in pleasure. The call to prayer swept through the air and the sun peeked its head above the horizon as Ripoli faded.

CHAPTER SEVENTEEN

They traveled through the day, stopping once to get gas from a tanker moving along the highway. The heat moved in waves but Lovell didn't remove his clothing and sat in his sweat. He could smell himself, and the driver. He thought to himself this was no Lawrence of Arabia, riding on a camel. He was in the back of a pickup truck with a shitting mean greedy donkey and a turbaned Berber who kept studying him from his mirror and hadn't said a word. There was a woman with her face covered in the truck who fed the driver and burlap bags of something the mule didn't bother to touch. They drove until night, and after the woman had made a fire, he led the mule out of the truck, gave him food, water, and then approached Lovell, squatting in front of him. His breath was sour like the sweat on his body and his English was mixed with Arabic and French words.

"Here, drink some of my water."

Lovell dropped his head.

"I'm not worthy of drinking with you sir. But I hope you'll drink with me."

He pulled the bottle of Courvoisier from his backpack and gave him the bottle. The Berber's eyes expanded.

"Shokran. Suliema, fire."

He dug in the sand with his hands, placed something over the hole and placed the burning wood over it. Squatting, he drank from the bottle. "I'm Ahmed, and you're an American."

Lovell nodded affirmatively. Ahmed guzzled the liquor and rocking sat on his butt with both legs stretched out, waving the bottle in the air.

[423]

"I own this desert and I know all its secrets. What I don't know, I don't want to know. Do you understand me American?"

"Yes sir."

"I am a sir and this is my kingdom. This is my kingdom, Tehenu, and that is my woman and my donkey."

He began to sip and switched into Italian.

"My kingdom is rich, look at its gold."

He took a fistful of sand and let the uncountable colors flow through his fingers. The people are like the sand Abdul had said. They look the same on the surface but underneath they're very different. And this one was funky and he'd never turn his back to him. Ahmed was staring at the dollars on Lovell's wrist. Lovell pulled off a one hundred dollar bill and gave it to him. Nodding thanks, he held the Courvoisier bottle in the air and the fire created an image in the brown alcohol.

"There is life here in my kingdom and when it gets difficult, I know what to do."

He'd drank half the bottle and rested on his elbows. His feet stank.

"You see that woman there and my mule?"

Lovell followed Ahmed's finger.

"If I run out of water or I'm stranded, what do you think I'll kill first?"

Lovell looked at the mule.

"You're wrong. I'll kill my woman first because it takes more to take care of her and I can do the same thing with my mule as I can do with her."

He gave Lovell a toothless grin and twisting the bottle so it wouldn't fall, crawled to his woman and using her shoulder to pull himself up, pulled her by the hand into the darkness, his grunts filling the air. The air grew quiet, and leaning on her, he came back to the fire and fell on a blanket, snoring.

[424]

His woman placed a blanket over him and with her back to Lovell, her knees up, legs open and facing the fire, she turned, raised her veil and showed him her face. She was no more than eighteen and he thought she looked like a light skinned Cicely Tyson. Ahmed turned over and when his eyes returned to her, her back was all he could see. Feeling exhaustion weighing on his eyes, he chewed the kat, sucking the juice from the bitter leaves, and felt his heart begin to run fifty yards dashes. His mouth was as dry as paper. Removing the stone, he sipped from his water bottle, and observed her add more firewood and then stand over the snoring Ahmed and spit on him. She never turned towards Lovell and wrapping a blanket around her, lay in the opposite direction as Ahmed. Lovell's fingers and toes opened and closed involuntarily and rising to his knees, back to the sleeping couple, he peed in the sand, and then, walking five steps from them, dug a hole with the Iraqi's knife, defecated, cleaned himself with the paper he'd brought and covered the hole. He was dry back there and thought the Arabs have it correct for the desert, water works better. Moving to the truck and sitting with his back against it, the Sahara sky beckoned him, with its canvas of stars stretching down to the earth. He saw red glowing eyes float across the savanna and clutched his knife, the kat putting his nerves at attention. The firelight showed loping tan hills with deep gullies, and winding sand castles. He wanted to take off his shoes and run, the amphetamine charging through his blood, but the engine of a car, and Ahmed's leaping to his feet and kicking the girl shouting Suliema, pushed reality into his face. He pointed to the truck and she got inside just as a big truck pulled up, lights still on. Two Berber's got out, rifles across their shoulders. The three Tuaregs kissed on both cheeks. Ahmed walked past Lovell, and grunting, took one of the burlap bags to the

[425]

men. Money exchanged hands. Laughing, Ahmed got
another bag and carried it to them. One pointed his rifle at
Lovell and Ahmed said "American." They laughed again
and left. Ahmed turned his back to Lovell, counted the
money, and then made his way over to the bottle he left on
the sand. Taking it, and a hit, he cradled the bottle, leaving
the woman in the truck, as he curled up in the sand. Eyes
wide open and his mouth working and hearing Ahmed's
crackling snores, he watched as the woman creeped from
the truck, and lay on the other side of the fire, her eyes
narrowed and focused on Ahmed. The mule made a sound
and he rose, knife in hand, to see if anything was near it.
Head up and moving from side to side, the animal glanced
back at him and Lovell jumped out of the range of the
mule's kick. It showed its teeth, nose flaring. Lovell eased
beside it and dropped a handful of the nuggets in its feeding
bag. Placing the bag over the mule's head, he froze, feeling
someone behind him. Raising both hands in surrender, he
turned around to find the woman in front of him. She
placed her hand over his mouth and motioned her head to
the left for him to move. They walked three steps and she
angled her body to be able to watch Ahmed.
"I'm Irish and I've been his slave since I was eleven. I'm
eighteen now. If you help me kill him we can get away."
She opened her top button showing alabaster skin. "You'll
learn how I got here tomorrow. Get some sleep. I'll let you
know if there's danger."
Her voice had maintained the Irish accent. Walking on her
tiptoes around the back of the truck she got back inside.
Her face was visible in the side mirror and she mouthed I
hate him. Please help me.   Watching her, watching him,
Lovell recalled the words from something he'd read. I love
you, but I hate you, and therefore though I hate you. I'll
defend you and help you. His head bobbed twice from

exhaustion. Hearing the truck door open, he rose and walked around to the other side of the truck to relieve himself. The sun was ascending, and hearing footsteps going in the direction of the mule, he bumped into Ahmed coming around the front of the truck. Ahmed blew his nose as he passed Lovell and continued walking, carrying a gallon water container in his left hand.

"Stop!"

Lovell looked at the oasis, hearing Ahmed grunt then use the water to clean his hands, and everything else. Lovell covered his nose to keep the smell of fresh shit from entering. Hearing the truck door close, he returned to the back of the truck and the open gate. Lifting up the gate, which the mule kicked, he climbed in and stepped on a knife. She had placed it there and leaning out pretending to look for Ahmed, who stood facing the road smoking a cigarette, Lovell saw her wink in the side mirror. His stomach did somersaults. The air was blazing, and he covered his head with his jacket, sipping water, and put on dark glasses to conceal his eyes. He'd been napping for a while because the sun was in the one o'clock position, and leaning over the side rail pretending to vomit, she raised her eyebrows as the truck turned right, almost throwing him over the side. Ahmed laughed inside the truck as they drove down a narrow road to a flattened area with a ranch style flat-topped building. It had open stalls covered only by a tarp in front. Trucks and custom made limousines were parked to the side of the building. Ahmed parked the truck, and rushing to the back, let down the walkway. He jumped in and guided the mule backwards down it. The mule's tongue hung from its mouth and Ahmed tied it to a post and ran inside the building. Lovell followed him inside and choked down the bitter leafy acid trying to escape from his mouth. Men and women, all white, blond, red haired,

[427]

auburn and dark haired, hands bound behind their backs, faces smeared with dirt and tear streaked, were being auctioned.

Sheiks dressed in silk, head scarves, men in designer business suits, some in Jalabias, raised their hands at the prices being said for each person, or groups of people, who were then led outside. A veiled woman stood outside each stall and as the women were led in, the veiled women went in and examined them. The men examined the men. He walked by each stall and moving the tarp enough to see, watched the slaves being stripped, examined, and led away to limos, trucks or vans. Passing by Suliema she whispered. "This is how I got here."

Hand to his head, aching with ancestral memory, Lovell followed his feet, which stepped on each other, until two hands on his wrist righted him. "Please help me! Please help! I heard them call you an American. Don't let them take me!"

A blond haired boy with eyebrows almost touching, with an angular nose and well cared for teeth held onto his arm. Reality shifted and the buyer's eyes shifted to him.

Suliema, her head bowed, shook and two men wearing dark glasses stepped towards him. Lovell pulled his knife and sliced the young man across the fingers, the blood wetting his hand.

"I can't help you."

Screams of Neine, Neine! snatched the attention away from Lovell and he turned to see a beanpole blond woman being pushed into the stall where Suliema stood. She opened the partition, stepped inside, and closed it. Slaps could be heard from inside, then muffled crying. Suliema opened the curtain and led the sniffling German woman by the hair, her head hanging like a dead weight, to the truck. Jumping in the back, she pulled the German woman up by the hair and flung her down into the mule crap. Passing Lovell who stood by the truck, she said see and returned to her place outside the stall, staring at her feet. Ahmed emerged a few minutes later, dragging a red haired little girl, around eleven, by the back of her dress. The child kicked, sand covering her pale legs.

"Mommy, mommy. Please don't let them take me! Daddy please, where are you? Why are you letting them do this to me?"

The kat poured from Lovell's mouth and he held onto the truck's back flap to keep from fainting and walked to the little girl. Suliema, a dribble of blood creeping down her lip, followed him. They lifted the kicking child into the back of the truck. Suliema looped a cord around the girl and woman's arms, tied it to both sides of the truck and got inside. Ahmed, smiling, took the three remaining burlap bags from the truck, and carrying each one, put them inside the truck where the boy Lovell had cut, sat, his eyes closed and face facing upward, moving his mouth. Ahmed then got the mule, its tongue now hanging out and blue, and tried to pull it. The mule took two steps and fell sideways, knocking Ahmed against the building. He pulled himself up and stood over the convulsing animal, which frothed at the mouth, then ceased to move. Everyone outside grabbed their stomachs and sides laughing. The truck driver with the truck and the bags, and the boy, approached Ahmed, shaking his head and laughing. Ahmed pulled Lovell's arm and pointed to his wrist, whispering.

"Dollars. Dollars. No dollars I kill. I sell."

The approaching Berber stopped mid step, seeing Ahmed pull Lovell's arm. Lovell thought he saw every gun and knife in the market, so he removed the rubber band, and counted out ten one hundred dollar bills into Ahmed's hand. Ahmed took five and handed them to the man, now facing Lovell. The men held up two fingers and Ahmed gave him two more. A kiss on both cheeks from both of them sealed the transaction and Ahmed went back inside the building.

"God's going to punish you for being a slave trader you fucking nigger."

The boy shouted as the truck carrying him pulled off. Feeling as if a left hook had slammed into his stomach, and spitting out the pain, Lovell entered the building where the bidding continued.Turning, Lovell heard the word Siddiqui (friend). A man, Muhktar's height, wearing a smudgy Jalabia, and a Kufi, spread his arms, and didn't attempt to wipe the grief spewing from his eyes. Twin girls reaching his chest with thick hair stood in front of him, and a woman, almost his height, her head rising and falling stood next to them. Lovell nudged Ahmed, who studied a fair skinned woman with bright lipstick, and in shorts, being auctioned off on the stage.

"Sir, can I sell them again?"

He spoke to Ahmed in broken Italian mixed with Spanish. Ahmed spit on the floor.

"You won't get much for them. We have plenty of them. They're cheap."

The auction became clearer. They wanted whites because they were a rarity in this area. Blacks were all over the North African and therefore of little value. This included him.

"You can have them all for two thousand U.S."

The voice spoke Castilian Spanish. Lovell turned around, saw no one, and then looked down. A cream skinned man with a white derby, mirrored sunglasses, and wearing a short-sleeved white sports jacket with shoes to match smiled displaying gold-rimmed teeth.

[430]

"I've been here all day and I've had no offers. Your partner's a pig, but I see you have a keen eye. Two thousand and they're yours. You can sell him to a farmer and the others as maids, or breeders. Give me cash and they're yours."

Lovell touched his heart and nodded to the head of the family, then spoke in Spanish.

"I will buy you."

The tiny businessman pointed to the family and a fat man wearing a fez and mirrored glasses, put handcuffs on the father, which had a chain that connected the family. They walked slowly because their ankles were manacled. He led them outside following Lovell and the owner.

"Here are some papers, sign this."

Lovell read and signed a receipt of sale, taking the one thousand from his wrist, plus another thousand from the top of his sock. He counted the money into the little man's hands, who then shook Lovell's hands, and gave Lovell the key to the cuffs and manacles. Lovell checked the locks by opening and closing them, and walked away laughing, along with the people in the market place. Ahmed ran out of the building screaming and cursing which made everyone laugh more. Lovell made out he was saying Lovell hadn't paid for all these people, and he couldn't feed them and something else. Bending down and pulling more one hundred dollar bills from his sock, Lovell spread them out, silencing Ahmed and the crowd. Using his jacket, he swept the mule shit from the back of the truck and spoke to the family again in Spanish.

"Get in the truck."

The family shuffled along and dragged each other to the truck. Lovell bought open baskets of food, and put it in the back of the truck with the slaves. His chest sticking out, Ahmed entered the truck and drove away from the market.

[431]

Reaching the paved road, he stopped the truck. Lovell got out and spread out five one hundred dollar bills. Ahmed, licking his lips, took them and got back in the truck, returning the way they'd come. Studying his watch, and watching the sun, Lovell figured they were near where they'd camped last night. Ahmed had turned off the highway once, about fifteen minutes before, stopped the truck, left on foot, and returned carrying something in a long box. They returned to their campsite and Lovell pulled the family away from the German woman and little girl, removed the cuffs from their hands.

"I need to keep these on your ankles to fool this Berber."

"Thank you my, uh, sir, uh. Thank you. You have saved our lives."

Lovell studied Ahmed, who did something in the truck, and glanced into the sky before exiting it. Suliema lit the fire as night crept over the desert. She fed the German and the little girl after feeding Ahmed. Ahmed took a cup to the truck and closing the door, carried it to Lovell.

"Drink with me. You are my new business partner. It is good."

Lovell reached for the cup as one of the twin girls screamed and jumped up. Lovell used the excuse to drop the cup. Its contents spilled in the sand. "Excuse me sir. Please honor me again by having my drink."

He pulled another bottle of Courvoisier from his bag and passed it to Ahmed, who held the bottle up to the light, and passed it back to Lovell.

"You drink some first."

Lovell opened the Courvoisier and turned the bottle up. The black space in Ahmed's mouth showed when he smiled, and taking the bottle, he returned to the fireside and facing Lovell, began to chug the cognac. Lovell's watch said seven o'clock when Ahmed's head bent forward. Getting a running start, Suliema swung a pointed shovel down on Ahmed's head, splitting it in half. One half fell to the left, and his body to the right. She continued to swing at the body until the blood coming from her hands made the shovel too slippery to hold. She spit at Lovell.

"You thought I was on his side didn't you. You thought I was going to stab you in the back. I told you I wanted to kill him and I did. Now what? I know him. He'll have them come here when the moon's high, around 9 o'clock. They were going to kill you and sell that family. Now what? I can't drive and we'll never get down the highway."

She wiped the blood from Ahmed off her face and the blood from her hands on her dress. Lovell unshackled the family's ankles.

"Untie them and gather everything you can to eat and drink. We're out of here."

"Do you know the way?"

Lovell glanced from Suliema to the man he'd just purchased.

"My name's Lovell and all I know is to keep the moon on my right. Where are you from and what's your name?"

"We're from Spanish Morocco and my name's Saed. These are my children, Naila and Noorah, and this is my wife, Nafisa."

They gathered all the food and found high powered lights, and the rifle Ahmed had brought back, with ammunition, and more flares in Ahmed's truck. Together, they set off into the night. Sharing his kat with Saed, they walked in front with Suliem, Nafisa, and Gretchen, the German woman and the little girl behind, each with a child in hand. The moon brightened the desert, but the two men still used the high powered lights for guidance. Suliema smacked Lovell's back.

[433]

"You should turn off those lights and let the moon guide you because if Ahmed's friends come after us, they'll follow the lights. Plus, we need to save the power for the future. There's no telling how long we'll be out here."
Lovell turned off his flashlight and translated for Saed.
"I was thinking the same but you're our leader and I was following you."
Looking up at the direction of Saed's voice, Lovell could only see his profile
"Then don't let me be the leader because I know nothing about the desert. You're a man from the desert and you should lead."
Saed turned his head around, spoke in Arabic and Lovell felt the group pull closer.
"He knows what he's doing. I was thinking the same thing. We need to stay closer together and keep our voices down. There's another world out here and it's very dangerous."
Suliema spoke to Saed in Arabic after speaking to Lovell. Saed snorted, then stopped, pulling Lovell down into the sand. The others followed and Lovell heard the faint sounds of motors. It faded and Saed stood. Suliema passed Lovell and Saed pistols. Gretchen whimpered and he heard a slap.
"Be weak out here German and the desert will eat you up. You tried to smuggle drugs like everyone else here, and you got caught. Now toughen up because if you become a burden, I'll kill you before I'll be a slave again."
She translated to Saed who said "la", no in Arabic, and one sentence. He spit the out the kat.
"I was sold for the debt I couldn't pay educating my children."
His long stride set the pace for their walking. Lovell checked his watch after he and Saed had finished the kat. They had been walking for forty five minutes. It had taken Ahmed thirty minutes to reach the highway when they'd

[434]

left Ripoli. He knew they had to make it back where he'd started before sunrise because of the heat, and whispered this to Saed. Saed patted Lovell's chest with four fingers twice, meaning 8 hours and walked faster. The group moved with him until Suliema pulled on Lovell and Saed's shirts.

"Listen!"

They all flattened themselves on the sand. This time, the engines came from behind them and were getting nearer. Putting the children, Nafisa, and Gretchen behind them, they readied themselves. "Can you shoot Yank?"

"Better than you girl."

"If you miss, I think we're dead. I'll take one headlight and you take the other. I know he can so he'll take the men in the seat. They won't drive with anyone behind at night. Give Saed your big light." She translated into Arabic, and Lovell heard the dials on the lights turn to the right. Full beam. A truck's engine was nearing and his mouth dried. It came over a dune, headlights throwing arches into the air and as soon as they flattened, they fired, hitting the lights. Glass and metal shattered and the hand lights showed four men trying to get out of the truck, then being hit, with two falling and the other two jerking as the bullets hit them. They slumped in the truck's seat; one man tried to crawl through the sand but Suliema stopped him with one shot. "Ahmed taught me that."

They walked in the beams to the truck and inspected the dead men. Saed examined the truck's engine by lifting the hood, and then had Lovell start it. The motor hummed and leaving the Berbers in the desert, they loaded the children, Nafisa and Gretchen in the back, and got in the front. Suliema first sat between Lovell and Saed, and then nudged Lovell.

[435]

"Let me out. I can't take being sandwiched between two men, like a prisoner, plus they need me back there."
Lovell placed the high-powered light on the dashboard to guide them. Two hours later he set off a flare and they waited. A flare lit the sky in the distance and Saed, thanking God drove in the direction of the flare. Five minutes later they heard Edwin Starr's "War" coming from an approaching truck, which stopped in front of them. They could see men with black covers on their faces in the front seat, and heard people walking. Something was stuck in the ground on both sides of the truck and lights came on, making the area look like daylight. Matt walked into the brightened area and Lovell joined him, doing the Philly Dog, until they embraced rocking back and forth.
"Negro what you doing traveling with all these people? It was only supposed to be you. What would you have done if there wasn't enough room?"
They sat outside a dome shaped limestone building. Everyone except Lovell had gone inside.
"I don't know. It wasn't planned."
"With you it never is. Damn bro, you kinda ripe. And you a little wired."
Lovell could smell himself, and the kat hadn't run through his system.
"Yea, ripe and I haven't slept in days."
Matt angled his head towards Suliema, who'd come outside and was leaning against the building, drinking from a bottle of scotch.
"What's up with her? She sunburnt like a muthafucka and hard as that wall she's leaning against. And she can drink too. Look at her."
Lovell turned to Suliema who raised the bottle to him.
"She been a slave for seven years bro. Do I need to say more?"

[436]

Matt bit his lips.

"Naw."

"And how long you been out here, Mr. Johnson?"

Matt pulled the kinks from his beard. His fingernails were dirty.

"Since I got out of dodge. It's not my fight bro. Now that you're alright. I'm heading west."

"Where you going?"

Lovell flicked a bug off Matt's shoulder.

"Recife. I'll die there. And you?"

"My first stops Rome. I have a family now. Then I don't know."

A Winnebago with darkened windows pulled into the yard and Mukhtar, in a gray business suit with a white silk collarless shirt, walked from the open door, his arms open for an embrace. Lovell rushed to him.

"My warrior brother, I knew you'd be alright. I've heard of your bravery."

Matt joined them. He'd taken off his guns.

"Thank you Mukhtar, but now I need to go home."

Mukhtar raised his glasses, displaying those moon eyes.

"I would expect no less. Now let us all go."

Saed's family, Gretchen, Doreen, the eleven year old Irish girl, Matt, Suliema and Lovell rode in the air conditioned vehicle for an hour, then boarded a plane to Egypt from some small airport, in an unknown country. They left Mukhtar at that airport, his arms raised in a V, for victory.

A limousine took them to the U.S embassy first, and stopped outside. Suliema came to the back of the vehicle where Matt and Lovell sat.

"You're always welcome in Edinburgh."

She gave him a vice grip hug, which Lovell returned and stepping away from Suliema, spoke out loud.

[437]

"My name's Lovell Pendleton and you can always find me through Duchess Marguerite in Rome. She'll know where I am."

He followed her to the front of the bus and hugged Gretchen, who kissed the top of his head and little Doreen, who kept mumbling thank you into his chest. Saed and his family stood together. Lovell removed his money belt, took out the traveler's checks, and extended it to Saed, who raised his hands in refusal.

"I can't take this mi amigo. I should be giving you something. Don't insult me."

Lovell put the belt over his shoulder and handed Saed the papers he'd been given. Nasifa and the girls bent to the floor in front of Lovell, their hand's touching his shoes. Nasifa lifted her head.

"I'm with child and my husband and I will name him Lovell for you."

"Please ask them to stand Saed."

"No mi amigo. You must pass over them."

Lovell stood looking down at the two girls and the woman. "Since your son will bare my name, then I'm his godfather. And as his Godfather, I give him this gift to celebrate his birth. I want to give it to all of you."

They got up and Lovell placed the money belt across Saed and Nasifa's extended arms. It didn't reach the girls. Saed opened his mouth, but Lovell's raised hand silenced him. "You can't refuse Saed. I'll be the boy's godfather." He turned around and squatted to Doreen's height, then took all the money from his hiding places and gave it to her. Suliema turned away from him, but her body shook. The family parted and allowed Lovell and Matt to leave. Breathing the Cairo air, he knew the Winnebago would take Doreen and Suliema to the Scottish embassy, Gretchen to the German embassy and Saed and his family to the

[438]

Morroccan embassy. Lovell and Matt stood in front of the American embassy. Matt raised his hand for a high five.

"Shit, we don't need to go in there. You have your passport, I got mine, we both have traveler's checks and money to burn, so let's get a shower, a drink, and then make that call to the Duchess Negro."

Hailing a taxi, they checked into the Luxor, and got separate rooms, agreeing to meet in an hour. Lovell shredded the clothes he wore, sat on the bed, and called Miss Marguerite's direct line.

"I'm in Cairo, and I need you to send someone to get me." She giggled and swallowed. It was after 2 p.m., and he knew she'd started drinking.

"They're already there, Mon Amie."

She hung up the phone. Lovell stayed in the shower until the steam filled the bathroom. After drying off, he stood watching the Cairo traffic, and thinking he had nothing to wear. Not even underwear. There was a knock on the door and he heard Matt popping his fingers.

"Open the door. I bought you some clothes."

Opening the door, he was pushed back into the room. Khadijah put the clothes bag on the back of the door and closing it, shed her clothes and walked Lovell to the bed.

CHAPTER EIGHTEEN

Lovell was awakened by a hot towel cleaning his member, the slush of water, and then another hot towel moving over his body.

"Turn over Habibi."

"Khadijah, my love, let me take a shower. I'll wash back there."

Khadijah took a free wet hand and covered his mouth.

"There is no time Habibi. You know the Countess. She's prompt and when she's ready to leave, we leave. Now clean your mouth quickly. We have to go now."

Rolling out of the bed, Lovell put on the white linen suit and shoes laid out for him, and walked to the bathroom. Emerging, he and Khadijah walked between four cream skinned Egyptian men, mustached, with dark glasses, dressed in sky blue business suits, carrying walkie talkies. They escorted Lovell and Khadijah from the elevators, turned left to a set of stairs which led to a back door, and out into a waiting limousine. Riding through the Cairo night, looking through the tinted glass of the limousine, Lovell blinked with Cairo's blinking lights, which passed in a stream. The limousine stopped on an airport tarmac, and the guards exited first, hands in their pockets, their heads looking in all directions. Lovell could see the plane in front of him, with the Count's insignia, a black eagle with wings spread and talons wide, ready to attack its prey. The bird's white eyes though, were painted aqua, softening them, as if observing something it loved. The limousine's doors opened quickly, and they were pulled out and flat palmed pushed up the plane's stairs. Lovell heard a baby crying before turning into the plane, and his eyes teared upon seeing Miss Marguerite, dressed in pink from head to

[440]

toe, pink pearls wrapped through her bee hived hair, rocking the crying baby.

"Please let me hold my son."

The baby boy's head turned hearing Lovell's voice, and he stopped crying. Lovell gave his son a first finger, which he grabbed, smiling, and Lovell's emotions plummeted from his eyes. The baby boy started to cry. Miss Marguerite raised her eyebrows at Lovell.

"You cry. He cries. That's the connection between a parent and a child. Now stop crying and he will Lovely."

Miss Marguerite stroked Lovell's ear, then removed her hand when Khadijah stepped forward. She showed all her teeth in a smile, nodded to Khadijah, and swished down the aisle.

"Hey Negro, you finally made it. You are one crazy mutha fucka."

Aisha walked down the aisle, rocking a bit because the plane had started to move, and arms open, kissed Lovell, while guiding him to his seat. Looking as he walked, Matt, Abdul, and Suliema, held their hands up in high fives. Lovell paused upon seeing Suliema.

"What are you doing here and how'd you get here before us?"

Suliema angled her lips at Ms.Marguerite.

"I need to adjust before I go home Lovell, and the Scottish embassy called Miss Marguerite who arranged everything".

Lovell gave her the thumbs up sign as the plane ascended and Lovell and Khadijah sat in their seats, facing their friends who sat in the lounge area of the plane. Once the plane leveled, Ms. Marguerite emerged carrying a tray of champagne glasses, and served Lovell first. She then offered Khadijah a glass, giving her a wink, then Matt and Suliema, Aisha, and last, Abdul.

[441]

"This is for our returning brother, friend, and lover Lovell, whom we salute."
They stood in salute to Lovell, who kissed, then rocked his son, holding back the joy brimming within him.

The End

www.ingramcontent.com/pod-product-compliance
Lightning Source LLC
Chambersburg PA
CBHW070547030726
47505CB00001B/195